love you better

ALTERNATIVE COVER EDITION

BRIT BENSON

Love you Better

BRIT BENSON

Special Edition Cover Design by TRC Designs by Cat

Editing by Rebecca at Fairest Reviews Editing Services

Proofing by Sarah at All Encompassing Books

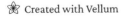 Created with Vellum

This one is for 8-year-old me.
It might not be the kind of book we initially imagined, but I like
this one better.
We freakin' did it, girl.

playlist

Salute- Little Mix
R U Mine?- Arctic Monkeys
Lovebug – Jonas Brothers
S.L.U.T. – Bea Miller
A Little Bit Yours- JP Saxe
Older than I Am- Lennon Stella
Bruised Not Broken – Matoma
I Wanna – The All American Rejects
A Little Less Sixteen Candles- Fall Out Boy
Sugar- Maren Morris
One Kiss – Dua Lipa
Like No One Does- Jake Scott
Poetry- Wrabel
Watermelon Sugar High- Harry Styles
Give it to You – Julia Michaels
I Think I'm OKAY – Machine Gun Kelly
Come On Get Higher – Matt Nathanson
Love You For A Long Time- Maggie Rogers
Here (In Your Arms) – Hellogoodbye

Intentions- Justin Beiber
5 More Minutes- Jonas Brothers
God is a Woman - Ariana Grande

Follow me on IG, @britbensonwritesbooks, for the extended playlist.

content note from the author

Please be aware: this book contains references to sexual assault that may be upsetting to some readers. Though the assault does not take place on page, it is discussed briefly, and some emotional effects of the trauma are shown.

If you've been a victim of sexual assault, I encourage you to contact a professional who is trained to help. Call the National Sexual Assault Hotline at 800.656.HOPE or speak with someone online at Rainn.org

ivy

MASCARA SMEARED. Heels in hand. Not-so-attractive post-coital bed head.

Another Saturday morning.

Another walk of shame. Without the shame, of course.

I've definitely gotten smarter about it, too. Checking the weather beforehand is probably one of my proudest planning maneuvers. I learned that lesson the hard way when I had to haul my sopping wet behind three blocks in the pouring rain at 6 a.m. a few months ago. And packing travel ballet flats in my clutch next to my pepper spray and condoms is a pretty genius move, if I do say so myself.

Not every Friday night ends in a hookup, but when they do, I'm nothing if not prepared.

Most weekends, it's just me and my friend Jesse, dancing and people watching, releasing the tension from a long week of classes, internship hours, volunteer shifts, and the like. Some nights, I'll act as J's wing woman, and occasionally, like last night, someone will strike my fancy and, *voila!*, the potential for a late night playdate. Then I have to decide between the comfort of my apartment or an *excursion*.

Meaning, we head back to his place for the night.

Meaning, I rock the walk of shame instead of sleeping on my 800 thread count Egyptian cotton sheets.

If I go back to his, I don't have to worry about disturbing my roommate, soiling my precious sheets, or engaging the awkward morning after exchange. I can sneak out whenever I want. And, while my apartment is cozy and familiar and *mine,* the idea of bringing some random into my personal space still makes my stomach twist, and not in a good way.

So far, excursions have always won out.

Last night went well, too. After my pep talk, I only had to do one grounding exercise, and that's a big improvement from some of my previous evenings. I suppose if I'm going to keep this up, attempting to bring a guy back to my place would be a logical next step.

Just to see how it goes.

I should take a closer look at the pros and cons. Compare my notes from the last few times. I'll have to work it all out tonight. My head is too fuzzy to make sense of it now, and I'll need a couple of cups of coffee in my system before I can really dive in.

As I continue the trek up the block to meet my Uber, my phone vibrates in my clutch.

I don't even have to look at the Caller ID to see who it is.

Six a.m. on a Saturday and my best friend is still on top of my mess.

Before I even say hello, Kelley speaks.

"Ivy."

"Kelley."

"You're on the move."

I smile at his matter-of-fact tone and the way his voice is still gravelly from sleep. Low and growly. The idea of being the first person he speaks to after waking makes me feel warm in a way that I choose to ignore.

"I am. You're tracking me."

"Of course. It's in the best friend code: don't let your bestie go home with the beefy dudebro with an undercut from the bar unless you're stalking her promiscuous ass on Friend Finder."

I snort, and it's unfeminine and unapologetic. He's right, though, and I love him for it. It's been our code for the last eight months, and I'd do it for him, if he ever stopped being a stick in the mud and went out once in a while.

"How do you know he was beefy with an undercut?" I ask, curious.

"You have a type, Ives. It's always the same kind of guy. Undercut, gym rat, tan. It's like you want to fuck the cast of Jersey Shore."

I flinch a little at his observation, but the smile I can hear in his voice soothes the offense. He didn't mean anything by it. If he knew...*well*. He doesn't know, so I shake it off. He's always teasing me and giving me a hard time, but he never judges, so I play along.

"Oh my *gosh*, Kelley! Don't be crass."

"I call 'em like I see 'em, Ives. And anyway, I made Jesse send me a picture of him."

I laugh again, louder and fuller this time. Jesse isn't just my weekend wingman; he's also Kelley's roommate, which means even if Kelley doesn't come out with us, he's still pretty well-informed. I shake my head and grin. I love our friend group—me, Kelley, Jesse, and my roommate Bailey— even if we do tend to get a little too up in each other's business at times.

"Oh boy. That's next level."

"Only for you, Ivy."

I can picture him leaning on his kitchen counter, that infuriating little side smirk on his face as he sips his morning coffee. He's probably shirtless, defined abs on display, sweats riding low on his hips. I give my fuzzy head a little shake.

"This is a little late for you, yeah?"

"I couldn't get an Uber any earlier. The shortest wait was half an hour."

"Damn. What'd you do?"

"Hid in a corner of the apartment lobby for 20 minutes and played Farm World on my phone until I got the text that my Uber was close. I didn't want to wait on the curb."

He laughs.

"What are you doing today?" I ask him.

Tonight is Netflix and Fill, our standing weekly hangout where Kelley and I take turns cooking each other dinner and then veg out on the couch. Our Saturday evenings are set, but his Saturday days are usually more fluid than mine.

"If Jesse comes back soon, Imma hit the gym with him."

"Hate to break to it to you, Kell, but I doubt that will happen." I giggle. "Pretty sure J went home with two *very* willing partners last night."

"Of course, he did," Kelley deadpans, and I can practically hear his eyeroll. "Then it looks like I'll be flying solo at the gym today."

Kelley takes two things very seriously: his education and his physical fitness. If he's not studying, he's playing soccer or lifting weights or working through his modified marathon training program. As a result, he not only has a 4.0 GPA, but he also has a lean and ripped body that has the potential to make me think very unfriendly thoughts about my best friend. If he weren't my best friend, that is.

"No training today?" I ask.

"Nope. Today is a rest day. Yesterday was 18 miles."

"Ick." I shudder, and he laughs at me. I don't understand why anyone would want to run that far for that long. It's just...*ick*.

"Hey, I gotta go." I love him, but I need some time inside my head to plan for my day at the office. "My Uber just pulled up. Love you."

"Love you back. Text me this afternoon."

"Kay. Byeee."

I put my phone in my clutch and slide into the light blue Prius that's waiting for me on the curb. My driver is a girl, probably a college student. She gives me an empathetic look and smiles shyly, but other than a soft "good morning," she lets me ride in silence. I know I look like death, but there's no judgment in her eyes. I offer her a latte and an extra five bucks on the tip if she takes me through the coffee shop, and she obliges. I drink the whole latte before we even get to my apartment, and I send a little thank you to the Ride Share Goddess for blessing me with an accommodating driver.

My Uber pulls up outside my building, and just before I slide out, I have a thought. It's the same thought I usually have anytime my Uber driver is a woman, and I take a deep breath to control the anxiety I feel creeping up.

"What's your name?" I ask.

She startles at the abruptness of my question.

"Clara...?" She's timid and sheepish, no doubt confused and probably a little suspicious about my sudden interest.

"You ever drive at night, Clara?"

She nods. "Most Fridays and Saturdays. The pay is really good."

I nod. I figured as much. I do a quick scan of her keychain and the center console and make up my mind quickly, snapping open my clutch and pulling out my hot pink bottle of mace.

"Here," I say as I hand it over to her. "Keep it on your keychain or in the side pocket of your door. Somewhere easily accessible, okay, Clara?"

She reaches out slowly. "...Thanks?"

"Gotta be safe." I shrug. "There are a lot of creeps out there."

"You sure?"

"Of course. I've got more," I reassure her as I nod my head to the apartments. "We women have to look out for each other, right?"

A smile takes over her face. "We definitely do."

I nod and return her smile. "Have a good day, yeah?" and then I head toward my apartment.

The scent of fresh coffee embraces me when I open the door, and I say a heartfelt thank you to Yesterday Me. Programming the coffee pot before I went out last night was another win. I'm definitely crushing it at life.

Ivy Rivenbark, sultry temptress by night, pragmatic adult by day.

Bailey is asleep, so dropping my shoes at the door and stripping off my clothes as I go, I pour myself a cup of coffee and take it into the shower with me. I've got to be at the office at nine for internship hours, and I am never late.

* * *

Pulling open the mirrored glass doors always fills me with pride. There's something so empowering about working for one of the top general practice law firms in the city, and even though I'm only an intern, I still feel like I belong.

Checking my reflection in the windows of the vestibule, I'm confident in how official I look. My dress slacks and button down are wrinkle-free, my blonde hair is pulled into a sleek and stylish high bun, and my makeup is fresh, feminine, and fierce.

Geoff greets me enthusiastically from the front desk.

"Good morning, you dangerous mountain lion of greatness! Amelia is already in the conference room pulling files."

I roll my eyes with a smile at another one of his unusual greetings. They're ridiculous but they always brighten my mornings.

"Mountain lion of greatness is a new one. I like it. It's agile and graceful but also deadly." I nod my head toward the conference room. "How long has she been here?"

"About fifteen minutes," he replies, popping open the side drawer of his desk and pulling out one of the fancy espresso pods he reserves just for us. "You're going to need this. I heard her mumbling a minute ago and I think today's tasks are going to be *nah-stay*."

He passes the pod to me, and I hug it to my chest as I make my way over to the instant coffee machine in the corner.

"Bless you, Saint Geoffrey. You are my salvation."

He winks. "Good luck, V."

Coffee in hand, I stride into the conference room, eyeing Amelia cautiously.

"Fifteen minutes ago, Ames? Really? How hard did you have to hustle to beat me?"

She pops a perfectly arched brow and smirks. "I spilled coffee on my pants, and I'm pretty sure I lost an earring between my front door and my car."

I flick my eyes to her dress slacks, scanning for a coffee stain. "At least they're black?"

"Yeah, and it's French vanilla, so my thighs are gonna smell scrumptious today." She flips her braids over her shoulders and gives them a little shimmy, and I can't hold back my giggle.

Amelia is one of the reasons I love it here. She's a paralegal at the firm and oversees most of my internship tasks. She's also taking law school classes online and a mom, and I honestly couldn't have dreamed of a more perfect mentor. She's hardworking, she's knowledgeable, and she makes the days more enjoyable. She also shares my passion for law, so her drive fuels mine.

Becoming a lawyer has been the ultimate goal since the summer after ninth grade. I went to Kelley's house to swim and saw Ms. Pierce coming home from work. She was wearing a sleek pencil skirt and carrying a black leather briefcase; she looked like the most empowered woman I'd ever seen. She was a stark contrast to my own mother, who was always ragged and exhausted and disheveled after pulling doubles at the diner. I didn't know women could look so powerful.

So professional.

So *awake*.

After that, I wanted to be just like Ms. Pierce. I wanted to be an empowered, successful woman, and I spent the next three years peppering her with questions about her job. When I wanted an internship to give my law school applications a competitive edge, *Pierce, Pierce & Associates* was the obvious choice. A paid undergraduate legal internship is a rare find, and I'm not ashamed to say I took full advantage of my connection to the Pierce family.

Their general practice firm employs lawyers who specialize in a variety of fields, providing me with loads of experience-gaining opportunities, and Ms. Pierce happens to be the firm's prestigious family law attorney, which is the field of law that I'm interested in. It couldn't be more perfect.

I take one of the files Amelia has stacked on the desk and flip it open, sliding my glasses on so I can better scan the details on the page.

"What's on the agenda for today?"

"Well, Ms. Pierce said we're to review and update the Harrison estate account, which is the file you've got in your hands, and..." She pauses, and I meet her eyes.

"....and?"

"And...it's also these files." Her hands span out like Vanna White over what appears to be a pile of twenty additional file folders.

"Jeebus. That's a whole forest."

"I know. They had Geoff print out everything for you to go over. Past tax forms, a list of assets, financial records, his will, insurance policies, et cetera. The whole nine."

She slides me a fresh legal pad, a tray of Post-it flags, several highlighters in assorted colors, and a stack of file folders.

"It's a lengthy estate, and Ms. Pierce wants it ironclad because Mr. Harrison received a terminal diagnosis, and he has a feeling his son is going to contest. It's got the potential to get ugly."

"Good gracious." I study the table in front of me, my eyes wide, both overwhelmed and excited to dive into the sea of documents. I'm already mentally organizing my tasks for where and how to begin. Usually, I work with more of the firm's family practice cases, but I relish any opportunity to gain experience in all fields of law.

Amelia and I marvel at the files once more, and then steel our resolve for what's about to be many hours of work.

"Welp," I exclaim, downing the last of my coffee, "let's jump on it! We are dangerous mountain lions of greatness. Let's show these file folders who's boss."

Several hours, multiple cups of coffee, and two turkey pesto paninis from my favorite café later (praise Saint Geoffrey for his heroic lunch run), Amelia and I are ready to call it a day. It's been exhausting, and I think part of my cerebrum has gone numb from overuse, but we've done good work today.

"Thanks be to the Goddess of Espresso and Endurance, for we have succeeded!" I declare dramatically, throwing both hands up and tilting my head to the heavens. "We covered a lot of ground today. I'm proud of us."

"I'm proud of us, too, V. We make a good team."

"We do. Will all my colleagues be as awesome as you?"

Amelia laughs and shakes her head. "Girl, no one is as awesome as me." She gives me a wink, grabs her leather satchel, and shoots a text to Ms. Pierce, letting her know we're leaving for the day. Then we walk out of the office together.

"What are your plans for tonight?" Amelia asks as we make our way to the side lot. "You out on the prowl?"

"Nope." I pop the P and shake my head with a smile. "I did that last night. Tonight's Netflix and Fill with Kelley."

"Ah, yes, Kelley Pierce. The prince of the *PP&A* dynasty. Sexy ginger and exceptionally boring bachelor."

I laugh. She's not wrong. My best friend is friggen gorgeous. Auburn hair, hazel eyes with bright flecks of green and gold, plus a body that I'm pretty sure a lot of the students on the Butler University campus want to lick. Professors, too, probably. He's a regular Irish Adonis, but dang if he couldn't try to have some fun once in a while.

"When are you going to hook him up with one of your friends?" She waggles her brows at me, and my stomach twists. "A fine specimen like him shouldn't go to waste. Hell, if I weren't happily married..."

I know she's only joking, but I can never stop the initial jolt of discomfort anytime Kelley's love life comes up (no matter how non-existent it may be). It's unfair and irrational, especially given my personal weekend proclivities, but no matter how much I fight it, it's always there. That nagging sting of jealousy and anxiety. It's always hiding in the dark recesses of my mind, ready to strike at even the slightest hint of competition.

Ugh. I'm such a cliché.

We reach our cars, and I glance up, finding Amelia's eyes on me, a curious expression on her face.

"What?" I ask. "Why are you studying me like I'm Mr. Harrison's 2012 tax returns?"

She sighs and shakes her head. "I don't know why you won't just admit it. I'm no fool, Ivy."

I scoff. "What? No. I don't know what you're talking about."

"Sure." She unlocks her car, opens the door, and slides in, popping that infuriating perfectly arched brow at me once more. If she doesn't watch it, I'm going to shave it off. "You're in denial, Ivy. And your face is turning bright red. Better blast that AC before you get home to Kelley for Netflix and Chill or your secret won't be a secret anymore."

"It's Netflix and *Fill*, Ames!" I shout as she shuts her door and puts her car in drive. "*Fill*! There won't be any chilling!"

My protests are futile, though, and she waves at me as she pulls away. I bet her eyebrow is still popped.

Curse the Gods of Overly Opinionated Friends.

kelley

"GOOD MORNING, MR. PIERCE!" Matthew, one of my eighth graders, calls out as he approaches me. I'm writing the day's objectives on the board and waiting for my supervising teacher to show up. He's usually late, but I like knowing that he trusts me with the classroom even though I've only been here a few weeks.

"Morning, Matthew. How was your weekend?"

"It was good! I went to my friend's house, and we played video games and I hit a new high score and his mom ordered pizza."

"That sounds like fun."

"It was. Don't worry, though. I finished the study guide." He plops his Trapper Keeper on my desk and starts riffling around in it, digging through an unorganized stack of crumpled papers.

"Here!" he shouts as he pulls out last week's study guide and hands it to me. "My mom says sorry about the coffee stain."

I can't help but laugh. We're not supposed to have

favorite students, but any teacher who tells you they don't is lying.

Matthew is one of my favorites. The kid can't sit still to save his life, and more often than not he speaks as he's raising his hand instead of waiting to be called on, but his enthusiasm for learning is unmatched. If my mind wasn't made up to teach high school history, students like Matthew might make me consider teaching middle school.

"You tell your mom that it's fine. I can still grade it with the coffee stain," I grin. "What else did you do this weekend?"

"Just hung out with my friend and played his video games. It was only supposed to be for Friday night, but Mom asked if I could stay Saturday night, too." Matthew shrugs, a little less excited but there's still a buzzing energy around him

"Alright, well we're still on for lunch today, right?"

"Yeah," he nods, the excitement returning. "I brought fruit snacks and some granola bars."

"Nice. I love fruit snacks," I say with a grin. "Now go take your seat. Mr. Miller will be coming in any minute and then the fun begins." Matthew laughs at my use of the word fun, but he eagerly heads to his desk. He enjoys this class even if he tries to pretend like he doesn't.

This semester's student teaching assignments are in seventh and eighth grades, while next semester the university will place us in a high school. The program I'm in to get my bachelor's degree in education requires that we get both middle school and high school experience in order to graduate with a secondary teaching certification. It makes sense, but I already know where I belong. High school is the end goal, but right now I'm just happy teaching in a classroom.

The only thing I look forward to more than my student teaching days is my Saturday night Netflix and Fill date with Ivy. Two nights ago, we watched this, in Ivy's words, "tasteless comedy aimed at entertaining man-children," and while she tried to pretend that she hated it, she about pissed herself laughing, and I about pissed myself laughing at her laughing.

Writing the agenda on the board, I'm lost in my thoughts of the oversized, off the shoulder sweatshirt Ivy was wearing on Saturday. The freckles on her back that I dream about tracing with my fingertips dance in front of me like stars in my vision. I only snap out of it when my supervising teacher comes lumbering into the room smelling like a mixture of coffee and cigarettes and grumbling something unintelligible. He's a grumpy fucker in the mornings.

"Good morning, class!" Mr. Miller booms, and the students greet him back randomly, some with giggles and some with disinterest. "And good morning, Mr. Pierce."

"Good morning, sir."

"How was your weekend?"

"It was good. Almost finished with my project for Educational Psychology."

He nods. "And training as well?"

"Yes, sir. Nine weeks until the marathon."

I know what question he's going to ask next—he asks the same one every Monday.

"And how about socializing? Did you go out at all?"

I shake my head slowly and shrug. "Nah. Too busy."

Mr. Miller harrumphs and gives me a skeptical look.

"Have some fun once in a while, Mr. Pierce. It will be a lot harder to make time for it once you start teaching, so you might as well make the best of your last free year."

Before I can respond, he turns to the class and begins going over the day's agenda. This isn't the first time Mr. Miller has given me the *you're only in undergrad once* speech. Instead of overthinking it, though, I focus on today's lesson.

We're starting our unit on Industrialization, and call me a nerd, but I love this shit.

When the lunch period rolls around, I grab my bag from the fridge in the lounge and set up at Mr. Miller's desk. He always takes his lunch in the teacher's lounge after driving around the block twice to smoke a cigarette. I prefer to eat my lunch in the classroom.

At first, I did it because I could work on lesson plans or course readings, but a few days into my first week Matthew came wandering back into the classroom for something and found me sitting at Mr. Miller's desk. Since then, he's started eating lunch in the room with me, and we've worked out a nice little system.

"Ok, Matthew. What have you got?"

Matthew plops a crumpled brown paper sack onto the table in front of him and proceeds to dump out its contents.

"I've got three granola bars—two are chocolate chip and one is almond." I'm not sure what the granola bar ever did to him, but you'd think *almond* was code for *garbage juice* by the way he scrunches his nose up at it. *I'll definitely be taking that one.* "I also have two whole packs of fruit snacks and these cheese crackers!"

"Not too shabby," I say, nodding my head with feigned approval. As far as Matthew's lunches go, this one is pretty standard. A small, random selection of easy-grab processed shit shoved into a rumpled brown paper sack. Sometimes he has a juice pouch or a can of soda, and once in a while, he might have a piece of fruit, but I've never seen him with a sandwich or any consistency of healthy foods.

As disappointing as his lunch spread may be, there's always one thing that always brings a smile to my face.

"And what does it say today?" I ask with enthusiasm, and Matthew groans.

"Awww, Mr. Pierce, do I have to?"

"Matthew, it's very cool that your mom writes you those notes. It means she cares about you and wants you to have a good day," I press, and he rolls his eyes.

"No, for real!" I insist. "I think it's so awesome that I want to do it for my own kids when I become a dad someday. I wish my parents did it for me."

His grin grows, and he gives me side-eye. "You want to be a dad?" he asks with a giggle.

"Of course, I do! I'm going to be a cool dad."

"I wish you were my dad," Matthew says quietly, and I feel like someone kicked me right in my chest. I'm not even sure how to respond to that, so I go with honesty.

Reaching my hand out to pat his shoulder, I speak clearly.

"If I have a son as kind and smart as you someday, I'll be very proud."

I stay silent for a minute to allow him to fully absorb my words, and then I give his shoulder one last squeeze.

"Now on with it, man! Read it!" I nudge his bag toward him.

"Okay okay," Matthew relents, and pulls a napkin out of his lunch sack and begins to read from it.

"Almonds are good food.

Eat the granola bar, Matt

Growing strong, Love Mom"

I laugh at his mother's haiku as Matthew glares at the granola bar.

"I happen to like almonds," I say. "Do you think your mom would be okay if I trade you half my turkey sandwich and some grapes for the almond granola bar and some fruit snacks?"

Matthew's eyes light up. "I don't think she'll mind!"

"And..." I grin as I reach into my bag, "I have some cookies that my friend's roommate baked. I brought some for you, too." Ivy is always giving me little snacks to bring to Matthew. She knows all about the student I share my lunch with. He reminds her of her younger brother Jacob, I think.

"Thank you!" Matthew smiles big and organizes his new lunch in front of him.

"My pleasure." I slide Matthew the "extra" bottle of juice I got from the vending machine, we cheers, and then we dig in.

"You want to grab something to eat?" Cassie asks as we drive the thirty minutes back to campus. The school where we intern is about halfway between Butler University and my hometown, and only about fifteen minutes from my parents' firm. Cassie is another education major in my program, and we were placed at the same middle school for student teaching, so we ride together.

"Yeah," I say, checking the clock on the dash. "Jerry's?"

"Mmm, yes. Jerry's would be heavenly." Cassie rubs her stomach enthusiastically and closes her eyes. "I'm starved. I didn't get a chance to eat my lunch because we had hall duty."

"Hall duty sucks. I gave half of my sandwich to one of my kids, so I could definitely eat."

"Same kid you always share your lunch with?" she asks me playfully.

"Same one," I say with a laugh, as we pull into the Jerry's parking lot. It's a popular sub, salad, and soup shop just off campus, frequented by upperclassmen, and even sometimes grad students and professors.

"How's your Ed Psych project coming?" I ask after we order, sliding onto two stools on the wall counter.

"Good. I'm about halfway there. You?"

"Good. I've only got the annotated bibliography left."

"No kidding?" Cassie asks, her eyes wide. "How? It's not due for weeks yet!"

I shrug, not really wanting to get into the fact that my social life is almost non-existent, consisting mainly of Saturday nights with Ivy, soccer, and the occasional random gym session with Jesse.

"You need to get out more," Cassie declares. "Come out with me this weekend. The Sig house is doing a series of theme parties. We can dress up. It'll be fun!"

I take a sip of my Coke before I answer. "Nah, I'm not feeling it."

"Why not? It's not like you've got work. I'm in the same courses as you," Cassie presses. "Ed Psych is the only big thing assigned right now. Anything else doesn't need a whole weekend's worth of focus." She fixes her eyes on me and smiles, and I'm certain she's flirting. "Come out with me."

Cassie is stunning. She's smart. She's funny as hell. We have a ton in common. On Tinder, her bio would definitely be worthy of a right swipe, and I should be jumping at this offer. But I see Cassie almost every day. We're in all the same classes, and we're currently placed in the same school. It would be awkward as hell when it didn't work out, and I'm just not interested in trying for any type of relationship right now. Not even a casual one.

"I'll have to pass this time, Cass." I avert my eyes and focus on the sub in front of me.

I hear her sigh, a little sad but maybe more frustrated, and the topic drops. This isn't the first time she's invited me out with her, so it isn't the first time I've turned her down, and it likely won't be the last.

Despite what Jesse thinks, I haven't put my love life on hold for Ivy.

I'm not waiting for her to finally see me or whatever unrequited love bullshit he's comparing me to in those "best friends falling for each other and living happily ever after" kissing, sex books that Bailey's always reading. In those stories, there's always one sorry sap in the friendship who has been holding out hope that the other will fall in love with them and they'll run off into the sunset to have three kids and adopt a dog.

That's not me.

I'm not that sorry sap.

I'm not holding out hope because I know there isn't any. I took my shot senior year of high school and fucked it up, but contrary to what Jesse believes, I've come to terms with that. I accept it, and I want Ivy to be happy, even if that's not with me.

So, I'm not turning down Cassie's offer because I'm saving myself for Ivy. That would be fucking dumb.

But.

The heart wants what it wants, and right now my heart is still tied up elsewhere. I've talked to other girls, gone on a few dates, but I refuse to start dating as a method to "move on" or whatever. I won't do that to someone. It wouldn't be fair to them, and it wouldn't be fair to me.

And besides, I'm not like Ivy and Jesse—I just can't do the random hookups with random people thing. When I start dating again, it will be because I am finally free to invest myself in someone new. Until then, I'll be maintaining my 4.0 GPA and my friendship.

* * *

Wednesday nights are for soccer.

When I was on the BU soccer team freshman year, practices were regimented and much more organized. Now I just get up with a bunch of dickbags on Wednesdays who like to fuck around with the ball. We run drills, and when enough of us are free we scrimmage. Some nights, like tonight, we're able to get another group of dickbags together and we attempt to have something resembling a real game. It's not an official college team, but I like this better.

In middle school, when I ate, slept, and breathed soccer, I had every intention of doing whatever necessary to go pro. In high school, when my dream of teaching history started to form, I was okay with playing soccer here at BU instead of doing it professionally. Now, after everything that happened with my soccer scholarship, I'm content with weekly scrimmages and work out drills with my merry band of ball kicking dickbags.

We're a rag tag bunch, but we have fun.

After leading the team through some stretches, the student ref blows a whistle, and we post up, ready to kick ass. I don't want to brag, but I'm a brilliant midfielder, and "real" games like this one are the only time I can really unleash. So yeah, I'm confident we'll wipe the floor with these frat douches, because I didn't have a full ride soccer scholarship once upon a time for nothing.

Two hours later, I'm sweaty and physically spent in the *second*-best way. We ended up winning by a landslide.

"Good game, man," Brewer says as he slaps me on my back.

Brewer is a decent guy. A little rough around the edges, but harmless. He's a sophomore, a Poli Sci major, and a pretty good soccer player.

"You too, Brew," I say between gulps from my water bottle.

"They thought they had us there for a minute," Brewer

laughs, "but they didn't know they were up against a human rocket."

I laugh at the compliment and give a shrug.

"What can I say, man. I'm a beast," I joke back, and flex to show off a bicep. Brewer huffs out a laugh, and just as I'm about to toss out some more cocky bullshit, I hear my name called.

Ivy is waving at me from the side of the field.

I wave back with a smile, then turn to Brewer, ready to dismiss him, when I catch him ogling Ivy with a bawdy stare.

"Damn. I don't know how you do it, man. If I had that hanging around, I sure as shit wouldn't be playing Candy Land and making friendship bracelets."

"So you've said," I snap. I'm not having this conversation again.

"I'm just sayin', man. Word around campus is she's got a—"

"Stop," I growl, cutting him off. "Finish that sentence, Brew, and I swear I'll kick your ass. I mean it."

Brewer throws his palms up. "Fuck man, got it. I'm just sayin' what everyone else knows."

"And if I hear you repeat it, you'll have to have your jaw wired shut."

"Message received, Pierce."

"Fuck off, Brewer."

I make my way to Ivy, leaving Brewer without a goodbye or a second glance. I fucking hate it when guys think they can talk shit about Ivy to me just because she likes to party.

So, she hooks up. So what? So do lots of people. So do all the guys who comment on it. Do I like it? No. But is it up to me? Also no. And it's certainly not up to any of these judgmental fuckers, either. If she wants to go out every single night and troll for dick with Jesse, that's her business. But it doesn't give anyone free rein to talk shit about her.

"Ivy," I greet her stiffly, still keyed up from my exchange with Brewer.

"Kelley," she replies with a grin, dimple on full display, and immediately my muscles loosen. I'm weak for that damn dimple. She holds up a take-out bag. "Food to buy your love?"

I gotta laugh at the way her lips quirk up, but when my attention starts to slide down her body, I look away. The way the fabric hugs her curves... How can she be this gorgeous in just leggings and a t-shirt? *My* t-shirt.

After the busy day I've had, seeing Ivy is the sweetest kind of torture, and all I want to do is sweep her into my arms and kiss her, passionate and deep.

But I can't.

So instead, I settle for a friendly side-hug and another dimpled smile.

Being in love with your best friend means being painfully aware of the line and constantly toeing it. Giving yourself just enough to take the edge off, but never enough to satisfy the craving.

I've gotten good at repressing most of these feelings over the last few years. Somedays, I can *almost* forget that Ivy is my own personal siren and nearly everything she does turns me on.

But then other days, she struts up to me wearing tight yoga pants, one of *my* t-shirts, *and* carrying food, and I'm a goner. I have to swallow before I respond.

"Depends on what it is," I joke.

"Burger from Mac's Grille."

"Cheddar cheese?"

She nods seriously. "Lettuce, onion, pickle. No tomato or mayo."

"Steak fries?"

"Kelley, I'm not a monster. You know I got the steak fries."

"I don't know. You forget I've seen you before coffee. You could give Freddy Krueger a run for his money."

She gasps out a laugh and elbows me in the side.

"Or when you've pulled a series of all-nighters? You walk just like Mike Myers and you've got a temper to match."

She puts on an angry face, but her lips twitch at the sides.

"That time you got a cold during midterms, you were something straight out of *The Ring*, I swear." I'm not exaggerating this one. She didn't shower for days, so her hair was a mess, she was pale as a ghost—more so than usual—and her voice was so scratchy that it did kind of sound like TV static. Still beautiful, but kind of scary, too.

"Fine," she snips, squaring her shoulders. "If you think you've got jokes then I'll just eat this myself." She starts to walk away, but I grab her and slide my arm around her shoulder.

"Okay, okay, I *suppose* I can spare some love for a cheeseburger from Mac's."

"Ick. You're all sweaty and you smell." She gives me a light shove, failing to hide her smile. I snatch the bag from her hand with a grin, and she rolls her eyes.

"You just leaving the library?"

"Yeah. I've just about finished all of the free study materials, so I'm going to move on to practice tests next."

I pull a fry out of the bag and hand it to her.

"You're ready. You could probably take it tomorrow and score a 180." I mean it, too. Ivy is smart as hell, and she's one of the hardest working people I know. There's no way she won't blow the LSAT out of the water.

"I'm not ready yet, but I'm almost there. I'll be ready in

23

four weeks." I don't even have to look at her to know her face is set with an expression of determination and focus.

Ivy Rivenbark is a force.

"I'm here if you need any help, you know. Study buddy. Accountability partner."

She smiles. "I'm good, but I appreciate it."

"You're gonna crush it, Ivy. Seriously."

"Thanks, Kell," she says with a smile, and when she looks up at me, we have a moment of eye contact that gives me chills. The kind that stretches out and fills with something deeper, something *more,* and makes my heart pound into my ribcage.

If she was anyone else, I'd read into it. I'd reach up and tuck a strand of hair behind her ear and let my fingers trail down her jaw in a caress.

But she's not someone else.

She's my best friend.

So, when Ivy blinks and breaks eye contact, giving her head a little shake, I change the subject. Because she doesn't feel that way about me, and there's no point in trying to see something that isn't there.

"What are your plans for tonight? J is supposed to be home. Wanna come hang out?"

"I'm going to pass," she says, and my heart sinks a bit. Because I'm an idiot. "Bailey is off tonight, and I haven't seen much of her lately. I'm going to stay in and see how she's been."

"Girl code for pillow fights in your underwear?" I tease, and she raises her eyebrow mischievously.

"Pillow fights *naked,* Kelley," Ivy says with a laugh, and I change the subject. The thought of Ivy naked is sure to get my dick hard, and that's not a situation I want to deal with right now.

"How's your ma and Jacob?"

"Fine. The same. Mom's working too hard as usual, and Bug had some little weasels at school giving him a hard time, but I called the principal and I think I got it straightened out. He sounded better when I talked to him this morning."

"Are these the same little shits from last time?" I'm ready to kick some sixth grader ass. Ivy's younger brother Jacob is awesome, but he's got some learning struggles and kids can be dicks, so he gets picked on for being different.

I hate it for him. He's honestly the kindest and coolest kid. He's funny and clever, and he doesn't deserve the shit these little punks keep putting him through. On top of that, I know it kills Ivy. She feels helpless, and she can't stand seeing him upset. She's taken care of him since he was born, so not being able to take care of him now is troubling her deeply.

"Yeah, it is," she says with a sigh. "They were stealing his homework and making fun of his handwriting. Calling him Blind Bat Boy. Stupid immature stuff, but it hurts him, you know?"

Hearing the despair in her voice crushes me. I throw my arm around her shoulder again and draw her close, pressing a kiss to the top of her head. This time, she doesn't shove me away.

"You're a good sister, Ives. He knows you love him, and he knows you'll fight for him. He's strong because you've shown him how to be strong. Try not to worry too much about it."

She stops walking and wraps her arms around my waist, so I gather her into a tight hug. She buries her face into my chest, and I can feel her deep breaths through my shirt, counting her inhales and exhales, so I close my eyes and wait, trying my best to provide the comfort she needs from me.

With a final deep breath, Ivy releases my waist and takes

a step back, my arm dropping down to my side. I miss her immediately.

"It's going to be okay. I'm okay," she states firmly, and that same look of determination is on her face.

"I could always hire another little punk to mess with them," I tease. "Itching powder in their underwear. Tampons in their lockers. Whatever other shit will embarrass those little middle school asshats."

She barks out a laugh. "I'll consider it and get back to you."

As I drive her to her apartment, we argue about what movie we're going to watch this Saturday, and I keep my voice light and playful. Anything to brighten her mood and lessen the weight on her shoulders.

"SO, WHAT DO YOU THINK?" I ask my best friend Preston as we're filtered into the gym and onto the bleachers. "You see anyone you know?"

"Yeah. Brandon from South Middle is down there." He points to the other side of the gym. "We go to the same sleep-away camp. And Bobby Flemming goes to church with my cousin. He's over there." I swing my eyes between the people Preston just pointed out. "What about you? See anyone?"

I scope out the gym again. It's the first day of ninth grade, and both local middle schools filter into Morgan County High School. Preston and I both went to North Morgan Middle, so we're already familiar with the teachers and the school layout, but there are also incoming ninth graders from South Morgan Middle starting today.

"I know Gavin is gonna be here. We played him in baseball this summer."

"Oh yeah, Gavin. The dorky kid with the braces." Preston laughs.

"Yup. He's cool, though. He hit that homerun off Baker Kennedy and Kennedy was pissed for like weeks."

27

Preston and I scan the crowd from our seats on the bleachers as hordes of freshmen filter in through the doors for the assembly.

"Hey," I nudge Preston with my elbow. "Down there. Is that Chris Moore? From the summer soccer camp?"

I'm trying to get a good look at who might be Chris when I feel someone sit down next to me. I glance over my shoulder, thinking maybe it's someone else I know, to find a girl with a blonde ponytail digging through a messenger bag.

A girl I definitely do not know.

"Hey," I say to her. "You've got your head shoved so far into that bag that you could be wearing it as a hat."

She startles and sits up straight, whipping her head around and fixing me with a glare.

"Excuse you?" she huffs.

"I said, you've got your hea—"

"Yes, I heard what you said. What I want to know is why you felt the need to say it?"

Well damn.

"Sorry," I shrug. "I was just kidding around."

"Oh." Her eyes soften, and her lips turn up into a small, embarrassed smile. "Well, okay then. I get a little grumpy when I'm hungry." She waves a granola bar in front of her, which must have been why she was digging around in her bag.

"It's cool. My ma says I get hangry, too. I'm Kelley." I point to my chest and smile real big. "Everyone calls me Kap, though. I'm from North Middle."

"Ivy," she says with a smile and pushes her glasses up the bridge of her nose.

Just as I'm about to pester her with more questions, the principal starts talking into the microphone to begin the assembly.

He talks about the student handbook and dress code and conduct expectations. All crap we've heard before. I just want to get to my classes so I can see who's in them with me. I also want to get up with some of the guys from the summer soccer workshop. Tryouts are in two weeks so if I wanna make varsity as a freshman, I need to see who I'm up against, maybe see if anyone will run extra drills with me. My dad tries but he's terrible at sports. Golf does *not* count.

Just as the principal is closing the assembly, I feel a tap on my shoulder, and I turn to find the blonde girl—Ivy—looking up at me with determined eyes.

"Kelley," she starts.

"Ivy."

"Um, I was wondering if you could show me to the locker bank nine?" She looks a little nervous, but her voice is steady and kind, and I feel weirdly proud of her. My mom always tells me to face my fear and work through my nerves—it's how I made it through the travel baseball league tryouts two summers ago. It's not easy. I'm still figuring it out, to be honest. But Ivy obviously can do it, and my chest warms all funny-like.

"Yeah. I'm in eight so you can just follow me." As we head out of the gym, I tell Preston I'll catch him later. He's in bank four so he's heading the opposite direction of us.

"Let me see your schedule," I say to Ivy, and she quirks a brow at me but hands it over. "Rivenbark." I roll her last name off my tongue, accentuating the *v* and the *k* sounds. "I'm a Pierce. That's why our banks are close." I study her schedule some more. "You're in English with me." I grin over at her and she gives me a small smile.

"Cool. It will be nice to know someone."

"You don't have any classes with anyone from your middle school?"

29

"Oh, no. I'm not from here."

Oh. That makes sense why she would be sitting alone at the assembly, then.

"Where'd you come from?" I ask her, genuinely interested, and she laughs a little.

"Bowen? It's about two hours south of here."

"Never heard of it. But that sucks having to move right before high school," I say, and she shrugs.

"It is what it is."

"Well, don't worry Ivy Rivenbark," I say loudly, tossing my arm over her shoulders as we round the corner into locker bank nine, "I'll help you settle in and be your first friend."

She looks up at me, a warm smile slowly stretching over her face, making a dimple pop on her left cheek and her blue eyes—very blue eyes, like Gatorade blue—shine through her glasses, and something weird pinches in my gut.

"Thanks, Kelley Pierce," she says through her toothy smile. "I could use a friend."

All day, I wait impatiently for English with Ivy. I keep looking for her in the halls but haven't seen her yet. Every time I see a blonde ponytail, my gut does that weird pinching thing again, but it's never her. Eyes are never blue enough or dimples aren't deep enough or the facial expression doesn't contain enough determination. Nope. None 'em are *enough* to be Ivy Rivenbark.

When fifth period finally rolls around, I hustle into the classroom and put my stuff on one of the two-seater tables near the front. I drop my notebook onto the chair next to me, and then I watch the door.

"'Sup, Kap," Sam Benning calls out to me when he walks in the room. "How was summer?"

"Good, man. Travel soccer and we went to Wisconsin Dells for a week," I reply, but I don't take my eyes off the door.

When I don't ask Sam about his own summer, he mumbles something and tries to sit next to me.

"Seat's saved, Sam."

"Oh sweet, is Preston in this class, too," he asks about my best friend.

"Nah. It's for someone else," I tell him, and just as I'm about to tell him that I'm helping out a new student, I see a flash of blonde hair walk through the classroom door, and Sam Benning is forgotten.

"Ivy!" I practically shout, jumping up from my chair and waving at her. She startles and flushes, and I immediately feel like a jerk for embarrassing her, but then her lips turn up in a small smile that erases my self-doubt and she walks toward me.

"Kelley," she says with a playful grin that makes her dimple pop, clutching her books to her chest.

"Ivy," I grin back. *Is it weird that I like that she's using my real name?* "As your first friend at Morgan County High," I take my books off the chair next to me and pull it out for her, "I saved you a seat. First friends are always table buddies."

She raises her eyebrows at me. "They are?"

"Yeah, here they are. I don't know how you guys did it in Boatin—"

"—*Bow*en."

"Yeah, Bowen, but here at Morgan, we are always table buddies with our first friends. It's in the handbook. Were you paying attention this morning at the assembly?" I tease.

Ivy laughs and rolls her eyes, but she sits down in the seat next to me and I'm hit with the same zing of triumph I felt when I scored the winning goal in the final soccer game this summer at camp. *What the hell is that about?*

The teacher tells us all to settle down. Her name is Mrs. Jolie, and I think she's probably like eighty or something but she's real cool. She comes to all the home sports games and dyes her hair a different color every year for homecoming. I lean over and whisper this to Ivy and she giggles, putting her hand up to her mouth to try and hide it.

Zing. Triumph again.

"So, since there's a good chance there are some unfamiliar faces in the classroom right now, we're going to do a little activity," Mrs. Jolie says. "You're going to be interviewing someone in the class whom you do not already know, and then you're going to be using what you learn to write an essay about them. Don't just learn the basics—make your essay interesting. You have sixty seconds to find your partner."

I immediately look to Ivy. "We don't really know each other yet since we only just met this morning. Want to be my partner, Table Buddy?"

"I believe I'd like that, Table Buddy." *Zing.*

Over the next thirty minutes, Ivy and I take turns asking each other questions. I learn that her middle name is Jean (mine's Allen); her name means "ivy plant," which she says is boring (mine is Irish and was my great gran's last name, which Ivy says is cool); she has a four-year-old brother named Jacob (I'm an only child); she loves horror films (I hate them, but I didn't tell her that because I don't want her to think I'm a wuss); her favorite subject is math because she's really good at it (mine's history because I like how it answers a lot of my questions); her favorite dessert is everything (I told her she had to pick one and she threatened to break up our new friendship because she refuses to discriminate against dessert) and her family just moved into a house two neighborhoods from mine.

When she told me she lives in the Crenshaw Village neighborhood, I was thankful she was writing in her notebook so she didn't see the momentary shock on my face.

Crenshaw Village is, well, *not nice*. It's not bad, but it's kind of junky, and the houses and yards are smaller and usually not well-maintained, and there are no sidewalks, and most of the streetlights don't work. Crenshaw isn't far from my neighborhood—I can easily ride my bike there—but it couldn't be more different.

I do a quick survey of her outfit: ratty black Chucks, plain jeans, a plain blue t-shirt, plain black-framed glasses. Except for the shoes, there's not a single label on any of her clothes that I can see. It's polar opposite to my brand-new Under Armour shirt, brand-new Abercrombie jeans, and brand-new Under Armour slides.

"You're not far from my house," I say in an attempt to mask my surprise. "Maybe we can hang out."

Why did I just say that? I can't hang out with anyone. Soccer tryouts are in two weeks. When I realize my mistake, I open my mouth to specify that I meant hang out *after* tryouts, but Ivy beats me to it.

"That could be fun!" And she's so excited that I forget all about running drills to prep for tryouts and decide I'll hang out with her whenever and wherever she wants.

"This weekend?" I ask.

"Oh, maybe. I have to ask. My mom is probably working doubles since we just moved here and all, so I'll probably have to watch my brother."

"Can't your dad do it? Or is he working too?"

She stiffens a little, and I immediately know I said the wrong thing.

"My dad died when I was five," she says with a shrug. Her voice is equal parts sad and resolved, and I'm surprised at how, I don't know, *adult* she sounds.

"I'm sorry." I pat her back awkwardly and she gives me a small smile.

33

"It's okay. Car accident. Drunk driver," Ivy shrugs again and sighs. "It is what it is."

In an attempt to lighten the mood, I ask the first thing that pops into my head. "Where's your mom work?"

"She's a shift manager at Pat's Diner. What does your mom do?"

"My mom and dad are lawyers. They own *Pierce, Pierce, & Associates*." I beam with pride. "It's the top general practice law firm in the city."

"Wow," she says, eyes wide. "That's awesome. That's a huge accomplishment." With a morbid chuckle, she adds, "we get excited when we can make the rent before the three-day grace period is up."

We sit in awkward silence for what feels like freaking forever. It's terrible, but I don't know what to say. Each tick of the clock makes me feel more desperate to put a smile on her face, to smooth her scrunched eyebrows and bring out that stupid dimple.

"What if I come over and hang out with you and your brother both this weekend? And I could walk home with you after school today since we're going in the same direction."

She nods, but then says, "Maybe. I have to pick Jacob up from daycare after school, though."

"I'll come with!" I cringe a little because I know I'm on the verge of sounding too eager and maybe a little stalker-y, but I can't turn back now, so full-steam ahead. "I can come with to pick up Jacob. First friends need to know each other's siblings and you said your brother is, and I quote, the coolest tiny human on the planet, so I feel like I should definitely meet him."

She studies me for a minute, her face freakishly blank, but I can tell from her eyes that she is considering the whole thing. Probably trying to decide if I'm serious, or if I'm worthy of meeting her brother, and I feel my whole body tense the same way it does whenever I'm about to hear who made the team after tryouts.

When the side of her mouth lifts into a half-smile, I heave a sigh of relief.

"Okay, Kelley Allen Pierce. I'll meet you after school."

Zing.

At last bell, I hustle back to locker bank nine and waited for Ivy. When she comes around the corner and sees me waiting for her, her face splits into the widest grin and her dimple pops real deep-like. I bet I can fit a whole pencil eraser in that dimple.

"Ivy."

"Kelley."

"You ready? You said your brother is at the daycare down the street?"

"That's the one," she responds as she tugs her messenger bag from the locker and stuffs some books inside.

Ivy walks with me to the bike racks where I unlock my chain, and then, rolling my bike next to me, I follow her to the daycare.

When we get there, I wait outside while Ivy goes in to sign her brother out, and a few minutes later she comes back out with him in tow.

He's short, like all four-year-olds, has jet black hair and the thickest glasses I've ever seen. He's carrying an orange water bottle and is wearing a black shirt with a pumpkin on it and khaki shorts. When he looks up at me, his brown eyes are magnified in his glasses. He looks absolutely nothing like Ivy, and maybe it's nerves but I just blurt that out.

"He looks nothing like you," I say, and then wince.

"Well, he's technically my half-brother," she says. "But that doesn't mean anything. He's my whole brother where it counts," she adds firmly, no room for dispute, so I just nod and smile like a dork.

"Wh-who are you?" Jacob asks as he clings to Ivy's leg.

"I'm Kelley. I'm Ivy's friend," I say. "Who are you?"

"I'm J-Jacob," he says back. "I'm her b-b-brother."

"Cool," I nod and grasp for something to say. He's just standing there, blinking at me through those thick glasses. I can feel Ivy's eyes on me, and it's making me nervous.

"Sooo..." I point to his shirt. "You, uh, like pumpkins?" The minute the words are out of my mouth, I cringe again and can hear Ivy stifle a laugh. *Real smooth, Kap.*

He blinks.

"No." Blink. "I like *Hallow-ween.*" He's got a little bit of an attitude.

"Right," I breathe out and start fidgeting with my bike handles. This is awkward. "Well," I start again, but trail off when I find him surveying me. And then he blinks at me some more. Like a little judgmental owl.

"C'mon, Bug," Ivy interjects, saving me from looking even more like an idiot. "Kelley is gonna walk home with us."

On the walk to Crenshaw Village, Ivy asks Jacob—or Bug, as she calls him—to tell her what he learned in "school." That starts him jabbering about a sand table and tornado bottles and other kid crap, but he's got this little lisp and a thick stutter and I gotta admit that he's kind of adorable. I always wanted a younger brother but so far Ma and Pop have told me nope.

When we get to Ivy's house, I notice that the yard is better maintained than the neighbor's, and there's even some sort of orange and purple flowers planted around the front. She and Jacob walk inside, and I don't really know what to do. I'm not ready to say goodbye just yet, so I lean my bike on the side of the porch and follow them in.

Ivy and Jacob slide off their shoes, so I do the same, and Ivy tells Jacob to go wash his hands. Then, I watch as she places a cutting board, knife, and apple on the small counter jutting from the wall in the kitchen and begins peeling and slicing the apple. She puts the sliced apples on a plate, pours a small cup of milk, and puts them on the small kitchen table in front of a booster seat.

And I just stand there and gawk at her. Because she's doing *mom* things, and I've never seen any of my friends do parent-y things like this before. Because the *parents* do them. Sure, I fix snacks and junk for myself. Open a bag of Doritos. Drink a Gatorade. Throw some pizza puffs in the toaster oven. But I'm pretty sure I've never seen anyone peel and cut an apple before who wasn't a mom.

Jacob comes running into the kitchen and clambers up onto the booster seat.

"Don't run in the house, Bug."

"S-sorry, Bean," he says through a mouthful of apple.

And I am still gawking.

Shaking myself out of the weird sense of awe I feel, I ask her, "So, like, why do you do all this?"

She pops a brow at me, the same fire in her eyes that I saw this morning on the bleachers, and I know I said something dumb again.

"Excuse you?"

"No, I mean, like, how long have you, like," and I lower my voice to a whisper so Jacob won't hear, "been taking care of him?"

"He's four. So, for four years? When my mom is working, I'm glad to do it." Her glare is challenging. "Why spend rent money on a babysitter when I'm capable? And anyway, I *want* to take care of him. He's my brother." And then she turns her

37

back to me and starts washing off the cutting board and knife.

"No, yeah, of course," I sputter out. "It's just, I don't know. Surprising? No, impressive. It's impressive," I say with more confidence. "You impress me, Ivy Jean Rivenbark."

She studies me from the other side of the counter, her face that same blank mask from before, and my chest constricts. Once again, I feel like I'm trying out for something, and I really, really, *really* want to make the team.

And then a smile starts to spread over her face, and when that stupid dimple pops, I let out a breath.

"Thank you, Kelley Allen Pierce," she says with a huge grin. "I'm really glad you're my first friend."

Zing.

FOUR

JESSE and I got here about twenty minutes ago, and it took us about that long to find and claim a table by the wall that wasn't already in use or covered in spilled beer.

Keggers is packed, one of the most popular spots on the Butler University campus for their Friday night wing and pitcher specials, and open seats are in high demand. Your shoes might stick to the floor a little when you walk, you'll probably hear "In Da Club" by 50 Cent at least twice, and a twenty-minute wait to use the ladies' bathroom is pretty standard, but on Friday nights, Keggers is the place to be.

Since it's my weekend to get the drinks, I head up to the bar and leave Jesse to guard our table and scope out the crowd. As I weave my way through the crowd of bodies, "Mood" by 24kGoldn comes on, and soon, everyone is bouncing to the music. By the time I get to the bar, I've stepped in one giant puddle of what I hope is beer and narrowly missed two separate spillage incidents. Pretty successful, actually.

Stepping up on the bottom rung of the stool next to me and leaning my body as far over as I can, I hold up my debit card in an attempt to grab the bartender's attention. I've seen him here before. The guy is pretty attractive. He kind of looks a little like Kelley, actually. Similar height and build, but Kelley's got a better jawline and better hair. I look him over more closely as I wait. Kelley also has better biceps, I decide, and I'm not sure but probably better hands, too. The bartender is very good looking, but he doesn't hold a candle to my best friend.

When the guy finally makes eye contact, my calves are straining from being on my tiptoes and I'm sure the edge of the bar has left a permanent bruise on my hips from how I'm propped over it.

"What can I get you?" he asks as he simultaneously makes what looks like a vodka cranberry with a lime garnish.

"I'll have two pints of the draft special," I shout over the music as I hand him my debit card. "Just run it. I don't want to leave it open."

"You know," the guy says as he takes my card, "our draft special also includes pitchers tonight. $6.25 for the pitcher. It's a better deal."

I raise my eyebrow and stifle a grin. I can't be mad, though, because the poor guy probably has no idea.

"Actually, it's not," I say to him, and he looks back at me with confusion all over his face.

Here we go. My time to shine.

"You see, the standard pint is 16 ounces, which you guys always fill quite full—thanks for that," I beam, and he smiles back at me.

"Anyway, I'm paying two dollars for it. That's roughly 12.5 cents an ounce. The pitchers are 48 ounces, and that's when they're filled full, which you guys tend not to do." I nod at the pitcher the second bartender is currently passing to someone a few stools down. "That's probably only at about 42-ounce capacity. But let's say for sake of argument that it was filled to 48 ounces, that would still be roughly 13 cents an ounce. So you see? It's really not a better deal. It's basically the same. In fact, the standard pint is even a slightly better deal, even if it's just a matter of half a cent."

The bartender, wide-eyed and amused, shakes his head and turns to run my card. When he slides back my card and the two pints, I take a sip and smile.

"Thanks!" I say sweetly and turn away with satisfaction all over my face.

Ivy Rivenbark: Blonde hair. Big boobs. Bigger brain.

Jesse is leaning on the wall next to our table, his foot propped on the stool. He's got one hand messing with something small, probably one of his fidget toys, and the other is scrolling his phone. When I plop the pints on the table, he looks up with a smile.

"Why are you grinning like that? You look like you just made a frat boy cry." He smirks as he takes his beer.

"The bartender offered me a pitcher of the draft special."

Jesse barks out a laugh. "You're such a nerd. Of course, you'd get a boner from spitting math facts."

"Guilty," I sing-song, and slide onto the stool next to him. "He also looked a little like my Kelley."

"*Your* Kelley?" He eyes me with a smirk, and it takes me a second to realize what he's talking about. "Freudian slip?"

"Hush, you know what I meant." I wave him away airily.

"Yep. I def do." I ignore him and go back to scanning the crowd.

Jesse is almost a foot taller than my 5'5", and even sitting on the high-top bar stool, my eyes are still only about level with his armpit. After a few minutes of people watching, he nudges my shoulder with his elbow.

"You sure you're good with two weekends in a row?" Jesse asks, and I nod.

"Yeah. Things went well last weekend. I want to test it out." I'm still riding the high of progress, but I don't want to take the risk that last weekend's success was a fluke.

"Cool cool. Okay, how about that dark-haired guy at the pong table? He's got that douche bag look you been goin' for."

Jesse laughs, but I'm not offended. He's right. One hundred percent, I go for the d-bag look right now, and while Jesse has a vague understanding of *why* I do what I do, he doesn't know everything, so I let it slide right off me. Water off a duck.

I narrow my eyes and study the person he's pointed out.

"Ummm, J, I think I've met him already."

"Worth a replay?"

"Meh, I suppose everyone deserves a second chance." I laugh, and he tosses me a grin. "But let's keep him on the bench for now."

"Sure thing, Coach."

We scope out the crowd a bit longer as more people pour in the front door, singing along to the music and making idle chitchat as we wait. My week was grueling, though, so I don't have the energy for small talk, and Jesse can tell. One test, a pop quiz, and a paper I turned in this morning has left my mind a bit mushy for socializing. Not to mention yesterday's brain busting session of LSAT practice tests. I did pretty well on them, but my accuracy wasn't as consistent as I would have liked.

Anyway. This week has been *a week*.

"Ooooh." I lean into Jesse and bring my beer to my lips. "I want that one," I say, nodding my head to the muscular guy a few tables down from ours. I go through my mental checklist:

Athletic build, *check*.

Around six feet, *check.*

Smooth shaven, *check.*

Dark hair that's longer hair on top than on the sides, *check.*

And there's something about his clothing—tight jeans, a Colts t-shirt, Jordans, and a black, backwards ballcap—that sells me on him. He's exactly what I'm looking for.

Yeah, he'll do nicely.

Jesse tears his eyes from the short skirt he's spotted and drags them to my conquest.

"Damn, girl. You've definitely developed a type." He gives me a wink. "I think I'm going with her." He nods back to the redhead in the skirt, currently dominating at the beer pong table.

Another reason Fridays are so popular at Keggers—they set up beer pong tables in the back and host first-come-first-served games. It makes for a rowdy crowd and definitely contributes to the stickiness of the floor.

I check Jesse's girl out. She seems confident and has two girlfriends in tow, so she's not fending for herself. Smart. I watch as she tosses the ball into the other team's cup and then throws some sassy remark I can't hear at the guys on the side of the table. She cocks her head to the side and pops her hand on her hip, a small smirk on her face as the guys say something back. Yeah. This girl could work.

"I like her. Meet back here in twenty? Text if you need more time."

"Yesss," he says, drawing out the 's' so he sounds like a snake. "Imma go secure you some *D* for that *P*, V."

I snort out a laugh and bump his fist with mine, and we each head toward the other's prospective company for the night.

I sidle up to the girl and watch as she finishes handing the frat guys their butts. Then, I get to business.

"Good game," I say, before taking a sip of my beer.

"Thanks," she smiles confidently. "They were easy to beat."

I nod and laugh with her, unable to contain my grin. "What's your name?"

"Bianca. You?"

"I'm Ivy."

Her smile is warm, her eyes focused and interested. She's not drunk, so that's a notch in the pro column, and she seems like a straightforward woman, so I cut to the chase.

"Alright, Bianca, I'm going to be blunt." She pops a brow at me, suddenly suspicious. Another notch for the pros. "First, how much have you had to drink?"

She jerks her head back, no doubt ready to put my nosy self in my place, and I find myself liking her even more. I throw my palm up in an effort to show her I'm harmless. *Mostly.*

"No judgments here. Totally respect your right to party however hard you want. I have a purpose, I swear," I say, and her shoulders relax a bit. She studies me a moment before defiantly taking a sip of her beer and responding confidently.

"This is my second beer. I got a paper to write tomorrow so I'm just here to let loose some steam and kick some ass at pong." She winks.

I nod my head and can't hold back the mischievous grin.

"Perfect. Okay, Bianca. I'm playing wing woman for my friend over there." I nod my head toward Jesse. "He's the tall, tan, sexy one talking to the guy at the corner table."

She slides her eyes over to J, and I watch as she assesses him while sipping her beer. Then a smile forms on her face, and she brings her gaze back to me.

"And what's your sexy friend have to do with me?" Her grin is almost predatory, and I know I've got a winner.

"Well, Bianca, I'm pretty sure he wants to provide you with a few orgasms tonight."

She barks out a laugh at my bluntness and spits some beer out of her mouth. I should have waited for her to swallow before delivering that information.

"No shit? And why should I follow through with this opportunity?"

"I'm glad you asked," I say with a smile. "He's a great guy. Word is he knows his way around the female body. Respectful. Safe. Clean. A little goofy, but he's fun. And he's 6'3"." I punctuate his height with a wink, and her eyes widen with humor. "But he's not wanting a relationship, and he only takes home women who are sober, single, and well-informed on his intentions."

I know I've sold her when she nods appreciatively and slides her eyes back to J. She eyes him greedily and takes a few more small drinks from her cup before looking back to me.

"Alright, Ivy. I'm in."

"Great!" I say, clapping my hands in front of my chest. "Cool if I hang out here until he's done securing my company for the night?" I waggle my brows at her and we both giggle.

"Nice." She laughs, and we watch Jesse until he looks over at us and sends me a wink.

"That's my cue, Bianca. Have fun tonight. Your orgasms will arrive shortly."

"Thanks, Ivy." She smiles, I smile, and I head over to meet the brunette jock in Jordans. My *company* for the evening.

I've been chatting Brock up for the last ninety minutes and so far, so good. He seems like a decent guy, albeit a bit dull.

Several times I find myself wishing Kelley were here to liven up the conversation, but my best friend doesn't go out. It's for the best, anyway.

With the exception of some shoulder rubs and a light hand on my hip, Brock hasn't gotten gropey, so I've been cool, collected, and flirty. I think this might actually be the night I beat it.

But then it happens.

Brock slides his hand up to my waist and gives it a squeeze as he lowers his lips to the shell of my ear.

"Want to head to my place?" he asks, and I feel the familiar drop of ice skate its way down my spine, leaving pinpricks in its wake. My breath catches and my pulse thunders in my ears.

To anyone else, I could definitely pass as aroused, and I can tell Brock assumes as much by the way he slips his fingertips into the back band of my jeans. I shut my eyes and take a deep breath in, letting it out slowly. I'm sure Brock thinks I'm being coy, but that's better than him knowing the truth. I recite the Attorney's Oath in my head, and just like last weekend, I only have to say it once before I've calmed my heart rate. I take that as a good sign.

I raise my eyes to his and ask, as playfully as I can muster, "where's your place?"

"South Campus."

"One of the frats?"

"Yeah. A Sig. Is that a deal breaker?"

I shake my head slowly. South Campus is only an eight-dollar Uber ride to my apartment. Definitely worth not having to dirty up my sheets. I've got travel ballet flats and makeup removing wipes in my clutch, and the weather app says tomorrow is supposed to be clear and rain-free. Plus, still not feelin' the idea of a stranger in my space. So, his place it is.

"Sounds good," I say, trying to hide the shake in my voice. "Just let me head to the bathroom first. Meet you out front?"

Inhale slowly through my nose, exhale slowly through my mouth.

"Yeah, great." Brock smiles eagerly, and I try to focus on that. He's been kind and decent and this will be fine. I remove his hand from my waist and walk quickly to the bathroom.

Once inside, I shut and lock the door and rush to the sink. I wet a paper towel and run it over the back of my neck.

"You got this, Ivy," I say to myself in the mirror. "This is all you. You're a dangerous mountain lion of greatness. You're in control. Just a regular hook-up like a regular twenty-one-year-old college student." I close my eyes. "This is sex. You enjoy sex. You want to be able to have *good* sex again. Everything will be fine."

I take another deep breath through my nose and release it slowly through my mouth, then open my eyes and look at myself one last time in the mirror. "Orgasms," I say firmly with a nod.

Opening my clutch, I take inventory.

Pepper spray, *check*.

Condoms, *check*.

A single white pill, *check*, but only as a last resort.

Once my heart rate is settled, I take out my phone and share my location with Jesse for the next twenty-four hours. He sends me a thumbs up emoji followed by an eggplant emoji, which makes me snort out a laugh, and I head out to meet Brock in front of the bar.

You've got this, I tell myself again. *You're in control.*

Brock gets a little handsy in the back of the Uber, but I don't mind. He doesn't breech the clothing barrier, and he's a pretty decent kisser. He knows how to work his mouth, and if I can get him to take that tongue a little lower, I'll probably get at least one orgasm tonight. I'm not naïve enough to expect one from the *penile penetration* part of the evening. I stifle a laugh at the thought. I can practically hear Kelley poking fun at me for the clinical terminology.

Just say dick, he'd tease. *C'mon, Ivy Jean. You can do it. You can say the D-word.*

I roll my eyes with a smile and give my head a little shake. *Focus on the task at hand, Rivenbark.* Right. Head in the game.

Once in his room, I take off Brock's baseball cap and toss it in the corner, raking my fingernails over his scalp. I pull my tank top over my head and throw my arms around his neck.

Brock pushes me lightly onto the bed, and I watch as he takes off his shirt and jeans. He's standing in front of me in just a pair of boxers.

When did he take off his shoes?

I scan the room for the black and grey Jordans but don't see them. Did he leave them downstairs? Surely, he wouldn't irresponsibly leave his shoes in the common room of a frat house. There are probably around one hundred guys in this frat, so at least one of them is bound to be untrustworthy. Those Jordans had to be worth a pretty penny—my mom would have had to pull doubles for a week to get those shoes. I know because Jesse has a sizeable collection, most of which he refuses to even take out of the box. I can't for the life of me understand spending so much money on shoes that you won't even wear, but to each their own, I suppose.

Perhaps they appreciate in value?

I make a mental note to research the investment opportunities with a Jordan collection. Then I give myself a pat on the back for the involuntary direction my thoughts went. Musing about over-priced tennis shoes is much better than having to force a grounding exercise to keep my fight or flight response in check. It's a good sign.

Brock drops himself on top of me and presses his mouth to mine, effectively silencing my inner monologue. When I place my hands on his shoulders and lightly try to guide him downward, I hear him laugh lightly.

"Eager?" He breathes into my neck.

"Yes," I say, and push a little harder. This time, Brock doesn't resist and starts sliding down my body, kissing me as he goes. He pops the button on my jeans and pulls them off. Just when I think he's going to settle between my thighs, he climbs back up and latches his lips to mine. I huff out a frustrated breath through my nose and press his shoulders once more, but he resists again, and I give up.

Welp, I guess oral is out for tonight.

I reach between us and grip him, pleased at what I find. He grunts and drops his lips to the swell of my breast, and I'm ready to get this show on the road.

"Condom?" I ask, and he freezes for just a moment.

"Hmm?" He murmurs as he slips his fingers into my underwear.

"Condom," I say more firmly, and he lifts himself up to meet my eyes.

"I actually don't have any," he says with a fake innocence. *Baloney.*

"That's okay," I say, and he visibly relaxes. Then I roll out from under him and add, "I carry my own." I saunter over to my discarded clutch and pull out a foil packet.

As I walk back to the bed, he sits up and hits me with these big, ridiculous puppy dog eyes, and I'm already over him.

"Babe," he says, and I start scanning the room for my clothes.

"Babe," he says again. "How about we skip the condom? I can't feel you as good with it."

I scoff and put a hand on my hip. I'm standing in front of him in just my bra and underwear, and he rakes his eyes over every inch of my body. I know I look good.

That's right, Brock. Look your fill. That's the extent of what you're going to get.

Despite my *are you kidding me right now* glare, Brock continues his pointless pitch.

"I don't want anything between us, babe. I want to feel you when I make you come."

"Yeah, I imagine sex without a condom feels great," I coo seductively, and he nods eagerly. "But you know what also feels great?" He pauses his nodding and watches me carefully. Yeah, he knows he's not winning this one. "Not having some random frat boy's semen dripping from my vagina." I start to put on my jeans. "Also, not having herpes. That also feels great, Brock." I slip my shirt over my head and pick up my heels.

Brock is standing now with his hands on his hips, his semi-erect penis still visible beneath his boxers.

"Don't be like this. I'll wear the condom."

"Too late, Brock. Any guy who is going to try to manipulate a girl into riding him bare isn't the kind of guy I want inside me."

I start out the door when he calls behind me.

"Fine. I don't want to fuck your fat ass anyway."

Ha. Just like an insecure boy to try and insult a woman's appearance as a last-ditch effort to feel like a man.

I stop at the landing at the top of the stairs and look over my shoulder at him.

"That's too bad," I croon as I slide my hand down my body and stop at my butt cheek. "I might have let you have it," and I give it a squeeze to emphasize my point. I'm totally lying, but he doesn't need to know that.

I pause, letting the implication sink into his thick skull, and flick my eyes back to his visibly tented boxers. Goodness knows what kind of infections this man-child has going on down there.

Praise to the Goddess of Safe Sex for allowing me to dodge this STI-ridden bullet.

When I'm sure he thinks I'm about to run back into his giant arms—*fat chance, dudebro*—I drop my hand and descend the stairs, throwing my middle finger up behind me.

"Good luck with your chlamydia, Brock!"

And then I walk my *sexy* fat behind right out the door, the sound of his frat brothers laughing in my wake.

FIVE

kelley

MY ROUTINE for most Friday evenings includes checking the Friend Finder app before I hit the sack, so I know where Ivy landed for the night.

When Jesse texted me the picture of the douche-canoe she went home with an hour ago, he said she was likely heading to a fraternity on South Campus. When I check the app, though, her icon is moving three blocks away from South Campus frat row. The hair on the back of my neck stands on end, and I immediately start to worry. This is exactly why we have the app. It's one in the morning. What the hell is she doing walking in that area at night? Is she with him? Is she okay? Just as I'm about to call her, a text comes through.

Ivy Bean: You awake?

I heave a sigh of relief and dial her number. She picks up immediately.

"Hey, did I wake you?" Her voice is strong, and aside from sounding irritated, I'm sure she's safe.

"No, I was up. What's up? Is everything okay?"

"Yeah, everything's fine. Except it's a two-hour wait for an Uber and I don't really want to walk through that creepy Campus Grove."

Campus Grove is a four-acre stretch of trees and trails and randomly placed picnic pavilions. It's great during the day, but it's definitely not safe to walk through at night. A year ago, the campus put safety lights and call boxes along all the trails, but it's still not somewhere you want to find yourself at one in the morning alone, if you can help it. It's fucking creepy.

"Yeah, no, don't do that. Sit tight, I'll come get you."

"Thank you, Kelley. I owe you big."

"Nah, it's fine. See you soon."

"Love you!"

"Love you back."

I hang up, pull on some sweats and a t-shirt, and head out to play the gallant knight in a silver Jeep Wrangler.

Fifteen minutes later, Ivy climbs into the passenger seat of my Wrangler, and I'm immediately assaulted with the nauseating and overpowering smell of men's body spray. As if I needed one, it serves as a reminder of her activities for the evening.

"Thanks for this, Kell. Seriously, I owe you." She heaves a sigh and settles back into her seat as I pull a U-turn.

"What cut your night short? Is everything okay?"

"Yeah," she shrugs. "The guy just ended up being a bigger jerk than I wanted to deal with."

My hands tighten on the steering wheel.

"What happened? Did he try something? Did he hurt you?" I shoot off a rapid fire of questions, my fury obvious with every word. I will fuck him up.

"No, nothing like that," Ivy says quickly, placing a calming hand on my forearm. "He just didn't want to wear a condom."

I stiffen at the mention of Ivy and condoms and other men, but she's staring out the front window and doesn't notice.

"I'm not trying to catch something for twenty minutes of what was sure to be lackluster sex and the hope of a possible orgasm," she states. "Gosh, I'm exhausted."

"What time do you have to be in tomorrow?" I ask, happy for the change of topic.

"Nine. At least now I'll get to sleep in my own sheets."

"Yeah, at least there's that," I whisper. There's more melancholy in my voice than intended. It's one thing to hear about Ivy's Friday nights in abstract from Jesse; it's something else entirely to be this close to the actual event, and I don't know how to process it.

The rest of the drive to her apartment is silent.

When I pull my Jeep up to the curb, Ivy unbuckles her seat belt and grabs her small purse thing off the floor.

"I'll see you tomorrow night, yeah?" she says as she reaches for the door handle. "And don't forget, you promised to teach me how to drive stick on Sunday night."

I can't help but return her smile.

"You know, there's a joke there..."

"Oh my *gosh*, Kelley. No. No phallic stick jokes." I bark out a laugh at her exasperation.

"No worries, Ives. I haven't forgotten. I'll see you tomorrow."

Ivy leans over the center console to give me a hug, and I hold my breath. For some reason, I'm overcome with a deep sense of loss, and I know that even smelling her fruity shampoo mixed with that douchey body spray is likely to push me over the edge. But even with my eyes clamped shut, I feel the unavoidable warmth and crackle of electricity I get every time we touch. I tighten my arms around her because,

54

apparently, I'm a glutton for punishment, and the pain in my chest sharpens.

She lets me hold her, and I feel her fingers twist in my t-shirt, the caress on my back shooting small sparks of heat over my skin. She turns her head slightly, and I feel her breath skirting over my collarbone, feel her loose hair stick a little to the scruff on my jaw. When my heartbeat starts to thunder, I mentally reproach myself for any sneaking hope that this is *more* than just a hug between friends.

"Thank you," she whispers, and she's so close that I can feel her lips moving. I swallow.

"Anytime."

I turn to press a kiss on her head at the same time Ivy tilts her chin up to kiss my cheek. When her lips land on the corner of my mouth, I can't breathe, and she breaks away quickly. She says goodbye without making eye contact, and all I can do is nod as she hops out and jogs toward her apartment building. When I finally inhale, my chest burns.

I sit in my Jeep and watch her, waiting for her to get in the door before I drive off, and I'm consumed with a familiar sadness.

She's unaffected, completely and totally fine, and I'm anything but.

Ivy Rivenbark is my power source. She is my light and my energy and my everything, but she will never be *mine*.

Not like *that*.

And as I put my car in drive and head back to my place, I tell myself again that I'm content with my BFF status and platonic Saturday movie nights.

* * *

I'm finishing up dinner for Ivy and me, and the oven timer goes off just as I hear the knob turn on the front door. *Right on time.*

"Honey! I'm home!" Ivy calls sweetly from the doorway. "Gosh, it smells divine." Her voice floats into the kitchen, and I can tell just from the cadence that she's exhausted. Work probably kicked her ass today. I'm sure the moment the clock strikes eleven, she'll be down for the count. As usual.

I hear the jangle of her keys as she hangs them on the hook next to the door and then the shuffle of her feet as she kicks off her heels. I turn my back to the doorway, intentionally busying myself with the pizza, so I don't see her enter the kitchen.

Instead, I try to imagine what she's wearing today. A crisp, modest button down, the blue one that matches her eyes, just fitted enough to hint at the delicious curves underneath. Black dress slacks that cling to the flare of her hips, bare feet since her sexy heels have been discarded by the door.

In my mind, her hair is up in a bun, strands framing her face from where they've fallen loose thanks to a day of resting her cheek in her palm. Her glasses will be perched on top of her head, her eyes will be soft with fatigue from poring over files all day, and her plump lips will be pulled into that gentle side smile that does twisted-up things to my stomach.

"Kell, did you make pizza? It smells amazing." I listen as she walks into the kitchen and drops her bag on to the counter. "When did you get here?"

"About an hour ago," I reply, my back still to her. "Bailey wasn't here, so I used my key."

I slide the pizza from the oven to the stove top, put the oven mitt back in the drawer, take a deep breath, and then turn to face her. She's leaning against the kitchen island, eyes downcast as she scrolls through her phone.

I run my gaze over her, taking inventory from toe to head. Bare feet, check. But that was an easy one since I heard her take her shoes off by the door. Black dress slacks, check. Fitted button down, check, but I lose points on this one. She's wearing a gray shirt, and I had guessed blue. *Wishful thinking*.

I got the hair and glasses right, though, right down to the errant tendrils framing her face. That just leaves...

"How was your day?" I ask, willing her eyes to meet mine.

Slowly, her gaze lifts from her phone and locks on my face, and there it is.

Soft eyelids, lined with red from staring at papers all day, making her gorgeous irises shine an impossible blue. Ivy is exhausted. But even dead on her feet, she's a goddess.

"It was good," she says on a long exhale. "A lot, but good."

"What's the old battleax got you doing now?"

"Kelley!" She laughs, her tired eyes lighting up in the exact way I was hoping. "Don't talk about your mom that way. You know I adore her."

"You adore everyone."

"Because there are so many people worthy of my adoration." She bats her lashes and smiles, genuinely sweet. "Speaking of adoration, what did you make for me?"

"Margherita pizza." I watch as her eyes flash over my shoulder, studying the pizza on the stovetop with obvious hunger.

"Mmmm. Did you add Italian sausage?" She runs her tongue over her bottom lip, and my groin heats. *Fuck*.

"Of course."

"Good, you know how I need my meat." She whips her eyes back to mine and wiggles her brows playfully, wearing a smirk that could be considered flirtatious on anyone else.

"Yeah, yeah, you hussy. I get it. You're a sausage fiend." I wave her off, trying my best to fight a laugh and failing. I place three slices of pizza onto a plate and set it in front of her.

"Can't help it. I'm a growing girl with an insatiable hunger," she says as she plops down onto the barstool and lifts a slice to her mouth.

I have to force myself to turn around, double-check that the oven is off, grab two beers from the fridge, anything to keep myself from watching her eat.

If I thought for one second that making a move wouldn't ruin our friendship, I'd do it. I'd tell her how I feel, and then I'd spend every minute afterward showing her. But I learned the hard way that anything more than friendship between Ivy and me is impossible. It's torture, but I can't picture my life without her, so I take what I can get and stoically bear the pain.

"So, what's the plan?" she mumbles through a mouthful of pizza. I crack open a beer and set it in front of her, then open my own and take a long pull before answering.

"Well, we could start that new cheesy horror film that came out last week. The one set in the high school and the teenagers are played by grown fucking adults?"

"Mmm, that could work. I'm down for gore, and older actors make me feel less skeezy about drooling over the hero."

"Ha, right. Or, we could watch *Becoming*, that documentary about the former First Lady."

"Always my First Lady," she says and lifts her beer to me.

I knock my can with hers. "I'll cheers to that."

"Well," she says after taking another drink of her beer, "my brain is tired. I need something I can pay minimal attention to and possibly fall asleep in the middle of."

"Sounds like you'll take twenty-seven-year-old teenagers for 1,000, Alex!"

"Yes!" she exclaims around a laugh, hopping up to put her plate in the sink. "C'mon, chef. My tummy has been sufficiently filled, and Bailey is bartending, so she won't be home until late. Let's get to the Netflixin' part of the evening. I know you probably have to run one hundred miles in the morning, so we don't want to keep you up too late."

I chuckle. "It's actually only six miles tomorrow."

"Ick." She shudders and saunters into the living room, and just like I've been doing since we were fourteen, I follow.

When I get back to my condo later, it's midnight.

Ivy, like usual, fell asleep before eleven, during a stupid gory ass slasher flick. I don't know how she does it. I was crawling out of my skin, using all my energy not to shriek like a small child. If she hadn't maneuvered her sleeping body onto my lap, I might have actually screamed.

The nights with more touching are torture. They are the best and also the worst possible thing. Tonight, when she fell asleep on my shoulder, her mango body wash engulfed me like a drug. An opium cloud of her scent. Thick and sweet and intoxicating.

When she sleepily moved so her head was in my lap, I forgot about the movie entirely. The weight of her head on my thigh and her warm breath slipping through the fabric of my thin joggers was enough to drive me crazy. By the time she rested her small hands on my leg, I was running my fingers through her silken hair and mentally reciting the Preamble to the Declaration of Independence to keep my dick in line.

I can't get that contact out of my mind.

Even with the physical distance between us, I can still

smell her shampoo, can still feel her fingers grasping onto my thigh, and I'm hard as stone. It doesn't matter how many amendments I recall; my erection isn't relenting.

Fuck.

It's not the first time I've taken matters into my own hands with Ivy on my mind. It definitely won't be the last.

I try not to.

I feel like such a shitty best friend when I do.

But I'm weak, and she's powerful, and I'm horny as hell. When I step into the shower and wrap my hand around my hard cock, it's her face in my fantasies.

I squeeze, letting the hot water cascade down my body, the soap allowing my strokes to glide smoothly up and down my shaft. I rest my back on the shower wall and slide my other hand down my torso, pressing on my abs.

I try to think about someone else.

Someone her polar opposite.

Someone who doesn't have blonde hair, blue eyes, curves for days, and the best fucking dimple in the whole damn world. Megan Fox. Ciara. Jessica Alba. Mother fucking Beyonce. After two, three strokes, a swipe of my palm over the swollen head of my dick, they all change into the one woman who owns me.

Ivy Jean Rivenbark.

Fuuuck.

In my head, I don't touch her. I never let it go that far. If I said what I really wanted to say, or put my hands on her how I craved, I couldn't come back from that. It would be the ultimate high. I'd never leave my fantasies.

Instead, I watch her.

I imagine her touching herself. Her delicate fingers pinch her nipples, and she whimpers. Her breasts are full and heavy, her nipples the same soft pink as her plump smile. My mouth waters. I want my lips on them. I want to suck those nipples into my mouth and lave them with my tongue. Bite them lightly. Mark up her perfect skin with my teeth.

But I can't.

So, I close my eyes tighter and watch as she massages and tweaks and writhes.

I squeeze my cock harder. Stroke it faster. A low groan escapes me, swallowed up by the steam.

Her small hands slide into black lace panties. She rubs her clit, swollen bottom lip between her teeth, desperate, needy blue eyes on me. I want to replace her fingers with mine, glide them through the slick folds of her pussy and press them inside. I want to feel her contract around me. I want to be the one to make her come.

Her hand moves underneath the lace of her panties. Her wrist bends slightly, fucking herself with her fingers. Her hips buck, her other hand massaging her breasts, and her eyes never leave me. I hold back from commanding her how I want, from urging her on. I clamp my mouth shut, both in reality and in my fantasy, and let her do as she pleases.

What I wouldn't do to taste her. To tell her all the dirty things I want to do to her. To have her hips moving like that against my face.

I flip around and brace myself on my forearm, drop my chin to my chest, and jerk my dick with her moans in my ears.

My balls tighten, my abs contract, and when I spray my release onto the shower wall, it's Ivy's name on my lips.

* * *

The next morning, I'm up with the sun.

So far, Sundays have been my favorite training days. The modified marathon training schedule I've been working through has me set so every Sunday, for the last seven weeks, has been six miles at an easy pace. Honestly, it's been therapeutic, and when I spend my Saturday nights with Ivy, it's necessary. I need an outlet. With the right playlist, I could do this session in my sleep.

I step out of my apartment, take a deep breath in, and drop to do a few more stretches.

Six a.m. is my sweet spot. I've always been a morning person. I'm that crazy idiot who likes eight a.ms on my class schedule every day. Ivy likes to joke that my affinity for mornings is why I'm getting my degree in education. I'm not going to lie, that actually went into my decision but being a teacher has always been end game.

Ma and Pop would have been overjoyed if I shared their love for law, but that just isn't for me. Ivy has the brain for that shit; I like lesson plans about dates and facts and cause and effect timelines. I like analyzing varying perspectives about the past to learn about the present, and I like knowing that I could be making a difference in the lives of my students.

Luckily for me, my parents aren't a bunch of controlling assholes who would try to force me into taking over their company or some other antiquated bullshit. They own a general practice law firm, not some Fortune 500 real estate investment banker empire or whatever. They're happy I found something I'm passionate about, even if that something means likely enduring piss-poor pay and governmental disrespect.

But I digress.

Finishing my quad and calf stretches, I pop in my earbuds and push play on my Sunday Marathon Playlist. Then, I slide my phone into my pocket, set the timer on my watch, and start my training session. I always do the first two blocks at a brisk walk before picking up into the guided run of the day.

Sundays—six miles at an easy pace. And I can breathe properly again.

Rounding the corner on mile five, I catch a glimpse of Jesse coming out of the student union. I don't know what he's doing up this early, but I can't say I'm not glad to see him. With the exception of the "*hey fucker are you alive?*" text I sent him when he didn't come home last night (to which he replied with a bunch of water and eggplant emojis), I haven't seen or talked to his ass since Friday morning, and I've got questions to subtly throw his way.

"Jesse!" I call out, slowing to a walk and pushing stop on my watch timer. "Hey, man."

"'Sup, Kell. Training morning?"

"Yep," I reply. "Halfway through the program." I rest my hands on the top of my head and work on steadying my breathing. I'm barely winded, but my heart rate is still elevated above resting.

"Damn. The marathon is getting close, yeah?"

"It is," I say on an exhale. "I'll be ready."

"Hell yes, you will." He nods with a grin. Jesse is a natural hype man. It's in everything he does. He's always the life of the party and the loudest one cheering in your corner.

"What are you doin' up so early on a Sunday?"

"Picked up a volunteer shift at the hospital, but I wanted to turn in this paper first." He holds up a stack of papers and nods toward the end of the quad. "This philosophy elective is kicking my ass, but it's interesting."

"The unexamined life is not worth living," I say in my best scholarly voice.

"Socrates. Nice." He chuckles. "Okay, out with it, Kelley. I know you didn't halt your training for bullshit small talk and to quote dead philosophers."

Busted. So much for subtlety.

"I don't know what you're talking about," I say, feigning innocence. "I love quoting dead philosophers."

He shakes his head slowly, leveling me with a no-nonsense stare. "I'm not spillin' shit until you grow a pair and ask, man."

"Fine," I say on a defeated sigh. "Tell me about Friday." I look away, hoping he can't see the apprehension on my face, but I can see him exaggeratedly roll his eyes in my peripheral.

"Same as usual. She nursed a drink, cozied up to a dudebro in a shirt two sizes too small, disappeared to the bathroom for fifteen minutes, and then left with the guy."

I nod my head slowly.

"You gotta get over this, Kelley. It's not gonna be you if you never shoot your shot. And for being her bestie, you're still damn clueless when it comes to Ivy."

"What?" I sputter. *What's that supposed to mean?* "I'm just looking out for her, J. Honestly. I don't want something happening to her."

"She's a grown ass woman, man, and she can handle herself. Trust me. If anyone can handle themselves, it's Ivy." He repeats the same thing he always does every time we have this conversation.

"I played the creep and took the picture, you've got her tracked on that stalker app, and I'm always there. You need to stop worrying. Maybe get out once in a while and have some fun."

"Not my thing, J."

"Yeah, I know," he says around a laugh and shrugs. "Can't fault me for trying. It would be nice to have a wing man in addition to my wing woman."

"I don't understand you two. Doesn't going out every weekend get old?"

"Nope. We make a good team." He winks like a jerk,

bouncing back and forth on the balls of his feet while he taunts me. "She reels me in some company, I vet hers, and we both go home happy. Nothing wrong with that." Jesse laughs at what I'm sure is a disgruntled look my face.

And on that note, I'm done.

"Alright, J. I gotta get to it," and I head away from him without a goodbye.

"Later, Kelley," he shouts at my back. "Come out Friday and I'll make sure you get your dick wet!"

I toss my middle finger up over my head and round the corner with his loud laugh echoing in my ears.

Later that night, I pull up to Ivy's apartment building in a truck I borrowed from a friend to give her the first lesson on how to drive stick. For a brief moment, my mind goes to her handling a different kind of stick—*my stick*—but I chase that thought away with a shake of the head.

Maybe I'll recall it tonight when I'm alone in my room, but it's best I don't have hand jobs on the brain when I'm stuck in a car with Ivy. Even if her delicate fingers would probably look sexy as hell wrapped around my dick.

A few weeks ago, after watching one of the *Fast and Furious* movies, Ivy decided that she wanted to learn how to drive manual.

When I asked her why she wanted to since her car is an automatic, she launched into this very *Ivy* tirade, listing all of the reasons why *all* women should know how to drive a manual transmission vehicle *if they want to.*

"But Ives, you've never owned a stick shift, and neither has anyone we've ever known—"

"Vicky Spencer's older brother had that muscle car in

high school and I'm pretty sure that was a manual," she interrupted.

"Okay. I stand corrected." I laughed. "But how many times did you even speak to Vicky Spencer's brother? Hell, how many times did you even speak to Vicky Spencer?"

"That's irrelevant. The point is that if the opportunity ever *had* come up with Vicky Spencer's brother, I would have missed out. And *you* know how to drive a manual transmission." She huffed, flustered and indignant and totally adorable.

Like a little pissed-off kitten.

"And anyway," she continued, "don't you know that manual transmission cars are easier to maintain, *and* they get better gas mileage—a significant two to five mpg! That can lower a vehicle's cost by up to $1,200!—*and* they're cheaper brand new?"

She had her little hands on her grippable hips, and her head was cocked to one side, her toes tapping in her Chucks. I half-expected her to hiss at me, and I was having a hard time fighting back my laughter.

"*And,*" she added, "manuals give the driver a better sense of control, and you know how I like control, Kelley. And even though only approximately thirteen percent of the vehicles in the U.S. are manual, that still means there is a thirteen percent chance of coming across a manual transmission vehicle in the event of an emergency or something like that."

I raised my eyebrows at her.

"In the event of an emergency? And what kind of emergency would lead you to needing to drive a stick shift?"

"All sorts."

"Really?"

"Yes, really."

"Ivy."

"Kelley."

"Name one."

If I thought I'd stump her, I was very, very wrong. Ivy Rivenbark doesn't go into any decision without having thought it out and done research. Preparation is key.

Ticking off on her fingers, she started listing.

"Well, there could be a natural disaster limiting the variety of available safety vehicles. I could get stranded in the middle of a road trip and the only rental is a stick. I could need to drive someone to the hospital and their car is a stick. Or the apocalypse, Kelley. Zombie apocalypse, alien invasion, volcanic eruption, fascist governmental coup. The possibilities are endless."

She leveled me with a stare, daring me to contradict her.

"Zombie apocalypse? Alien invasion? Do you believe those would happen?"

"No, of course not, but I needed to list as many things as possible," she said matter-of-factly, waving her hand in the air as if this conversation was completely normal.

"Plus, driving a stick would make you feel like a badass, empowered woman who 'don't need no man and anything he can do, you could do better'?"

She grinned widely.

"Most definitely. I want to learn to drive stick, and you're going to teach me."

And that was that.

Which is why, instead of working on my reading for my history class, I am about to spend my Sunday evening sitting in a truck I borrowed from a guy I play soccer with, in a vacant parking lot, teaching my best friend how to drive stick shift.

The last time we were in a vehicle in this capacity, we were in high school and I was helping her practice for her driver's test. Ivy doesn't handle being told what to do very well, and at sixteen, I didn't really know how to give instruction without sounding like a condescending asshole. We ended up not speaking for three days, and that was fucking *torture*. We may have grown up a bit since then, but I'm still nervous as hell.

Please let our friendship survive this.

"Okay, Kelley. Ask me to recite the steps of driving a manual transmission vehicle."

"Ivy Rivenbark, please recite the steps of driving a manual transmission vehicle."

"First, I put the gear in neutral, then I press the clutch all the way to the floor with my left foot."

"Correct."

"Then, I turn the ignition key."

"Yep. Continue."

"Then, I make sure the parking brake is off, and press the brake with my right foot."

I nod and gesture for her to keep going.

"I put the car into first gear, take my right foot off the brake and move it to the gas pedal."

"Yep. Now comes the hard part," I tease, and she flicks her eyes in my direction and scrunches up her nose.

"I slowly begin to take my foot off the clutch with my left foot and gently transfer that pressure onto the gas pedal with my right foot until I am only pressing the gas."

"Congratulations! You're hypothetically driving in first gear. Now let's put it into practice."

"Don't you want to know how I switch gears?"

"Let's just master first gear right now, Ives. We can learn shifting next time."

"Fine. Okay. Yes," she says while nodding her head, and

then mumbles to herself, "You can do this. You're a powerful, fierce mountain lion of greatness." I bark out a laugh.

"Hush," she scolds me. "Geoff came up with it, and I like it so I'm keeping it."

I put my palms up. "Okay, Ivy Mountain Lion, let's see what you've got."

She takes another deep breath, grips the steering wheel, presses hard on the gas, and then promptly kills the truck, jerking us both violently in our seats.

"Whoa, buddy, what was that? That didn't happen in any of the YouTube tutorials."

"That was you effectively stalling the engine."

She looks at me with wide eyes. "Is it okay?"

"Yeah, Ives." I laugh. "It's fine. Now chop-chop, try again."

She blows out a breath, fixes her face into a determined glare, and tries once more.

After four more attempts, and four more violent stalls, Ivy succeeds, and we crawl around the parking lot in first gear.

"Woohoo! Look at me! Danica Patrick, I'm coming for you!"

"You're ridiculous."

"Whatever, you love me, so you'll deal with it."

I laugh and nod. She's got me there. "Only for you, Ives. Only ever for you."

"Can we try to shift now?" She dances excitedly in her seat.

"Yeah, Ivy," I say with a chuckle. "Shift away."

I've got reading to finish and lesson plans to review, but right now, there's no place I'd rather be.

"YOU'RE BACK EARLY!" Bailey chirps from our kitchen table as I walk into our apartment on Tuesday evening.

"I didn't feel like starting another practice test," I say as I kick off my shoes and head toward my bedroom. "Plus, I knew you were off tonight, and I haven't seen you in almost a week."

"You just saw me this morning before you left for class." Bailey laughs.

I walk into my bedroom, drop my bag next to my desk, and promptly change into some yoga pants and an oversized sweatshirt. Heading back into the kitchen, I fill a small mason jar with white wine from the box in the fridge and grab some cookies from the dish on the counter.

"Seeing you in passing doesn't count," I say through a mouthful of chocolate chips and caramel. "We need some girl time."

"I am always down for girl time. Are you ready for the Indy 500?"

"Not yet. Kelley wouldn't let me leave the parking lot, but

I can shift all the gears without stalling." I hold my glass of wine up in the air and mime shifting gears with my other hand, doing a little shimmy and just narrowly avoiding a spill.

"Nice. Zombie Apocalypse, do your worst." She laughs with me, and then gestures toward the plate full of cookies. "What do you think?"

"They're good," I say enthusiastically.

"Yeah?"

"Yeah." I nod and stuff more cookie into my mouth. "Like, *Praise the Sugar Goddess* good. I think these are my favorite so far."

"Really? That's great. This is a new recipe. I took the chocolate chip cookies I made last weekend but kind of combined it with those caramel cheesecake bars that the guys liked."

I widen my eyes, thoroughly impressed, and take another bite. "They're really good, Bailey. I think Kelley would love these, too. You think this is the winner?"

"I don't know yet." Bailey shrugs. "I've got a few more recipes I want to try."

"Well, as always, I volunteer as tribute to taste test any and all of your concoctions," I say with a smile, and she grins back at me. "I also brought you a new legal pad for your recipes. I noticed your old one was almost out."

"Oooh, thanks." Bailey bats her eyelashes at me. "You're too good to me."

I met Bailey Barnes sophomore year. We both transferred to Butler University, and she was my random roommate placement in the dorms. I've heard horror stories about nightmare roommates, but Bailey and I hit it off right away. We got along so well that we decided to room together again junior year, and then this year, we got this apartment.

Appearance-wise, we're opposites. Where I'm a plain light blonde, Bailey's hair is a dark brown, probably only a shade away from full-fledged black, and she currently has the ends dyed a bright turquoise. Bailey's skin is permanently sun-kissed, and I'm pale and freckled. My eyes are a common shade of blue, and Bailey's are golden amber framed by the longest, thickest, blackest eyelashes. I love her eyes. They honestly sparkle.

Kelley likes to joke that Bailey and I are like symbolic images of good and evil in human form. Last year for Halloween, she and I dressed up as the angel and devil on Jesse's shoulders. I have a picture framed on my dresser.

"How's work been?" I ask as I fill her a glass of wine and top mine off. The one I fill for her is a pint glass from Keggers. Pretty sure she stole it.

"Good. Since Jada promoted me to a lead bartender, I've been getting more hours, but I've had to get creative with balancing homework and baking." Bailey and I take our wine into the living room and sit on the couch.

"I'm not complaining about waking up to find you've baked three dozen cookies miraculously overnight, but don't overwork yourself. And let me know if there's anything I can help with."

Bailey has been working as a bartender at Bar 31, one of the popular campus bars, since last year. At the beginning of this semester, one of the bakeries in the city announced a cookie baking contest open to all the students on campus. The winner gets a $2,000 prize and their cookie will be included on the shop's menu for a month. I've never seen Bailey so excited. Since then, she's been trying new recipes whenever possible.

"When are the submissions due?" I ask, even though I

already know because the date is circled in purple highlighter on the calendar hanging on our fridge.

"October third," she says excitedly. "The submission and judging are both on October third. It's going to be broadcast live on *The Morning Show* on Channel 5 News, too." She looks at me, nervous excitement all over her face. "You're still coming, right? I know the LSAT is the next weekend, but you're not going to be too busy cramming last minute practice tests to come watch me, right?"

"Bailey, I wouldn't miss this contest for anything. Besides," I add, "if I don't know what I need to know for the LSAT by then, there's no hope for me."

Bailey looks at me earnestly and smiles. "You're gonna crush the LSAT, V."

"Thank you, B." I smile back. "And you're gonna crush this cookie contest." I mean it, too. Bailey is freaking talented. The recipes she comes up with are always creative and delicious.

"Oh, I almost forgot," I say with a grin, "are you going to tell me where you were the other night? You weren't here when I got home...or when I left for class..."

She pops a brow and smiles coyly. "I checked in and shared my location with you."

"Ha, yeah, and you were off campus in a townhouse! I Google Earthed it."

She rolls her eyes at me with a smile. She knows I'm overprotective and a worrier. I'm not ashamed of it. Hence why we always share our locations and send check-in texts.

"Well," she takes a slow sip of her wine, "I might have met someone..."

I widen my eyes excitedly and can't help my suggestive smile. "Why didn't you tell me the second it happened? Name? Credentials?"

"It's not a big deal." She takes another sip from her glass and shrugs it off in a very *Bailey* way. "I met him in the baking aisle at the grocery store, and we had a good time."

"You gonna see him again?" I ask. Bailey dates, but she doesn't get invested. Guys are a fun pastime, a stress reliever, and that's it.

"Dunno yet." She crinkles her nose, and I watch her eyes flick to where her phone sits on the coffee table. *Interesting.*

"Oh, I wanted to ask," she blurts suddenly, "what happened Friday? You were already home when I got home from work, but it didn't sound like anyone was with you..." Bailey trails off and raises her eyebrows, effectively turning the tables on me.

"Ugh. I came home early. The guy I went home with was terrible."

Bailey laughs. "Oh no! What do you mean terrible? Like he had a small peen?" She wiggles her pinky finger, causing me to lose it in a fit of giggles.

"No! Gosh, no. He was, um, definitely fine in that department." I widen my eyes for emphasis. "But he ended up being a bigger jerk than I wanted to deal with."

"Oh, ew. That's worse than..." and she wiggles her pinky finger again.

"True. I'll take an average-sized, uh, tool over a tool *bag* any day. Big doesn't always equate to good."

"Truth. Sometimes big is just some meathead throwing it around in all the wrong ways thinking he's a baller." She flails her arm around in front of her in demonstration and I laugh when she splashes wine on her shirt.

"Shit!" She giggles and swipes at the spill with her other hand. "See? No finesse."

"Right? Like, you can take your extra inches and trade them in for some skill and basic knowledge of the female anatomy. Ya Neanderthal."

"So anyway," Bailey says after our giggles have faded. "What did the big dick dumbass do?"

"Well, first, he wouldn't go down on me, which okay whatever, that's not all that unusual," I say with a sigh. "But he tried to act like he didn't have a condom!"

"What! Like, he *lied*?"

"Yep. He lied and then fed me the 'I can't feel you good with a condom' line." I try to say it in my best pea-brain caveman voice, which is now how Brock sounds in my memories.

"Gross. What did you do?"

"I told him no way in heck was I having sex without a condom."

"Good. We don't want no STDs or baby dumbasses!"

"That's not even the end of it. When I told him I was leaving, he called me fat."

"What the fuck?"

"I know! Well, actually, he said I had a fat *ass*," I whisper the cuss word and raise my eyebrows for emphasis.

Bailey snorts. "You do got a fat ass, though."

I giggle and take a sip. "This is true."

"Cheers to fat asses!" Bailey exclaims and holds her glass up to clink with mine.

"Why do guys do that, though? Resort to insulting a woman's body if they don't get what they want?" I muse with a huff. "And why does everyone act like fat is a dirty word? It shouldn't be."

"No, it shouldn't be. And the guys who do that do it 'cause they think that a woman's appearance is the only thing valuable about them and they want to feel superior by doing the most damage in the shortest amount of time." She flashes me a smirk. "Joke's on them, though, because we're wising up and realizing that we're worth so much more than how men see us. And fat ass bitches like you and me? We're gonna dismantle the patriarchy, one big dick dumbass at a time."

"But, B, you don't have a fat butt."

She barks out a laugh. "Revision! Fat ass bitches and skinny ass bitches are gonna dismantle the patriarchy!" She lifts her glass again. "Cheers to the rise of all ass-having women. Fuck the patriarchy."

"To women!" We both take a giant gulp, and then Bailey's face contorts with disgust.

"What a douche." She shakes her head and I sigh.

"Yep."

"So, you just took an Uber home?"

"I tried, but the wait time was crazy, so I called Kelley for a ride."

Bailey gets quiet, and when I look over at her, she's looking at me skeptically.

"What?"

"You called Kelley to come pick you up from a failed hookup," she states for clarification.

"Yeah. I texted first. He was still awake. What? Why are you looking at me like that?"

Seriously, why is she looking at me like that?

Bailey sets her wine glass on the coffee table, and then meets my eyes. "Ivy Jean Rivenbark, that man is in love with you. And normally I'd say that's his problem and not your responsibility, because it *is* his problem and *not* your responsibility, but you act like you don't know."

"You've been reading too many of your romance novels," I say with a forced chuckle, trying to laugh it off. For being so cynical about her own relationships, Bailey certainly loves a good fictional love story. Now she's trying to create her own with me and Kelley as the main characters.

"Maybe you need to start reading them," she says pointedly, and I roll my eyes. "Ivy, you can't tell me you don't know that he's in love with you."

"He's not in love with me, Bailey. We're just friends." I pick up my glass and take a drink, tracing my fingers over the etching on the side. "We've been friends forever."

"V. He's in love with you, and I'm pretty sure you're in—"

"No." I put my palm up and cut her off. "We aren't having this conversation, B. I love you but listen, Kelley and I are friends. We've been friends since we were fourteen. The only time we weren't friends was when we let hormones get in the way, and that cannot happen again. And I do not have the time, energy, or emotional stability to commit to a romantic relationship anyway. I have no desire to try, okay? We don't see each other like that. We *can't*. So please drop it. Okay?"

I hold my gaze firmly on her. I don't blink. I don't back down. This is a line for me; I will not cross it. I *can't*.

Finally, she nods and lets out a long sigh.

"Wanna watch a serial killer documentary?" she asks, and I silently send up a thank you that she took mercy on me and changed the subject.

"Yes, please. Serial killer documentaries, cookies, and wine; these are a few of my favorite things."

Bailey laughs, picks up the remote and flips on the television, and the tension that was once suffocating dissipates. I send up another thank you to the powers that be that I have someone like Bailey in my life and settle in for a girls' night with my other bestie.

* * *

"Hey, Mom," I say into the phone as I walk to the library after classes on Thursday. I've talked to Jacob a few times this week, but this is the first time Mom's been around when I called. "How's work?"

"The usual, sweetie. Beth Anne quit finally so I got some of the girls training someone new. And Frank—you know Frank? The older gentleman who works in the kitchen—well, his daughter had her baby, so he took off the weekend to go see 'em and I had to move Nicky from fry to line and move Josiah from bussing to fry. You know. It's always somethin'."

"Jeez, Mom. When was your last day off before today?" I ask, and when she starts to answer, I add, "I mean a real day off; not a day when you only work a single instead of a double."

She barks out a laugh, followed by a cough, and I wince. I wish she'd quit smoking, but at least she doesn't do it in the house or in the car anymore. Jacob's asthma put a stop to that. Curse those nasty nicotine demons and the hold they have on my mother.

"My last full day off was ten days ago, but someone's gotta make sure the place don't fall down, Ivy Jean. That someone's gotta be me." I hear her deep inhale, probably taking a drag from a cigarette. "The only employee I can trust is Allison and she's got a son and that deadbeat husband, so I can't be expectin' her to be there all the time."

"I know, Mom." I hear this every time. "Just make sure you're not working yourself too hard, please. Jacob needs you. He shouldn't be home by himself all the time."

"Ivy Jean, I'm the parent here. I know what I'm doin'," she spits out. "I raised you just fine and you turned out alright. Trust I can take care of Jacob. He is *my* son."

I bite my tongue. She and I have gotten into it over this before, and it's a sore subject. I love my mother. She's worked harder than any person should have to, to provide for Jacob and me. Life's dealt her a really difficult hand and she's playing it the only way she knows how. But sometimes, a lot of times, I get frustrated with it all, and I grow resentful. I basically raised myself, and Jacob too. I have to remind myself that she's sacrificed so much—after my dad died, and then Jacob's dad took off, and then with everything that happened with me my senior year of high school. I'm lucky she's my mom. But sometimes I wonder if it couldn't be different.

There's an awkward, lengthy pause, and then I hear movement in the background.

"Is Jacob home?"

"He just walked up. I'll put him on." She takes a deep breath. "Ivy Jean, you know I love you."

"I do, Mom."

"Bigger than the sun..." she says.

"...and the moon and stars, too," I finish. Then she hands the phone to Jacob, and I can't stop the smile that takes over my face.

"Bean!" Jacob exclaims. I just talked to him two days ago, but he always acts like it's been forever.

"Hey, Bug! Did you just get home?"

"Yep. I stopped at the library on the way home. I got this book about dragons and a dragon rider and there are elves, and it's a series and the books are *huge,* but I'm gonna start it tonight." He's so cute when he's excited.

"That's amazing, Jacob! Maybe I'll check it out, too, and we can buddy read."

"Yeah! You can read it with Kelley and me!"

"You're reading it with Kelley?" I ask, and I feel my smile grow until I'm a grinning fool. I absolutely love that Kelley and Jacob are close. The way Kelley is woven into my life fills me with feelings I shouldn't feel, and I work quickly to mentally stomp on all of them. *Take that, butterflies.*

"He's the one that told me about it. He says he's read the

whole series like three times and now he's reading it with me so it's his fourth time." He's so excited that I don't think he's taken a breath.

"When did you talk to him?"

"Oh, he called to see how I was doin' a couple days ago…" Jacob trails off. Kelley must have called to ask him about those bullies at school.

"How *are* you, Bug?" I ask.

"Fine." His answer is clipped and quiet, and my defenses go up.

"How's school?"

"F-fine." As soon as he stutters, I can tell something is wrong. He used to stutter all the time when he was younger, but now it only comes out when he's flustered or nervous. Sometimes when he's scared.

"What's up, Bug? Those kids messing with you again?" I press.

Silence.

"Jacob. Answer me."

"It's n-nothing, Ivy. Th-they're j-just assholes."

"Jacob Lee Rivenbark, you do not curse," I admonish, and I can hear him huff indignantly. "Tell me what's going on. Are they taking your homework again?"

"N-no."

"Are they calling you names?"

"N-no, Ivy."

"Jacob," I say more softly. "Tell me what's happening. You can tell me."

He sighs loudly, resigned to finally give me what I want.

"They t-took my P-P-P.E. clothes. P-pushed me around a little. Then t-told everyone in the g-gym that I pee my p-pants." I hear him sniffle. Furious tears fill my eyes in response. I cannot stand the thought of him being so sad.

He's one of the most amazing people I know, and I don't understand how these kids don't see that. I would absorb every ounce of his pain if it meant he only ever felt happiness.

"I'll take care of it."

"No!" he shouts, making me jump. "No, Ivy. P-please don't call the school again. It will j-j-just make things w-worse."

"But I could—"

"—N-no, Bean. Please," he pleads, and my heart cracks right in half. "Please don't. It will be f-fine. I'm fine."

I hesitate. It goes against all my instincts to agree, but I don't want to add to his trouble. I won't call the school this time, but I make a mental note to add this incident to my file. Just in case.

"Okay," I relent. "Promise you'll tell me if things get worse?"

"I promise." His voice is strong, and I can almost picture him standing his ground, a determined set to his jaw and his brows furrowed seriously.

"Okay. I'm at the library now, so I'm going to have to let you go, Bug. But I'll talk to you tomorrow and I'll see you soon."

"Thank you, Ivy."

"For what, Bug?"

"Just for being my sister," he says, and my eyes fill with tears again. "I love you big, big, Bean."

"Bigger than the sun and moon and stars, Bug."

I hang up with Jacob, enter the library, and head straight to the study carrell I reserved for this afternoon. I set out my computer, my LSAT prep books, and plug in my phone.

Then I take a deep breath and allow myself a few moments to feel sad, worried, helpless, lost—all the things that come with knowing my brother is hurting and I can't fix it. I graze the surface of those emotions, acknowledge them, and then compress them into a tiny box and file that box away in my brain to be dealt with later.

If I think too much about it, I will lose myself in sobs, and I don't have time to cry. Right now, I need to focus on what I can control, and that is my preparedness for the LSAT. Because I *will* ace this test.

Tonight, Jesse and I have found ourselves at the Sig Chi fraternity. They're having a heroes and heroines theme party, so we dressed up like Danny and Post-Peer Pressure Sandy from *Grease*. We don't usually go out on Thursdays, but I need a distraction from my phone call with Jacob earlier. Kelley and I have decided to drive home this weekend, so when J asked if I would hit up this party with him, since we won't be going out tomorrow, I said yes.

Jesse is really feeling himself in his leather jacket and wayfarers, an unlit cigarette propped behind his ear. He's got his dark, curly hair gelled into the traditional T-Bird style, and with his cuffed jeans and white shirt, he definitely passes for a Greaser. I'm surprised I fit my butt, thighs and hips into these leather pants, but I'm feeling myself tonight too.

"J, you're looking spicy tonight," I say playfully as we walk up the steps of the house. He bounces up and down on the balls of his feet, and even though he's 6'3" and probably 200 pounds of solid muscle, he looks like an excited little boy on his birthday.

"I'm feeling spicy, V," he says. Then he quirks his upper lip, splays his palms out at his sides and swivels his hips. "I'm a hunka hunka burnin' love."

I bark out a laugh. "Noooo, J. You're Danny from *Grease*." I'm giggling so hard right now. "You're not Elvis."

He freezes, leaving his hands out and lip quirked, and pops a brow at me. "Huh?"

He looks absolutely ridiculous, and I'm tearing up from laughing.

"*Grease!*" I shout. "John Travolta? Olivia Newton John? The T-Birds!? The Pink Ladies?"

I'm actually shocked, because there's not a single ounce of recognition on his face. He's just standing there in the same position, lip still quirked, looking like a wax statue that was molded to be Elvis but was dressed like Danny Zuko and then given a really dark tan. I take out my phone and snap a picture, which makes him break into a smile.

"Looks like we're gonna have to have a movie night, V. I need more of these *Pink* Ladies," he says with a wink.

"Ew, J." I laugh.

"And send me that picture," he adds as we walk in the frat house. "That's gonna be my new profile pic."

About an hour later, Jesse is cozied up to a pretty brunette on the couch and I'm officially off duty. I'm here strictly as his wing woman tonight, so I'm not looking for company. Two weekends in a row was a lot for me. Add in the phone call with my brother earlier, and I'm mentally and emotionally drained. Instead of mingling, I'm sitting on the counter in the kitchen scrolling TikTok and sending Kelley the videos that make me think of him.

So far, I've sent him ten, and he's liked almost all of them.

No matter how many times I try to ignore it, I still feel a bit giddy when I know I've made him laugh. I tell myself it's normal to want to make your best friend happy, and then I promptly squash any of those pesky tummy butterflies who don't get the *Just Friends* memo. The dang pests are persistent, though.

Apparently, my RBF and phone scrolling don't send a

strong enough message, because soon a guy with blond hair and biceps for days is sliding up beside me.

"Hey," he says. Real smooth. Poetic. A regular Wordsworth. I stifle a laugh.

"Hey," I reply without looking up from my phone.

Go away. I'm not interested.

"I've seen you before."

"I go to school here. It's not that big of a school," I deadpan while watching a video of a dancing cat wearing a party hat. It's so funny. I shoot it to Kelley and wait for his reaction.

"No, that's not it," he says, and moves in front of me, bracing his hands on the counter, boxing me in.

"Excuse you," I snap, and glare at him in warning, but he doesn't back off.

"You were with my brother Brock last weekend."

"Oh, you mean Chlamydia Brock?" I say with attitude. He's too close and can't take a hint, and if he gets any closer, I am going to show him just what four years of self-defense training has taught me. "Yeah, I remember him. He's your brother? Just how close are you? Do you share STDs?" I say the last part loudly hoping he'll finally get the message and leave me alone.

"Don't be like that, Ivy," he croons, and I bristle at the fact that he knows my name. "Brock is a dick. He doesn't know how to treat a girl like you. But me?" He winks at me and I get a sick feeling in my stomach, anger and unwanted fear swirl violently. "I could treat you real good."

He leans in, invading my space even more, and I'm about to tell him to kick rocks, maybe knee him in the nuts, when I get a whiff of a spicy, expensive, and absolutely terrifying scent that sends me reeling.

My chest tightens, my skin pricks, and I can feel sweat

dotting my hairline. I push his chest away with my hands and squeeze my eyes shut, but my panic intensifies when flashes of memory play out on the backs of my eyelids. The same flashes I haven't seen in almost a year.

A dark mesh jersey.

A low rumbling voice.

Dark hair.

Navy curtains.

Pressure.

And now a new one.

A spicy and cloying blend of leather and ginger.

It's a rapid-fire viewfinder playing back my nightmares.

"What cologne are you wearing?" I choke out, unsure if he can hear me over the blood pounding in my eardrums, and he chuckles.

"You like it?" he says in a way that I'm sure he thinks is seductive, but if I don't get out of here soon, I'm going to vomit all over his too-small t-shirt.

A dark mesh jersey. A low rumbling voice. Dark hair.

"What is it?" I press again, trying my best to breathe through my mouth, to avoid the stink, but it's getting harder to do. My heart is racing, I'm feeling dizzy, and I can feel the kitchen cabinets closing in on me. It's getting louder by the second. My skin is tight and itching. I try to recite the Attorney's Oath but can't even recall the first sentence.

Navy curtains. Leather. Ginger. Pressure.

"It's *Juego Voss*... Hey are you okay?" The guy moves his hand to my shoulder, but I shove him off.

Jersey. Dark. Pressure. Pressure. Pressure.

"I'm going to be sick," I say, and he steps back quickly as I jump off the counter and rush to the stairway. I clutch the railing and stumble up the stairs, steadying myself on the wall for a moment once I reach the top. Then, hurriedly, I bypass the line for the bathroom and push past the girl coming out the door.

"Sorry!" I force out with a scratchy voice to the pissed-off coeds, and then slam the door and lock it behind me. I have enough sense to send Jesse an SOS text before I puke my guts out in the toilet.

In a matter of minutes that feel like hours, Jesse is banging on the door to the bathroom.

"Let me in, Ivy," he calls through the door, and I stumble over to unlock it. When he steps in, he immediately gathers me in a hug, and I start sobbing. I still can't remember the Attorney's Oath, so I switch to memories of Jacob.

Teaching him to ride a bike. *Breathe in.* Taking him for ice cream. *Breathe out.* Reading Percy Jackson together. *Breathe in.* Helping him bake cupcakes for Kelley's birthday. *Breathe out.* I put a picture of him in my mind and go over each of his facial features. His eyes. His smile. His floppy hair. *Breathe in and out.*

I vaguely feel, as if through a thick wool blanket, Jesse maneuver me to the floor, his hand rubbing gently up and down my back in a comforting gesture. I think I hear someone banging on the door, but Jesse bangs right back and yells something that I don't pay attention to. I don't know what he says, but the angry commotion from outside the door stops, and when my ragged breaths quiet, I unfold myself from the slouched position I'd been sitting in.

I'm still itchy, my skin still crawling, but I'm no longer on the verge of vomiting again. I'm teetering, and Jesse can tell, because he grabs my discarded clutch from the floor and pulls out my emergency Lorazepam. He hands it to me, and I take it dry.

Breathe in. Breathe out. Brown eyes. Thick glasses. Crooked smile... Breathe. Breathe. Breathe.

"What happened, Ivy?" Jesse asks quietly after about fifteen minutes. "Did that guy do something?"

I shake my head and wipe the tears from my cheeks. "No. No, he was a jerk, but it wasn't anything I couldn't handle."

He eyes me skeptically. "This hasn't happened in almost a year. What caused it?"

"His cologne."

"His cologne?" Jesse pauses for a minute, confusion etched over his face. "His cologne triggered a panic attack?"

I look at him and nod my head slowly. His eyes grow wide.

"You think it was a memory? A memory from—"

"I don't know," I respond quickly. "I don't know for sure, but I think so." I shrug once more, and the tears return. A loud hiccup breaks from my chest, and Jesse pats my back again.

"Why, Ivy?" he says sternly. "Why do you do this to yourself?"

I freeze.

"What do you mean?" I'm confused. He can't mean what I think he means.

"Why do you put yourself through this? I know it's hard for you. Why do you put yourself in these situations if you know this can happen?" His voice is broken, and though he's asking out of concern for me, it doesn't stop the anger from coiling tightly in my chest.

"Don't, Jesse," I growl as I scoot away from him, trying to keep another wave of tears at bay and failing. "I won't let one bad night ruin me." I tug my hair out of my ponytail. "It wasn't my fault. I'm not going to suffer for it for the rest of my life. I won't!" I press my fingers hard on my forehead.

At Jesse's shocked expression, I shut my mouth. He's never seen me like this, frantic and shouting and full of angry desperation. Even with the panic attacks, I'm never mean. I

87

never lash out. Tears are cascading down my face, but I take a deep breath. Jesse doesn't deserve my wrath. When I open my mouth to speak again, I keep my voice low and as calm as possible.

"I can't undo what happened, Jesse. I can't change it, but I refuse to believe that the damage is irreparable. I won't let these scars shadow everything I do. I'm not going to let him take away my ability to live my life. I wasn't given a choice before. I'm taking that choice back now."

"But is this the best way to do it?" he questions, and my anger flares hotter and my tears flow faster.

Curse my overwhelmed, chaotic emotions.

"Don't you dare judge how I deal with my trauma," I scold him. "Because I *am* dealing with it. I see a therapist. I'm in a support group. I've taken years of self-defense classes. It happened, it's part of me now, and I've accepted that. Now, I'm *choosing* to do what I think is best for me. I've *chosen* to come back stronger. It's *my* choice, Jesse, and you don't get to tell me how to heal. You don't have a say in how *I choose* to conquer *my* demons."

"I know," he says on an exhale and gives my shoulder a light squeeze. "I know, V. I'm sorry. You want me to take you to Kelley?"

"No. Definitely not." I shake my head quickly. My best friend would definitely soothe the ache in my chest, but I'm not ready for him to see me like this. I'm not prepared for him to know everything. "I'm sorry I ruined your night." I apologize to Jesse with a shrug. "You can go back out there. I'm okay now."

"Nah, girl. Queens before Peens."

I snort out a laugh, and he grins.

He gives my shoulder one last squeeze, then gets off the bathroom floor and offers me his hands.

"What do you say we head to your place and see what magical cookie concoction Bailey has conjured up?"

I smile and grab his outstretched hands, letting him pull me up off the floor, literally and metaphorically.

"I think that sounds great."

Hours later, I wake up in a cold sweat with tears streaming down my face, my breath ragged and gasping. I can't recall the dream, but I never can.

Sometimes I wish there would be a lingering memory of the nightmare that has such a violent effect on my body, for answers or closure or regaining some semblance of power. But tonight, I'm happy for the darkness. I grab my phone off the nightstand and check the time.

4:06 a.m. It's always 4:06 a.m.

It's been a while since this has happened to me. Eight months, to be exact, and I feel a niggling worry that tonight's events have caused a regression in my progress. I take a few steadying breaths to calm my racing heart and decide there's no way I'll be able to go back to sleep.

I guess there's comfort in this breakdown, considering it's always the same. Triggered panic attack, followed by the nightmares and a few extra therapy sessions with Dr. Joyner. It's just been so long since it's happened that I started to let myself believe I was over the worst of it.

Naive, really.

Dr. Joyner has always been clear on that topic. There is no real cure, and all I can do is work to manage the symptoms.

My first desire is to call Kelley—just the thought of hearing his comforting voice calms my nerves a bit—but I remind myself of all the reasons that's a bad idea. I'm not ready for him to know, and I definitely don't want to disclose it all when I'm a mess like this.

Instead, I open the browser on my phone and click the bookmark for my support group forum. After posting on the forum, I click over to my email app and send a message to Dr. Joyner's office, my therapist in Bowen. It's been a few weeks since our last check in, and I know she'll want to know about this episode.

When that's done, I pull up an LSAT practice test and do my best to block everything else out.

ivy

I'M AT LUNCH, sitting at my table in the back and flipping through the magazine I "borrowed" from the health department last weekend. I say borrowed because I'll probably return it on Saturday. I'm starting to feel guilty. I don't want to be the reason some poor single mom has nothing to read while she and her three kids are waiting to be seen.

At the time I didn't consider that, though.

I was irritated because I had to wait with Jacob for two hours before anyone would see us, and then I had to throw a fit to even be seen without a parent.

Never mind that I'm almost eighteen; they didn't seem to care about that fact.

Mom was working a double and Jacob's fever was 102, even after I gave him ibuprofen. We can't afford for her to leave a shift and risk being fired, so I brought him in myself. It took up most of my Saturday for them just to tell me to that there was nothing they could do.

"Give him ibuprofen every four hours and make sure he's getting a lot of fluids," they said.

Just keep doing what you've been doing, this trip was a waste, is what I heard.

So yeah, I was bitter.

And then I stole the magazine.

But now? Now I'm feeling guilty, and I'm cursing whatever genetic defect it is that makes me so empathetic that I can't even enjoy the spoils of my thievery. A life of crime is unfortunately not for me.

"Ivy!" I hear Kelley yell from across the cafeteria. I smile, but I don't bother looking up. I know he's walking over here with everyone's eyes on him, and honestly, I absolutely love it when he draws attention to our friendship.

"Ivy," he says again as he plops onto the bench beside me, draping an arm over my shoulders and snatching the magazine out of my hands.

"Ugh, get off me. You smell," I lie. "I told you not to hang all over me unless you've showered after gym."

I half-heartedly shrug off his arm and grab back my magazine, setting it next to my lunch tray. He then uses his free hand to steal what's left of my pizza and shoves it all in his mouth. I'm certain he's just returning from getting lunch off campus, so how he's still hungry is beyond me, but I let it slide. I also glance around to see if any of his friends or his girlfriend will be joining us, but he's alone.

Thank you for going easy on me, Gods of Unwanted Company.

"Here's your calculus homework," I say, sliding the papers in front of him. "You got three wrong. I fixed them, but I'll show you how to do them tonight."

"Ivy, you're the best," Kelley says around a mouthful of pizza. "Can I come over when I get out of practice?"

"Of course. It'll just be me and Jacob. Mom's on the closing shift all week."

Nodding his head, Kelley slides his arm back over my

shoulders in a side-hug. "Thank you. Seriously. Whatchya reading?" He makes a grab for the magazine again, but I swat at his hand. He laughs loudly.

"Just a magazine." I make eye contact, push my glasses up on the bridge of my nose and state matter-of-factly, "I was getting tips for how to give mind-blowing oral."

Kelley's eyes go wide, and he coughs violently, so I pat his back and slide him my lemonade.

"You asked." I shrug.

He chugs my drink and starts to laugh. "What the fuck, Ives? Lemme see." He grabs for the magazine once more, and I quickly shove it under my butt. I hear the sound of ripping pages and cringe. I hope the single mom with three kids doesn't mind a few torn pages.

"Leave my magazine alone, you heathen," I say, and make an attempt to shove him backward. "I don't want your greasy pizza fingers all over it."

Suddenly Kelley's laughter stops, and when I meet his eyes, there's a slight glare in them, as if he's angry with me.

"Wait, are you serious? Why are you reading about blowjob tips?" he interrogates, lowering his voice like the topic requires secretive discretion.

"Many reasons." I shrug and pop a grape in my mouth. "Why do you care?" I ask while chewing.

"I don't care. I just don't know why you'd need it." He lifts a brow at me while his statement trails off. I can guess what he wants to know, but I'm not giving him any answers until he asks the question.

Our gazes remain locked for several seconds, and when he widens his eyes at me, I mirror the expression. *Spit it out, Kell.*

He scoots closer and lowers his voice to just above a whisper.

"Are you..." He runs his hands through his hair nervously,

and his eyes scan the cafeteria as if checking for eavesdroppers. "You want these tips for *him*?"

I sigh and give a sympathetic smile.

"No, Kelley, I'm not interested in these tips for *him*," I reply, my voice at a normal speaking volume, and Kelley visibly relaxes before I catch him off guard with my next statement. "I am interested in these tips *for me*. Because I would like to be able to give mind-blowing oral. But I'm sure Tyler, *my boyfriend*, will benefit from it."

The mortified look on Kelley's face makes me huff out a laugh. It's not often I'm able to shock him. Usually, he's the one rendering me speechless, and since I am enjoying this victory far too much, I add, "I'm sure the last few times I've gone down on him were great and all, but there's no shame in wanting to improve my technique."

I smirk and return my focus to my grapes, popping two more in my mouth since the barbarian beside me stole my pizza. I can feel his stare on the side of my face, but I say nothing and refuse to look back at him. Instead, I slide the magazine back out from under me and open it.

I start flipping the pages and try to feign interest, but I can't focus. At first this was funny. I thought it was playful, friendly. But if it is playful, then why isn't he laughing? Why isn't he teasing me about the magazine? Why is he still staring holes into the side of my head? And why am I overthinking this? *Why do I feel guilty?* I almost sigh with relief when he puts his hand down on the magazine, halting my aimless page-turning.

"Ivy," he says firmly, and I turn so my eyes, once more, meet his.

"Kelley."

"Ivy, have you...*ya know*...with Tyler?" He widens his eyes and stares at me with apprehension.

I have a feeling I know what he wants me to say, and it's times like these when I get so confused. Kelley is my best friend. I should be able to talk to him about this stuff without this weird tension, but instead, he looks like he's in pain. It doesn't make any sense.

I shake my head slowly, maintaining eye contact. "No," I say, and I see his body sag slightly, but the tension returns to his shoulders when I add honestly, "not *yet* anyway."

"What do you mean, *not yet?*" Kelley raises his voice, and this time, it's me scanning the neighboring tables for anyone who might be paying too close attention to our conversation.

"Ivy, you can't be serious," he sputters. "With Tyler? But he's...*Tyler.*"

And now I'm offended.

"Actually, Kelley, I am serious." I puff up my chest and straighten my shoulders, preparing for the argument that's bubbling inside me. "And what exactly do you mean, *he's Tyler?* I am well aware of who he is, Kelley. I've been dating him for four months."

"That's exactly what I mean! Only four months, Ivy. That's it. You tryin' to tell me that you love him enough to lose your virginity? To him!?" Kelley is nearly irate at this point. His face is a mixture of complete shock and pure agony, but at least he hasn't gotten any louder.

"Oh my gosh, Kelley, we've been over this. I may not love Tyler, but I like him, and I trust him, and I am very attracted to him. He's kind, and he cares about me." I lower my voice to a whisper. "I want to have sex. Why not with Tyler?"

Kelley's face is turning bright red, and his eyebrows are scrunched so tightly that they're practically meeting in the middle, giving him an almost-unibrow. It's like I can see the wheels turning frantically inside his head, smoke pluming out his ears.

"But what if you get pregnant?" he whisper-yells. "What about STDs?"

My best friend is losing it, and for fear that he might actually combust, I soften my approach.

"Kelley...I know how to buy condoms, and I'm on birth control."

"What!" he shouts, and I jump at the outburst. Now, several of our classmates have their eyes trained on us, no doubt dying for some sign that there's trouble in our paradise.

Kelley looks around and lowers his voice once more before continuing, "Why? Since when? Why didn't you tell me?"

I'm silent for a few seconds. I'm honestly surprised by Kelley's sudden line of questioning and his intense interest in my budding sex life. We've talked about sex, kind of. We discuss our relationships, and we've even, at times, talked about the things we've done within those relationships. But this is the first time that Kelley has reacted like this.

I take a deep breath, and then another.

This is weird. This feels weird, and I respond carefully, as if I'm tiptoeing through a mine field and each of my words is an errant boot in danger of blowing the whole thing to smithereens.

"Since about a month and a half ago. And I don't know why I didn't tell you. It just never came up."

"Why?"

"Why did it never come up?"

"No, why did you go on birth control a month and a half ago?"

I give him an *are you serious right now* type of glare and answer slowly, "...because I want to have sex, Kelley. I'm ready, so I want to be prepared." I shrug.

Why does he look like I just told him that I ran over his grandma?

He starts to say something else, but before he can even get the first word out, I interject. I know what he's going to say, so I might as well just cut to the chase. This whole conversation is filling me with anxiety and the sooner it ends, the better.

"It's really not that big of a deal, Kelley. It's just sex. It's not like I'll actually be *losing* anything by having sex with Tyler. Virginity is a social construct. I'll still be the same person the next day. I'm not going to become someone entirely different just because I'm going to ask him to insert his penis into my vagina."

Kelley winces, but he's listening.

"I'm informed, I'm prepared, and I'm ready for this," I state, watching him closely. When he doesn't respond, I reach out my hand and place it over his. Quietly, I reassure him, "it's not going to change who I am, Kelley. I'll still be your best friend. I'm not going to drop you."

He's not looking at me anymore. He's staring down at the cafeteria table when he pushes out, just above a whisper, "But you're not in love with him. Don't you want your first time to be special and with someone you love?"

"Just because I'm not in love with him doesn't mean it's not going to be special, Kelley." I'm frustrated. It's times like this when I feel like I'd be better off with a girl as my best friend instead of a boy.

Am I in love with Tyler? I don't think so. But I care about him a lot, and I trust him. I'm ready to have sex. Isn't it a good thing that I do it with someone I care about and trust after taking the time to prepare and become informed?

Heck, I feel like I deserve a pat on the back for how mature I'm being about this whole thing.

Why can't Kelley be supportive?

I'm just about to ask him that question when something dawns on me, and instead of ending the conversation like I probably should, I voice the thought that's come to my mind.

"Kelley, are you upset because you haven't had sex yet? Are you mad that I'll be doing it first?" I watch him carefully as I wait for his answer.

I'd always just assumed he was having sex. He'd never told me for sure that it happened, but Shelby made a big scene about it in the locker room earlier this year. Shelby and Kelley started talking over the summer, and the fact that the relationship lasted this long—albeit on and off—is unprecedented. Kelley dates. *A lot.* But never keeps a girl around for long.

"What? Jeeze, Ivy, no."

"So, you're not a virgin?" I press.

Kelley laughs loudly, and it sounds like he's mocking me. I've never, ever felt hurt by Kelley until right now, in this moment, because of the way he is laughing at me, and I find myself rubbing at an ache in my chest.

"Are you fuckin' kidding, Ivy? You know I'm not."

He stands from the table and grabs my empty lunch tray, but I remain sitting. Kelley's been getting snappier lately. Easily irritated. But usually with his parents, Shelby, his teammates. Never with me. I don't like how it feels.

"Okay, so then why are you being such a jerk about this? Awfully hypocritical of you, right? Unless you're telling me you're in love with Shelby?"

Kelley looks down at me, and for a brief moment, all I see in his eyes is agony. Loss. Grief. But in an instant, he blinks, and all those emotions vanish.

"You're right, Ives. I'm being an asshole," he says, but he's not sincere. He's being condescending, and as he stoops down

to pick up his backpack, he adds, "Let me know when you're tryin' to fuck Tyler and I'll give you some of my condoms." With my empty lunch tray in his hand, he walks away without a backward glance.

And I'm left sitting with a pain in my chest, watching him go and replaying every word of the strange conversation we just had. Questioning everything I thought I knew about Kelley. Questioning what I thought I knew about our friendship.

kelley

WALKING INTO IVY'S APARTMENT, I'm hit with an aroma of chocolate and something sweet and find Bailey in the kitchen wearing the Wonder Woman apron Ivy got her for National Cookie Day. We all thought it was a holiday Ives made up but turns out there's actually a National Cookie Day in December.

"What are you baking, Bailey?" I ask her as I slide up to the kitchen island. There are rows of chocolate cookies cooling on wax paper, and when I reach out to grab one, she smacks my hand with a plastic spatula.

"Ow! Fuck, Bailey!" I cradle my hand to my chest and flash her a shocked glare.

"Oh, that didn't hurt, ya baby. Don't touch 'em." She points to me with the spatula and then to the cookies. "They have to cool first. That way you can experience the proper texture and consistency."

I pout at her, and she laughs.

"Nope. That shit doesn't work on me like it does V. Go point that lip at someone else."

"You're stingy," I tease. "Is she getting ready?"

"I think she's finishing up. I offered to help, but you know how that goes." Bailey flashes me a grin and then mimics Ivy's voice when she says, "I'm good. But thanks!"

I chuckle. "Sounds about right." Ivy only accepts help when it's something she absolutely cannot do herself. "So, for real, what are these?" I point at the rows of cookies again, and Bailey smiles, her body vibrating with excitement.

"They're double chocolate cherry cookies. I used a fudgey brownie recipe but tweaked it so it's a brownie/cookie hybrid, and then added chopped maraschino cherries. I think they're going to be very yum."

"They smell very yum," Ivy says as she appears around the corner, and I have to work to tame the look of appreciation that takes over my face.

Ivy is wearing tight yoga pants and one of my old soccer t-shirts with the bottom tied up on her hip. When she leans over the island to snatch a cookie, a sliver of her skin shows, and I look away.

"Hey, wait! How come she can take one, but I got attacked?"

"Because she loves me more." Ivy giggles and takes a bite of her cookie. I turn my pout on her and she rolls her eyes. "Ugh, fine, you big baby. Here," and she shoves the cookie in my mouth.

I turn to Bailey and flash her a gloating smile while chewing. She snarls at me in return.

She points the spatula at us. "You two are barf."

"These cookies are not barf, though, B. They're amazing."

"Really?" Of course, that turns her mood around. "They're not too brownie-y?"

"No. They're the perfect cookie/brownie hybrid," I say through a mouthful. "They'd be killer if I was high."

"It's true!" Ivy sing-songs. "They're delish! Chef's kiss!" She kisses her fingers. "Can we have some for the road?"

Ivy turns wide, pleading eyes on Bailey, and I fold my hands in prayer beside her and do my best impersonation of that sad cat from that movie with the ogre.

"Pleeeeease?"

She rolls her eyes and blows out a puff of air.

"Yes, fine. Now go away before you eat them all."

Ivy puts some cookies in a Tupperware container, then we say our goodbyes and head outside. When we reach the parking lot, she notices that it's not my Jeep parked on the street, but my soccer buddy's truck. She turns a wide smile on me, dimple out for all the world to see, and my heart leaps in triumph. *Because I am a fucking moron.* I toss her the keys, and she fumbles them, letting out a stupidly adorable squeak, and I stifle a laugh.

"You think I'm ready for the interstate?" she asks with a little dance.

"I do. You've mastered the streets of campus town. You can handle the one-hour drive back home."

"Oh yikes," she says, and raises her hands to the sky. "Please watch over me, Road Goddess, for I am an interstate virgin." Then she kisses the keys and hops toward the driver's seat like she isn't the most fascinating person in the world.

The hour-drive back home is, well, *eventful.* When Ivy pulls the truck up to the curb in front of her house, she puts it in park and then turns to me with a sheepish look.

"Well, that wasn't so bad?"

I chuckle. "Are you sure? Because you don't sound sure."

"I was doing really well until we got into town. I didn't realize how much hillier it is here than it is on campus," she protests. "I haven't practiced hills yet."

She's frustrated because she thinks she failed by being unprepared. Ivy hates being unprepared.

"Honestly, I think you crushed it, all things considered," I say earnestly. She really did do a fine job. "You were thrown to the sharks and swam, Ives."

"Yeah? Tell that to the big jerk who honked at me." She huffs and folds her arms over her chest. She's probably cursing that stranger in her head.

"To be fair, you did stall at the stop light and start rolling backward toward his car."

"*Inches*, Kelley! It was only a few inches, and I would have gotten it started and over the hill faster if he wouldn't have been making me nervous with his honking. He really should learn some patience."

"Don't worry. I'm sure he learned his lesson when you yelled out the window at him to 'hush' and called him a 'big rude bully.'"

I laugh at the memory, but what makes it even better is that I know without a shadow of a doubt that Ivy would have firmly put that man in his place had he been standing in front of her and not in the shitty Ford Focus behind us. You don't mess with a pissed-off, determined Ivy Rivenbark. I pity the fool who tries.

"Ugh, whatever. He *is* a big, rude bully, and he *should* hush."

"You're right, you're right. But seriously," I reach over the seat and rub her shoulder, "you did a great job."

She studies me for a minute, no doubt searching for any hint that I'm placating her, but I know she doesn't find it because soon a smile is blooming on her face and *pop*!, out comes that damn dimple that I hate to love.

"I did do pretty great, didn't I?" She shimmies a little and pumps her fists in the air. "Dan-i-ca Pa-trick!"

I shake my head, grinning like a dumb ass. "Let's go inside, speed racer. I'll grab your bags."

We walk up the cracked sidewalk side by side, and when I swing the door open for Ivy, she calls out for her little brother.

"Bug," she shouts, louder than necessary for the tiny house, but that's because Jacob probably has headphones in. "Jake-a-bug!"

"Ivy Bean!" he shouts from his bedroom, and then comes lumbering out in worn jeans and the Pokémon t-shirt I got him for his last birthday. "What are you doing here? Are you staying?"

"We're home for the weekend! Ms. Pierce gave me Saturday off, and you said you needed help with math, so I'm at your service," she exclaims and wraps him up in a tight hug.

"Thank you," he whispers into her shoulder. Even though he's only twelve, he'll be taller than Ivy soon, and I can't get over how much he's changed from the little four-year-old boy I met eight years ago. There's the same solemn tone to his voice that I heard when I called him the other day, and I know Ivy hears it too. I don't know if he's struggling in his classes, or if he's lonely, or if those little punks at school are giving him trouble again, but my heart breaks a little.

"You okay, Bug?" Ivy asks as she tightens the hug. "Do I need to threaten some more flea-bag jerkfaces?"

He snorts and pulls away, shoving his thick glasses up on the bridge of his nose. "You can't go threatening everyone who fucks with me, Bean."

"The heck I can't. And don't cuss."

He shakes his head. "I don't want to talk about it. I'm j-just glad you're home."

Jacob used to be cool with all of his classmates, but it's like last summer a few of them came back to school soulless, and Jacob's thick glasses and asthma make him an easy target. And even though he's almost mastered his stutter in normal conversation, the kids know it comes back when he's overwhelmed or nervous, so of course they provoke him because they're assholes. They also make fun of him because he stayed back in kindergarten an extra year, so he's a little older than the rest of his class. I want to break their fucking kneecaps.

"Alright, well, Mom said she only works 'til eight tonight so I got stuff to make dinner!"

Jacob's face pales. "No, Ivy."

"Hush, you. I'm not that bad."

"Please. Just...no. We can make sandwiches or have hot p-pockets."

"It's only pizza, Bug," she pouts, and I laugh. "And anyway, I was going to let you and Kelley do most of it."

At that he heaves a sigh of relief and then turns to me.

"Whaddup, Kell?" He puts out a fist like he wants me to bump it, but I fake him out and pull him in for a hug.

"Don't try to fist bump me, kid," I tease as I headlock him and ruffle his hair. He's laughing when I let him loose. "We're family. We hug."

"Yeah, yeah, yeah." He rolls his eyes. He's showing more and more of an Ivy attitude each time I see him. It's brilliant.

"Alright, Jake. What do you say you and Ives get started on that math, and I'll start the pizza? Sound good?"

"Yup!"

"Extra sausage!" Ivy sings.

I shake my head at her. "Fiend," I tease, and she sticks her tongue out at me.

* * *

I was right.

Saturday night Netflix and Fill, and Ives, as usual, is asleep by 10:58 p.m. She's curled up in the corner of the couch, wearing my 10th grade soccer hoodie, and snoring lightly. Jacob is sprawled out on the floor under her with a Halloween-themed blanket draped over him. I gave him that blanket for his fifth birthday. I look them over, committing this moment to memory. No matter how many times I see her asleep, no matter how often I catch her wearing my clothing, it never affects me any less. And seeing Jacob curled up in a gift I gave him fills me with so much warmth. We might not be blood, but that kid couldn't be more my brother even if we were.

Since we came home this weekend, we did Netflix and Fill at Ivy's house with Jacob, and we were all able to cook dinner together. These nights are my favorite, even though Ivy can't cook for shit. It always ends up with me doing the cooking and she just hands me the stuff I need when I ask for it. She's got a soft spot for Italian food, so tonight we (see also: I) made spaghetti with homemade meatballs and homemade marinara sauce. She put the store-bought garlic bread in the oven (it was only a little burnt), and Jacob set the table and grated the parmesan cheese like a champ.

My chest constricts as my gaze falls to her pouty lips. They're parted slightly, and I once more find myself sinking into the memory of the time in 12th grade when I almost kissed her. It's my biggest regret, and not just because I likely missed my only chance to taste her, to feel if her lips are as plush as they look. I regret it because of the chain of events that followed. How it led to more than a year of silence. How for fifteen months, she was lost to me, and when I finally got her back, she was different.

She's mine again, but not.

She's the same, but not.

We don't talk about that time, and I've never told her that for fifteen months I couldn't breathe right. That not seeing her every day caused a physical ache in my chest that still, after over two years of strong rekindled friendship, hasn't quite disappeared. It's why I'll never make that mistake again. I'll never attempt to cross the line, no matter how badly I may want to. Because I can't lose her. Not again.

Second semester sophomore year, when we started the Netflix and Fill tradition, we were both in student dorms and the evening usually consisted of ordering pizza or subs from a campus restaurant and watching ridiculous comedies with our roommates. My roommate would always get tanked and pass out, and Ivy's roommate, Bailey, would usually leave around 11 p.m. to go to a party. It always ended up being just Ivy and me, if you didn't count my drunk-ass, snoring roommate. This was before her internship and before she started really cramming for the LSAT, so we'd stay up talking until sunrise. It was therapeutic, and it patched up our broken relationship one shitty comedy at a time.

I bend down and nudge Jacob awake, and he sleepily stumbles to his room, blanket draped around his shoulders like a cape.

"Ives," I kneel next to the couch and whisper, brushing her hair off of her face and massaging her shoulder. "Ivy, move to your room. You're gonna be miserable tomorrow if you sleep out here." I graze my thumb over her cheek, and she leans into the touch. She's warm and soft and *fuck*. I trace my fingertips up to her ear, tucking a strand of hair, and then slide my hand back to her shoulder, giving another soft shake.

Her eyes flutter open, and she looks up at me in a way that

makes my heart race and my groin heat. Her eyes are a deep, sparkling blue, and I can't look away.

"What time is it?"

"Eleven. You didn't even make it into episode two," I tease, and she scoffs sleepily.

"Whatever. Math is exhausting." She stands and stretches her hands above her head. My old hoodie is baggy and long on her, but it rises slightly, showing off the bottom curve of her ass in her yoga pants.

"Are you leaving? You can stay on the couch, you know."

"I'm going to head out. I told Ma and Pop I'd have breakfast with them since we're home. You and Jacob can come, if you want."

"I think we'll stay here and toaster some Eggos. But tell your parents we said hello."

"Sure."

She nods, making her way to her bedroom and doesn't even glance behind her as she replies, "Drive safe, Kell. Thanks for dinner." As she disappears into her bedroom, I hear her call out, "love you!"

"Love you back," I say quietly. Then I leave, locking the door on my way out.

I do my marathon training on the streets of my hometown the next morning, making it a point to run past several nostalgic places of interest. The elementary school where I met Preston and he became my first best friend. The middle school where I discovered my love for soccer. The practice fields where I spent weekends and summers, and the arcade where Preston and I probably still hold the Mortal Combat high scores.

When I run past the high school, I'm inundated with

memories of Ivy. The assembly where we met on the first day of ninth grade. She wowed me, and I walked her to all of her classes for the first month of school. I ended up with too many tardy slips and Ma grounded me from video games for two weeks, but it was worth it. The first time she came to one of my games, she'd painted her face and ironed my jersey number onto her t-shirt, and I swear my chest puffed up to twice its size with pride. It was my best game that year.

And then there was Senior Prom.

I run down Main Street and turn right on Franklin Avenue so I can see the ice cream shop where she and I take Jacob in the summers. I pass the pizza place where we went after homecoming in 10th grade. I thought it was a date. I *wanted* it to be a date, but that didn't end up at all how I'd wanted.

Not for the first time, I roll my eyes at myself. I need to stop doing this shit. It's borderline obsessive, and I'm pretty sure my balls are shrinking from all the mental pining.

As I turn the corner back onto Main Street, I hear someone calling after me, so I stop and turn around.

"Kap!" Preston yells from the window of a BMW. "Kap, man. Hold up, I'm going to park."

I press stop on my watch timer and head to where he's parking. Other than some likes on social media here and there, I haven't talked to Preston since the summer before sophomore year of college. He went out of state to Stanford. His parents are loaded, and when I said I was glad my parents aren't the type to force me into their chosen profession, I mostly meant I am glad my parents aren't like Preston's.

"What up, Kap?" Preston walks over and shakes my hand. "How you been?"

"I'm good, man. Been good. Student teaching. Got a marathon in a few weeks. You?"

"Great. Had to come home this weekend to sit in on

some meetings with my dad." He's got the same cocky grin I remember. "You know, preparation and all." I watch as he smooths down the lapel of his suit jacket, and I'm pretty sure he did it just to flash the shiny ass Rollie on his wrist.

"Cool. You headin' back today?"

"I fly out this afternoon. I wish I'd known you were in town, man. We could have gotten drinks."

"Yeah, definitely. Or next time you could come back to my campus. I know it's not Ivy League," I mock jokingly, "but we had fun when you visited freshman year. You'd like my roommate. We could get some guys together for a pickup soccer game."

"That would be great. You just home for the weekend?"

"Yeah, we're heading back tonight. I teach in the morning."

Preston cocks his head to the side. "*We?* Who's *we?*"

"Oh, yeah, Ivy. I'm here with Ivy."

Preston lifts an eyebrow at the mention of Ivy. Last he knew, she and I weren't on speaking terms.

"So, she's visiting from her aunt's?" he says slowly.

"Her aunt's?" *What the fuck?* "No, she transferred to BU sophomore year. She goes to school with me."

"Ah," he nods his head slowly, "so that's why you dropped off the face of the Earth."

"No, man," I huff. "I dropped off the face of the Earth because I needed to pull my head out of my ass and focus on school and because you go to fucking Stanford 2,500 miles away."

I think Preston's always resented my relationship with Ivy a little. He thinks Ivy is why he and I stopped hanging out in high school, and I'm sure now he thinks she's why we lost touch in college. In reality, we aren't close anymore because he can be kind of a stuck-up douche sometimes and our priorities are vastly different.

"What do you mean *her aunt's*? Ivy doesn't have an aunt." I change the topic.

"Yeah, Kap. She does." He scrunches his eyebrows at me as if *I'm* the one who is mistaken. "You know how she left right after graduation? She was down in Bowen with her aunt, going to the community college there. Deferred her BU acceptance and scholarship and everything."

I stare at him blankly.

I don't know where Ivy was freshman year. I don't know why she came back. We never talk about it. The first time I tried, she clammed up, and I was just so relieved to have her back that I never asked her again..

"You didn't know that?" he asks incredulously. "I thought everyone knew that."

I shake my head slowly. "Nope, not everyone." How the *hell* does he know? His parents are pretty involved in the community, but why the hell wouldn't he have told me?

"Shit, Kap. Sorry." He shrugs, obviously not sorry. "Maybe you need to have a talk with your girlfriend, then. See what she's hiding."

And this is why I stopped hanging out with Preston in high school. He's a dick.

"She's not hiding shit from me, Preston." I start to pop my earbuds back in. "And we're just friends."

"Fuck, still?" His laugh grates in my eardrums. "I thought by now you'd have gotten your di—"

"—Don't finish that sentence, Preston," I warn. He throws his palms up and flashes a smarmy grin.

"Just joshin', Kap." His jokes stopped being funny a long time ago. "I gotta get to the airport, though, so I'll be seeing ya. I'll call and we can plan my visit to campus."

"Yeah, sure." *Hell no.* "It's been a pleasure." *You're an asshole.* "Have a safe trip back." *I hope your pretentious ass BMW gets rear ended and you spill coffee on your $1,000 suit pants and get first degree burns on your dick.*

I don't wave goodbye as I continue my run.

The drive back to campus is tense at first. When I mention I ran into Preston, Ivy just nods and asks how he's been. I want so badly to tell her about what he said, to ask her how the fuck he knows where she was freshman year of college and why I don't.

But I clamp my mouth shut.

I respect her privacy, because if she wanted me to know, she'd have told me the first time I asked. She'd have brought it up sometime in the last two years. We would have already talked about the time between high school graduation and sophomore year of college when it was complete radio silence between us.

If she wanted to share that story, I would already know where she disappeared to and why.

And truthfully, what it comes down to the most is that I'm okay with the secrets. They're *safe.* I don't push it because I don't want to hear that I was the reason she dipped on all our plans. And I definitely don't want to talk about what went down *with me* during that time, so I can't expect her to play show and tell when I have no interest in joining. Am I willing to risk everything just to satisfy some juvenile interest that was sparked by petty jealousy?

No. I'm not.

This might be an instance where curiosity really would kill the cat, or at least our friendship. Sometimes, secrets are better kept secret. *Fucking Preston.*

So instead, we talk about Jacob. We sing along to the radio. We plan our next Netflix and Fill. By the time we pull back into campus town, the encounter with Preston is just an annoyance that I brush off.

My relationship with my best friend is solid. I'm stupid for even questioning it.

When I walk into my condo after dropping Ivy off, I find Jesse on the couch wearing the Cookie Monster pajama pants Ivy and Bailey got him for his birthday with a cup of tea sitting on the coffee table next to his basket of yarn. His foot is bouncing, his right hand is twirling a knitting needle, and his left is scrolling on his phone.

"Ay-oh," he calls out when he sees me. "Come here, man. How do you feel about little poofy balls on your slippers? Yay or nay?"

I laugh and kick off my shoes. This is definitely the kind of company I prefer to keep.

ivy

MONDAY AFTERNOON, I have a video call with Dr. Joyner. An assistant in her office responded to my early morning email on Friday within two hours and insisted we set up a check-in meeting. This was the earliest Dr. Joyner could see me.

Dr. Joyner's image comes over the screen when the call connects. She looks exactly how she always does. She's sitting at her desk, a bookcase brimming with books and her framed degrees and certifications can be seen behind her. Her short black hair is styled perfectly, not a flyaway to be seen, her red-framed glasses are perched on the bridge of her nose, and on her ageless face is the same warm yet serious expression I'm used to.

The familiar sight of her on the screen helps me to relax before I even noticed my own tension.

"Good afternoon, Ivy," she greets. "I am recording this session. If you are not comfortable with that, I will turn off the recording and take handwritten notes."

She starts every session this way.

"I'm okay with it."

She nods. "How are you feeling today?"

Dr. Joyner is decidedly no-nonsense. She doesn't beat around the bush and she doesn't coddle. I think that's why I was able to open up to her so quickly. I appreciate a direct woman. I was determined to get my head straight, and she was determined to help me.

"I'm feeling better. Much better, actually," I say honestly. "I've been messaging with some women in the forum, and it's helped to know that what happened isn't unusual and doesn't mean I'm backsliding."

"That's good. I'm glad you joined that group." I can only see her body from the chest up, but I know she's behind her desk with her legs crossed and her hands folded in front of her. "Have you been doing preemptive grounding exercises?"

"Yes. I start and end each day with a breathing exercise and reciting my mantra."

"Good, good. I'd like for you to tell me what happened on Thursday night. What triggered your attack. Would you like to do that?"

I nod. I need this.

"I would. Jesse and I went to a fraternity party. While we were there, a guy got into my personal space. I handled it well, despite a bit of fear at first. I was prepared to use a self-defense move if I needed to. But then his cologne just, kind of, *derailed* me."

Dr. Joyner nods again, her face stern and focused, but listening intently.

"Was the fraternity party meant as a CBT exercise?"

Dr. Joyner doesn't ask this question with judgment, despite the fact that she was not exactly happy with my decision to independently attempt cognitive behavioral therapy. When she saw that I was determined, she warned me of the risks and provided me with some literature on how to effectively perform CBT. But she also made sure to state that she was *not* recommending the treatment. She's been nothing but helpful, though, especially when I started making positive progress, and I am grateful for that.

"No. But my previous CBT exercises have been successful. I've noticed marked improvement. This is the first time in eight months that I've had an episode."

"I want you to describe the episode for me," she states firmly, and I take a breath and swallow.

"Okay. Yes. So, it started the same as usual. Sweating, rapid heartbeat, pounding in my ears. I tried to do a grounding exercise at first, but it intensified quickly, and I couldn't focus. I started to feel like the room was shrinking, and then I started to get the flashes of memory. The curtains. The clothing. The voice. But this time, there was a new memory. The cologne. I was able to isolate myself in a bathroom where I threw up, and then did breathing and visualizing exercises until I was able to take medication."

She steeples her brown hands under her chin, her red lips pursed, surveying me.

"The vomiting is new."

"Yep. The scent of the cologne, it was so strong. Stronger than it should have been. Even after I was in the bathroom, after I'd vomited, I could still smell it. It was suffocating."

"What do you think that means?"

"I think it's a memory from that night."

She nods again. "And how do you feel about that?"

"Kind of relieved, actually. I feel like it's another clue? I know that we've moved beyond my quest for justice, and I *have* moved past that, but this feels like a step toward clarity. I'll probably never have all the answers, but now I have one more, and that makes me feel powerful."

"I like that you're choosing to see it that way. Have the nightmares returned?"

"Twice," I say, and I can't keep the defeat from my voice. No matter how hard I work on controlling my fight-or-flight responses while I'm awake, I relinquish that power as soon as I fall asleep. "One Thursday night after the panic attack, and one last night."

"There is a chance you will have more in the coming weeks, but it's important to remember that this is not a failure. These nightmares do not mean you have regressed in your progress." Dr. Joyner speaks this with conviction, and the tightness in my chest, the disappointment I've been feeling with myself, eases a bit. She doesn't say things just to pacify me.

"I'm very pleased with how you've handled everything, Ivy. You did everything right in that situation, and you likely made the attack less severe."

I take a deep breath and smile grimly. It's nice to hear, but it's a bittersweet kind of praise.

"Ivy. I need you to understand and accept that there will always be a chance that something will trigger a panic attack or nightmares. There is no true cure for PTSD or for anxiety. We can use what we know to manage the symptoms, but we cannot cure it."

I jerk a nod and stare at my hands. I hate this fact. It never gets easier to hear.

"Ivy, I would like your eyes on me for what I am about to say, if you're comfortable with it."

I take two deep breaths and raise my eyes to hers.

"This is not a failure. This is not a loss of control. You are not a failure, Ivy. You are not out of control. I'd like you to nod if you believe me, and I'd like you to repeat that back to me if you agree."

I grit my teeth and take two more deep breaths, letting the truth wash over me.

"This is not a failure. This is not a loss of control. I am not a failure. I am not out of control."

"Thank you. How do you feel about our meeting?"

"Good. I feel mostly good."

"Do you feel you would benefit from a prescription to aid with sleep? I could contact your psychiatrist."

"Not yet. I'll email you if I change my mind."

"Have a good day, Ivy."

"Thanks, Dr. Joyner. You too."

* * *

On Tuesday, I head straight to the firm instead of attending lecture. Ms. Pierce told me I didn't have to make up the hours I missed this weekend, but I'd much rather be helping out here than sitting in a class that I currently have an A in. I figure, the experience at my internship will be much more valuable to my future career than my ECON elective.

"How was your weekend?" Amelia asks when I walk into the conference room, a stack of file folders piled high in my arms.

"Good. It was good to see Jacob and Mom. I feel a little better now, you know, about everything with him at school."

"Mmhmm. Middle schoolers can be little assholes. I'm sure he was glad to see you too."

"Yeah, I think so. How about you? How was your weekend?"

"The usual. Devon is still on nights, and I had homework to catch up on. But Sunday we were able to have some family time, which was really nice and much needed. Destiney had us play a board game and then we watched some documentary on climate change."

I giggle. "Destiney picked the documentary, didn't she?"

"My little world changer."

Amelia's family is perfect. Her husband worships her, as he should, and they have an amazing eight-year-old daughter, Destiney. A marriage like theirs, a little family that is happy and loved—someday, I'd like to have that.

"I looked over the work you did last week. Your notes are good. Concise." Amelia hands me a packet of papers. "There were some places where your verbiage needed to be cleaned up. I highlighted them. Also, I printed out some examples of estate cases that were contested and went to court. I want you to look over those documents and write up the links to the Harrison case." She levels me with a no-nonsense look. "This has the potential to get messy."

"Are we thinking it won't be settled in mediation?"

"My guess? Definitely not. You spent last time organizing assets, so you haven't gotten to the will yet." Amelia raises her prefect eyebrows to punctuate her cryptic message, then takes her coffee and saunters out the door.

After a few hours, I'm in disbelief and calling Amelia back into the conference room.

"Mr. Harrison wants to leave everything, absolutely everything, to his thirteen-year-old grandson?"

"That's right."

"Nothing to his only son?"

"Not a thing. And that's not all. Did you look at the notes on the trust?"

"Yeah. He wants to put everything into a trust for his grandson and make the trustee the kid's mom. His daughter-in-law. Doesn't want the kid's dad, his own son, to be able to touch any of it."

Amelia nods slowly, and my wheels start turning. This could be tricky.

"I've got some ideas," I say absently, my mind whirring while I jot down some notes on my legal pad. "I have to do some research." Then, I get to work.

* * *

Bailey and I pull up to the intramural fields at 6:50 on Wednesday evening. Kelley's scrimmages usually start around seven, so the teams are just finishing up some warm-up drills. As we head toward one of the scattered sets of bleachers set up along the edges of the field, I hear my name shouted and the distinct sound of sprinting shoes on pavement behind me. I know what's about to happen, and I have just enough time to drop my messenger bag, freeze, and brace myself for impact before I'm scooped up and thrown over Jesse's shoulder.

"Ivy Bean has brought the par-taaaaay," Jesse shouts as he runs in circles around Bailey with me giggle-shrieking and gripping his waist for dear life.

"Put her down, you menace, before you trip and drop her on her head," Bailey yells. Jesse stops running, and I hear him gasp as if he's offended.

"I would never trip. I'm far too coordinated." He puts me back on my feet and lunges for Bailey. "I'll show you."

Bailey squeaks and kicks her foot out at him.

"Hernandez, I swear to god, if you try to pick me up, I will kick you in the dick."

"Ow, no." Jesse jumps back, one hand cupping between his legs and the other thrown up at Bailey likes she's a wild animal. "Loud and clear, Barnes. But if you put me out of commission there will be some very disappointed people on campus, feel me? This is the best thing I've got goin' for me." Jesse wiggles his hips a little and winks at us.

"You're disgusting." Bailey laughs.

"You love me."

"Ew, no."

"Hush, you two," I cut in. "Let's sit."

When we're settled on the bleachers, Jesse sitting between Bailey and me, I covertly reach into my messenger bag and sneak a bundle of yarn to Bailey behind Jesse's back.

I pull another out for myself and then clear my throat.

"Brrrr, it's getting a little chilly, isn't it, B?" I say, making a show of wrapping the scarf around my neck.

"Yeah, I'm a little cold, too," Bailey says theatrically and does the same.

"You guys are nuts," Jesse mumbles as he scrolls his phone, one leg bouncing quickly. "It's like sixty degrees out."

I clear my throat louder. "I said *it's chilly*," and when he doesn't look up from his phone, Bailey swats him on the back of the head.

"Ow, B, what the fuck! That hu—hey wait! Those are my scarves!"

Jesse goes from irritated to elated in a blink when he notices what Bailey and I are wearing. He's grinning like a goofball and grabs the end of mine, inspecting his handiwork.

"Hey, these are some sexy scarves. I did good."

"You did," Bailey says and nudges his shoulder playfully.

"You've come a long way from potholders and tea cozies," I add.

"Yeah, especially since those potholders didn't work for shit."

"Yeah, sorry about that, B." Jesse widens his eyes at her and makes a face that can best be interpreted as *whoops my bad.*

"I think I still have a scar," Bailey jokes, looking at her palm with wide eyes.

"Oh shit, really?" Jesse makes a grab for Bailey's hand, but she snatches it away with a laugh.

"I'm just fucking with you, J."

"Not funny. I still feel bad about that." Jesse pouts a moment, then returns his attention to the field, shouting through cupped hands. "Let's go, Kelley Baby! Kick some ass!"

I can hear Kelley's laughter from the field, and he throws both fists in the air. We watch as the teams move into position, a student ref blows a whistle, and the other team takes the kickoff.

Watching Kelley play has always fascinated me. Truthfully, I've never been able to keep up much with the actual game because I spend most of it with my eyes glued to my best friend.

The way he moves? It's criminal. It puts everyone else out there to shame.

Kelley weaves in and out of the other players with speed and precision. When everyone else seems to be chasing the ball, the ball seems to bend to Kelley's will.

His instincts are unmatched. His skill, expert.

And his body? Well, it's masterfully shaped and honed from years of athleticism and training. Simply put, Kelley is hot. A testament to the fruits of hard work and dedication. I watch the way his quad muscles bunch and stretch as he pushes his legs down the field, the way his arms pump and his biceps bulge.

Jeebus. Absolutely criminal.

Halfway through the game, Kelley takes off his shirt, and I can't help but stare at the planes of his defined abs. The way they contract when he kicks long sends funny tingles through my body. He really is a thing of beauty. Unfortunately, I'm not the only one to notice, and when a group of girls along the sidelines starts tittering and pointing at him, I bristle and have to temper my stare.

"Just go tell them he's off limits," Jesse snarks from beside me. "I don't think your death glare is getting through to them."

I huff. "Those women can drool over whomever they please, Kelley included. I don't have a claim on him." I tear my eyes away from the group of girls, and Jesse snorts.

"Sure, V. That's why you growled and started frothing at the mouth like a rabid dog protecting her favorite squeaky toy."

I shove Jesse's shoulder. "That's not true." I start to protest just as a cheer comes from the field. I whip my eyes back to find Kelley staring right at me, a triumphant smile on his face and his arms raised in celebration. He scored. I clap and cheer proudly, my smile likely bigger than his, and giddy butterflies do laps in my tummy.

"Mmhhmmm." Bailey chuckles from beside Jesse. "No claim."

"Hush," I scold, then tune them both out, ignoring the way my heart skipped under Kelley's attention.

He's my best friend, and he's an amazing soccer player. It's completely acceptable for me to be proud of him when he scores.

Kelley should be playing soccer for BU on scholarship. It's the only reason he came to Butler in the first place. I got an academic scholarship, he got a soccer scholarship, and we were supposed to brave freshman year of college together.

Except we didn't.

Instead, I spent a year at the community college near Bowen, leaving Kelley to experience the college life as a star athlete without me. But when I transferred back, I found that

Kelley was no longer on soccer scholarship. He's never told me why, and I don't press.

We both have our secrets, and I don't know when, if ever, I'll be ready to share mine.

No, Kelley and I are solid just how we are. Our friendship is pretty perfect as it is. Why do or say anything that could change that?

The game wraps up with Kelley's team scoring the final goal off of his assist. Bailey, Jesse, and I cheer loudly and watch as the teams do their good game fist bumps or whatever.

One guy shoulder checks Kelley, and my hackles rise, but Kelley brushes it off. I watch as the two exchange a few words. The guy Kelley is talking to looks kind of familiar, but I can't quite place him. I squint to see him better, and then the guy gives Kelley a shove.

What the heck?

They're obviously arguing about something. The game, maybe? Curse the distance. They're too far away for me to eavesdrop. I should really learn to read lips.

The third time the guy rams his shoulder into Kelley, I'm livid. Then I realize why he looks so familiar.

"Bails. That's him. The guy from the other night. Brock."

"Brock?" She questions, but quickly her eyes widen, and she sits up straighter, squinting back at the field. "Wait. The BDD?"

I nod and she snarls in his direction.

"Wait, what? Who? What's a BDD?" Jesse jumps in.

"Big dick dumbass."

"Ha! That's a good one," Jesse barks. "Why do we hate him?" he asks, still laughing.

"He tried to tell Ivy he didn't have a condom like two weekends ago. Tried to talk her into boning bare."

"Oh no he didn't." Jesse's smile drops, and he turns a glare toward Brock.

"And he told me I had a fat *a-s-s*," I whisper.

"What?" Jesse jumps. "What, like, as an insult? He said you had a fat ass as an insult?"

Bailey nods, and we reply at the same time.

"Mmhmm."

"Yeppers."

"I'll kill him." Jesse stands quickly, but Bailey cuts him off.

"Looks like Kelley is handling it."

On the field, Brock and Kelley are in each other's faces, and though I can't hear what's being said, I can tell from the tense set of his shoulders that Kelley is furious. When Brock gives Kelley yet another forceful shove, I'm off the bleachers and marching toward the middle of the field.

"Oh, shit!" Jesse claps his hands once and scrambles up behind me. "You sure fucked up now, man!"

"Shut up, J," I hear Bailey say to him. He then starts humming *Eye of the Tiger* but promptly stops with an *ooof*. I'm betting Bailey elbowed him in the stomach. If I wasn't prepping a speech in my head, I'd laugh.

I stomp up to where the guys are facing off, plant my feet, and cross my arms.

"Brock. I see you've met my friend, Kelley. Kelley, this is Brock."

Brock turns his snarling face toward me, and a smarmy grin takes it over. The look turns my stomach and I resist the urge to snarl back.

"Hey, Ivy. How you been, baby?" He licks his lips, and it's gross, but I maintain my poker face. I can practically feel Kelley's anger emanating off of him, and I send a silent plea to whatever gods and goddesses are watching that he lets me handle this myself.

"I'm good, Brock. I'd ask you the same, but I don't particularly care." Jesse and Bailey stifle laughter behind me.

"Don't be like that, babe. I know you regret the other night." He takes a step toward me, but I hold my ground. I won't be intimidated. I'm a fierce mountain lion of greatness, and he is an idiot man-child of sexually transmitted infections. "I would have showed you a real nice time."

"No thank you, Brock. I like not having chlamydia." I raise my voice and hear laughter coming from the teams. I almost forgot we had an audience on the field, and this makes Brock visibly angry.

"Whatever. I was slumming with you."

I plant my hands on my hips and raise an eyebrow.

"Please," I scoff. "Literally no one cares what you have to say, Brock. You're full of crap and your ego is bruised so you're lashing out. I know an insecure boy when I see one."

He's spitting mad, now.

"I wouldn't touch your fat ass if you begged me."

"I'm grateful for that. If you have sex the way you play soccer it would be a total waste of my time."

"Oh yes she said it." Jesse laughs out loud behind me. "You best walk off before she makes you cry."

"Shut the fuck up," Brock shouts at Jesse, which just makes Jesse laugh harder.

"Just go home, Brock, before you make a bigger fool of yourself," I tell him with a sigh. "Nobody likes a sore loser."

Kelley steps next to me then and throws his arm over my shoulder.

"Bye, Brock," Kelley says with a death glare.

"This isn't over," Brock points his finger in Kelley's face.

"Yes, it most definitely is," I shake my head. "And make an appointment with campus health. Wouldn't want your diseased dick to fall off."

I turn and walk away with Kelley's arm still slung over my shoulder and Jesse and Bailey trailing behind, still laughing.

"Ivy Jean Rivenbark," Kelley says with a grin, "did I just hear you say dick?"

"Hush." Kelley barks out a laugh and tightens his arm around me.

I press myself into Kelley's side and pretend to ignore the heat coming from his bare skin. The way he smells of sweat, grass, and the nighttime air of early fall is a combination that I love, and I shiver. I flick my eyes to where the group of girls from earlier was standing and see that two of them are watching us leave, eyes fixed on Kelley, so I slide my arm around his waist, hook my thumb in the band of his shorts, and send the girls a small smile.

I know that I don't have a claim on Kelley. I *cannot*, because that would suggest we are more than just friends, and we aren't. We *can't* be. But, well, that doesn't mean I can't seek comfort in our platonic affections while we're both single. That's all I'm doing. Friendly hugs and smiles. If those girls see it and get the wrong idea...well, that's not my fault...

"Hey, V," Jesse's voice is suddenly serious, "I'm sorry I didn't vet that douche better."

"It's not your fault, J."

"Yeah," Bailey adds. "Guys like him treat other guys differently than they treat women."

"Yeah, but still. Next time I'm saying condoms and respect, or I'll break his dick."

kelley

"ALRIGHT, Matthew. Show me what you have today," I say with extra gusto at lunch on Thursday. Something has been wrong with Matthew. I can tell because he didn't raise his hand even once in class today, and it was my lesson, so I was expecting extreme excitement from him. He's been withdrawn this week, so I've been doing what I can to perk him up at lunch.

"Um, I forgot my lunch today. But I grabbed a granola bar from the cabinet before I left." Matthew won't make eye contact with me. He remembered to grab a granola bar but not his lunch bag? I'm not buying it, but I'm glad that I made it a point to pack some things that will boost his spirits.

"That's okay," I say with a nod and a conspiratorial grin. "It's actually probably better this way because look what I brought."

I pull out a foot-long gourmet sub from *Jerry's*, the sub shop off campus, two bags of chips, a container of grapes, two bottles of juice from the vending machine, and of course, the container of Bailey's cookies that Ivy packed. Matthew's eyes grow wide, and he starts to smile, but then the grin drops.

"I don't really have anything to trade, though."

"Pffft, that's fine," I say with a shrug as I start to divvy up the food. "Consider it a thank you for always coming to keep me company at lunch. And if you want to repay me, you can just make sure to ask a few questions next time I teach. I know you had some in your brain today."

"I did," Matthew says before taking a giant bite of his sub. "I just didn't feel like talking."

"It's cool. Sometimes I don't feel like talking in large groups either. But you know you can always talk to me if something is bothering you, right?"

Matthew pauses and looks at me while he chews, and suddenly I'm hit with the memory of Jacob the first day I met him, with his assessing blinks, vulnerability, and silent strength. Just like that first day with Jacob, I hope Matthew knows that my words are genuine.

"I mean it, Matthew. You can talk to me about anything. And if there's a problem that I can't help you with, we will find someone who can."

Matthew nods and gives me a small smile.

"I know, Mr. Pierce. Thank you. For the lunches and for everything."

"Good. Now how about you ask me those questions you didn't want to ask in class today. The Progressive Era was a pretty big moment in American History."

Matthew and I finish the lunch hour discussing my lesson, and soon enough he's smiling and laughing like his usual self. I only hope he's still smiling next time I see him.

The day goes by quickly, and I manage not to think too much about the comments that douche Brock made at the soccer scrimmage for most of it, but I wasn't so lucky on the drive back to campus.

"So how was soccer last night?" Cassie asks, and I can't

help the grimace that takes over my face. "Oh no. Did you lose? I was gonna come cheer you on, but I needed to work on my Ed Psych project."

"Nah, we didn't lose. We kicked ass."

"So then what's up?" She turns in her seat and I can feel her eyes on my profile. I don't like it.

"Nothing big," I shrug. "Just some dick on the other team trying to get under my skin. Didn't work."

"Who was it?"

"Some frat prick named Brock."

"Brock Mohler," Cassie says, and she's not surprised. I turn my head and look at her.

"You know him?"

"Yep. He's in a business frat with my roommate's boyfriend." She hesitates, and I can tell she wants to say more.

"What?" I urge, and she takes a breath.

"Was it about Ivy?" she asks quietly. "That how he tried to get to you?"

"Yeah." I shake my head, disgusted with the memory of the way he talked about my best friend. "How'd you know?"

She shrugs and looks away. "Just a guess."

"Right." My answer is clipped, and I'm more irritated than I probably should be at her assumption. At her *correct* assumption.

My skin crawls at the thought of that asshat Brock putting his hands on Ivy. The way he talked about her body yesterday makes me sick. Not just because of how he disrespected her, but because I'm also fucking jealous, and I hate it. I try to ignore the way my stomach roils, but I can't, and all I want to do is drop Cassie off and go for my run.

When I pull up in front of her apartment complex, I'm ready to mumble a goodbye and speed home for my training session, but Cassie reaches over and puts her hand on my forearm.

"You're tense. You're angry. I get it. I would be, too." I'm not quite sure what she thinks she *gets*, but she sounds sincere, so I meet her eyes and listen. "I really think you should come out with us tomorrow. Before you say no—"

"Okay."

"Really?" Cassie's eyes are wide with surprise, and a shocked smile is on her face. "You'll come out with me?"

"Yeah," I nod, and her smile makes me smile. My abrupt acquiescence startled her, and me too, to be honest. But I need to stomp out these feelings—feelings for Ivy—that are coursing through me, and a night out sounds pretty damn good right now.

"Okay! Okay, cool. Tomorrow. I'll text you."

"No frat parties, though."

"That's fine. We'll bar hop. It's gonna be great." Then she squeals a little and leans over to hug me goodbye, which catches me off guard. "Thanks for the ride, Kell. See you tomorrow!"

I feel both lighter and more weighed down on the drive back to my condo. It's not lost on me that I'm border-line pathetic and practically whipped when it comes to Ivy Jean Rivenbark. I would probably do anything in the world she asked me to, and I would do it with a smile.

And normally, I'm okay with that—more than okay with that—for two reasons.

One, I know without a shadow of a doubt that Ivy would drop everything and come to my aid If I needed her. It's the kind of relationship we have. The kind of relationship most people would kill to have. It's rare and special.

And two, I can't for the life of me understand what's wrong with worshipping the woman you love. I don't buy into that toxic masculinity bull shit that a man has to be an aggressive, possessive, closed-off, emotionally-stunted dick. I'm a lover always, a fighter when I have to be, and I save the aggression and possessiveness for the bedroom where it belongs.

But, more and more, I'm being reminded of the not-so-small fact that Ivy *doesn't* return my feelings. She loves me, sure, but not the way I love her, and maybe she's not the woman I should be worshipping.

Maybe it's time I take a giant step back—go to Ivy Rivenbark rehab—and give myself some space to work on knocking some sense into myself.

When I get home, I change into my training gear and crank my playlist. By the end of the first mile, I've convinced myself that distance is exactly what Ivy and I need. By the end of the second, I'm almost excited to bar hop with Cassie and her friends. And when I'm doing my cool down stretches, I'm determined that tomorrow night, I am going to go out, have fun, and blow off some steam like a normal college student.

A few hours later, I'm sweaty as hell but I feel refreshed in a way that only a good, challenging run can do. I go to open the door to my condo and find that it's already unlocked.

"Jesse," I call, kicking my shoes off on the *New Apartment, Who Dis* doormat Ivy bought us. "What happened with st—"

"It's me!" A voice coming from my bedroom cuts me off, and I can't stop the smile that takes over my face. I tell myself to shut it down, to smother the warmth that bum-rushes my chest and sets my heart racing, and I just about manage it.

Baby steps.

Ivy skips into the kitchen, looking like my fantasy in jeans and a t-shirt, and maybe it's because I'm physically exhausted from my run, or because I'm emotionally wrecked from yesterday's encounter with Brock the Beefy Buttface, but I don't let myself look.

"They let us out of lecture early, so I thought I'd bring dinner for my two favorite men." A smile takes over her face, her dimple popped and adorable, and she slides a large brown paper bag in front of me. As usual, she's completely oblivious to my inner turmoil.

"*Two* favorite men? What about Jacob?" I tease and peer into the bag.

"Hush." She rolls her eyes. "He's not a man yet, so he doesn't count. And anyway, he's my favorite *human*. That's different."

"Of course. So, what did you bring me?"

"China Wok. Your fave. Beef and broccoli and some dumplings," she says as she sets containers and chopsticks in front of me.

It smells phenomenal, and if I gave in to my impulses, I would totally kiss her right now. But I don't give into my impulses, *ever*, and the punch to my gut it creates is exactly why I need to go out with Cassie tomorrow night. So instead, I smile and take the chopsticks from her hand, making sure that our fingers brush just enough to create the zing of barely-there energy that I crave like an addict. Because I am still a man in love with his best friend.

"I got J that fried rice he likes," she continues unbothered. "Where is he? I thought he had an early bio-chem lab on Thursdays."

"Yeah, he does. But he's got a study group tonight," I answer.

"Dang. Oh well, more for me," Ivy chirps, and she picks up her food and carries it into the living room.

The condo I share with Jesse is nice. Much nicer than

most undergrads can afford. It's in a private building and the majority of the residents are older, established townies or PhD students. Between my parents and Jesse's parents, the monthly payment is chump change.

"Do you want to watch a movie?" Ivy asks. She's perched herself on the black leather sofa, the tie-dye throw blanket she keeps here is spread over her lap, and she's moved Jesse's yarn basket to the floor, so she could set food up on the coffee table in front of her.

Once again, I'm struck with just how perfect she looks in my personal space, how perfectly she fits in my life. And, once again, I squash those thoughts as fast as possible and remind myself that she is my friend. *Only* my friend.

"Definitely. Just let me shower, first." I set my food down on the table next to hers and turn toward the bathroom. "I just ran fifteen and a half miles."

"Ick." She shudders, and I laugh at her.

"Cue it up. Romantic comedy? Action? Period drama?"

"Hmmm. I vote horror," she says impishly, and I groan.

"Of course you do," I say, and she wiggles happily on her cushion. "You're only doing this because you like to see me squirm."

"That's not true! I love blood and guts and ghosts and such."

"Fine." I give in with a sigh and hand her the remote so she can pick a film, then head to the bathroom for my shower. "I'll be right out."

One hour into the movie, and I know it's going to happen.

I can feel it. I'm on the edge of my seat, heart racing as I watch the dumbass on the TV walking down a dark hallway lined with closed doors. He's escaped death twice now; there's no way he'll do it a third time.

As the guy reaches for a doorknob, I dig my fingertips into my thighs. This is it. This is definitely the room where the knife wielding psychopath is hiding. My heart feels like it's going to burst out of my ribcage.

I fucking hate horror films.

When the guy flings open the door, I jump, but there's nothing inside, and I heave a sigh of relief right along with the dumb ass on the screen.

I glance over at Ivy. She's got her knees pulled up to her chest, her arms hugging them to her body, and the blanket draped around her shoulders. Her eyes are wide, and her breath is heavy as she stares at the screen. She gasps as the guy in the movie opens another door, and I whip my eyes back to the television.

This is it.

This one has to be the one.

Third door. Third time's a charm.

Dude is toast.

The movie music gets louder, more ominous, and I suck in a breath. He turns the knob and—

"Fuck!" I shriek, jumping off the couch and running to the edge of the living room while Ivy's hysterical laughter fills my ears. "What the hell, Ives!"

My side burns from where she poked me, and she's hunched over laughing, tears welling in her eyes. Even though I was just about ready to run for my fucking life, I have to hold back a smile.

"That's not fucking funny, Ivy," I say between gasps. "You know I get jumpy during these stupid movies."

"I know," she pushes out, "I know. I'm sorry. I was just

going to have you pass me my beer. Oh my gosh, Kelley! You should have seen your face!"

She's laughing harder now, but she attempts to twist her features into a terrified expression and lets out a high-pitched squealing noise.

"I don't fucking sound like that," I protest, still trying to catch my breath.

"Yes, you do!"

"No, I don't," I shout playfully and toss a couch pillow at her.

The pillow smacks her in the face, but it just makes Ivy laugh harder, and she makes the squealing noise again.

Shit, I really hope that's not how I sounded.

"You did that on purpose, didn't you?" I accuse.

Ivy shakes her head back and forth quickly, biting her lip to keep from laughing more. "No, I didn't. I swear."

"You're lying," I say, and I stalk slowly toward her.

Ivy's eyes get wide, and she sits up straight, inching her body farther down the couch, away from me.

"I'm not," she says again, breathless and fighting a smile.

"Lies," I say, and with a predatory grin, I lunge for her.

Ivy lets out a stream of shrieking giggles and jumps over the arm of the sofa, just as my knees land on the cushion. She tosses her tie-dye blanket over my head and tries to make a break for the hallway, but I'm faster than she is.

I throw the blanket off and catch up to her just as she's rounding the corner into my bedroom. With a burst of laughter, she spins and tries to shut the door, but I crouch down and wrap my arms around her waist, hoisting her up so she's half thrown over my shoulder.

Ivy is writhing with uncontrollable laughter, and I can't remember the last time I had this much fun.

"Admit it," I say, walking backward away from the door. "Admit you scared me on purpose."

"No!"

"Admit it," I repeat, and I give her side a playful squeeze, causing her to squeal with laughter.

"Never," she shouts again, so I squeeze her side once more. Her body jerks in response, the sudden movement causing me to fall sideways, landing on my bed with Ivy sprawled on top of me.

It all happens so fast.

At first, Ivy is laughing and I'm laughing, both attempting to out-tickle the other, both refusing to surrender.

And then, somehow, the playfulness vanishes, and it's replaced with an overwhelming sense of intimacy.

I become aware of our situation milliseconds before she does, because she's still writhing and giggling when I freeze.

I'm lying on my back on the bed, one hand on Ivy's upper arm and the other gripping her waist as she lies next to me with her leg hitched up and draped over my body.

Everywhere her skin is touching mine becomes hyper-sensitive, and I try not to focus on the way her thigh is hooked across my hips, precariously close to my now rock-hard dick, or how her chest presses into mine with every inhale, or how her warm breath fans over my neck with every exhale.

I squeeze my eyes shut, attempting to get myself under control, and tighten my grip on Ivy's waist to stop her wiggling. If she moves even an inch, I won't be able to hide the effect she's having on my body.

"Kelley," she breathes out, and I snap my eyes open to find her gazing down at me, face still alight with laughter but her brows are furrowed, questioning.

We look at each other, and I watch the confusion and

laugher fade from her features as something else takes its place. Something less playful. Something more complicated.

"Kelley," she says again, and I feel her tightening her grip on my shirt. Her pink tongue darts out to wet her plush lower lip, and my breath quickens.

Her pupils are blown wide, and as I drag my fingers up her arm, she closes her eyes and lets out a shuddering breath. I trace my fingertips up her neck, across her jaw, and she leans her face into my palm.

"Ivy," I whisper, and I hardly recognize my own voice. It's raw and gravely and full of barely restrained desire.

She opens her eyes slowly, and everything I'm feeling is reflected back to me. I've seen that look in her eyes once before. I thought for sure I'd never see it again. But there it is. Want. Lust. *Need*. For me.

Despite all my talk mere hours earlier, only one thought comes to mind.

I won't survive another minute if I'm not kissing this woman.

I tighten my grip on her waist, and slowly, painfully slowly, I begin to bring my lips up to meet hers.

But they never touch.

"Ayyy," Jesse calls from the living room, and the sudden interruption causes Ivy to jump off me. "Who got Chinese?"

What the actual fuck.

I hear his footsteps heading toward us and Ivy scrambles off the bed, fixing her shirt, running her hands through her hair, and looking at everything in my room except for me.

"I'm going to go get Jesse his dinner," she says quickly, her voice high-pitched and airy. She runs out of the room as if she's just narrowly avoided disaster, and I'm left lying on my bed, alone, with my hands outstretched, reaching for something that's no longer there.

I squeeze my eyes shut and allow myself to recall the jolts

of electricity that exploded through my body when we touched. The way all of my nerve endings vibrated with excitement. So much more than our barely-there finger brush. More powerful and more pleasurable and more torturous than anything I've felt in my life up to this moment.

Then I let myself replay her reaction when I leaned up to kiss her. The way her gorgeous blue irises were nearly swallowed whole by her pupils. The emotions I watched flash over her face. I didn't imagine it. The way my body burns is proof it wasn't a dream.

She wanted me.

She needed me to kiss her, maybe as much as I needed it.

I know because I've seen that look on her face once before. And I'll be damned if I mess it up this time around.

kelley

"I LOOK LIKE A FUCKING IDIOT," I grumble as my mom fixes my tie.

"You look very handsome," she says, finishing the knot and stepping back to survey me. "You look like an adult in this tux, but don't swear. It's pedestrian."

I roll my eyes at her. If she only knew how *pedestrian* my fucking mouth can be.

"I just don't understand why Shelby picked out this fu—" Ma glares and raises her hand like she's gonna smack me. She won't really do it, but I still throw up my palms, ducking away really fast, and correct myself.

"Fugly! I was gonna say *fugly*! I don't know why she picked out this *fugly* pattern. I look like a circus clown."

Ma hits me with her *I'm not impressed with your antics, young man* expression. "Fugly is no better than the other word. But, no, you do not look like a circus clown."

I turn to look in the hallway mirror and grimace at the maroon tux and pink and maroon polka-dotted tie. What the *fuck* was Shelby thinking? Was she fucking high when she selected this from the catalogue? I shake my head in disgust and turn away.

"What time is Ivy getting here," I ask my mom and check my phone to see if she's texted.

"She and Jacob should be here in about 10 minutes," my mom calls from the kitchen. *Good*, I think to myself and walk into the foyer to wait for them.

Things have been weird with Ives and me since our, uh, *spat*? Yeah spat. Since our *spat* in the cafeteria two weeks ago. Basically, I fucked up and spazzed out on her and now I think she's punishing me with the cold shoulder. It sucks.

I was actually dreading tonight until she called and asked if my parents could watch Jacob. Her mom has to work a late shift last-minute, and Ivy doesn't want to miss prom. Of course, my mom and dad said sure, and now Ivy and Tyler are doubling with me and Shelby.

It's gonna be awkward as hell.

Shelby and Ivy don't get along—well, Shelby doesn't get along with Ivy—and Tyler is fucking annoying. But at least I get the chance to try and patch things up with Ives. I hate this weirdness between us. I just want my friend back.

Headlights flash in the driveway, and I walk over and open the front door, just as Ivy and Jacob are climbing out of their mom's car. Ivy looks absolutely stunning in a dark blue dress. The straps that go over her shoulders and tie behind her neck are covered in sparkly diamond crystal things, and her waist dips in and her hips flare in a way that makes me choke on my own spit. When she turns to shut the car door, I see that her back is bare almost to her ass, and I have to look away or else I might actually die. Best friends shouldn't be allowed to look that good.

"Hi, Mrs. Rivenbark!" I divert my attention to Ivy's mom

and smile at her. She leans over to look at me through the passenger window and throws me a thumbs up.

"Hey, Kelley. Tell your momma I said thanks for watchin' Jake. I'd hate for Ivy Jean to miss her prom 'cause my employees are unreliable," she calls from the car. She's got a smile on her face that looks a bit like Ivy's when she's sad but trying to act like she's not sad, and I smile back to make her feel better.

"It's no problem, Mrs. Rivenbark. Don't work too hard."

She laughs and waves my comment off. "I told you before to call me Pam, Kelley. Now you behave yourself and stick close to Ivy Jean." Ivy's standing next to me now and rolls her eyes at me. The playful gesture lessens the tension coiled in my stomach.

I glance down at Ivy and smile as I say, "Ives can take care of herself, Miss Pam."

"Oh, I know it," Pam calls out. "I mean stick close so she can keep an eye on you. I know you're not as sweet and wholesome as you act, Kelley Pierce." She points her finger at me with a smirk and then pulls out of the drive with Ivy and Jacob suppressing giggles at my side.

"Okay, okay, ha ha, very funny. Get inside."

"You look kind of ridiculous," Ivy says quietly as we walk into the house.

"Hush, you," I respond, and when she giggles, I feel like things are going to be fine.

I lied. Things are not fine. They aren't even in the same area code as fine. I'm fucking fuming.

It started in the limo on the drive here.

Every time Ivy laughed at one of Tyler's stupid fucking jokes, I had to grit my teeth to keep from telling her that his jokes actually aren't funny. *At all*. And then Shelby made it worse because every time Ivy spoke, Shelby would sigh really loudly or talk over her or try to make out with me, and that's petty shit that I just have no patience for.

But that's not even the worst part.

When we got to the Silver Pines Country Club, the swanky ass banquet hall our school rented out for prom, Shelby pranced off to talk to some friends and brag about how she and I are probably going to be crowned Senior Prom King and Queen, Tyler excused himself to the bathroom to probably adjust the socks he has stuffed down his pants or guzzle some mouthwash or take a bath in more fucking Axe body spray, and me and Ivy settled in at a table on the side of the dance floor. It was going good. Great, even. I was excited to have a few minutes alone to talk to her—to apologize in person for being a dick in the cafeteria two weeks ago. But then Ivy took her phone out to check in on Jacob, and when she opened her small purse thing, something horrible caught my eye.

Foil packets.

Condoms.

And not just one condom. Not even two. But *three*.

Three fucking condoms.

The fuck does she think two virgins are going to do with three condoms before curfew? I rarely even wank three times in a single night.

I'm seething.

I'm grinding my teeth so hard I think I'm in danger of cracking a molar.

When Dad Joke Tyler comes back from the bathroom, I'm irrationally pissed that his fly isn't down and there's no pee stain on the crotch of his pants. He looks dumb and happy, and I want to punch him in his tiny little throat. When Ivy smiles at him and takes his hand, I want to take off my stupid freaking circus tie and strangle him with it.

This night fucking sucks.

Of course, I dance with my girlfriend, and I do the obligatory prom pose and smile for pictures. When the Cupid Shuffle comes on, I go out on the dance floor and make a show of it because that's what people are expecting. But no matter how hard I try to avoid it, my eyes always find Ivy. And she's always laughing with Tyler or holding hands with Tyler or her dimple is fucking popped for fucking Tyler, and all I can think about are those damn foil packets.

I can't let her do this.

She doesn't love Tyler. She can't lose her virginity to someone like Tyler. He's not good enough for her. He can't even make her laugh *for real*, because I know when she's fake-laughing and that's what she's been doing every time Tyler cracks one of his lame as fuck dad jokes.

When Ivy gets up to use the bathroom, I make the decision to follow her. If I get her alone, I can talk to her and hopefully make her see reason. Luckily, Shelby is in a group with some of the other volleyball players and doesn't even realize I'm leaving.

I make it out to the hallway, just in time to see Ivy walk into the restroom, so I post up on the wall across from the door and wait. In a few minutes, she comes back out, and when she sees me standing there, a confused-but-happy smile plays on her lips.

"Kelley."

"Ivy."

I walk up to her and take her hand, quickly leading her down a hallway away from the room where the dance is being held. She follows without hesitation, which makes me feel way better than it should, and she doesn't ask questions until

I pull her into a smaller room on the opposite side of the building.

"What's going on?" she asks as she looks around. "Where are we?"

"It's a men's lounge," I tell her. "I knew where it was because Pops and my gramps come here sometimes." Yeah, my parents belong to this swanky ass country club. "They also use it as a groom's room when there's weddings here," I add so I don't feel like such a douche.

"Oh," she breathes, and she runs her fingers over the back of a gray leather sofa. "Why are we here?"

She looks at me then, and my heart jumps into my throat. She must be wearing her contacts tonight, because her eyes are unobstructed and bright. The color of her dress brings out every shade of blue in them. Her irises are a kaleidoscope of blues, and like a magnet, I'm pulled to her. I've spent most of the night looking at her, watching her with Tyler, with irritation clouding my vision. Now, in the silence and privacy of this room, I'm seeing her with clarity, and she's absolutely beautiful.

With each step toward her, more details come into focus.

Her eyes are lined with some sort of silver makeup, and her lashes look darker and fuller and longer than I've ever seen them. Crystals matching the ones on her dress are dangling from her earlobes, and when I'm mere inches in front of her, I reach up and touch one. The warmth coming off her body is a direct contrast to the cool, metallic material of the earring, and it feels fragile on my fingertips.

"They're not real," Ivy whispers. She's barely breathing, and my eyes flick to her mouth. "They're fake. Costume jewelry."

I know she's talking about the earrings, but now her lips are the sole focus of my attention. They're a soft shade of pink, almost nude, but slightly darker than normal. *If I kiss them, will they feel as pillowy as they look?*

Ivy's mouth opens slightly, and her tongue sneaks out to wet her lips, making the plump lower one glisten. Somehow my left hand has found its way to her waist, and my right hand slides to the back of her neck and I slip my fingers into her hair. Everywhere my skin touches her is buzzing.

"Kelley," she whispers. I look up to meet her gaze, but her beautiful eyes are closed, and I miss them. I want them on me.

"Ivy," I say and press our foreheads together.

"Yes?" Her voice trembles. I graze my nose along hers.

"I want…" I lick my lips.

"…Yes?" Her soft panting breaths fan over my face, and I pause, willing my heart to stop pounding.

I'm going to kiss her.

I'm going to kiss her and I'm never going to stop.

"Ivy, I want to kiss you." Her tiny hands grip the front of my suit jacket and my stomach tenses. I can feel her knuckles pressing into my abs.

"So do it," she says, and I'm momentarily struck dumb.

I can't move. I'm frozen. I'm an idiotic circus clown statue.

When the meaning of her words finally sinks into my numb skull, that Ivy Rivenbark just gave me permission to kiss her, I lean forward, brushing my lips lightly over hers. It's the faintest of touches, but it ignites a fire in my gut. I kiss the corner of her mouth, mustering up the courage to connect our lips for real. To do it right.

And then my phone rings.

What the fuck.

"Crazy in Love" plays loudly from the pocket of my suit

pants, the ringtone Shelby set for herself without asking me, and I'm assaulted with our reality.

I have a girlfriend. Ivy has a boyfriend. Ivy is my *best friend*, and I was just milliseconds away from saying, "I don't give a fuck," to all of that.

We break contact and step away from each other at the same time, but I don't reach for my phone. We're locked in a silent staring contest when the song stops, and we're still staring when the song starts back again.

Ivy looks away first, clamping her eyes shut, and I know she's counting her breaths.

"Answer her," she commands. There are no emotions in her voice. Just business.

I hesitate.

"Answer her, Kelley," she insists.

With my eyes set on Ivy, I answer my phone.

"Yeah?"

"Kap, where are you? They're gonna announce Prom King and Queen any minute!" Shelby exclaims on the other end. She's been excited about this for weeks.

Ivy still isn't looking at me. She's picked up her purse from the floor and she's running her fingers through her hair to fix where I mussed it up, and I want to stop her. I want to tell her to leave her hair alone—to stop erasing the evidence that just moments ago my fingers were there, buried in those golden strands, massaging her scalp and making her breathless.

I blink hard and look away, focusing back on the music from the dance pounding through the phone.

"Yeah, okay. Be right there."

"Yay! Hurry!"

I put the phone back in my pocket and watch as Ivy walks to the door.

"We should go," she says, voice still devoid of emotions. "Shelby is waiting for you, and I'm sure my boyfriend is wondering where I went."

My teeth grit at *boyfriend*.

"Ivy—"

"No, Kelley. We're dating other people, and this could have been really, really bad. We're not these people, Kell. So, let's just go back to our dates and forget this happened."

Fat fucking chance I'll ever forget this.

"But, Ivy... You almost kissed me back. You told me to kiss you. Don't you think that means you shouldn't...*ya know*...tonight?"

She looks at me like I'm speaking Pig Latin. She doesn't know what I'm saying but she is pretty sure it's offensive.

I take a deep breath and try again.

"I saw the condoms in your little purse thingy. Ivy, you can't lose your virginity to Tyler. You don't love him. You wouldn't have been okay with me kissing you if you were in love with Tyler."

Her soft face goes from shocked, to hurt, to straight pissed the fuck off within seconds, and I know I said something very, very wrong. When she opens her mouth, I flinch, expecting to be hit with an explosion of rage.

Instead, what I get is calm, steady, and vicious.

I'd rather have the rage.

"Is that what this was about?" she asks, and her cold, calculating stare studies my face. My heart is now racing for an entirely different reason, and I start to sweat under her scrutiny. "The condoms. Is that why you tried to kiss me? As some sort of a trap? A test?"

That's what she thinks?

"What? No. That's not why I tried to kiss you." She lifts

her eyebrow and hits me with a glare. "It's not! But you can't have sex with him!"

"Excuse you? I can do whatever the heck I want, Kelley Allen Pierce."

Shit. I fucked up again.

"No, of course, I know. That's not what I meant."

"It's what you said, is it not?"

"No. I mean it is what I said, but I didn't say it how I meant to say it."

"Just spit it out, Kelley." Her hands are on her hips, her blue eyes are glacial, and I have one more chance to get her to hear me.

"I just meant that, well, don't you think that if you wanted me to kiss you that you shouldn't be losing your virginity to Tyler? You wanted me just now, not him. You wanted *me*, Ivy."

"So, I should lose my virginity to you, then? Is that what you're saying?"

"No! I mean...no? I don't know. But it shouldn't be Tyler."

God how the fuck did we get here? How the hell do I fix this?

For the first time in what feels like years, Ivy's face finally drops the emotionless blank slate expression, but what replaces it guts me. I watch as sadness and disappointment move across her features briefly, before settling on disgust. She inhales a shuddering breath, and on the exhale, she lets out a morbid, sad little chuckle.

"It doesn't matter anyway, Kelley. I wasn't planning to lose my virginity tonight. Because Tyler and I are not virgins anymore."

I can hear my blood rushing in my ears. I don't know if I want to cry or punch something. Or cry while punching something.

How could she do this?

Why would she do this?

Why do I feel so...*betrayed*?

It's not until she takes a step toward me that I realize I've stopped breathing, and I sway on my feet from the force of my gasp.

"Kelley?" She goes to put her hand on my arm, but I jerk it away.

Suddenly, I'm furious.

Furious at Tyler. Furious at Ivy. Furious at myself.

And I want to hurt her. I want her to feel how I feel right now, because I hate the pity and shock that I see on her face. I hate that I just made myself vulnerable without even realizing it and it punched me in the fucking throat. I'm hurt and humiliated and just fucking *furious* because of it all.

"I can't believe you'd be so stupid, Ivy," I spit. She jerks her head back and drops her jaw.

"Excuse you?" Her voice is a whisper, but it doesn't conceal the anger and hurt within it.

"Tyler is just using you. He doesn't care about you. He just wants someone to fuck."

Ivy's eyes go wide, and I swear she growls.

"Are you freakin' kidding me right now, Kelley? Two seconds ago you were upset because you thought I didn't care enough about Tyler to have sex with him, and now you're saying *he's* using *me*?"

"So, you're saying you're just using him?"

The venom dripping from my words turns my stomach, and I know I'm going to regret what I say next even before I say it. But it's a slow-motion train wreck I can't stop. Verbal diarrhea I have no control over. My emotions are driving and I'm just along for the ride, fuck the casualties.

"I don't even know you right now," I sneer. "Making these

dumbass decisions. For what? For *a fuck*? You want to end up just like your momma?"

Ivy flinches like I slapped her, and I know my words hit their mark when I see tears well in her eyes. But instead of apologizing like I should, pride or fear and fucking stupidity clamp my mouth shut, and I say nothing.

"How *dare* you," Ivy hisses. A single tear rolls down her face, and she furiously wipes it away. "I've never known you to be cruel, Kelley. I thought we were friends."

"Guess not," I snipe. "Not if you're gonna throw away who you are for Tyler. You're gonna throw away *me* for Tyler. You're being stupid and selfish."

"That's not fair," she snarls, and I watch another tear fall. "All you do is date. All you *do* is mess around with girls, and I have to hear about it in the lunchroom and the locker room and on social freaking media. And you have the *audacity* to turn this around on *me*? You say I'm throwing away our friendship, but friends don't speak to each other the way you just spoke to me. You crossed a line—you said something you knew would hurt me. Bringing up my mom? That's low, Kelley."

She takes a deep breath, swipes her hands under her eyes to get rid of the tears, and erases every emotion from her face. Dread fills my stomach.

"I hope you have a great night with *your girlfriend*, Prom King. I'm done with this conversation."

"If you go back out there to Tyler, then you're done with me, too," I threaten. I don't even know why I said it. I'm desperate and grasping and digging my hole even deeper.

She shakes her head slowly and shame hits me right in the chest. Then with one last impassive look, her face in that blank mask that I hate, she turns on her heel and walks out.

Ivy doesn't spare me another glance. Just lets the door shut softly behind her.

After she leaves, I have to sit down on one of the leather sofas because I'm pretty sure I might pass out. I want to run after her. I want to apologize. But she just chose Tyler, right? I fucked up big. I don't know if she'll ever forgive me. If I'll ever forgive myself. The pain in her eyes—the pain I inflicted on purpose—I can't stop seeing it. I'm going to have nightmares about it.

When I finally return to the dance, I have ten missed calls from Shelby, and I find that she's had the chaperones hold off on announcing Prom King and Queen until I got there.

When they call us up to be crowned, I search the crowded dance floor for a dark blue dress, bright blonde hair, and piercing eyes, but she's not there.

She's gone.

TWELVE

I WAIT up for Bailey to get off work. It's 2:30 in the morning when she finally gets home, and by then I've had three freak outs and probably a quarter of our box of wine.

After showing Jesse the Chinese food I brought him, I shouted goodbye and hightailed it out of their condo. I was going to send an SOS text to Bailey but remembered she was closing the bar tonight, so instead I went home and paced the apartment and drank. When she walks in, I could cry with relief.

"Thank the Goddesses you're here," I say and crush her in a hug.

"Whoa, hello. I'm happy to see you too!" Bailey laughs as we break apart. "Wait...are you drunk? You never get drunk."

I shake my head. "I'm not. Not really. Maybe just moderately buzzed." She raises her eyebrow at me, a mix of concern and amusement in her smile.

"What's up?"

"I almost kissed Kelley," I blurt.

"What!" She shouts on a laugh.

"It's not funny! This has the potential to be bad."

"What do you mean you *almost* kissed him?"

I start pacing again, trying to recount the moment for her, but everything about those memories makes me feel flushed and woozy, and I can't get my head to de-fuzz.

"Well, he also almost kissed me. We almost kissed each other? He was going to kiss me, and I think I was going to let him. Actually, no, I was definitely going to let him. I was going to let him but then Jesse came home and I just kind of freaked out and ran away."

I halt pacing and whip my eyes to Bailey.

"Ohmigosh, Bailey, I just *ran away*. I was such a spaz. What am I going to do? I can't want to kiss Kelley. Last time we almost kissed, it ruined everything."

I start pacing again.

"Well, to be fair, Kelley was a total prick last time because he was young and immature, and his pride was hurt because you'd just unknowingly broken his poor little prick heart. Do you think that would happen again?"

"No." I shake my head. "Probably not? But that's not the point."

"Ivy." Bailey grabs my arm and maneuvers me to the couch. "You gotta stop walking around me in circles, babe, it's making me nauseous."

"Sorry," I say absently, and sit on the couch.

"Okay, so what's the point?" Bailey asks, and I jump back up again.

"The point is that I think I wanted him to kiss me, B. And that can't happen. It cannot happen. I cannot kiss him."

"Why not?"

I stop pacing and throw a bewildered glare at where she's perched on the couch.

"What do you mean *why not*? Because!" I throw my hands

in the air and slap them back down at my sides. "Because!" I say again and punctuate it with a stomp.

"Wow. That's a real compelling argument, there, counsel. Much logic. Such convince."

I groan, and throw myself onto the couch next to her. "See? I can't even think straight. My brain is much broked."

"Deep breaths, V." Bailey reaches over and rubs my shoulder. I count my inhales and exhales until the fuzz clears a little, and then I sit up. "Okay, babe. Lemme hear it. Why can't you and Kelley lock lips?"

I sigh and shake my head.

"I'm still so messed up, B. I just had that panic attack, and I've had more nightmares. I have to give myself a pep talk before even attempting to have sex. I'm not emotionally stable enough to be in a relationship. And I can't risk trying something with Kelley and it failing, which is inevitable. It will explode epically in my face."

"Okay, well, we'll table the doomsday mindset for now. Did you experience anxiety tonight?" she asks, and I widen my eyes and gesture to my hunched over, obviously stressed-out form.

"Does it look like I'm hunky-dory, sniffin' flowers and singing songs, Bailey?"

She rolls her eyes and laughs at me. "No, I know you're freaking out now, but this isn't a panic attack. I mean earlier. When Kelley almost kissed you. When he touched you and was all up in your personal bubble—did you feel any anxiety then?"

I think about it for a second, place my hand on my heart, and shake my head slowly. "No," I breathe out. "I mean, my heart was racing, and my breathing was labored, but it wasn't panic. It was—"

"Because you were turned the fuck on and wanted to hop on his dick?"

"Bailey!" I bark out a laugh and give her a shove, and Bailey cackles. "You're reading too many of those books."

"Maybe you're not reading enough of them." She pops a brow, then lowers her voice. "You don't have to control everything. Everything won't implode if you loosen your grip on the reins, V."

"I know," I whisper, then drop my head into my hands. "I know. It's just so hard and I can't stop the spiral of *what-ifs*." Bailey reaches over and squeezes my hand, and for a few minutes we're quiet.

When my breathing has slowed, Bailey breaks the silence. "I bet he's a beast in bed."

I snap my head up. "Kelley? No... You think?"

She shrugs and smirks. "You think just because he's responsible and studious—"

"and respectful and kind and considerate," I interject.

"Yeah, yeah, all those things. You think just because Kelley presents in public as a Mr. friggen Rogers, that he can't do you the best kind of dirty in the bedroom?"

"Oh my gosh, just stop talking," I squeak and throw my hands over my eyes. *No, no, no,* cannot see Kelley like this.

"Shouldn't judge a man by his metaphorical cardigan, V."

"No. Nope."

"It could definitely be a beautiful day in his neighborhood, if you catch my drift." She thinks she's so dang hilarious.

"No, no, no."

"And we've seen him in sweats, V. That dick print is..." she whistles for emphasis.

"Please, please stop. I get it." I'm begging, and she snickers at me. Jerk.

"Admit it, V. You're turned on. You want him."

I peek at her through my fingers and sigh. "I admit it."

"So, what's the problem?"

"You mean besides the fact that he's my best friend and sex is guaranteed to change things?"

"Besides that."

"Bailey," I say quietly, "he doesn't know about any of it. At all."

She blinks. She opens her mouth and then closes it. And then blinks again, shocked.

"I know," I relent, trying to explain myself. "But when I first got back, I couldn't talk about it with him yet. I wasn't ready to talk to *anyone* about it other than Dr. Joyner. The only reason you know is because you were my roommate and I had nightmares. Then, after a while, our friendship was getting back to normal, and then so much time had passed, and I just... I don't know. I guess I didn't want to risk things changing again." I shrug. "Kelley's always treated me like I can do anything—like I can conquer the world. He's always looked at me like I'm this pillar of strength. He makes me *feel* stronger. I don't know what I would do if that changed. If he started to see me as a victim..." I release a shuddered breath.

"Ivy. You know he wouldn't. You know. He wouldn't because you aren't. You are strong, and everything that's happened only further proves that."

"Maybe."

"Fuck *maybe*, V. It's the truth." Bailey speaks with such conviction that my confidence is bolstered slightly and my mouth quirks up into a soft, sad smile.

"It still doesn't change that I've got a plan from which I will not deviate. Law school. A practice. I can't be in a relationship. I can't let anyone distract me from those goals. I know what happens when women let romance drive them. I've seen it."

"That's a weak argument. Yours and your mom's situations are totally different. Kelley isn't like your dad, or Jacob's dad, and you're not your mom. You're not the kind of person to let anyone derail your plans or throw you off course. And anyway, Kelley would never try. He's, like, your biggest cheerleader. Hell, I'm even jealous sometimes because I know there's no damn way I could ever usurp his Number One BFF throne."

I laugh. "Hush, I love you."

"Yeah, and I love you. And that's why I'm totally cool coming in second to Kelley, because he loves you big, too, and you deserve the biggest love."

"Too many of those kissing books, B," I joke with a smile.

"Not enough of them, V." She points at me and winks, then gives me an encouraging smile. "Loosen the reins, babe."

I lean over and hug her tight. "I don't know what I would do without you, Bailey."

"Yeah, yeah, thank the Roomie Placement Goddess or whatever." She rocks side to side playfully as she hugs me, and I giggle, but then she pushes me back, gripping my shoulders and hits me with a serious look.

"But I swear, Ivy, I better never come in behind Jesse in the BFF hierarchy. He might have scarves and shitty potholders, but I have cookies and I'm freakin' boss at girl talk. Plus, I'm the only one who willingly watches creepy shit with you."

I snort out a laugh and she giggles with me, then she picks my jar of wine up off the coffee table and takes a sip.

"So, what are you gonna do?"

I answer honestly. "Avoid him until I figure it out."

"You still hunting for hanky-panky tomorrow with J?" She waggles her brows and I roll my eyes.

"Meh. I'll go to fulfill wing-woman duties, but that's it. Hey, do you work tomorrow?"

"I do, but I can see about switching. Why? You want me to come turn you and J's twosome into a threesome?"

"Yes, please!" I clasp my hands under my chin and bat my eyelashes.

"I'll see what I can do."

* * *

Bailey was able to switch shifts with another bartender, and I'm so grateful. She walks into Keggers with me and Jesse, and the tension I've been carrying in my shoulders all day loosens.

Of course, "In Da Club" is already blaring from the speakers, my heels are already sticking to the floor, and I can hear cheers coming from the pong tables in the back. The atmosphere is so familiar, so normal, and I draw comfort from it. It's nice that some aspects of my life are still dependable, and I'm determined to enjoy this night.

I hate being confused, and I hate not knowing the solution to a problem. And make no mistake, this whole thing with Kelley has **WARNING: PROBLEM!!!** stamped all over it.

Usually, I puzzle over every detail and piece together an answer. It's just how I am. I research, and I problem-solve, and I logic my way out of any tangled web. I'm basically a less-eccentric version of Sherlock with a vagina. But I cannot bring myself to dissect my complicated feelings for Kelley. It's just too much. Just makes me *feel* too much. But now my second instinctive coping mechanism is also failing me—no matter what I do, I can't ignore this.

Honestly, it's annoying.

After my chat with Bailey early this morning, I attempted to get some sleep without success. My dreams were inundated with replays of the *Almost Kiss* with Kelley—both *Almost Kisses*. My anxious brain decided it would be a great idea to torment me with images of last night mushed all together with images from the destructive evening from Senior Prom four years ago.

Every single version of the dream ended with us both in tears, a giant irreparable chasm between us. My brain has been fighting off ominous thoughts all day.

"I'm gonna grab drinks," Jesse shouts over the music. "Draft special?"

"Actually, J, can you get me a vodka cranberry with lime?"

Bailey lets out a celebratory whoop and Jesse flashes me a grin.

"You gonna get buzzed tonight, V? We gonna have to carry your tipsy ass home?" Jesse shimmies his shoulders and I roll my eyes at him. He's such a goof.

"I'll complete my wing-woman duties first, but yeah, I think I'm gonna let loose a little."

"Nah, V. You're off the hook tonight. Queens before peens, remember?" Bailey looks up from her phone and snorts a laugh. Jesse turns his mischievous grin on her. "I'm gonna hang with my best girls and we're gonna get our dance on. BRB."

Bailey and I watch as Jesse dances his way up to the bar, both smiling like fools. Praise the Goddess of Friends because I've got some great ones.

"He's such a goofball," I say to Bailey as we huddle together off to the side of the dance floor. We got here a bit late, so there was no chance of snagging a table. No matter, though, because I plan on dancing all night.

"Yeah, he's definitely a goofball. He's gonna make someone very happy someday." She says on a wistful sigh.

"They'll wear matching scarves, and they'll get a cat and he'll knit the cat little sweaters."

"He'll probably name the cat something ridiculous, like Dog or Pig."

"Or Steve Carrell."

We both let out big laughs. "He'll definitely name it Steve Carrell." This night is going to be exactly what I need.

"I love this song!" I shout to Bailey as "my ex's best friend" by Machine Gun Kelly comes on, and when Jesse comes back with our drinks, we head out to the dance floor.

For as off-kilter as I've been feeling, I still went all out tonight. Black distressed skinny jeans, shimmering silver stilettos, and a white flowy silk tank that shows just a hint of my stomach when I raise my arms. My hair is half-up in a top knot with the rest curled into beach waves, and I'm rocking siren red lipstick and thick winged eyeliner. Basically, I look freakin' hot.

I'm starting on my third drink, feeling relaxed and floaty, when Jesse checks his phone and disappears. Bailey and I are dancing and singing along to some '90s boy band throwback when Jesse slides back up next to us, and I watch him hip check Bailey. They share a conspiratorial grin that confuses me for all of two seconds before I learn exactly what they're smiling about.

I feel him before I see him, and the rush of emotions that floods through me is both exhilarating and terrifying. He slides his hand over my hip, his thumb grazing the exposed skin just above my jeans and presses his chest to my back.

This type of touch isn't new, but the way it sets me on fire is nothing like I've felt before. Goose bumps travel from where his hand is resting and cover every inch of my body. The sensation is so sudden and erotic that my breath catches, and my eyes fall shut. When he lowers his mouth to my ear, my head involuntarily falls back onto his chest.

"Surprise," Kelley whispers. "You look amazing."

"Thank you," I say back, but he probably can't hear me over the music. I wonder if he can feel my heart pounding.

Gods, why am I electrified?

I take a deep breath and turn around, forcing myself to take a step back, causing his hand to fall from my waist. I'm both relieved and aching from the loss.

"What are you doing here?" I feign bravado and flash him a grin, trying my best to get a handle on myself. "Did Mr. Serious finally decide to cut loose and have some fun?"

"I did," he nods, mouth quirking in a sexy smirk that sets my pulse skyrocketing.

What in the world? What is happening?

I can't stop myself from looking him over. My gaze rakes down his body, exploring and discovering details I've somehow been missing, and my body releases a sigh of relief. It's as if my eyes are rejoicing in finally being allowed to *see* him fully. To *appreciate* the view in a way that they've previously been denied.

Gosh, he looks good.

I've always known he is attractive. I'm not blind. But this new recognition? This is next-level.

Kelley's auburn hair is styled in that *un*styled way that looks like someone just ran their fingers through it. I have to clasp my hands into fists to keep from trying it out for myself. His hazel eyes are sparkling with mischief, his plump lips still sporting that infuriating and extremely hot smirk.

Curse that smirk. I frown. I'm too tipsy to handle it.

I let my eyes drift downward. The top two buttons on his dark grey Henley are undone, exposing a sliver of smooth, golden chest. The shirt fits him just snug enough to draw attention to his defined pecs and biceps, and his long sleeves are pulled up slightly, to show off his forearms.

Frankly, it's borderline indecent.

The way he's flaunting his forearms for everyone in Keggers to see. The way his biceps are outlined through his shirt. If I stare hard enough, I could probably see the indention of his six-pack. I'm surprised we're not swarmed by thirsty women and men trying to sneak a peek. And I am the biggest hypocrite.

When I let my eyes fall down to his tight, dark wash jeans, I hear him laugh. It's low, rough, and seductive. I feel it *everywhere*.

"You're acting like you've never seen me before." I can hear the cocky grin in his voice.

I lift my eyes to his. *Who is this unbelievably sexy man in front of me, and what has he done with my best friend?*

"Maybe I haven't."

A boyish, giddy smile engulfs his face, and he tucks his chin and looks away briefly. If that isn't a sight to memorize. Kelley Pierce is embarrassed. I take a mental picture and hope that I'm not too buzzed to store it properly.

"Hey, Jesse! Hi guys!" A female voice infiltrates the imaginary, secluded bubble I'd been standing in with Kelley, and I remember suddenly that we are in the middle of a crowded bar. I glance at my friends, and they're both watching us with huge, troublemaking smiles. But there's a third person standing with Jesse and Bailey, and she definitely isn't in on their joke.

"Hiya," I say and raise my hand to wave awkwardly. I am the smoothest. The Queen of Cool. Definitely do not need another vodka cranberry.

"Ivy, you've met Cassie, right?" Kelley gestures toward the gorgeous girl standing next to Jesse. She's got to be 5'10" and her legs are probably twice the length of mine. A plump, glossy pout. Sleek and shiny dark brown hair. She looks like a dang Jenner. The model one, not the other one.

"I have not met Cassie." I shake my head and force a confused smile. What in the hello...are they here together? On a *date*?

"Well, I feel like I've met you," Cassie chirps, and she smiles sweetly up at Kelley in a way that makes me grit my teeth. "Kelley has told me a lot about his best *friend*."

Before my buzzed brain can decide if that was supposed to be a dig, Kelley slides his arm over my shoulder and presses a kiss to the side of my head. In my mind, I picture him getting a face full of my stylish top knot and I snort out a giggle.

"Ivy's my best girl," I hear Kelley say, and I watch as Cassie's smile falls a little. The butterflies in my stomach do a little victory lap that I refuse to analyze, and I giggle some more.

Good grief, I'm floaty.

"Cassie, this is Bailey," Jesse cuts in.

"I'm Ivy's roommate, and I think we all need to dance," Bailey exclaims, then she hooks her arm with mine and pulls me farther out onto the dance floor.

I can feel the bass pulsing up through my stilettos as I move my body to the music. Surrounded by people I love and trust, the crowded dance floor feels like the safest place in the world. No stress. No anxiety. No baggage. Just a carefree twenty-one-year-old woman enjoying her last year of undergrad.

Cassie has turned out to be pretty freaking cool. The two friends that came here with her and Kelley—So *not* a date, thanks—joined our group a few hours ago, and we've been laughing and singing and dancing together all night.

I absolutely love seeing Kelley having fun. He never comes out with us, and Bailey rarely does anymore, so this has been a perfect night.

Well, except...

I'm struggling with a niggling sense of disappointment deep in my stomach. Kelley hasn't been outside of an arm's length from me all night, but our physical contact has been minimal. I've felt his eyes on me way more than his hands, and that *disappoints* me.

Ugh.

Every so often, our arms would brush, or I'd feel the heat from his body behind me as we danced, but despite the way the connections electrified my blood to boiling, every encounter has been...friendly. He's acted the same with me as he has with Bailey and Cassie and even Jesse tonight.

But the looks?

The looks have been anything but *friendly*.

Sultry. Suggestive. Sexy. But definitely not friendly.

My head is spinning.

Just a few hours ago, I was insisting to Bailey *and myself* that I have no interest in Kelley outside of friendship. I would never, ever, see him in any way other than platonically.

But then he had to come waltzing into this bar with his stupidly adorable hair, and his damned lickable biceps, and that infuriatingly perfect little side smirk—also lickable, I've decided—and now I don't know what side is up.

I've been blindsided by feelings I've repressed since Senior Prom, and I can't seem to cram them back into the lockbox where they belong.

Who the heck let them out in the first place?

I blame the Henley. Why are Henleys so hot? A sleeper-seduction technique, for sure. Sex disguised as cozy cotton loungewear. The guy who designed them is probably a playboy genius.

It's unfair, really.

I'm going to take all of Kelley's Henleys and burn them.

No wait. I'll donate them. Either way, they need to go.

As the song ends, I turn to Bailey. I need a shower and sleep and possibly some pros/cons lists and data charts to figure out just exactly what's happening in my head tonight. Not necessarily in that order.

"I'm ready to head out when you are," I shout over the crowd. She nods.

"Sounds good. I'll go close my tab."

"Coolie. I'm gonna go to the bathroom, then we'll say goodbyes."

"Hey, so, I might actually go to Bar 31 and meet up with Alex, that guy I told you about. You wanna come?" Bailey seems nervous but excited, which is out of character for her. Men don't make her giddy, and she's never intimidated.

"Are you asking because you want me there or just out of the goodness of your heart?"

She scrunches up her nose and gives me a sweet smile. "The latter?"

I pretend to be insulted and shake my head with a mock pout. "Then definitely not. My feet hurt. But make sure you share your location with me and send me a picture of him. Or a social media profile, or a license plate or something."

"Of course! Go pee and then I'll wait with you for your Uber."

I make my way toward the back of the bar, dodging bodies and crossing my fingers that the line isn't ridiculously long. When I reach the restrooms, I'm pleased to find that there are only eight girls ahead of me, so I'm able to get in and out in only fifteen minutes.

When I walk out of the bathroom, stepping out of the doorway to allow another girl access, I look up and find Kelley leaning on the opposite wall. There is a small smile playing on his lips, and his arms are crossed in front of his chest in way that makes his biceps bulge and displays his pornographic forearms directly in the center of my vision. I puff out an excited breath, then immediately frown at my reaction.

"Ivy."

"Kelley."

Without another word, he steps up to me and grasps my hand, then leads me down the darkened hallway and into a small room. When he flicks on a light, I see we're in a storeroom of sorts. Boxes of cleaning supplies and toiletries are stacked on metal shelving units along the wall, a mop and bucket stand in the corner. Everything smells clean, like fresh linen and citrus.

"What's going on?" I ask, arching a brow and trying to tame my intrigued smile. "Why are we back here?"

"We're in a storeroom," he states the obvious, and I get the feeling there's a punchline I'm not quite grasping.

"I can tell." I roll my eyes. "But why are we in a storeroom in the back of Keggers?"

"Zack, from my soccer team. He works here. He unlocked it for me."

He takes a step closer to me and my skin burns in the best way.

"*Ooookay...*" I look up at him, confusion and exhilaration coursing through my veins.

I wait for him to tell me more, to fill me in on what I'm missing, but instead he takes another half-step toward me. Our toes are almost touching, and I watch his hazel eyes as he looks me over. He settles his gaze on my mouth. I lick my lips

167

on instinct, and his prominent Adam's apple bobs in his throat. I have an urge to kiss it.

My heart is beating so fast.

He drags his eyes to mine and every green and gold fleck in his irises are set ablaze. My breath catches in my chest, and without breaking eye contact, he raises his hand to my ear and brushes his fingertips over my dangling faux-diamond earring.

I feel the touch all the way to the pointed heels of my stilettos, and I curl my toes and breathe out the first thing that comes to my mind.

"They're fake."

"Hhmm?" Kelley hums in question, lightly grazing the pad of his finger along the back of my ear. I gasp and snap my eyes open, meeting his heated stare punctuated by a tiny smile.

"I said, they're fa—"

I halt my words, a wave of memory washes over me and my eyes flare. Kelley's pleased smile takes over his face.

"They're fake?" he finishes playfully. "Costume jewelry?"

I can't help the giggle that escapes my lips, and I nod.

This is so surreal.

Still smiling, Kelley brings his other hand up to my face and threads his fingers in my hair, so I'm cradled in his palms. His feet are straddling mine now, our chests just barely touching, and I wonder when he got so close, and how can I get him closer.

I lower my eyes and watch as I slide my hands slowly up his chest, around to his shoulders, and down his arms until I'm gripping his biceps, marveling at the way my fingers impress upon the soft fabric of his shirt and the solid feel of him beneath. When I lift my gaze back to his, his eyes are filled with mirth and heat and promise, and I shiver with anticipation.

"Ivy," he rasps.

"Kelley," I whisper back.

He rests his forehead on mine and flutters his eyes shut, and before he can say anything else, I raise up on my toes and press my mouth to his.

For a moment, I'm suspended in time, weightless and breathless, floating somewhere between seventeen-year-old me and now. I sink into him without a second thought, warmth and comfort and tingles washing over my body. His lips are so soft. I open my mouth a little and run my tongue along his plump bottom lip, and he groans, tightening his grip in my hair. It shoots straight from my mouth to my core, and I'm aching for him.

In a freaking storage room in the back of Keggers.

Next to bathroom cleaner and paper towels.

Jeebus. So dang floaty.

Kelley opens his mouth and when his tongue brushes over mine, I can't help the whimper that escapes. I fist his cursed Henley and press my knuckles into his hard chest. The feeling that takes hold of me is one of ecstasy and awe, like I'd been waiting for this moment for years, only I didn't know it until just now. Like a dream I'd had often, but could never remember, was coming to life.

When the desire to let him bend me over the box of toilet paper crosses my mind, my heart races faster, stealing my breath completely, and I can't tell if it's panic or arousal. In an effort to get a handle on my body, I slow the kiss, smoothing my hands down his torso and resting them on his hips, and he follows my lead.

Resting our foreheads together once more, the kissing

stops, but his lips don't leave mine. When I feel him smile against my mouth, I return it and let loose a giggle.

The panicky feeling in my gut is gone. All that's left are intoxicated butterflies.

"I've been wanting to do that all night," Kelley whispers against my lips.

"Yeah?"

"Yeah," he exhales. "You look stunning. Watching you dance and laugh. Seeing you carefree with our friends. That's when you're the most beautiful. I'm stuck in your orbit, Ivy Rivenbark."

Oooof. This man.

His words circle my body, caressing every part of me, and I kiss him once more. Soft, sweet, and sexy. Like us in this moment.

"I know you're going to overthink this later. I know you're going to want to take a step back and analyze it until you think you have everything planned and figured out," he states, and I'm smacked upside the head with just how well he knows me.

"Just, promise you won't avoid me. I'll give you some space if you need it, but try not to overanalyze, okay? Let's just let this…unfold. Let's see where it goes."

His voice is soothing and hopeful, but I also hear a hidden plea woven into his words. Anyone else might have missed it, but just like he knows me, I know him. Kelley is full of promise with a hint of fear. *Same.*

"Okay," I agree.

"Yeah?"

I nod, and take a step back, giving him a small smile. "Yeah."

I head toward the door. "We should go. Bailey is waiting for me." He nods back and grins. All of the ways this could go wrong, how feeling like this for Kelley is not at all what I'd planned, claw at my mind, but I shove them back. I box them up. I'll revisit them later. With a pros/cons list, probably.

Right now, I just want to drift on this euphoria some more.

"You still gonna come over tomorrow night? We can watch one of those murder shows you like."

"I'll be there," I answer, and smile bigger.

When we leave the storeroom and head back toward the main bar, Calvin Harris and Dua Lipa's "One Kiss" is blasting from the speakers.

I glance at him and he looks back, and we both break out in shy, knowing smiles.

And I'm floating again.

Good grief.

kelley

SATURDAY MORNING, I hit the campus gym hard. I have way too much excitement and tension built up so heavily in my body that I might combust. My muscles are tight as a bow string, my brain working overtime.

I know Ivy, and I know she's probably already created at least two pros/cons lists and possibly a complicated flow chart or Venn diagram to try and analyze what's happened between us over the last few days. It's who she is. It's how her brilliant mind works, and fuck, I find it so damn sexy, but I'm nervous as hell. I just have to hope that whatever she determines works in my favor. Because after that kiss...

After that kiss, I'm sprung harder than ever for Ivy Rivenbark.

I've replayed the entire scene nearly a hundred times since she left the bar last night. The way her blue eyes sparkled with desire, the way her tiny hands pressed into my chest, fisting my shirt when I kicked up the heat of our kiss. And those whimpers? *Fuck*. They've been on repeat inside my head. I jerked my dick last night to the memory of those whimpers, and once again this morning. I'll probably have to do it at least twice more before she comes over tonight.

If she comes over.

Ivy's not one to run from her problems. She studies them until she knows how to best them, and then she faces them head on. She's fierce and fearless.

But her *feelings*?

Yeah, she avoids those until she's ready to feel them. Anything that makes her feel vulnerable or confused, she boxes it up and ignores it until she feels prepared to deal with it. Anything that makes her feel *too much*, she packs away until she can face it with a steady, clear head. She's been like that for as long as I've known her—the product of having to grow up too fast, the responsibility of a sibling to help raise and a house to help run. I admire the way Ivy handles things, but I'm fucking worried.

I know she must be feeling overwhelmed.

Hell, *I'm* feeling overwhelmed, and I've been in love with her for years. This is all brand-new and unfamiliar for her.

I just hope it's not too much that she decides to box *us* up and avoid it until she's ready.

I'll wait. I said I would give her the space she needs, and I mean it. I'll respect any decision she comes to. But damn it, I really, *really* want it to work out in my favor.

My strength training day is supposed to be lower body and core, but I throw in some upper body when the rest isn't succeeding in calming my nerves. I was hoping to talk to Jesse this morning, but he's got a shift at the hospital and probably won't be back until later tonight. So, it's just me, the squat rack, and however many bicycle crunches I can do before my abs turn to jelly and leak out of my pores.

After the gym, I hit the grocery store. If Ivy is coming over tonight, I'm going to be prepared. It's my weekend to cook, so

I'm going to make her favorite: chicken carbonara. I'm not so much trying to impress her as I am trying to make sure she's comfortable. If she's overwhelmed and confused by the new, uncharted territory we've found ourselves in, I'm going to do my best to make things seem...normal? Familiar? Shit, I don't know. I just don't want to freak her out.

"Hey, stranger," Cassie calls from the end of the pasta aisle where I'm grabbing a box of pasta.

"What's up, Cassie?" I ask with an awkward smile. I'm not exactly sure what to expect from this conversation. While last night was not a date, I'm pretty sure Cassie had some hopes for how the evening would go, and I'm certain none of them included me disappearing for twenty minutes with Ivy and then leaving immediately after. I've never led Cassie on, but I understand first-hand the pains of unrequited affections. In short, they suck.

"Not much. Just doing the weekend grocery shopping." She sidles up next to me with a smile and lifts her grocery basket. "You?"

I give the pasta box a little shake. "Grabbing stuff for dinner tonight. I'm making chicken carbonara."

"Nice. Are you cooking for Ivy?"

I'm caught off guard by how casually she asks about Ivy, but what's really confusing is the genuine smile she's sporting. Something on my face must betray my skepticism because Cassie continues, "I had a great time meeting her last night. I like her a lot. I can see why you do, too."

"We've been friends forever." I lift my shoulder and give her a hesitant smile, but Cassie laughs.

"Right," she says with a teasing eye roll. "Friends. Look, Kelley. I like you. I think you know that. But I don't want things to be awkward. I thought at first that maybe if I got you out, I could show you how much fun we could have together." She shrugs and twists her mouth up into an embarrassed grin. "But I know better now. I saw how you and Ivy are together. I get it."

I stare at her for a moment, replaying her words over in my head.

"How we are *together*?" I question, and she widens her eyes and nods.

"Yeah, *together*. What you feel? It's not one-sided. I saw that last night. You two are hot for each other and I'm not risking third-degree burns by getting in the middle of it."

Cassie snickers at her own joke, and I blow out a relieved breath. I'm probably a coward for admitting it, but I was hoping to avoid any sort of conversation like this with Cassie. The fact that she's the one that initiated it and she's being so cool about it all is a huge worry off my shoulders.

"Thanks, Cassie."

"Anytime, *friend*." Her smile is genuine and she adds, "see you Monday," before walking off to finish her shopping.

I make quick work at the store, filling my basket and checking out in record time. I'm so jittery the whole time I'm making dinner, checking the stove clock and my phone every few minutes, that I almost burn the fettuccini.

Says a lot about the kind of mess I am, almost burning damn pasta noodles.

When my front door finally opens a few hours later, I can't help the immediate relief. My muscles sag with it. I'd been restless and anxious all day, with each minute closer to 6 p.m. increasing the tension in my body.

I honestly wasn't sure if she'd show tonight.

"Hi," she says brightly and waves as she kicks her shoes off at the door, and of course, she looks beautiful. She must have stopped off at her house and changed out of her internship clothes, because she's wearing a pair of grey leggings and a BU hoodie. The sweatshirt is not one of mine this time and I stifle the niggling disappointment. "It smells amazing in here, Kell. Is that chicken carbonara?"

"It definitely is." My chest swells with pride and I eat up her praise, and for once, I don't feel the need to check myself. Is it pathetic? Am I a fucking idiot? After last night, I'm pretty sure the answer to both is no.

I pour her a glass of wine as she sits at the breakfast bar. I keep my eyes on her, trying to covertly assess what's going on in her head. For all intents and purposes, she's acting...well, surprisingly *normal*. I'm not sure if I should be worried. I wouldn't put it past Ivy to ignore everything that happened last night until she could process it.

"How were internship hours?"

"Busy. We've got this estate case that is pretty challenging, but I'm learning a lot. Plus, I love your mom and Amelia, so it's great."

Ivy takes a sip of her wine and watches me as I plate up the food. It seems as though she's in full-on denial mode. I want to give her the space and time she needs, but I also don't know how well I can mask my feelings. At some point tonight, I'm going to have to bite the damn bullet and have the "so, like, um, where do we stand?" talk.

Fuck.

After dinner, we settle onto the couch for a movie, but I haven't been able to pay attention to anything happening on the screen. Some light and fluffy romcom about friends who hook up and then act like they didn't.

The irony is not lost on me.

At first, I thought Ivy was just going to pretend like everything between us is just as it's always been. I mean, even the way we're sitting on the couch, with her legs pulled to her chest and her body curled into my side, is normal. All friendly comfort and zero sexual tension—from her, anyway. But as soon as the actors on screen kissed, her body language shifted. The changes were subtle, but I am always so tuned into her that I swear I could even sense when she blinked if I tried. Her muscles tightened, her spine straightened, and her breathing grew shallow.

Now, instead of watching the movie, I've been watching her watch the movie.

With every touch and kiss and romantic encounter on screen, Ivy's reactions grow more obvious, to the point where I know she's uncomfortable. Her back is rigid against my side, her hands are fisted together in her lap, and she's spent more time holding her breath than she has actually breathing. I can't see her eyes, but I am willing to bet she's been squeezing them shut. She's probably freaking out right now, cursing herself for clicking the top suggested movie without reading the description or watching the trailer first. She's definitely regretting our kiss, and this movie is making it impossible for her to ignore it.

Shit, I feel like such an asshole.

I should have just said something right away so we could have avoided this tension.

I shouldn't have asked her to come over tonight.

I should have said, "It's okay, Ivy. Nothing has to change. I'm still your bestie for the restie. Just friendship bracelets and Candy Land forever," or whatever the hell she needed to hear from me so that she wouldn't be feeling whatever terrible things she's feeling right now.

Will it break my heart? Yes.

But it hurts just as bad seeing her in pain, and I'd rather us not both be miserable. And then I move forward with my plan for distance. At lease now I won't have to wonder *what-if.*

When the scene on the TV quickly turns sexual, Ivy begins to practically vibrate with discomfort, and I can't take it anymore. I have to fix this.

Moving my arm from where it's resting on the couch back behind her, I gently place my hand on her shoulder. I'm about ask her if she's alright, if there is anything I can do, if she'd like to go home, when she turns her eyes to mine, and I'm struck dumb.

I was wrong.

Ivy isn't distressed because of fear or nerves. She isn't freaking out and regretting everything.

No.

Her cheeks are a rosy red, and the blue of her irises have been all but swallowed up by the black of her pupils.

She's not apprehensive. She's turned on.

I know she can see the shock and awe on my face when our gazes lock, and when she draws her plush bottom lip between her teeth, I have to hold back a groan. I know exactly how good those lips feel. I'm never going to forget it.

Ivy unclasps her hands from her lap, places one on my thigh, and slides the other up my chest without breaking eye contact.

"Kiss me?" she asks, her voice demanding yet unsure. I respond by crashing my lips down onto hers.

This kiss is different from the one last night in the storage room. Last night's kiss was sweet, tentative. This one is carnal, fueled by raw need and years of repressed desire.

I move one hand to the back of her neck and grip her waist with the other. When she opens her mouth and bites my lower lip, my body shudders and I pull her in closer. My dick is throbbing in my sweats and all we're doing is kissing. I open my mouth wider and caress her tongue with mine, and when she moans, my grip on my control slips.

Grabbing her thigh, without breaking our kiss, I drag Ivy's leg over mine until she's straddling my lap, the contact with my already hard dick making me release a deep groan. Ivy tugs on my hair and grinds her hips over me, moaning and nipping at my lips as she creates the delicious friction and, fuck, does she feel amazing. I run my hands up her thighs and back to her shoulders, caressing and grabbing and committing to memory every soft, perfect part of her body that I can reach. I slide one hand under her shirt and palm her breast through her bra, rubbing my thumb lightly over her peaked nipple and she arches into me.

My hands aren't big enough or fast enough. I want to touch every part of her all at once. She feels so damn good.

Our tongues glide and tangle, the kiss growing more heated and frenzied with every grind of her perfect body over my dick. I continue teasing her nipple with one hand and grip her ass with the other, pressing her body into mine. I meet each glide of her hips with a hard thrust from mine, and I swear if we move any faster, the friction from her leggings on my joggers will ignite flames. I can feel the heat from her pussy through our clothes. It's making me crazy.

I want to pinch myself to make sure I'm not dreaming. Ivy and I are dry humping on my living room couch like a damn pair of horny teenagers, and I fucking love it.

Ivy moans into my mouth and it takes all of my control not to flip her onto her back and fuck her senseless. The visual in my head makes my dick painfully hard, and I pinch her nipple, causing her to moan louder. I know if I slide my hand between us and palm her pussy that I'll feel her arousal through her thin leggings, and suddenly that's all I want.

"Are you wet, Ivy?" I rasp into her mouth. I move my lips to her ear and nip, whispering, "If I put my fingers on that pretty pussy, will I find it dripping for me?"

Ivy gasps, no doubt shocked by my filthy words, and I pull back to watch her face.

"Surprised?" I smirk.

She slows her movements and bites her lip, giving me a small nod.

"I've been repressing fantasies starring you for years, Ivy. Better get used to it, because I'm not planning to hold back."

Her eyes flash with heat. "Don't hold back," she whispers. "Please don't."

Jesus Christ, this is literally all I've ever wanted.

I take my hand off her breast where it's been massaging and teasing her nipple, and she whimpers at the loss of contact.

"Shhhh, baby." I laugh lightly and kiss her lips. "I'm going to see if you want me as much as I want you." Slowly, I skim my fingertips down her torso and her breathing grows ragged.

"Look at me," I command quietly, and trace my middle finger lightly around her belly button. I can feel the goose bumps rising on her skin, but she drops her head back and hums, keeping her eyes squeezed shut.

"Ivy," I growl, and grip her hips with both hands. I need her eyes on me. I need to see her seeing me the first time I worship her pussy. "Look. At. Me," I say more firmly, and I dip my thumbs into the waistband of her leggings.

Slowly, she raises her head, and those deep blue eyes connect with mine. Her face is flushed, her breath is coming out in pants, and she looks so sexy that I have to grip her hips tighter to still her movements. I'm in the sweetest sensory overload, and any more stimulation, I'll be blowing early in my joggers.

"Keep your eyes on me," I say, and move my left hand into

the back of her leggings to squeeze her naked ass. She's not wearing panties.

Fuck me.

"I want to see your face when I make you come for the first time. I'm going to make this pussy feel so good, baby."

Ivy's eyes flare, and she gasps. She might be surprised by my dirty talk, but she loves it, and that turns me on so fucking hard.

"You want that?" I ask, toying with her. I slide my right hand between us and graze over the apex of her thighs through her leggings. "Yeah, you do. You want me to make this pussy feel good."

"Yes." Her voice is breathy and raw, and when my thumb glides over her clit, her eyes fall shut. I halt my movements and squeeze her ass hard.

"No," I say. "Eyes on me. Eyes stay on me." She huffs back at me, but her eyes snap open and meet mine with a glare. I rub my thumb over her clit in response.

"That's right, Ivy. You want to feel good? You keep those gorgeous eyes on me. You close them, and I stop. Understood?"

I rub her clit faster, and she moans and nods quickly, "Fine, okay. Yes. I understand." Irritation and desire are warring in her brilliant blues, and I'm fascinated.

"Good girl," I say with a devious grin, and she rolls her eyes. She's a panting, writhing, gorgeous mess grinding shamelessly on top of me, but she's still got sass in spades. My control is an illusion—she's given me the reins only temporarily—so I'm going to make it count.

I move my hand into the front of her leggings, finding a thatch of short hair, and I let out a deep guttural groan. *God, could she be any sexier?*

Ivy smirks at my reaction.

"Surprised?" she purrs, mocking my earlier words, so I give her hair a soft tug and she gasps.

"This is so fucking hot. I can't wait to see you naked and spread out for me." I graze my fingers over her once more and then move to her clit. Ivy presses herself into my hand, and I laugh softly.

"You're so impatient," I say with a smirk.

"This is nothing," she responds, her eyes narrowed in playful warning, so I give her what she wants. I slide my fingers down through her folds, groaning loudly when I find exactly what I was hoping for.

"*Fuuuck.* You're soaked for me."

I keep my gaze locked with hers as I glide my fingers through her arousal and drag them back up to her clit, rubbing firmly, and she rewards me with a moan.

"Yes," she murmurs on an exhale. The desire in her eyes, the heat coming from her, and the scent of her arousal are a heady combination, and I can feel precum leaking from my dick.

This. Her. Us. It's my damn wet dream come to life. It's *everything*.

I take my cues from Ivy, watching her face as I get her off with my hand. Alternating firm presses and circles, fast and slow. I watch as her mouth gapes, and she struggles to keep her eyes open. The soft whimpers and gasps that she makes are my new favorite sounds, and I want her making those noises for me every single day.

With my hands on Ivy—having her, touching her—I realize that every girl I've been with up to this point was just practice, prepping me for this. Readying me for this woman. Everything I know, I learned for the purpose of pleasing her.

Ivy rides my hand, and as her pace quickens and she

presses into me, I know she's about to come. I circle her clit faster and squeeze her ass cheek harder with my other hand.

"Just like that," Ivy forces out between pants. "Just like that, Kell. I'm gonna come. You're gonna make me come."

Fuck, I've never heard anything sexier than Ivy Rivenbark telling me that I'm going to make her come.

"Come for me then," I say, and kiss her lips quickly. She leans forward in an attempt to deepen the kiss, but I evade her, and she whimpers. "No. I want to see your face when I make you come."

And just like that, her body tenses, and her mouth falls open with the hottest breathy moan. I massage her clit faster, giving it a little pinch, and she moans louder, tossing her head back and finally giving in to the heavy droop of her eyelids.

I watch, fascinated, as she rides out her orgasm. I swear I will never forget the look on her face. It's the sexiest, most beautiful thing I've ever seen, and I continue rubbing her clit, extending her pleasure, until she jerks back and stills my hand with hers.

"No more," she pants. "It's too good." She rests her forehead on mine, eyes still closed, and our heavy breaths mingle as our lips ghost over each other. "It's so good, Kell."

"Mmmm," I murmur, and glide my fingers back through her folds, coating them in her arousal. I bring my fingers to my mouth, and she watches with wide, heated eyes as I suck on them.

"I'm going to taste you next." I lean in and kiss her, tangling her tongue with mine so she can taste herself on me, and she hums in appreciation.

"I'm going to tongue fuck that pretty pussy until you're coming on my face," I rasp into her mouth.

"Oh my God," she gasps, greedily swallowing my words.

"I'll have your cum dripping down my chin before I'm done with you."

She grips my shirt in response, digging her nails into my pecs, and then slides her hands down my chest.

"I want *you* in *my* mouth," she whispers and closes one of her tiny hands around my hard dick.

"Yeah?" I ask with a smirk and thrust my dick into her palm. I try to remain calm and confident when inside I'm losing my shit like a giddy kid in an arcade. This is more than I ever could have hoped for. I never even let myself fantasize about this. "You want to wrap your pretty lips around my—"

The sound of the deadbolt unlocking on the apartment door startles us into silence, and we have just enough time to move our hands into more respectable positions when the door swings open and Jesse walks in.

I knew I should have taken her to my room.

Ivy is holding her breath, an embarrassed blush mixing with the lingering flush from her orgasm, red from chest to forehead, and she squeezes her eyes shut. I watch over her shoulder as Jesse scrolls through his phone and drops his bag on the floor by the door without looking up.

"Kelley?" he shouts into the condo, eyes still on his phone as he kicks off a shoe. "You home? I ran into Cassie in the Student Unio—"

Jesse stops abruptly mid-sentence, one shoe off, when he looks up from his phone and sees Ivy and me on the couch. I keep my face blank and watch as his surprised eyes take in the scene: Ivy straddling me, my hands on her waist, our hair mussed, and my lips swollen from kissing. Thank god I hadn't taken off any of her clothes.

"So..." he says, "what exactly is going on here?"

Ivy opens her eyes and slowly looks over her shoulder at him.

"Heeeeey, Jesse," she squeaks, her cheeks and neck burning red, and for the longest second ever, we all just sit there, stuck in a staring match, holding our breath, and waiting for someone to say something to make this less awkward.

Then, slowly, a smile starts to creep over Jesse's face.

"Has this been going on long?" His question is all playful humor, and Ivy and I answer at the same time.

"No!"

"It's new."

Jesse nods, and his grin grows. Ivy lets out a slow breath, and I watch as a matching smile takes over her face.

Then, Ivy giggles and Jesse throws both hands in the air.

"MOM AND DAD!" he shouts. "Finally, my family is whole! A child of a broken home no more," he jokes proudly as he kicks off his other shoe. "Your dick better not be out, Kelley, because we're gonna have a family cuddle," and he launches his 6'3" frame on to the couch, tackling Ivy and me.

"Owwww," Ivy yells through her laughter. "J, you're squishing me!"

"Get your big ass off, Jesse," I joke and give him a shove, turning in an attempt to take some of his weight off Ivy.

"Shhhh." He wraps his arms around us both in a giant, awkward hug. "Embrace the love. This is the happiest day of my life." Ivy is in a fit of giggles, and I'm smiling so big my cheeks hurt as Jesse snuggles his face into Ivy's hair.

"This is nice," he says on an exhale, and we lie there for a few seconds, laughing at his giddiness.

"This is nice," Jesse says again and pushes himself up so he's propped on one arm, "but it smells like sex in here and that's hella weird."

"Oh my gosh!" Ivy screeches between laughs, and I use all my strength to shove Jesse off of us and onto the floor.

His big body lands with a thud, but he hops back onto his feet quickly and his laughter booms through the condo. I throw a pillow at his head and it hits him smack in the face, causing us all to laugh harder.

"I'm gonna let you guys have a minute," he says as he jogs toward his room, a shit-eating grin on his face. Then just before he walks through his door, he calls over his shoulder, "maybe open a window or something, though, to air out the sex smell."

"Jesse!" Ivy yells. I hurl another pillow at him, but he makes it inside and shuts the door, the pillow hitting the wood with a hard thump.

"Oh my gosh, I cannot believe that just happened." Ivy giggles. She's lying on her back beneath me, and her hands are covering her face while her neck and cheeks blush crimson.

"You can't believe I made you come harder than you've ever come in your entire life with just my thumb?" I tease, and she elbows my shoulder.

She spreads open her fingers and peeks at me through them.

With a sigh, she says, "This changes everything, doesn't it?"

I nod slowly and can't contain the suggestive smile that takes over my face. My voice is gravelly, and the way her breath catches in her throat fills my head with all sorts of filthy promises. She has no idea the things I plan to do with her.

"I sure as fuck hope so."

FOURTEEN

ivy

SUNDAY MORNING, I hear a knock at the front door. My guess is that Bailey is just getting home and either she doesn't have her key, or she's got her arms loaded down with more sugary baking supplies.

After Jesse busted in on Kelley and me last night, I came home electrified and ready to talk it out with B, but she wasn't here. When I texted her, she said she was out with the mysterious Alex and after a fairly vulgar and extremely hilarious exchange of emojis, she went dark. I'm not only excited to hear about this guy who seems to have caught her interest, but I am desperate to talk to her about last night. I need to tell someone else before my brain overheats and melts out of my ears.

I swing my legs out of my bed and pad toward the door just as another louder knock sounds.

"Patience, B," I call out as I unlock the deadbolt. "It's early and I haven't had my coffee yet."

I step back and swing open the door, but instead of seeing Bailey with a bunch of grocery bags, I see Kelley in his running clothes looking stupidly gorgeous for someone who probably just finished running a bajillion miles, and he's holding a to-go cup carrier with three coffees and a brown paper sack.

"Hey," I say quietly, and I can't stop the memories that flood my brain at the sight of his small, knowing smile. *Gah. Stop it, brain.*

"Hey. Brought you guys some breakfast."

He holds up the coffees and paper bag, and Jiminy Crickets can he just stop doing things that make him hotter? I stare at his hands—his big hands—clutching the coffee carrier and the bag. *Has he always had such big hands?* Then my eyes wander to his forearm, flexed slightly from his grip, veins popped and muscles rigid and *dang it,* I am blatantly checking him out. Did he notice?

Goddess of Attraction, please let him not have noticed.

I flick my eyes back to his, and his stupid little smirk is on his face, just being all stupid and attractive and smirky. Yep. He noticed.

"Can I come in?"

Oh, whoops.

"Yeah, yeah, of course." I stammer and step out of the way, awkwardly gesturing toward the kitchen as if he's never been here before. "Is that from Bakery on Main? The place where Bailey's contest is?"

"Yeah," he says as he sets the stuff down on the island. "I pass it on my runs sometimes. Figured I'd pick something up since I know you and Bailey like it." He gestures toward the hallway that leads to Bailey's and my rooms. "Is she here?"

"No. She hasn't come home yet."

Our eyes are locked in a heated stare. I know what he's thinking because I'm thinking it too. *His hands on me. Mine on him. Our lips locked. My soft body pressed against his hard one. His very hard one.*

I let out a shaky breath.

Kelley is the first to look away, reaching into the bag and producing the most mouth-watering and perfect looking muffin.

"I got you a cranberry orange," he says as he hands it to me.

"Thank you."

"And this one is for you," he adds, passing over one of the coffees.

I take a sip, and my eyes fall shut as the flavors burst on my tongue. I give myself a second to savor it, to imagine the caffeine flooding my bloodstream, and then my eyes fly open with a shocking realization.

"This is a cinnamon dolce latte," I say, blinking at him in awe. He nods and grins.

"With oat milk and an extra shot."

"How did you know this was my new order? You've only been out for coffee with me, what? Once? Since I switched."

I'm pretty sure I'm gaping. I don't mean to come off accusingly, but I'm just so...shocked? Confused? I'm definitely something.

Kelley shrugs sheepishly under my questioning. That's twice in thirty-six hours I've made him turn shy, and it's so adorable that I can't bring myself to feel remorseful. Kelley is never rattled; he's always so confident and sure of himself. I kind of like this bit of vulnerability. I like that I'm the one bringing it out of him. It's been years since I've seen it.

"I pay attention. I've always paid attention." His eyes lock on mine, and the heat from them, the thoughts I swear I can read, leave me covered in goose bumps and fighting a blush.

"Well, thanks, Kelley Pierce," I rush out, trying to diffuse the tension. The *sexual* tension. "You're a good friend." I grimace a little at my accidental drop of the *F-word*. Kelley quirks his eyebrow and cocks his head to the side with a smirk.

"Friend?" My body relaxes a bit at his playful tone.

"Are we not friends?" My tone matches his, and *ohmigosh* we're flirting.

Holy moley, I'm flirting with my best friend.

Wait, why is this so surprising? Last night I was dry humping him like a sex-starved lunatic. *Jeesh.*

"I was kinda thinkin' maybe we were a little more than friends now."

"Thinking?"

He takes a step toward me, his stare smoldering. "Hoping."

Oh man. Okay. His voice is sex and promise and dang it, I'm warm and tingling again. If he's trying to disarm me, it's working. I am never disarmed. I am unshakable. I am an impenetrable freaking arsenal of arms.

Get a grip, Ivy Jean Rivenbark. Where's your fierce inner mountain lion? Deep breaths. Two can play at this game

"Oh yeah?" I set my coffee and muffin on the island behind me and take a step closer to him. I drag my eyes down his torso and back up, biting my lip slightly when they reach his once more. "And why is that?"

His eyes flare as they drop to my mouth. I run my fingers lightly along my clavicle, and he follows the movement without blinking. I trace them down the collar of my shirt and send a thank you to Last Night Me for putting on a loose V-neck instead of my oversized t-shirt with One Direction on it. His breathing picks up as I reach the top swell of my breasts. I'm not showing any cleavage, but I'd bet he's getting hard anyway. I resist the urge to look.

This is a bad idea, the practical part of my brain whispers, but I shush it. I'll think about that later.

When I bring my hand back up and tuck a strand of hair behind my ear, I peek my tongue out just a bit, making my lower lip glisten, and his breath hitches on a quiet groan.

Take that, Kelley Pierce. I'm totally going to win this seduction game.

But then after a moment, he grins, it's salacious and wicked, and his eyes dance with something daring. *Oh shoot.* He pops a brow and I try to brace my body for whatever he's going to say.

"Do you usually spend Saturday nights grinding on your friend's dick?"

I can't help it. I wasn't expecting that, and I break with a loud laugh, my eyes wide and my jaw hanging open in shock. Kelley looks so dang smug, and at his loud laughter, I huff and stomp my foot.

"Kelley Allen Pierce!" I shriek out. "You stop that! That's not fair. You were grinding just as much," I protest. My cheeks hurt from smiling. "You were probably even more into it than I was!"

"Mmm, no way, Ivy Jean." He takes another step forward and I take one back, my laughter halting. "I pay attention, remember?" My back hits the kitchen island and he cages me between his arms. He licks his lips, a hungry tiger stalking his prey, and dang it, but I want to be devoured. *Frick.*

"Your heart was racing. I could feel it on my fingers when they were wrapped around your neck." He lowers his face to the crook of my shoulder and kisses my pulse point. My eyes fall shut, my breath hitches, and the jerk chuckles. "It was racing just like it is now."

Kelley places an open mouth kiss on the tender skin just under my jaw, flicking his tongue against it, and my head falls to the side to give him better access. "Your breaths were heavy and ragged. You were panting for me, Ivy." I try to scoff indignantly, but it comes out a strained groan. *Double frick.* He's winning.

He brings his hands to my hips, sliding them torturously up my sides, running his fingers just under my breasts, and my nipples pebble in response. "Yeah," he rasps. "Just like that."

He drags his nose up my jaw and grazes his lips over my ear, and he's right, I am totally panting for him.

"Your pupils were blown wide when you watched me touching you." His gravelly voice tickles my ear and shoots straight to my core. "You were dripping wet when my fingers were on you." I whimper, it's pathetic and embarrassing but I can't seem to care. "Your moans were loud when I played with your clit." My panties are drenched, and my hands move on their own to fist his shirt, desperate to feel the tight abs underneath.

My body has gone rogue. It's a sex starved fool. Mountain lion who? I am just a tiny purring kitten.

He rests his forehead on mine, and I realize I love it when he does that. When he speaks, his lips whisper over mine, and I rein in just enough control not to attack him. "You came so hard for me, baby. The way your head fell back, and the noises you made. Fuck, it was so hot."

He's won. He is the victor. Take me now.

I crash my lips on his, and his answering groan vibrates over my skin and sets me on fire. Every con on the pros/cons list I made is forgotten, and all I can focus on is his mouth on mine, his hands in my hair, and his...erection pressed into my hip?

I reach down and slide my palm up and down his length through his gym shorts. His hips thrust into my hand, and his tongue invades my mouth.

I hitch my leg around him because I'm apparently a

wanton harlot with zero dignity, but he feels so good that I just don't care. Did I say before that he won? Because I take it back. I definitely am winning. This is definitely winning.

Kelley runs his hands roughly down my sides and grips my butt. When he squeezes roughly, he lets out the sexiest moan I've ever heard.

"I love your ass," he grinds out, and I am prepared to jump him right here in the kitchen and let him take me on the counter.

But then he slows the kiss.

When he pulls away, I lean forward in an attempt to chase his lips and he dodges me playfully, a teasing smile on his face. I stick my lip out and pout, because why not? I've already gone full-on desperate, so I might as well lean in. I add a tiny whimper just for good measure and he hits me with a low chuckle that does stupid things to my sexy parts.

"I want to take you on a date," he says abruptly.

I blink at him. "Huh?"

"A date, Ivy. I want to take you on one. I know you've got to do law school stuff tonight, but this week. Maybe Wednesday? I'll skip soccer, and we can do something other than watch Netflix and try not to fuck each other."

I swat at his shoulder.

"Why are you alway so crass?" I ask, fighting a blush, and and he laughs at me. Jerk. I know he does it just to rile me up. "Wait. You want to skip soccer?"

He smiles and shakes his head, and I feel like I'm missing something.

"Yeah, Ives. I'll skip soccer to take you out." He presses a soft kiss to my lips. "What do you say? Wednesday?"

I look at him for a minute. I see the hopefulness, the eager excitement, and just a hint of trepidation in his eyes, and my stomach clenches.

This could end up being totally bad.

Like, blow up in my face bad.

Who even was I just now? Definitely not in complete control. He played with me, toyed with me, and I let him. But what's weirder is that I liked it, and I don't know how I feel about that.

More importantly, I can't lose him again. If this doesn't work, I will *most certainly* lose him.

But we've crossed too many lines to ever be able to go back to what we were before. I'm conflicted. I'm unsure. My body and my mind are shouting two very different things with two very different outcomes.

I still have so much left to tell him, secrets he should know, but a small voice from somewhere deep down, the one that I've locked up, boxed away and ignored for years, is telling me that I'll never know if I don't try.

I sigh, and his eyes light up. He knows I'm giving in. He knows me too freaking well.

"Okay. I'll be at the firm to sit in on a meeting, though. You can meet me after? Five-ish?"

"Yes. I'll pick you up at five." He kisses me again, deep and long, and when he pulls away, I want to pull him back. "I'll text you later."

And then he just walks out as if he didn't steal my breath, turn my insides into mush, and flip my world upside down in a matter of days.

Seriously, who is this man?

And more importantly, should I want to keep him?

* * *

Wednesday afternoon, as I'm getting ready to head to the firm, I get a text from Kelley. I haven't seen him since Sunday, but he's been texting me pretty steadily, which isn't out of the norm. But the flirty content of those texts?

That's new.

Kelley: I hope you learn a lot from your meeting today. I'll be there at 5 sharp to scoop you up. Tell the old battleax not to keep you late.
Me: Don't talk about your mom that way! I love her.
Kelley: You love everyone.
Me: Not true. Just the important ones.

The little chat bubbles pop up and then disappear, pop up, then disappear again. *What are you going to say, Kelley Pierce?*

Kelley: I've been thinking about you.
Me: Yeah? What about me?
Kelley: Our date tonight.
Kelley: And Sunday in your kitchen.
Kelley: And Saturday on my couch.
Kelley: And Friday at Keggers.

I feel giddy just knowing I've been on his mind so much, because he's been on mine, too. I had to actively force myself to stop reliving our Sunday encounter just so I could get some studying done. I should feel guilty about it, but I don't. It's not hurting anything. *Yet.*

I am still acing my classes and kicking butt at the firm. Thankfully, my law school applications are already near perfect, and I'm ahead in my study schedule, so I was able to indulge in a little bit of daydreaming...

Me: Those are some...provocative...thoughts.

Kelley: They are.

Kelley: I've been hard for days. *eggplant emoji*

Me: KELLEY!

Kelley: *winking emoji*

Kelley: I'll see you at 5, Ivy Bean.

Me: See you at 5, Kelley Allen Pierce.

My smile is so big that my cheeks hurt. My stomach is aflutter with butterflies, and I can tell I'm blushing like a schoolgirl with a crush. It's so *not me*.

This isn't at all in any of my plans, and I'd be lying if I said it hasn't been a point of anxiety in the recesses of my brain. I'm not good at living in the now, without considering how every move will affect the future, but I'm making a concerted effort to do as Kelley asked and take this a day at a time.

I know there are things I'm going to have to talk to him about soon—where I was for those fifteen months we didn't speak, why I left, what I've dealt with since.

I need to tell him, and I'm terrified of his reaction.

What if he treats me differently? What if he's angry for letting him think the fallout was his fault? I'm not too proud to admit that I would be heartbroken.

But I can't think about that yet. There's nothing I can do about it right now anyway.

So, like everything else that overwhelms me, I file it away in my mind under *For Later Review* and focus on the more immediate issues.

Like the meeting for the Harrison estate case.

I'm ahead in my classes and already squared today's absence with my professor, and Amelia said the work I've done for the case has been perfect. Today, I get to sit in on a meeting that is sure to be heated, and as nervous as I am, I'm eager for the experience.

I walk into *Pierce, Pierce & Associates* at 1 p.m. on the nose. Our meeting is at two, but I want to help Amelia, Ms. Pierce, and Mr. Davis, the attorney who specializes in estate law, prepare.

When we've been briefed and the files are all in order, Mr. Davis calls Geoff at the front desk and tells him to show Mr. Harrison to the conference room.

Mr. Harrison introduces his son, Brandon, his daughter-in-law, Allison, and his grandson, Matthew. Then for the next three hours, I sit back and listen to the two men argue about the will. Mr. Harrison tries to maintain his composure, but Brandon is full of rage, and several times Mr. Davis has to remind him to lower his voice.

The whole time, when I should be listening to Ms. Pierce and Mr. Davis discuss the legal options, I can't keep my eyes off the boy and his mom. His mother reminds me so much of my own. She's weary. Disheveled. Overworked. *Sad.*

And the boy? His despair hits me so hard that I have to fight off tears. He's not much older than Jacob. Does Jacob look like that when I'm not around? Lost and alone? Not for the first time, I'm overwhelmed with the guilt of leaving him.

This is exactly why I want to get into family law—to advocate for kids and mothers like them.

My life could have been very different if my family had someone advocating for us. Had my mother known about her options, maybe she would have left my father before he got drunk and wrecked his truck and left us destitute with credit card debt up to the ceiling. Or maybe, after Jacob's dad abandoned him to go back to his big city banker job and rich family, my mother would have known she could legally hold him accountable for a portion of Jacob's medical bills.

If someone was there to educate my mother and fight for us sooner, I wouldn't have had to shoulder so much responsibility as a child. Instead, she thought her only choice was to take it all on herself, and I was left to pick up the things she couldn't juggle.

I hope that after today, Allison and Matthew will have the advocates they need.

FIFTEEN

kelley

I HAVE BEEN WAITING IMPATIENTLY for this date all week. I have everything planned. I just hope I don't come on too strong, because I pulled no punches. Ivy's giving us a chance, so I fully intend on proving to her that it's worth it.

I have to hold myself back from jogging toward Ma and Pop's firm. It's ridiculous how badly I'm jonesing to see Ivy.

Now that I've had a taste of her, I can't get enough. It's like she's the last pint of craft beer on tap, and I just crossed the Boston Marathon finish line. I'd say glass of water after crossing the Sahara, but that's too cliché, and Ivy is anything but cliché. Ivy is definitely craft beer. Unique, high-quality, fucking intoxicating.

Pulling open the mirrored glass doors to the firm, I'm about bowled over by a big guy sporting a furious expression.

"Fuck off," he grumbles at me, and I step back and throw my hands up, but not before flashing him a look that says *what the hell is your problem, asshole*. When he stomps past me, I stride through the doors and up to the reception desk.

"Hey, Geoff," I greet my parents' front desk manager.

199

"Well, if it isn't Prince Pierce. What brings you in to our fine establishment today? Ready to claim your birthright and cross over to the dark side?"

Geoff chuckles at his own joke; he knows I would sooner string myself up by my baby toes for all eternity than become an attorney.

"You wish you could see my pretty face every day," I quip back. "I'm actually here for Ivy. She said she'd be done at five."

"They should be out soon."

I shoot the shit with Geoff for a few more minutes when I hear, "Mr. Pierce!" shouted from the hallway. Unsure if the call is directed at me or my pops, I glance up to see my student, Matthew, scrambling toward me. He gets within inches from me before slamming to a halt. The grin he's wearing takes up his entire face.

"Hey, Matthew. What's up, man?"

"Nothing," he shrugs, suddenly sullen, and gestures behind him. "Had to come to a meeting with my mom and grandpa." His face falls. "Dad was here but he left."

Just then Ivy, my mom, and a woman I assume is Matthew's mom come walking up the hallway. The sight of Ivy brings an entirely different kind of smile to my face, and she winks at me. The little flirt.

"Mom!" Matthew shouts. "This is Mr. Pierce. He's my teacher I told you about."

"Student teacher," I correct with a smile. "I'm interning in his Social Studies class this semester."

"Oh, so you're the man Matthew eats lunch with. I'm Allison." She assesses me with kind eyes. "Thank you. *Truly.*" I'm taken aback by her sincerity. "Come on, Matty. We have to go." She thanks my mom and Ivy, saying she'll be in touch, and then exits with Matthew.

I say a quick hey to my mom, give her a kiss on the cheek and tell her to say hey to Pop, and then I lead Ivy out.

"So that's the kid you talk about? The one you always share your lunch with?"

"That's him. One of my favorite students."

Ivy hums in response. "I'm not really allowed to talk about it, but whatever you're doing to make him light up like that around you, keep doing it, okay?"

Her cryptic message fills me with worry for Matthew, but as we round the corner into the parking lot, my attention is pulled right back to Ivy.

She jumps once and claps her hands. "Does this mean I get to drive?" she asks excitedly, and I feel a little zing of triumph that I called this one correctly.

"Sure does, Speed Racer. I borrowed the truck just for you." I toss her the keys and open the driver's side door for her. "Hop in. I'll be your navigator."

One hour later, Ivy pulls into the parking lot of our old school and turns off the engine. She does a quick survey of the area, and then turns to me.

"The high school?" She scrunches her nose and furrows her brow quizzically. "Why the high school?"

"Patience, Grasshopper," I tease. "C'mon."

On the outside, I'm all confidence and swagger, but on the inside, I'm shaking and sweating just like I did at my first ever soccer tryout. I take Ivy's hand and lead her to the back of our old high school building where there's a flower garden maintained by the agriculture class.

"Remember the first day we met?"

"Of course," she beams. "How could I forget? You were my first friend and table buddy. You were the only thing that made being forced to move schools tolerable. Enjoyable, even."

The sparkle in her eyes when she looks up at me fuels my confidence and my chest puffs out like a damn strutting rooster. A cocky cock, if you will.

"Well, what if I told you that you knocked me on my ass that first day? I had the biggest crush."

"What? I had no idea."

I give a wry chuckle and nudge her with my elbow, turning her toward the flower garden. "You were totally oblivious."

"How was I supposed to know?" she protests. "You never said anything. Why didn't you ever say anything?"

"Well, funny you should ask." I pause our stroll and survey the raised beds. The agriculture classes have added new landscaping projects over the years, so it takes me a minute to find what I'm looking for. But when I see it, I lead Ivy into the garden.

"So, after the first few weeks of school, I actually decided I was going to shoot my shot. Tell you I liked you." I glance down at her, and she's watching me with rapt attention.

"I even asked my mom for advice," I admit with an embarrassed grin.

"What did she say?"

"She said to make it special and be honest. So, with all my fourteen-year-old wisdom, I decided that *make it special* meant give you flowers. But I also had already spent my allowance on a new video game and way too much soda from the vending machine, so I had to improvise."

"Wait," she blurts out, then her eyes grow wide, and she looks around at the flower garden. "You didn't."

"I definitely did."

I stop her at a concrete bench and gesture for her to sit, then I head to the crop of blue flowers.

"So, Sunday night, I rode my bike here and picked a

bunch of these blue flowers. I didn't know what they were at the time, but they reminded me of your eyes." I hear a small gasp escape her, and I snap one of the flowers low on the stem. "Then I rode my bike back to my house, put the flowers in a Mountain Dew bottle filled with water, and had every intention of giving them to you Monday at school."

I sit down next to her and hand her the single stem. She brings it to her nose and takes a deep inhale of the tiny bloom.

"What happened? Why didn't you?" Ivy is twirling the flower in her fingers, staring like she finds it fascinating.

"What happened was I was an idiot." I shrug and sigh. "Monday morning, I was all set to bring the flowers to school, but when Preston showed up to ride with me, he started giving me shit about them."

"Oh no. He embarrassed you?"

"Hell no, I told him to fuck right off. But then he goaded me into racing him, and I was a dumb kid and felt like I needed to prove myself just a little to make up for carrying a froufrou bouquet of flowers to school, and I ended up crashing. Crushed the bouquet to pieces and scraped my elbow to shit, too."

"I remember that morning. I made you go to the nurse."

"That's the one. I was gonna pick you some more after school, but then Preston wouldn't shut the hell up about the flowers all day, and by last bell, I was doubting myself and feeling stupid, so I just forgot about it."

"Dang." Ivy's voice is quiet and contemplative, and we sit in silence for a moment. She's still sniffing and twirling the flower, when she asks, "so what is it?"

I take the flower from her and smell it.

"I learned in my 10th grade Intro to Agriculture class that

this is a blue cornflower, also known as the Bachelor's Button."

"Bachelor's Button?"

"Mmhmm. Apparently, in folklore, the blue cornflower was worn by bachelors who had fallen in love, and if the flower wilted quickly, it meant the one he'd fallen for did not return his feelings." I hold her gaze for a moment, letting her search my eyes for whatever emotion or secret she's trying to find. When she bites her lip, I lower my attention back to the flower and continue.

"It also has a lot of different symbolic meanings, but in some cultures, the cornflower is believed to symbolize hope and resilience." I flick my eyes back to her and add playfully, "and in ancient Egypt, they were used as décor for mummies. So basically, I tried woo you with ancient grave flowers."

Ivy rolls her eyes and laughs with me, but then she places her hand on my thigh, her penetrating blue eyes laying me completely bare—seeking my secrets and inner most desires—and I hold eye contact, because I want her to know everything. When she leans over to press a soft kiss on my lips, I accept it gratefully.

I stand and pull her up with me, then we make our way back to the truck. "Where to next?" she questions, and I get another *zing* at how dreamy she sounds.

"Now, we eat."

Walking into Maria's Pizza, the smell of garlic and tomato sauce makes my mouth water and fills my mind with yet more memories, all of which star the amazing woman beside me.

"I haven't been here in years!" I watch as Ivy looks around the place, letting her gorgeous blue eyes flit from the red-checkered tablecloths to the canvas paintings of Italy on the walls. "It hasn't changed at all."

"I know. It's nuts. Like walking into a time warp. I should be wearing my letterman jacket and skinny jeans." I flash her a grin, and she groans comically.

"Not the skinny jeans. Remember when you frosted your tips?" She scrunches up her nose and raises her eyebrows. "That was not a good look."

"It wasn't," I admit with a laugh. "But at the time I thought I was cool as shit. Almost as cool as you thought you were with those jeans with all the little patches on them."

"Hey, I loved those jeans." She sighs wistfully. "I'd still wear them if I could."

"The Dr. Who patch."

"That one was my second favorite. The patch with Rainbow Bright was my first favorite."

"Those jeans were basically rags by 12th grade. More patches than actual denim," I say on a laugh. Those jeans were a mess.

"Such a shame." She raises her water glass. "To my favorite jeans. May they rest in pieces."

After we order, we fill the time chatting about school and her internship. I tell her about student teaching and where I'm at with marathon training. We argue about the TV series we started watching a few weeks ago, and I laugh at how passionately Ivy defends the actions of one of the characters. I recall my latest book talk phone call with Jacob, and the smile on her face is pure happiness.

Conversation, like always, flows comfortably between us. She gets me, and I get her, and that's why we've been best friends for so long. Thank god it hasn't become awkward now that I know how her lips feel on mine. How she looks when she comes.

The only difference now is that when I want to touch her, I can. When I want to take my time appreciating the captivating features of her face, her striking blue eyes and that sexy as fuck dimple, I can. I don't have to look away. I don't have to stifle my impulses or hide the desire in my gaze. And it feels amazing.

"Remember when we came here after homecoming sophomore year?" I ask as we sip our post-pizza espressos.

"Yep yep," she says, studying me over her coffee cup. Then she arches a brow and her lips turn up slightly. "Why?"

"I thought it was a date. When I asked you to go with me, I meant for it to be a date." I drop the truth bomb, and she sets down her cup, gaping at me once more.

"What? But we were with half the soccer team," she declares in disbelief, and I shrug.

"Yeah, but I got us our own table. I ordered for us both. I was even planning to pay. In my head, that was a date."

"But you started dating that Tasha girl on the girls' soccer team, like, right after." Her statement is pointed, her face puzzled and slightly annoyed.

"Mmhm. Two days after. I actually called her that night after I dropped you off at home."

Ivy gasps at my confession.

"Ew! That's gross, Kelley," she admonishes. "Why would you do that? If you wanted to go on a date with me then why would you immediately call redheaded Natasha Winston, JV soccer team captain and one of the most popular people in our grade? It makes no sense."

Despite the obvious offense in her words, I can't stop the stupid giddy excitement that swirls in my stomach. Why does Ivy remember so much about my first girlfriend? I only dated Tasha for a month and she and Ivy were never friends.

"Ivy Jean Rivenbark, were you jealous?"

"Pfff, no. But Tasha was like you with boobs so of course I remember. I thought for sure you'd get married and have little ginger babies. They'd probably crawl out of her womb wearing soccer cleats." She folds her arms over her chest and looks away.

She was definitely jealous. I love it.

Instead of toying with her some more, even though I really want to know about this teenaged jealousy because I could have sworn she had zero interest in me in high school, I relent and do my best to hide my pleased smirk.

"You remember what you said to me when it came time to pay the check that night?"

Her eyes snap to mine, once again searching for the answer, her eyebrows crinkled in thought. "I don't," she admits finally. "What did I say?"

"You said that you needed to make sure to pay your half because you couldn't allow people to think we were on a date."

Her eyes widen.

"You said the cheerleaders would steal your gym clothes to retaliate if you 'claimed their favorite eye candy.' You told me that they'd already messed with you for spending so much time with me." I pause for minute to let that sink in. "So, I decided to make sure everyone knew we were *just friends,* even if that's not what I wanted."

I pay the check and grab her hand. We walk to the truck in silence, and her eyes are downcast. I don't interrupt her. This is a lot, and I know she's probably running through every memory, every decision, from the time we were kids to now.

She wordlessly hands me the keys, and I open the passenger door for her to climb in, then I jog around to the driver's side. For a long moment, we just sit together silently in the cab of the truck. Ivy picks the blue cornflower out of the cupholder and studies it while I study her.

After a moment, she turns those stunning, shining eyes on me.

"How did I not see it before?" she whispers. "How did I not know?"

I reach out to cup her cheek and she leans into it, eyes still swirling with questions and wonder. I swallow.

"You know now."

After taking her for ice cream at The Scoop, we make the drive home singing to the radio, and the only time I let go of her hand is when I have to shift gears. When I walk her to her door, she kisses me sweetly, and I resist the urge to press her against the wall and run my hands all over her body.

"This was perfect," she whispers against my lips.

"You are perfect," I whisper back.

I press one last kiss to her lips and step away. She opens her apartment door and steps inside, but her eyes never leave mine. Not until the door clicks shut.

I drive back to my condo with a stupid grin on my face, replaying every touch, every smile, and how she reacted to each of my confessions with awe. I'm a dopey lovesick fool and I don't give a damn. I've always been soft for Ivy, but I'm a marshmallow now.

When I get home, I jerk off to my mental soundtrack of her moans. Because my heart may be soft when it comes to Ivy Rivenbark, but my dick definitely isn't.

SIXTEEN

"I'M HERE!" Jesse says as he pops out of the crowd and squeezes in next to us. "Just in time! I got out the door but had to turn around because I almost forgot these." He holds up a reusable grocery sack, then reaches in and pulls out some scraps of yarn and hands one to each of us.

"What the fuck are these?" Kelley asks as he studies the knitted object. It's a circular strip of blue and purple yarn, with a white *B* knitted onto one side.

"What do you mean *what the fuck are these?*" Jesse puts the object on his head, positioning the B directly in the middle of his forehead. "They're sweat bands, man." Jesse flexes his biceps like a body builder and growls. Then points to the B. "With a B, for Bailey the Baking Beast."

"Oh, they're so cute, Jesse!" I say earnestly as I put mine on. "Here, I made you a t-shirt." I hand him over the tie-dye shirt that I decorated with little puff paint cookies and #TEAMBAILEY in all capital letters across the front.

"Sweeeet. Hashtag Team Bailey!"

As we stand in the back of the shop in our matching t-shirts and sweatbands, the excitement in the room is palpable. Bailey is set up behind a long counter, and she is next to four other contestants. Each contestant was allowed to invite up to four guests to watch the competition from inside the bakery. Everyone else has to watch it live on *The Morning Show* on Channel 5 News.

On the side of the room there is a panel of three judges, and the camera crew for the news station is set up in the corner, giving them a direct view of all the people participating in today's competition.

I keep my eyes on Bailey, willing her to look my way. She was so nervous last night, and was already gone when I woke up this morning, so I wasn't able to wish her luck in person. I did let her borrow my crappy car, though, because she couldn't risk carrying the baked masterpieces on her Honda. Plus, she said she didn't want to chance having helmet hair while live streaming on local television.

When she finally glances our way, I throw her two thumbs up and she smiles nervously. When Jesse sees her looking, he jumps out in front of us and throws up his arms.

"Go beast mode, Bailey," he shouts as he flexes his biceps and points to the B on his sweatband. "Hashtag Team Bailey!"

Bailey's eyes grow wide, and she scowls at him while subtly shaking her head. I roll my eyes at the exchange. I know Jesse did it for laughs, and Bailey might be embarrassed, but she's not actually mad. Their friendship dynamic is so weird. It basically consists of irritation, bickering, and sarcastic eye rolls. Like siblings.

My attention is grabbed by the guy sitting next to her. He looks so familiar, but I can't quite place him. He tries to stifle a laugh, which isn't unreasonable because Jesse is ridiculous, but Bailey pins the guy with a scathing glare. The intensity and hatred behind it I've never seen from her before—and Bailey can get pretty worked up when she's angry, so that's saying something. If Bailey could shoot lasers from her eyeballs, this guy next to her would be cinders on the ground.

When the contestants present their cookie submissions, the guy next to Bailey introduces himself as Riggs Stanton, and she scoffs and rolls her eyes. It's not loud or obvious, but I notice because I'm watching her closely. By the way Riggs stiffens, I can tell that he notices, too. *Interesting.*

The taste-testing and judging doesn't take long—maybe an hour total, thanks to the pauses they need to take for commercial breaks. When it's time to announce the winner, the atmosphere in the room is tense, and I lock my hands with Jesse and Kelley, squeezing tightly.

I'm positive Bailey is going to win.

I'm absolutely sure of it.

Her submission was the most creative, and I know for a fact it tastes divine. One of the judges actually let out a little moan when he tasted her oatmeal raisin and carrot cake cookie.

So, when they announce the winner as Riggs Stanton, I am legitimately shocked, and the blank look on Bailey's face gives nothing away. When she makes her way to us, Jesse throws his arm around her shoulders and pulls her in.

"Wanna go get high, Barnes?" he says, low enough so only we can hear.

Bailey nods slowly, as if still in disbelief, and says without emotion, "Fuck yes."

* * *

"What kind of name is Riggs, anyway?" Bailey spits the name from her tongue like it's poison, and I suppose right now it kind of is.

I'm relaxed on Kelley's chest, his fingers are lazily running up and down my arm, sending electrified goose bumps from my ears to my toes, and I release a small sigh of contentment. I feel a twinge of guilt, being so happy while Bailey is miserable, but the thought dissipates when I feel Kelley press a random kiss on the top of my head. He's so attentive and affectionate that I could cry. Who'd have thought?

Kelley passes the bowl down to me and I take a hit, relaxing as the haze blankets me. I let it quiet the questions in my mind, the *what-ifs* and the *how-tos* and the worries are silenced, and I let myself just *be*.

The only time I feel safe enough to do this, smoke weed or get drunk or do anything that could threaten my handle on reality, is when I'm with these three people. *Only* these three people. And with college ending, our lives changing, evenings like this probably won't be happening much longer. So, instead of organizing my mental to-do lists, I sit back and let myself enjoy this moment with these people.

The past week with Kelley has been nothing short of blissful. It's surreal and unexpected, but it feels like it's always been this way. Like it's how our relationship should have always been. I'm completely immersed in the ocean that is Kelley Pierce, only coming up for air to study and work.

I've managed to mostly ignore my concerns. When I start to feel anxious, I list out all the things currently going right in my life. I haven't dropped the ball anywhere, so I let myself enjoy the bliss. I'm allowed to. I deserve this.

On an exhale, I tread lightly and say to Bailey, "I thought you guys knew each other. He acted like he knew you at the competition."

"Nope," she says quickly, emphasizing the *P* with a loud pop. "I definitely have never met *that guy* before. Ever."

There's more passion in her voice than I think she realizes, and even though I'm high, I can tell she's hiding something. Because that picture she sent me from the night she went to Bar 31? The picture of the guy she was meeting? That picture was of Riggs Stanton, even if she won't admit it. She may have said his name was Alex, but I've pulled the text back up and studied it. It is, without a doubt, Riggs Stanton. I want to ask her more, but she's had a crappy day, so I let it drop for now.

"I can't believe he's a baseball player," I muse after a few seconds. "It's just so *unexpected*."

"He's not *a* baseball player," Kelley chimes in. "He's *the* baseball player. Pretty sure Riggs Stanton was courted last year by two different major league teams."

"Then why is he still here?" I question.

"Dunno," Jesse responds. "He just...turned them down, I guess."

I pass the bowl off to Bailey, and we're silent for a few minutes. I close my eyes and bob my head to the low music floating out of the Bluetooth speaker.

"Urrrrg!" Bailey yells, causing me to snap my eyes open and watch as she angrily blows out a huge puff of smoke, passing the bowl to her left. "I want to take his stupid *palets de dames aux raisins* and shove them down his stupid, ass-kissing throat and watch his beautiful stupid face turn purple while he chokes on them. And then I'll do a dance on his corpse. While wearing my biker boots."

I snort out a laugh at her horrible attempt at a French accent, and Jesse's eyes bulge as he takes the bowl from her.

"Whoa there, killer. Weed is supposed to make you calm, *Zen*, not turn you into Ted Bundy. Say it with me now, *woosah*." He reaches up and tries to rub her ear, but Bailey bats his hand away with a vicious growl.

"Hands off, Hernandez, or I'll bite you. I can't help it that I have a violent imagination." She sighs and adds wistfully,

"It's a fatal flaw. I'm self-aware enough to acknowledge it as a problem, but I don't care enough to do anything to change it." Bailey shrugs and shoves a whole fudgey brownie cookie into her mouth.

I reach out and take her hand. "I'm sorry, Bails. I know how hard you worked for this. Your cookies were really, really good."

"That's a fact."

"They were, B."

"Thanks guys." Bailey sighs again. "I just feel like the dick cheated. He only made *palets de dames* because he knew the owner is French. Like *from* France. And I guess she still owns a *patisserie* in Calais or something, too. It was a total brown-nose, sleazy move. I just know it. He probably doesn't even like French pastries."

"I mean, he did say his mom is French," Jesse says, but Bailey shoots him a death glare and he throws up his palms.

"Whatever," Bailey says with a scowl, mouth now full of cherry cheesecake bar. She's eating her feelings. "Mark my words. Riggs Stanton is a dirty dealing, boot-licking charlatan. He's no good, and he's gonna regret fucking with me."

No one says anything for a good minute, and then we all crack up, laughing at the same time.

"Who are you, Al Capone?" Jesse snorts. "Take it easy, Barnes. We don't need a murder on our hands." She tosses a pillow at his head and laughs when he's too slow to dodge it and it smacks him in the face.

"Seriously, thanks for being here, guys," she says quietly. "You're the best."

Hours later, after ordering a pizza, watching a movie, and sobering up, Jesse announces that he has to take an Uber home because he has a volunteer shift at the hospital in the morning.

"You can totally crash on the couch if you want," Bailey calls from the kitchen where she's washing the empty cookie containers. We demolished almost every cookie she'd had in the kitchen, and after her week of frenzied baking, it was a *lot* of cookies.

"Ha, no thanks. Last time I crashed here I woke up terrified, thinking I was paralyzed because I couldn't feel my feet. I'd cut off their circulation because I had to drape my damn legs over the arm of the puny couch just to fit."

"Our couch is a perfectly acceptable size," I defend.

"It's a couch for gnomes. Pixies. Itty bitty children. It is a couch for ants!" Jesse counters, laughing at himself. "How do you expect a man to sleep comfortably if he can't even fit on the cushions?"

"Zip it, Zoolander and get in your Uber already," Bailey yells around the corner, and Jesse guffaws and blows her a kiss.

"You comin' with?" he turns to Kelley who then looks to me. Kelley raises an eyebrow at me in silent question.

"He's gonna stay, J," I answer for him, then Jesse and Bailey both make *awwww* and *oooohhhh* noises in jest, which makes me blush. Basically, our friends are jerks. But I love them.

They've been extremely accepting of this new dynamic. In Bailey's words, "it's pretty much the same, except now you touch more and kiss, and you know what his dick looks like."

I didn't bother telling her that I actually don't know what his penis looks like, but I'm hoping to remedy that tonight. I've been waiting for this night all week. All my fun bits tingle just thinking about it.

When Jesse walks out the door, Bailey yawns dramatically and loudly announces that she is going to her bedroom to listen to music with her headphones in. I ignore her smirk and take Kelley's hand, leading him to my room.

He closes the door behind him, and for a moment, we just stare at one another. His eyes lick over every inch of me, and I fist my hands at my sides, trying to harness the intense excitement ripping through my body and warming my blood.

How much of this connection is pure attraction, and how much of it is *more*?

Do I *want* to know?

No. Not right now. I'll think about it later.

"Kelley," I rasp quietly.

His eyes are smoldering, his lips smirking, his hair sexily mussed, and dang it, I'm so turned on. He hasn't even touched me yet, and I'm already aching for him.

I've never, ever wanted a man like I want Kelley.

I've never craved anyone as fiercely as I am craving my best friend right now.

"Ivy," he growls in response.

His voice is gravel. Pure sex that tightens my nipples and heats me up all over. The fragile leash I had on my control snaps, and I launch myself at him.

He grunts, gripping my hips and lifting me up, capturing my lips with his. I wrap my legs around his waist and moan into his mouth when he moves his hands to my butt and squeezes. I run my fingers through his luscious auburn hair, tugging hard enough to make him groan. His tongue strokes over mine, hot and wet and soft, and I want to devour him. I want to taste every part of him, savor him, and then swallow him whole.

Thank you, Goddess of Sex, for making my best friend an erotic masterpiece come to life.

My nipples are hard, and I rub my breasts across his solid chest to create friction, but it's not enough. There's too much fabric in the way. I reach for the hem of my t-shirt, breaking our kiss only long enough to pull my shirt over my head and toss it. When I attempt to bring my mouth back to his, he pulls away, and I whimper.

"Hold on, baby," Kelley pants. "Let me look at you."

I watch his pupils engulf his hazel irises as his eyes eat up the view of my chest. "You're perfect," he grinds out, and then he places open mouth kisses to the swell of my breasts. Sucking and nipping, marking me up.

He hoists me up farther and closes his mouth around my nipple, sucking it through the thin, silk material of my bra. His tongue dampens the fabric, and his hot breath permeates through to caress my breast. Then he bites down, making me cry out in pleasure before moving to the other.

My panties are soaked, and I'm rubbing myself on him brazenly, pressing my center into his body and rolling my hips in an attempt to relieve the pressure between my thighs while he sucks on my nipples. He groans and moves his mouth back to mine. Tightening his grip on my butt, he presses me more firmly against him before lowering me down and then dragging me back up so that his erection is rubbing tortuously between my thighs. Even through our clothes, I can tell his length is impressive and rock hard, and I need to feel him on me without the barrier of clothing.

I shove my hands between us and snag the band of his jeans, ready to rip them off of him, when we fall backwards onto the bed.

How did we get here? Has he been moving this whole time?

I yelp on impact with my favorite sheets, then giggle when we bounce a little on the mattress, and I can feel his smile when he covers my mouth with his.

He raises up on his knees and pulls off his shirt, tossing it somewhere behind him, then lowers himself back over me.

His hands on either side of my head, his biceps straining to support his hovering form, and like a magnet my hands are drawn to his chest.

I run my palms roughly over his pecs, then down to his abs, taking the time to run my fingers through the ridges and grooves that define his sculpted six-pack. When I start to trace my fingertips over the deep V at the bottom of his torso, he lets out a shuddering breath and attacks my lips once more. He plunges his tongue into my mouth, then bites my lower lip, tugging slightly on it.

"Can I take off your bra?" he asks against my mouth.

"Take off your pants first," I force out, trying my darndest to be seductive but likely just coming off as lecherous and desperate. *Oh well.* His responding chuckle vibrates through my body and goes straight to my already throbbing clit.

I watch with rapt attention as he stands from the bed, that infuriating smirk that turns me molten on his lips. I'm a quivering mess of raw desire and he's over there exuding confidence and cocky sex appeal. He's a god, and I am a lustful supplicant worshiping at his altar. *Ugh*, and I'm not even mad about it.

I raise up on my knees and set my gaze on his big hands as his dexterous fingers unfasten the button on his jeans. Slowly, *painfully* slowly, he drags the jeans down his powerful legs. Then he's standing before me in a pair of grey boxer briefs, his erection, long and thick, outlined scandalously against his muscular left thigh.

I'm gawking.

I can't pry my eyes off his lower half, and when I bite my lip, his groan is tortured and sinful. I flick my eyes back to his and raise a brow, daring him to keep going. His eyes burn, and as he moves to take off his boxer briefs, I reach up and unhook my bra. Both articles of clothing fall at the same time, his hard length jutting forward proudly as my nipples pucker even more from the cool air.

"You're gorgeous," he murmurs, almost to himself, and I reach my hands out, beckoning him to me.

His erection bobs with each step, and when he is within reach, I grip his shoulders and pull him on top of me. His lips close over mine for one deep, sensuous kiss, and then move down my jaw and to my neck. He sucks hard on the tender flesh there, then laves his tongue over the hurt. His teeth graze over my collarbone, nipping and scraping, and then move once more to my breasts.

Kelley sucks one of my nipples into his mouth, assaulting it with his tongue and teeth while teasing and tweaking the other with his fingers. Then he releases my nipple from his mouth and moves to suck on the other. I'm kind of impressed by his determination to pay them equal amounts of attention, and I would giggle if I weren't so worked up.

When he starts moving his mouth down my body, dipping his tongue into my belly button, I start to squirm with anticipation. Just the idea of that tantalizing, talented tongue on my most sensitive parts has me teetering on the edge of sanity. After he slips his fingers under the band of my leggings, he makes eye contact with me in silent question, seeking permission.

He's perfect. How did I not see it sooner?

My heart melts, and my voice is shaking with both need and admiration when I answer him.

"Please, Kelley," I whisper desperately, and he pulls my leggings down, taking my panties with them.

"I've been dreaming about this pussy," he says as he drags his fingers over me, through me. "God it's even better than I imagined. Pink and perfect and fucking glistening."

He slowly brings his eyes to mine, as if dragging them away from the view between my legs is painful.

"Who made you wet, Ivy? Who did this to you?"

"You did."

"Say it again," he growls, his eyes back on the apex of my thighs.

"You did, Kelley. You made me wet."

My voice is a strained whine, and he moans when he lowers his body and licks me from top to bottom.

"I want to lick this pussy till you come all over my face." He slips one finger inside, and when I clench around him, his groan is deep and husky. *Holy dirty talk.*

His naughty words make me clench harder around his slowly thrusting finger. I never would have guessed strait-laced Kelley Pierce, the guy who reads books with my twelve-year-old brother and teaches social studies to middle school students who think of him as a hero, would have such a filthy mouth. It's the best surprise. I freaking love it.

He slips a second finger in and I cry out. "Yes, Kelley! Please."

He wastes no time descending upon me. His hands spread me wide, so I am completely and utterly exposed, and he flattens his tongue against me and licks me slowly from end to end before closing his mouth around my clit and sucking. My entire body shudders, and he hums his appreciation against me. The erotic sensation shoots straight up my spine, and I thread my fingers through his hair so I can pull him closer.

"Up and down," I force out, and he immediately obeys, flicking his tongue rapidly against my clit while his fingers thrust in and out of me. It feels amazing. It's never felt this good before, and soon I'm rolling my hips against his face, pressing into him, riding his tongue and fingers.

He moves his arms to my thighs and spreads me wider,

then slips his tongue into me and begins rubbing up and down on my clit with his thumb. The sensation ricochets through me, tensing all of my muscles, curling my toes.

"I'm going to come, Kell," I cry. "Oh fuck, Kelley, I'm going to come."

And he stops.

I snap up onto my elbows to find him staring at me from between my legs. The sight is erotic but infuriating. His face is surprised, and his grin is elated with boyish glee.

"Why did you stop?" I screech out, breathless. He laughs, and I smack the bed at my side.

Am I going to cry? I might cry.

My body is on fire, the tension and need for release bordering on painful. This orgasm tease is going to bring me to tears.

"Kelley!" I whine and my sexual frustration is evident.

"Did you just say fuck?" he laughs again in disbelief.

"What?" *What!?*

"Did I just make Ivy Rivenbark say fuck?" His stupid smile is huge and adorable, and I want to throw a pillow at him, but I don't think I can reach one.

Oh no he did not stop, right when I was on the cusp of orgasm, because I said a cuss word.

"Kelley. Now is not the time," I scold. "If you don't make me come right now—"

He cuts off my threat by launching a double assault, his mouth and fingers thrusting and massaging, sucking and rubbing. I moan, low and long, threading my fingers back through his hair.

"Yes, yes, yes," I chant in sync with my hips, rolling against his face. "Don't stop. Don't you dare stop."

His chuckle sends me over the edge, and my body bows, arching my back and attempting to clamp my thighs shut.

Kelley presses on them more firmly with his arms and continues to rub and lick and thrust until I'm trembling.

"No more. No more," I cry, and he slips out from between my legs and props himself up beside me.

When I finally open my eyes, he is staring down at me, his grin a sexy combination of pride and awe.

"Craft fucking beer," he says, shaking his head with a small smile.

"What?" I ask with a laugh. *That's random.*

He shrugs, and then leans down to kiss me. I suck on his lower lip, tasting myself on him. It's heady and thrilling, and I never want it to end.

Kelley deepens the kiss, sliding his hand into my hair, and I turn on my side to hitch my leg over his hip. I want him, I want this so badly, but when I feel his naked length brush over my bare center, the panic starts.

It comes on quickly and with no warning. One minute I am floating blissfully, and the next, I'm plummeting. The skin on my scalp starts to prickle, sweat dots my upper lip, and my heart races for a new, more dreadful reason.

No, no, no. Not now. Not with him.

I try to force myself to be calm, to get control of my body.

I tell myself that I'm safe, that this is Kelley, that my fear is unwarranted. But my frantic mind doesn't hear the logic over the sound of the blood rushing through my ears. I'm trying desperately to hold myself together, but I'm cracking from the inside out, my control fracturing into fragments that I can't grasp.

Why didn't I do my grounding exercises? How could I possibly think I could get through this without them?

God, I am so stupid.

I let my guard down. I was careless.

The anger I feel toward myself swells, taunting the anger I

feel about *that night* and *that person*. That person and night that broke me and turned me into...*this*.

I hate this. I hate this. I hate this.

I can't even have this, this one night with this one man who means so much to me. Fury and anxiety war within me. I go over the Attorney's Oath in my head and pray to whomever is listening that I can make it through this without him noticing. And maybe, with any other man, I could have hidden it.

But not with Kelley.

"Hey," he whispers, running his hand down my arm lightly. "You okay? You've gone all stiff on me, and your eyes are clamped shut."

"Yeah," I push out. My voice is strangled, and I want to cry with frustration at how pathetic I sound. Of all the nights for my body and mind to rebel... "I just need a minute."

He's quiet for a moment, and then he starts to play with my hair.

"Is this okay?" he asks as his fingers thread through my soft strands, and I focus on the sensation. The loving caress, the way it makes me feel cherished and solid and *safe*.

"Yes," I say on a sigh. I switch from reciting the Attorney's Oath to thinking about Kelley.

I focus on now, this very minute. How his fingers are in my hair, how he is the epitome of strength and kindness. I think about Wednesday and the thoughtful date he planned, his heartfelt confessions. I picture the way his hair flops to the left when he's gone too long without a cut. The way he gets positively giddy when he hits a new running personal record. How he makes sure to call Jacob once a week to catch up. How he speaks passionately about teaching and fondly of his students.

Everything about Kelley that I can recall, I focus on, until my breathing is no longer labored, and my heart is beating steadily.

"I'm sorry," I whisper. I don't want to feel ashamed or embarrassed, but I do. This vulnerable side? This *condition* that I've yet to fully understand—that I may never fully control? I don't want Kelley to see it. I don't want him to treat me with kid gloves.

"It's okay," he says earnestly. "We don't have to talk about it, but I'm here if you want to. When you're ready."

Those words hit me hard.

He has been here, hasn't he? This whole time, supportive and patient, until I was ready.

Even when it looked like I may never be.

"Thank you." My voice cracks and I stare at the ceiling.

"You don't have to thank me," he whispers back. "You want to be my little spoon?" I can hear the smile in his question, and I find myself smiling back.

"Yes, please."

kelley

WHEN THE TENSION in Ivy's body is gone, and I can tell whatever just happened has passed, I let myself relax. I don't know why it happened, but it was terrifying. My best friend was in agony, and I could do nothing to help her.

I want to ask about it. I want to know what triggered what I am pretty certain was a panic attack, but I don't want to make her talk about something if she doesn't want to. It kills me that there is something huge in her life, causing her turmoil, and I don't know about it. But I have to trust she'll tell me when she's ready.

It's that thought that spurs me to suggest we play our old game.

"Ask me a question or tell me a secret," I whisper playfully in her ear. She gasps and turns to me. The smile on her face reassures me that I made the right call.

"We haven't played this since, what, 11th grade?" She rests her cheek on her folded hands and tangles her legs with mine.

Question or Secret was Ivy's and my personal version of *Truth or Dare* growing up. The rules are simple—you choose to either tell a secret about yourself or ask the other person a question.

Questions have to be answered honestly, and secrets are open to follow-up questions, which also have to be answered honestly. We also agreed to allow each other to "pass" on questions if we wanted, but neither of us ever used the pass.

"Summer before 11th grade. At the last summer slumber party we were allowed to have."

"To be fair, I'm surprised our parents let it go on for that long."

"Me too." I chuckle. "You wanna go first?"

"You go," she says quickly, then scrunches up her nose.

"Ok, I'll go for secret." I lower my voice, my heart pounding. "Freshman year was the first time I had sex."

Ivy snorts a laugh. "That's not exactly surprising, Don Juan. I'll admit it's a bit earlier than I would have guessed, but it's not really a shocker."

"Freshman year...of *college*," I amend.

"What?" She snaps up to a sitting position. "But you were always dating. And Shelby hinted to everyone who would listen that you guys were having full-on penetrative sex."

I sit up to mirror her position, then shrug. "Shelby lied. We barely made it to third base."

"Wait, so no penetration?" I smirk at how clinical she is.

"Nope. Well, not with my dick," I joke, but she's too surprised to notice.

"But...but what about that argument in the lunchroom? You said...you suggested...you offered to loan me your condoms."

"Yeeeeah," I drag out. "I was an immature douche. I was a seventeen-year-old virgin waiting for love. You caught me off guard so I kind of panicked and then lied."

She grows quiet. "So... prom?" She looks at me with a newfound understanding in her eyes.

"I..." I shake my head. "Ivy, I am so sorry for what I said to you that night. You have to know I didn't mean any of it. I was stupid and heartbroken, and fuck, I said some terrible shit. I didn't mean any of it. I am so, so sorry. You have no idea how sorry."

"I know, Kell. I forgave you a long time ago. We were young and dumb, and it was a situation neither of us fully understood." She shrugs. "There are...there are so many *worse* things. I'm not going to waste my happiness on something as trivial as a juvenile high school argument." I heave a sigh of relief, and she changes the subject. "So, what changed? With sex, I mean. Or did you..." She hesitates. "Did you fall in love...?"

I consider my options. I could pass. I could keep this shame a secret, and I'd never have to suffer through the embarrassment or her disappointment.

But...

If I want this to last, her and I, then maybe there shouldn't be any secrets. And that means I have to tell her everything.

"Not even close," I say quietly. "I just stopped caring about it. Lost myself a bit. Went kind of crazy."

I glance at her, concern and confusion etched all over her face.

"I started drinking a lot. Fucking my way through campus. I don't even remember the first time. My grades tanked. I lost my soccer scholarship 'cause of it. That and showing up to practices blitzed off my ass."

"Oh my gosh, Kelley," she whispers, and we share a look that I hope expresses the truth of my freshman year behavior. How I lashed out because she was gone, how guilty I felt for pushing her away...

I consider continuing, laying it all out at once, but the pain in her eyes stops me. Too much, too soon.

I tuck a strand of her hair behind her ear and whisper, "your turn, Ives. Ask me a question or tell me a secret."

She takes a deep breath and forcefully puffs it out.

"I was in Bowen for freshman year of college, and the summer before. I went to the community college near there and lived with my aunt."

"I knew that, actually," I admit.

"You did? How?" Ivy isn't upset, just surprised.

"Preston actually told me two weeks ago when we were back home. When I saw him on my Sunday run."

"Preston knew? Huh. Curse small town rumor mills." She laughs sardonically, and I steer us back on course.

"So, you have an aunt?"

"That I do. My dad's sister. Ugh, it's this whole big thing, and I didn't know any of it until the summer after high school. Remember how I told you my dad was killed in a car accident?"

"I remember. Drunk driver."

"Welp, apparently, *he* was actually the drunk. And he was on his way to see his mistress. My mom never had much of a relationship with my aunt, and her marriage to my dad was not a good one, so after he died, she cut all ties." She shakes her head and scoffs. "I lived in the same town as my aunt for years and didn't even know she existed."

I take her hand, bring it to my lips, and kiss her knuckles. She sighs. "Your turn," she says pointedly.

I know what I want to ask, but I don't want to overwhelm her, and I'm not sure I'm ready to hear her confirm how badly I'd hurt her that night at prom. She doesn't hate me anymore, and that's enough for tonight. So instead, I go for a lighter secret.

"Samantha broke up with me because I was spending too much time with you." I grimace and raise my eyebrows.

"Samantha...?" Ivy cocks her head to the side and looks at me quizzically, before her face lights up with realization. "The girl you were dating when I transferred to BU? That was Samantha, right?"

"That was her."

"Oh man. I'm so sorry. I liked her. She was nice. Did she not realize we hadn't seen each other in over a year? I could have backed off."

"She understood at first. But she was right to dump my ass. One hundred percent, I was spending more time with you. I don't blame her, and it wasn't a messy breakup. No hard feelings. I think she's engaged to a mechanical engineering major now."

I lie back down on the bed, and Ivy curls herself in front of me. I pull her body into mine and breathe her in.

Everything about this woman lights me up and calms me down at the same time. I'm buzzing and energized, comfortable and content. She's the only person who has ever felt *right.* Ivy is the tranquility of home and the exhilaration of adventure. I won't need anything else in life as long as I have her.

"Something happened," she whispers after a while. "After graduation, I mean. Something happened to me. It's why I left."

"You didn't leave because of what happened with us? At prom?"

She shakes her head, and I feel something wet hit my arm. Tears.

"No," she says with a sniffle. "It wasn't prom. I kind of wish it was, but it wasn't. Something happened, and after I had to go to Bowen to kind of deal with the aftermath, I guess. I started seeing a therapist. I transferred back when I was ready. I promise I'll tell you all about it. Just not now, okay?"

I press a kiss to her head and hold her more tightly, my protective instincts in overdrive. Pieces of a puzzle start to come together. The panic attack. *If someone hurt her...*

"I'm here when you're ready. I'm not going anywhere."

"Just...when I tell you. I need you to promise you won't look at me differently. I don't want it to change how you see me." Her voice is pained, heartbreaking, and I pull her in tighter.

"I promise, Ives. I'm not going anywhere. No matter what."

* * *

"So how was your weekend, Matthew?" I ask on Monday as I pass him the extra sandwich I brought. I'm not even going with the façade of trading anymore. I'm just bringing him lunch.

Matthew averts his eyes. "It was okay."

I watch him as he takes a bite of his sandwich. "Just okay? Did you do anything fun?"

He shrugs. "Not really."

My mind flits back to my literal run in with his father last week at my mom and dad's firm. Matthew has been growing increasingly more withdrawn, and I've decided to speak to the school guidance counselor about him this afternoon. I spoke to my mom, so I know that she's been in contact with Matthew's mom, but Matthew needs all the additional support he can get.

"Hmm, well," I say nonchalantly. "I read a really great book this weekend that you might like."

Matthew snorts. "You read books?"

"Of course, I read books! Books are awesome. This one is about a dragon and a little boy who is a dragon rider, and there are elves and fighting and magic." Matthew is watching me, intrigued. "I can loan it to you, if you want." I pull the worn paperback out of my backpack and slide it to him.

"Are you sure?"

"Yeah, definitely." He snatches it up.

"I think my mom and dad are going to get a divorce," he says quickly as he's thumbing through the paperback.

"I'm sorry," I say back, even though I'm pretty sure his dad is mega asshole. Matthew shrugs.

"I'm happy about it. I don't like my dad." We sit in silence for a moment, because I honestly have no idea what to say, before Matthew adds, "My mom says we might have to move."

"Moving could be a great new adventure, you know? A new beginning."

"Yeah," Matthew says with a hesitant smile. "I guess so."

* * *

I've spent every single free moment this week with Ivy. Even when I'm not with her, I'm thinking about her.

I can't keep my hands off her.

I can't keep my *mind* off of her.

It's just intensified my need to keep her.

On Tuesday, I walked her to her morning lecture, strutting like a damn peacock because it was *my* hand she was holding, and it was *my* lips she kissed goodbye, and I didn't give any fucks that it looked like I was a love-sick, simpering fool. Because I *am* a love-sick, simpering fool, and I'm totally cool with it.

Wednesday, she met me after soccer, and we ended up making out and groping each other like teenagers in my car at the intramural fields. My windows were fogged, my dick was rock hard, and I had to jerk off twice in the shower after I dropped her off at home. It was torture in the best way.

Thursday, I surprised her at the library, barricaded us in her study room, laid her out on the table, and covered her mouth with my hand while I ate her pussy until she came all over my face.

Twice.

Tonight, I have every intention of repeating that in the comfort of my room, where I don't have to stifle her moans. Jesse is going out with some of his pre-med friends, so I have the condo to myself. She can be as loud as she needs to be, and I plan to make her scream.

Just thinking about this shit makes me hard, and I have to discreetly shift in my seat to alleviate the tightness in my jeans from my semi. While my educational psychology professor goes over the assignment that's due next week—the assignment I've already finished—I slide my phone out of my pocket and text Ivy under the table.

Me: So, I've been thinking about this girl.
Ivy Bean: What about her?
Me: When she smiles, she has this adorable dimple in her cheek that pops out.
Me: I fucking love that stupid dimple.
Ivy Bean: Yeah? What else?
Me: She has these gorgeous blue eyes that sparkle when she laughs. They get darker when she's turned on. I like being the reason her blue eyes get darker.
Ivy Bean: Keep going.

I grin proudly, knowing that Ivy is probably eating this up. I picture her staring at her phone, smiling really big, with her dimple on full display.

Me: I'm kind of hoping I'll get to see her tonight.
Me: I've got plans that are sure to turn her eyes to the darkest midnight blue.
Ivy Bean: I think she is intrigued by your plans.
Me: Really? How do you know?
Me: You know her?
Ivy Bean: .....
Me: Oh you thought I was talking about you?
Ivy Bean: ....
Me: Damn. You're so conceited.
Me: You give a girl two good tongue fuckings and suddenly she's obsessed with you...
Me: *Mariah Carey gif*
Ivy Bean: *middle finger emoji*
Me: *kissy emoji*
Ivy Bean: *crying emoji*

I laugh out loud at the exchange, and then immediately have to apologize to the people in the seats next to me when they shoot me irritated glares.

"Sorry, guys." I wave my phone a little. "Reddit."

Me: Seriously tho. Want to come over tonight? Jesse is going out with friends... *water emoji*
Ivy Bean: I'll be there.

I'm cheesing like an idiot, and I don't care who notices.

• • •

I'm walking to the student union to grab lunch with Jesse when my phone rings and I see it's Ivy. She never calls.

"Hello, gorgeous."

"I'm really sorry to ask this, Kelley, but can I borrow your Jeep?"

"What? Why?" Ivy is attempting to hold her voice clear and steady, but I can still hear the worry there. The waver of fear.

"I got a call from Jacob's school. There's been an incident, and they can't get ahold of my mom. I wouldn't ask, but I let Bailey borrow my car and I can't get ahold of her and I don't know how to drive her stupid motorcycle."

"Where are you? I'll come pick you up, and we can go together."

"I'm outside the library."

"I'll be right there," I tell her. "And Ivy?"

"Yeah?"

"It's going to be okay. We'll go to the school and we'll straighten everything out. Jacob is going to be fine."

She pauses and I hear her deep inhale and exhale.

"You're right. I'll see you in a few."

I hustle to my car and head straight for Ivy, picking her up from the library and starting the drive back home. For the entire hour-long drive, Ivy is distraught. She fluctuates between eerie silence and blaming herself for whatever has happened at Jacob's school today. We don't even know what it is yet, but she's certain it's her fault.

"I haven't spoken to him in over a week." The disappointment is evident in her tone. "I never go more than two days without talking to him, and it's been a week. Gosh, I can't believe I didn't realize I'd let it go this long."

She's scrolling through her phone. "He called on Wednesday and I missed it because I was too busy..."

She lets the sentence trail off, disgust coating her words. I know what she was going to say, though. On Wednesday, she was too busy with me, in my car, hooking up. She hasn't talked to Jacob in over a week because she's been so focused on spending time with me.

A feeling of dread coils deep in my gut. I know that her distress is due to worry for Jacob, but I'm worried that it's got something to do with us too.

"It's okay, Ivy."

"It's obviously not okay, Kelley. We wouldn't be having to go to Jacob's school if everything was okay."

"I realize that it looks bad, but I think that if we just try—"

"Can we just not talk for a while? I need to think."

"Sure." I wince and nod.

When we get to Jacob's school, Ivy is out of the Jeep and striding up the steps before I can even shut my door. I jog to catch up to her right as she's turning the corner into the office.

"Hi, I'm Ivy Rivenbark," she speaks hurriedly to the receptionist. "Principal Grey called me. I'm here for Jacob Rivenbark."

The receptionist gives Ivy a sympathetic smile. "Yes, have a seat please. Principal Grey will be right out."

Within minutes, a tall, balding man I do not recognize appears from behind the desk and asks us to follow him. He's wearing a rumpled black suit, a red tie, and bags under his eyes.

I place my hand on the small of Ivy's back as a show of comfort, to let her know I am here as backup if she needs me, and she sends me a tight smile. Then she turns slightly, forcing my hand to drop, and a chill of unease runs up my spine. *Shit.*

When we enter Principal Grey's office, there are four people waiting for us. Jacob, another young boy about Jacob's age, and a man and woman whom I am assuming are his parents.

The tension is thick, and I watch as the couple look Ivy over with distaste. I bristle at the attention, even though Ivy is unaware. This kid's parents probably see Ivy's messy bun, messenger bag, leggings, BU sweatshirt, and Chucks as a sign of immaturity. They are probably wondering why Ivy, of all people, is in this meeting to represent Jacob. They are most definitely underestimating her, and I have to hide my smirk.

Big mistake, assholes.

Ivy rushes to Jacob's side, and when he turns our way, I notice his right eye is starting to swell shut and his lip is busted. I am murderous, but it's nothing in comparison to the fury rolling off of Ivy in waves. She sends a glare at the family in the other set of chairs, and I notice the other boy has a bruise forming on his chin. *Good.* I hope Jacob got a hit in on this little shithead.

Ivy takes the seat next to her brother, and I take the seat next to her.

"Principal Grey," Ivy begins, "I would like to know why my brother looks like he just stumbled out of a cage fight, and I would like to know it right now."

"It seems as though Jacob and Kyle got into a scuffle in gym class. And as you know, we have a zero-tolerance policy for fighting."

Ivy flicks her eyes to Kyle, then to his parents. "A *scuffle*? And what started this *scuffle*?"

The principal opens his mouth to speak but is immediately cut off by Kyle's father. "Your brother," he sneers, "attacked my son. My son is innocent, and I want that boy," he flings a finger in Jacob's direction and glares at the principal, "*expelled*."

Ivy, cool as a cucumber, stares down the boy's father. Gone is the nervous, frantic girl who rode here with me. In her place is a glimpse of the stern, no-nonsense, fearless attorney she will soon be. My heart swells with pride. This woman is brilliant.

After a moment, Kyle's dad fidgets in his seat, and Ivy turns to Jacob. I don't have to see her face to know it's awash with compassion and patience.

"Is this true, Jacob?"

"No, Ivy—"

"It is so! He hit me! He—"

Ivy whips her head around to the boy and interjects, "—it is not your turn to speak, Kyle. Exercise some respect and restraint, please."

"You don't speak to my son that way!" the mother yells, and Ivy glares at her.

"If your son knew basic decorum, I wouldn't have to reprimand him. Now, wait your turn. I'd like to hear Jacob's side of the story."

Ivy turns, dismissing the woman. Kyle's mother is fuming, but she clamps her mouth shut and stares daggers at the back of Ivy's head. I smirk at her, and she huffs at the same time her husband sneers.

"Go ahead, Jacob."

"H-he s-stole my gym clothes again, Ivy. W-when I told him that I w-w-wasn't." Ivy puts her hand on Jacob's, and he takes a deep breath, never breaking eye contact. When he starts speaking again, his voice is stronger, and the stutter is barely audible. "I told him that I wasn't going to take it anymore, and if he didn't give them back, I would go to the office. He called me some names and blocked the door. When

I tried to push past him, he shoved me to the ground and started hitting me."

Ivy's body is tense, and I hear Kyle start to protest, but his mother halts him. Good thing, because I am about thiiiis close to snapping on them. How dare this little punk fuck with Ivy's brother, with *my* brother, because that's what Jacob is. He's family.

"Did you hit Kyle back?" Ivy questions.

"Yes. It's how I got him off me."

Ivy nods, then turns back to Principal Grey. "Jacob was acting in self-defense."

"Like hell! If this boy—"

"Sir, you need to calm down. You are acting irrationally, and if you cannot conduct yourself like an adult, I will have to request Principal Grey remove you." The man's eyes flare at Ivy and he grits his teeth, but she turns back to Principal Grey, who looks both amused and intimidated.

"Principal Grey, I am aware of your zero-tolerance policy for fighting. As per the handbook, I expect you to give Kyle the full three-day suspension for his aggression against my brother." When Kyle's mother starts to protest, Ivy throws her hand up in a "stop" signal, but never takes her eyes off of Principal Grey.

"Given the nature of this *scuffle*, as you called it, and the fact that Jacob was acting in self-defense, he will receive no punishment, and you will make sure that Kyle is instructed to stay away from Jacob for the remainder of the year. You will switch his classes immediately, as I have proof that this is not the first time Kyle has bullied Jacob. Kyle's behavior is becoming more violent."

She pulls a manilla envelope out of her messenger bag and hands it to the principal.

"In there, you will find documentation of other instances

when Kyle has bullied, insulted, taunted, and harassed my brother, and the dates of phone calls I have made to inform you of Kyle's behavior. There are copies of harassing notes that Kyle has left in Jacob's locker, as well as the names of witnesses—students and teachers—who were present when these events occurred. Principal Grey, you and your staff have allowed this to go on for too long. I understand that you are busy and there are a lot of students in this school, but bullying is a serious offense, and you have been negligent in your unwillingness to step up and stop it. There is no excuse."

Principal Grey looks shocked and effectively scolded, and I have to hold back my chuckle. I want to go full-on Jesse on this room and shout, "hell yeah, that's my girl," but I refrain. Because I am a teacher. Hah.

Ivy turns now to Kyle and his parents. "Make no mistake, what Kyle has done to Jacob is *assault*. I will be photographing his injuries and including them in my file along with the other evidence. You need to find a way for your son to harness and manage his aggression, because you are raising and enabling a bully. If you don't find an outlet for him and he uses my brother again as an outlet, I promise you that I will press charges. I will charge him for assault, and I will throw the book at you."

Ivy turns back to Principal Grey. "Thank you for having us in today. I feel this meeting has been effective, and I trust we should have no further issues. Now if you'll excuse us, I have places to be. Let's go, Jacob. We're done here."

And then she just walks out with me and Jacob in tow, leaving everyone else in that office utterly speechless.

"Can you really do all that?" Jacob whispers to her as we walk to the car.

She shrugs. "Maybe. The important thing is that they

think I can." They share a triumphant grin, and my chest warms.

I love this woman.

The ride back to Ivy and Jacob's house is ominously quiet.

Ivy plans to stay at her mom's tonight, and she and I will drive back early tomorrow, so she can make it to sit for her 9 a.m. LSAT. I completely forgot about her test, and I'm surprised she's so calm about it. When I pull up outside of the house, Ivy sends Jacob inside, and the sense of unease I've been harboring grows.

"Thanks for being there today. I really appreciated it." Her voice is almost robotic.

"Of course. You don't have to thank me."

Ivy takes a deep breath. The unfeeling coldness of her blue eyes punches me right in the gut before she even opens her mouth.

"Kelley, I don't think this— you and me—is a good idea right now. I think we need some distance."

I'm dumbfounded. "Distance."

"Yes. Distance."

"You need distance *from me*." I reiterate, and my eyes fixate on her fingers fidgeting in her lap. It's the only sign that this might be difficult for her.

"I really appreciate you coming with me today, but the truth is that this likely wouldn't have happened if I hadn't been so distracted over the last few weeks."

"Distracted. I'm a distraction."

Ivy at least has the decency to wince, but it's gone in a flash and back is her pointed stare. "Yes. I'm sorry, but yes. I've neglected Jacob entirely and that's unacceptable."

"Ivy, what happened with Jacob today was not your fault."

She shakes her head. "I was negligent, and this fight was

the result. I'm lucky it wasn't worse. I thought I could do this, balance everything and you. I thought I wouldn't fail in the other areas. But I was wrong, and I did fail, and it's because I lost focus. I have a plan, and I can't afford to waste time on a fling."

"A *fling*?" I spit the word. "That's bullshit, Ivy, and you know it. This isn't a fling. You've enjoyed every moment you've spent with me these past few weeks."

"Enjoying the time with you isn't the issue."

"Then what is? Because from where I'm sitting, it feels like you're running. I've made you feel too much, and you don't know how to balance it, so you're gonna push me away. I put your emotions into overdrive, and it terrifies you." She looks out the window, refusing to meet my eyes. "This thing with you and me," I continue, "was never a fling. It's always been more, and that scares you because you didn't plan for it."

"You're right," she sputters. The anguish in her voice crushes me. "I didn't plan for it because it can't happen. I can't let myself lean on you again, Kelley. I can't get lost in you. I can't need you. Not again."

"What do you mean *again*?" Her eyes are clamped shut, brow furrowed. "Prom? Are you talking about prom?" I watch as she tries to take measured breaths. "You said you'd forgiven me for that." The pain in my words is loud, echoing through the car.

"It's not..." she shakes her head and takes a deep breath, "It's not that. I just can't have a relationship right now. It doesn't fit. You don't fit."

I feel like she's slapped me.

"I don't *fit*? Where? In your life? In your plans? Where don't I fit, Ivy?"

"Anywhere," she croaks. "Not right now. Not like this."

Her voice is a broken whisper, her eyes brimming with tears she's fighting hard not to shed.

"Ivy," I plead. "I won't...I can't... I *cannot* go back to just being your friend. Not after having you like this. I *can't*. If you're saying what I think you're saying..."

My voice trails off and Ivy dashes another tear away from her cheek.

My chest physically aches. This is what real heartbreak feels like. I thought I'd felt it before, the first time she left, but I was wrong. The resigned, decided look that takes over her face? *That* is heartbreak.

"It's my decision," she clips out. "If you don't want to drive me in the morning, I understand. I will take care of it."

I gape at her, hurt and angry and wrecked. As if I would leave her hanging. As if I would *ever* leave her hanging.

"I'll be here at seven."

She nods curtly, all-business. "Okay. See you then."

And then she leaves me without a backward glance.

Again.

EIGHTEEN

kelley

One Month After Senior Prom

I WATCH Ivy walk by the soccer field, but like the cowardly, prideful asshole I am, I say nothing. We haven't spoken since prom. She hasn't reached out, and neither have I.

It's fine. I'm pissed that she left me for that lame-ass twerp after our argument in the lounge. I am definitely in the right, and she's in the wrong. Right? Like, she basically shit all over our friendship by choosing Butt Munch Tyler. I said some shitty things, and yeah, I felt terrible afterwards, but I dumped Shelby after prom, and Ivy still won't even look at me.

How are we supposed to fix things if she won't even look at me?

Yeah. This is all her fault.

But that still doesn't stop my eyes from tracking her every move.

"Trouble in Ivy and Kelley's perfect paradise?" I didn't even hear Preston come up next to me. "Can't help but notice you guys ain't been talking. Or sitting together. Or riding to school together," he pries. "D'you finally screw her?" He laughs, and I snap my eyes to him.

"Shut the hell up, Preston."

"Whoa, man, just asking. You've been laying that groundwork for years. Just thought maybe you'd finally pumped and dumped."

"What the fuck, dude?"

He laughs loudly, oblivious that I don't find his joke funny.

"If you're done with her then can the rest of us have a try?" He's taunting me. "Nice tits, big ass." I'm seething, and when he cups his junk like a douche, I lose it, and attack him. He's so surprised that I get three good punches in before he reacts.

The rest of the soccer team has to break us up, but not before I blacken Preston's eye, bloody his nose, and mess up the left side of his abdomen with a fuckton of knuckled body shots.

* * *

High School Graduation

I spent the last week of school on suspension for kicking Preston's ass. No one seemed to care that he deserved it, but I didn't care that I was suspended. At least I didn't have to see Ivy. Seeing Ivy hurts. I missed a call from her last week after the fight, but she didn't leave a message. I haven't worked up the courage to call her back yet.

She spoke to my parents briefly after the graduation ceremony today. Her salutatorian speech was amazing, and I had to fight to keep my eyes off her.

There's a huge graduation party out at Shelby's tonight. Despite the fact that I beat the crap out of him, Preston wants me to go, but I'd rather avoid my ex. Plus, I don't want to see Preston's dumbass even if his black eye and fat lip lighten my mood.

I tell myself my lack of enthusiasm for attending this party isn't because I know Ivy wouldn't be caught dead there. I turn my phone off and watch a stupid fucking horror movie and fall asleep by 11 p.m.

The next morning, I'm bored and watch a bunch of Instagram stories from the party. In the back of one of them, I see Ivy. I know it's her because I've watched the thing twenty times. It's from around 10:30 p.m., and there's not another sighting of her the rest of the night. I even went and stalked other people's stories. Anyone who I thought would be there, including Shelby and Ivy's ex, Tyler, I creeped on their damn social media, but nothing.

I wait five days before my curiosity gets the better of me and I drive to Ivy's house. Her phone has been going straight to voicemail, all of my texts are unread, and I'm done waiting. This has gone on long enough. I know she broke up with Tyler after prom. It's fucking stupid that we're avoiding each other. We need to just forget everything happened and move on. We're going to college together, for god's sake. We can't hate each other forever, right? She can't stay mad at me forever. *Right?*

Jacob is playing outside when I pull up, so I ask him if he can grab Ivy for me.

"She's gone," he tells me with a shrug. I ask where and for how long, and he says he doesn't know, and probably for the summer.

Okay, fine.

The summer. I'll give her the summer.

As soon as college starts in the fall, we'll fix this.

* * *

Freshman Year at Butler University

She's not here.

I've searched faces at every freshman welcome assembly. Stalked every dorm. Even checked over the student directory until my eyes practically bled.

She's not here. She's not at Butler.

Her phone is disconnected. I know because I've tried calling from mine at least a hundred times and from my roommate's probably a hundred more.

The next weekend, I head back home and straight to Ivy's mom's house. No one answers, so I go to the diner where her mom works.

I ask where Ivy is. I ask what happened to her cellphone. I ask why she's not at BU on academic scholarship like she should be.

"Ivy needs distance," her mom says. "Stop trying to contact her for now, okay, Kelley? She's going to be gone for a while. It's best you leave her be."

Distance? What the hell does that even mean? She just up and left?

Shit. How did I mess up so badly?

I drive back to campus that night, go to the first frat party I can find, and get absolutely trashed. And then I do it again the next weekend. When I find a blonde girl with blue eyes, I bring her back to my dorm and fuck her. I fumble through it, make a total ass of myself, and I'm not sure, but I think I called her Ivy.

And then I do it again the following weekend.

Then I start going out on Thursdays.

Then Wednesdays, too.

I move up from hooking up with only blondes to pretty much any girl who is willing. I get tanked on weekdays. I give zero fucks about anything else. Just getting wasted and hooking up. "Booze and broads," Preston says. He loves hearing about my downward spiral. I think it's probably the only reason we still talk. It makes my stomach churn, but I ignore it.

Then I get a letter informing me that I'm on academic probation. The same day I turn up to soccer practice blitzed off my ass and the coach kicks me off the team.

My parents are pissed, I'm embarrassed as hell, and Preston thinks it's the funniest fucking thing ever. Ivy would be so disappointed in me.

So I go out and get tanked again.

* * *

First Semester of Sophomore Year at Butler University

Samantha and I are leaving the student union, coffees in hand, and we're chatting about our geology professor. It's an elective we both have, and though we're in different sections, the material and assignments are the same.

I met Samantha over the summer, but we've only been dating for about a month. After my parents threatened me and forced me to pull my head out of my ass, I took a summer semester to make up the credits I lost when I was being a drunken dick bag. If they hadn't stepped in, I most definitely would have failed out. Almost did.

As Samantha and I head down the steps toward the quad,

a blonde girl with a messenger tote and Chucks catches my eye, and I about trip over myself. Without thinking, I walk toward the stranger.

It can't be.

It probably isn't.

But I need to know, just in case.

She's standing with one foot crossed over the other while reading a flier taped to a cement light post. I assess her as I walk. Her hair is in a messy bun, and she's wearing a yellow sundress and black Chucks. A girl with black hair with pink streaks standing next to her says something to make her laugh, and when she turns to look at her friend, I catch a glimpse of a dimple.

When I'm standing about five feet behind her, I hear her voice, and it knocks the breath right out of my lungs. I reach up and clutch my chest, trying to rub away the ache. I might be having a heart attack.

"Ivy?" I don't know how I manage anything more than a whisper.

She tenses, and then slowly turns to face me. Her familiar blue eyes are cautious, a tentative smile plays on her full, pink lips. I want her to smile bigger. I crave another sighting of that dimple. I didn't realize how much I missed it until right now.

"Kelley," she says back.

And for the first time in fifteen months, I breathe.

NINETEEN

AN HOUR after Kelley drops me off, Mom brings home burgers from the diner and we fill her in on the meeting we had with that jerkface Kyle, his parents, and Principal Grey. She apologized repeatedly for not being there; she was swamped at the diner and never even got the phone call.

She's so, so, *so* sorry, and I'm just...tired.

I don't know how I'm going to go away for law school and still be here for Jacob. I'm feeling guilty for wanting to leave, but I'm certain if I don't do it now, I never will. And aren't I too young to feel this exhausted?

"Ivy," Mom calls from the kitchen after Jacob has gone to bed. "Can I talk to you?"

"Yeah?" I lean against the fridge and watch as she washes the dishes. She still hasn't changed out of her diner uniform. She shuts off the tap and turns to me.

"I wanted to thank you for bein' there today when I couldn't."

"It's not a problem," I brush off. It's not a problem. It's *never* been. And it wouldn't matter if it was.

"It is a problem. You've shouldered too much here for too long, and I've leaned on you more than a mama should."

"Mom, it's okay. You did what you had to do."

She sighs.

"I'm so proud of the woman you've become, Ivy Jean. So proud of the woman you're growin' into. You're so strong. So smart. So much better than I was at your age."

"Mom, no. I am who I am because of you. You're the strongest woman I know. I'm where I am today because of your example, because of how you raised me."

Mom wipes away a tear. My mom never cries. We're silent for a moment, and then she wipes her hands on her apron and stands up straighter.

"Well," she begins. "I want you to know that I'm gonna be home more with Jacob, so you won't have to worry. The fight today...well, let's just say it's got me rethinkin' some priorities. There's a girl at the diner. I'm gonna promote her, and there's also somethin' I want to run by you. Somethin' I think will help, but I want your opinion." She eyes me seriously, so I nod. *Oh boy.*

"Okay, Mom. Let's hear it."

After talking with Mom, debating our options, and making a few pros/cons lists, I'm feeling optimistic. *Cautiously* optimistic.

Mom also reassured me that Bug's actually been in a pretty good mood the last few weeks, and my absence really wasn't detrimental to his well-being. He said as much, but I was so worked up after that meeting, full of guilt and frustration, that I couldn't tell if he was placating me or not.

When Mom heads to her room for the night, I'm left lying

on my old childhood twin bed doing my best not to think about Kelley.

Doing my best and still failing.

I'm not sure if I made the right call. I'm not sure about anything with him. I hate not being sure, and this throbbing pain in my chest hasn't eased since he drove away this afternoon.

Ugh.

The fact is, I was spending so much time with him that my focus in other areas was shifting. I was thinking about him at work. I was leaving study hours early to be with him. I didn't talk to Bug for over a week and barely noticed.

I *never* lose that much time.

Today in that meeting for Jacob, I realized how much I wanted Kelley there with me, and it was terrifying. I wanted to lean on him. Depend on him. Rely on him. I was starting to need him, and that's not okay.

This thing with Kelley? It's not practical. Relationships fail. They aren't dependable. I can't put so much focus and energy into something that's destined to end. The sadness and loss I'm feeling right now is nothing compared to how badly it will hurt if I let this thing between us progress. If we go any further, when it ends, it will crush me.

I don't know where I'm going for law school, and he wants to stay teaching around here. Then there's what happened the other night when we tried to have sex...

I need to stop thinking about this because it's confusing me and making me emotional, and I can't afford to be emotional right now.

Heck, I can't even focus on my LSAT prep and the exam is tomorrow. Instead of doing one last practice test, I've made three different lists of all the reasons why I can't be with Kelley.

And all the ways in which we've ruined our friendship.

Again.

I'm writing furiously when a text buzzes through on my phone.

Kelley: Come outside

He's outside? I stand up and look out my window, but I don't see anything.

Kelley: I know you're up. Your light is on. I'm at your front door. Come down here. We need to talk.

Frick. Maybe he'll think I fell asleep with the lights on? I can't handle this right now. I'm not ready for this yet.

Kelley: My messages say read Ives. I know you're awake. You never sleep with the lights on.
Kelley: Please come downstairs. Give me twenty minutes.

I take a deep breath. I can do this. It's Kelley, and I have to see him tomorrow anyway. I can't avoid it forever.

Me: Ok.

The early October weather is finally starting to feel like a Midwest fall, and when I open the front door, the cool air calms my warm skin. Kelley is leaning on the railing of the front porch, and *dang it all*, he's wearing a stupid Henley.

"Ives," Kelley says, assessing me. I feel his eyes on me. I always feel his eyes on me. I tell myself that the responding shiver is from the chill in the air, and not my body reacting to his nearness.

"Kelley." I stand taller. "Look, Kell, I don't think now—"

"Just hear me out, okay? Please. I know you're trying to avoid this, but what I have to say is important. You need to hear me out."

His eyes are pleading, a determined set to his jaw. I watch the muscles bunch under his scruff as he clenches his teeth. When he pushes off the railing and squares his shoulders, my eyes track over the way his shirt clings to his biceps and chest. A chest that just last night, I was resting my head on.

"Let me argue my case, okay? If afterward you still feel the same as you did earlier, I'll back off."

I nod and respond hesitantly, "Sure."

"Okay, take it out."

I raise a brow. "Take *what* out?"

"Your list. The list I know you've made trying to talk yourself out of being with me. And a pen, too."

Again, I'm floored by how well he knows me, so I walk back into the house and grab a pen and the papers off my bed.

Kelley sighs when he sees what I've brought down.

"Three lists," he mumbles. "Alright, fine. What's the first one?"

"You want me to read them out?"

"How else am I supposed to give my rebuttal?"

I pause. *What the heck.* These lists weren't meant to be seen by him.

Kelley takes a breath. His eyes are intense and burning with urgency and sincerity, so I brace myself, and read the first bullet.

"I need at least a 175 on my LSAT. You've been distracting me from prepping."

"I'm sorry for distracting you, but that's a non-issue because your test is tomorrow. Cross it off." I squint at him and slowly run the pen through the words. "Number two," he prompts.

"I need to maintain my GPA to remain competitive for law schools. I can't forfeit study time," I say firmly.

"Easy. We'll draw up a schedule. Set times when you need to study, and I won't bother you. Same with when you need to work on your applications. Cross it off and give me the next."

I huff a little, but I cross it off and read the next bullet.

"Okay. My internship. I need to keep getting the hours so I can earn the money to pay for law school, and so I can keep a competitive resume. Plus, I need the experience."

"Also easy. No more texting during internship hours and no more dates on days when you have to be at the firm. Hit me with the next one."

I'm getting flustered. I was so sure when I made these lists.

"Law school. I don't know where I'm going to be after this year." I pop my hand on my hip, but he shakes his head.

"That's months away, Ivy. That should be the last item on your list because it's not an immediate concern." I roll my eyes at him because I know he's right. "Keep it on there if you need to. In a few months, we'll revisit it. Next."

I'm overwhelmed with nerves that I can't explain, and with trembling fingers, I flip through the papers and try to find one that doesn't seem so easy to deal with.

"Next one, Ives," he says more softly.

"Jacob," I spit. "I missed calls from him because I was making out with you in a car like a teenager. That's not okay, Kelley. Today never would have happened if I'd kept him a priority."

"Not gonna stop making out like teenagers in cars, but I'll never be offended if you stop whatever we're doing to talk to

Jacob. Even if my face is between your legs." He flashes a smirk, and I bristle at the way my body heats in response. "But Jacob will never not be a priority, for either of us. I promise. We can come home on the weekends. You can tell me when you're gonna call him, and I'll do the same. If you've got something you need to do, I won't get in the way. Keep going."

"This is ridiculous," I huff. "You really just want me to pencil you into my life like an appointment? Schedule time with you in my planner?"

"Yes." He's so matter of fact. So firm and certain.

"And what about our friendship, Kelley? What about that? Romantic relationships aren't dependable. They're statistically likely to fail. What if we try this and it doesn't work and we let each other down and it all just explodes? We'll be crushed. *I'll* be crushed."

I blink back my tears and try to keep my voice from trembling.

Kelley shakes his head slowly and takes a step toward me. When he speaks, his voice is low and sincere. I'm embraced by it.

"I've been in love with you since ninth grade, Ivy Jean Rivenbark. I didn't always know it, and I tried like hell for a long time to ignore it, but it's true."

He takes my hands in his and pulls me closer before continuing.

"For years, I've been that damn bachelor with the cornflower pinned to my lapel, even when I tried to pretend like I wasn't. And here's the thing. I thought for certain that my stupid cornflower was wilted, that it was dead because you didn't return my feelings, and I was just an idiot holding on to some ridiculous dead symbolic flower. And I swear, I was okay with that. I had accepted it. But then you kissed me at

Keggers, and I realized I was wrong. You have feelings for me, too, Ivy. Maybe you always have, and you didn't know it, but you definitely do now, and there's no turning back. We're in it too deep."

He kisses my knuckles, and I shiver at his touch. His words wash over me, and I can feel their truth thrumming through my bloodstream.

"That, right there," he continues, brushing his lips over my hand once more, "the way your body ignites under my touch. The way you're drawn to me, like a magnet, craving me. I feel that same way. I feel it all. You can't fake stuff like this. And I know you're scared, and I know you're thinking of all the ways this relationship could fail or end badly, but you're not considering everything. I know you, Ivy. I know you better than anyone. I know your mind, I know your heart, and I know your soul as if they were my own. You know what that means?"

I'm speechless. My heart is racing. All I can do is shake my head and watch him, completely enthralled by this man. My best friend.

"It means I'm going to love you better than anyone can. The only person who will ever love you better than me is yourself, but I'm going to spend all of my life trying to match you. And when your self-love falters, when you doubt yourself or us, my heart will carry yours. I'll love you big enough for the both of us. I always have, and if you let me, I always will."

There's no stopping my tears now. I'm flooded with emotions, and I can't hold them back any longer. I don't even want to.

"You spend so much time taking care of everyone else, loving everyone with your big heart and your brilliant mind, but you don't have to do it alone. Let me take care of you, too.

I know it's not part of your plan. I know it's scary. I know it's unfamiliar territory, but we can navigate it together."

We're so close now that our chests are pressed together, and I can feel his heart beating against me. It feels like it's in sync with my own. Silent tears stream down my face, and he closes his eyes and leans his forehead on mine.

"Let me love you, Ivy," he whispers, his warm breath fanning over my lips, cooling the tear tracks on my cheeks. "I'll do it better than anyone else can. I swear it."

I swallow, my eyes closed tight, and we just stand there for a moment. Feeling each other, breathing each other in. Absorbing everything.

"That's quite the argument, Kelley," I say with a quiet laugh trying to lighten the mood, and I can feel his small smile.

"Was it enough to sway opposing counsel? Did I convince the jury?"

"Oh, Kelley," I cry, and then I kiss him.

Without breaking the kiss, I attempt to pull Kelley into the house, fumbling over the threshold and stumbling backward before he wordlessly lifts me, and I wrap my legs around his waist.

"Bedroom," I whisper, and on light footsteps, he carries me up the stairs toward my childhood room.

Both hands on my butt, he nudges the door open with his hip, walks us in, and then kicks it shut behind him. He trips over something, stumbles a bit, and I grip him tighter.

"Shit," he grunts.

"You almost dropped me!" I squeal, and we try to stifle our laughter.

"If you'd pick up your shoes, I wouldn't have tripped. Slob," he teases, and I bite his shoulder, making him laugh more.

"Hush." I giggle against his lips as he sets me on the bed. "I don't want to wake them."

My mom and Jacob are both asleep. My mom's room is downstairs, but Jacob is right across the hall, and I don't want anything to interrupt this moment with Kelley. This thrilling, amazing, perfect moment that's been a long time coming.

I scoot backward on the bed and he follows so that he's kneeling between my parted thighs, bracing his arms on either side of my body as I'm propped up on my elbows. He breaks the kiss to sit up on his knees and pull off his shirt, and I lift myself up and do the same. Kelley pauses, his eyes eating up every inch of my exposed flesh. I was wearing pajamas when he got here, so now I'm in front of him in only a pair of cotton boy short panties.

I watch him as I slide my hands up my body and pinch my peaked nipples. When he groans, I smirk. He reaches down and cups my breast with one hand, and palms his erection, squeezing tightly, with his other. My body flushes hot at the sight.

"Stand up," I command, and I barely recognize my voice for the rawness in it. When he does, I lean forward to place open-mouthed kisses on his stomach. He swears softly and runs his fingers through my hair as I trace my tongue over his cut abs. I bring my hands up to squeeze his tight backside, and then drag his shorts down his thighs.

His erection pops out of his shorts, bopping me on the chin, and I giggle.

"Whoops." He laughs, and I bring my eyes to his, lighting up with the mirth and playfulness there. "Sorry," he says with a smile, definitely not sorry.

My matching smile is mischievous, and without breaking eye contact, I wrap my hand around his hardness and stroke. His eyes flutter shut, his head falls back, and he groans.

"Ah ah," I tease. "Eyes on me, baby." He snaps his eyes open and the uninhibited heat in them is intoxicating. "Keep those pretty hazel eyes on me, Kelley," I say, repeating his words from before. He smirks and gives my hair a light tug before I lower my mouth to him.

I lick up his shaft, swirling my tongue around the tip before taking it into my mouth and sucking lightly. It's been years since I've given a blowjob, but his answering groan and the way his hands tighten in my hair tell me I'm doing something right.

I lave my tongue on the sensitive underside of his head, sucking him like a lollipop, then tighten my lips over my teeth and take him deep into my mouth, massaging his shaft with my tongue as I do. I pump the rest of him with my hand, using my spit as lubricant. Kelley gathers my hair into a ponytail on the top of my head and never takes his eyes off me, not even when I close mine and take him as deeply as I can into my throat.

"Fuck, Ivy. Fuck," he says, his words low, his moans muted in the effort to be quiet. His breathing is heavy and when I move my mouth back to suck on the smooth head and stroke his shaft with both my hands, he pulls me off him, his erection leaving my lips with a pop.

"If you keep going, I'm going to come in your mouth, and as much as I want to do that, baby, I've got overdue plans for your pussy tonight."

Whoa. My panties were already wet, but my core throbs from his words, his smoldering looks. He captures my lips with his, and I lie back, pulling him on top of me.

My legs are wrapped around him, his hardness heavy and hot against my core through the thin material of my panties. He runs his hands up and down my sides, cupping my breasts, and moves down to suck on my nipple. He bites lightly, making me whimper, then does the same to the other.

His lips are a lit match, dragging flames across the surface of my skin, warming me up on the outside as smoke unfurls in my belly. The feverish sensation spreads outward toward my limbs, sparking at my fingertips and toes. He drags fire from the swell of my breasts to my collarbone, up over the slope of my neck, pausing briefly at the shell of my ear. His breath is heavy and warm, causing my flesh to prickle despite the spiked temperature. He whispers my name in a voice thick with lust, and the sound is lightning straight to my core. When his mouth captures mine once more, I combust.

Pulling him closer, I deepen his kiss, clenching my thighs and rocking my hips against him. I bite his lower lip and tug, causing a deep growl to ripple through him, and he presses his erection against my center. He moves a hand between us and into my panties. When he runs his fingers over me, he moans into my mouth.

"You want this?" Kelley rasps as he massages my clit and then slides back down to circle my opening. "Tell me you want my fingers inside your pussy." He continues to tease me, tracing his fingers over me, circling around me, but never pushes inside.

"I want you," I gasp.

I'm swollen and soaking and aching for him, and I thrust at his hand trying to slip his finger inside. To get any kind of relief. He smiles against my mouth, pulls away slightly when I try to kiss him, and watches my face as he slowly slides two fingers into me. It's euphoric.

Kelley drops his head into the crook of my neck, sucking on my skin. As he thrusts in and out of me, I moan and clench around his fingers.

"Fuuuck," he says again, strained and breathless. I can

feel his erection pressed hard against my thigh, so I reach down and grab it. He groans, and thrusts his fingers faster, using his palm to put delicious pressure onto my clit.

"I'm gonna eat this pussy now," he growls into my ear, and then makes his way down my body. Licking, nipping, sucking. When he reaches my hips, he pulls my panties down my legs and begins peppering my inner thighs with wet kisses.

I watch him, his broad shoulders spreading my legs, his big hands wrapped around my thighs. When he sets his hazel eyes on mine, the sight is so erotic and sexy that my clit aches with need. He blows lightly over the heated skin at the apex of my thighs and a shiver wracks up my body.

"I haven't stopped thinking about this," Kelley says, looking up at me from between my legs, blowing lightly again on my clit. "I've been dying to make you come again."

"God, yes," I cry. I try to raise my hips to his mouth, but his arms keep me pinned to the bed.

"Remember how good it felt last time?" He kisses my right inner thigh, and I squirm. "How I sucked on your clit until you came." He nips at the other, and I whimper.

"Please." I nod my head quickly.

His answering smile is wicked, and when he swipes his tongue over my folds without breaking eye contact, I almost come right then. Kelley drives me wild with his mouth, playing my body like an instrument he's been mastering all his life, and when he brings me to orgasm, it's a full body crescendo of sensations.

I'm panting and writhing, a livewire of nerve endings, and I want more. I *need* more. I pull him back up my body and kiss him hard.

"I want you," I pant. "I want you right now."

"Are you sure?" Kelley asks. The desire in his voice is unmasked, but so is his genuine concern for me.

Ugh, my heart.

I nod my head. "More than anything. I want you, Kelley." There's no anxiety. No fear. Only a deep-seated need for him that I can no longer ignore.

The emotions I see swirling in his eyes are so much more powerful than lust, deeper than arousal. I roll out from under him, hurry to where my purse is discarded by the door to retrieve a condom, and rush back to the bed, practically tackling him.

"Here," I blurt, before attacking his mouth. He snatches the condom from me and flips me onto my back underneath him in the same motion, causing me to yelp in surprise.

"Hush," he scolds playfully and nips at my lips.

"You hush," I tease back before reaching down and gripping his length, giving it a pump. His answering growl is carnal, and my muscles quiver with excitement.

I snatch the condom back from him, pop an eyebrow, and push on his chest, making him sit up on his knees. He's smirking at me, and I laugh. I'm about to wipe that smirk right off his beautiful face.

Without breaking eye contact, I tear the foil packet open, remove the latex and roll it slowly down his erection.

Kelley's eyes are pools of black. "You're so damn sexy," he says before crashing down on me, laying me beneath him and kissing me with so much enthusiasm that my head spins. "You're sure?" he whispers once more, and I nod.

"Yes. Yes. Fuck me, Kelley."

His eyes flash with fire, and he reaches down and lines his erection up with my entrance. He rubs the head up and down on me, once, twice, three times, and just as I'm about to beg, he pushes inside, making me cry out, the sound fevered and throaty.

When he pulls out slowly and slides back in, he drops his head to my shoulder and lets out a guttural groan.

"Fuck, baby. You feel so good." His voice is strained, and his panted breaths are hot on my neck as he leisurely moves above me, stroking himself in and out of my heat in long, deep, torturously slow thrusts. I can feel every single thick, delicious inch of him.

"Oh my god, Kelley." I moan. The feel of him stretching me, hitting me just right, the weight of his body pressing mine into the mattress, my sensitive nipples dragging over his hard chest as we move together, his plush lips worshiping mine. It's all so perfect that my heart aches.

I kiss him harder and rock my hips to meet his thrusts until we're moving in sync. He stands up on his knees and grips my waist, speeding up until he is pounding into me. I'm all but lost in the sensation until I hear the rickety bed screeching loudly and the old metal headboard thudding into the wall.

"Shit," Kelley hisses at the same time I whisper-yell, "stop!"

He halts his movements, and I can't help but giggle at his wide-eyed shocked expression. His answering smile is wicked, and he lets out a groan that's both tortured and comical.

Curse this stupid old bed.

"The floor?" Kelley suggests, and I nod through my stifled laughter.

"Stay," he says as he pulls out, and he quickly lays my comforter on the floor before scooping me up in his arms like a bride on her wedding night. With the same graceful speed that he showcases on the soccer field, Kelley has me off the bed and on the floor in a blink. In another breath, he's back between my thighs and plunging into me. I gasp and release a strangled cry of relief at being reunited. He kisses me once, sensual and deep, before picking up speed and returning to steady, powerful thrusts.

I have to bite my lip hard to keep from moaning, and when he lifts up onto his knees so I can no longer paw at his chest and back, I grip my breasts instead. His fingers dig into my hips where he's holding me, leveraging my body so he can hit deeper, harder.

It feels so good. Almost too good, but still not enough.

I think I might never stop wanting him like this.

"I wish you could see how sexy you look right now," Kelley says, his eyes licking tracks of fire up and down my torso as he continues to buck into me. "Your face is all twisted up in pleasure, your pussy sucking my dick in, taking all of me. Your breasts bouncing with each of my thrusts. Fuck, baby, you're a fucking goddess."

Kelley licks his thumb and brings it to my clit, rubbing up and down on the sensitive bundle of nerves. I clamp my hand over my mouth and moan loudly.

"You like that, yeah?" He puts more pressure on my clit.

"Just like that. So good." He's driving me crazy.

"My baby likes being touched when I fuck her." He rubs faster, pumps harder. When I clench around him, he releases a shuddering groan and squeezes his eyes shut. He falls back down, caging me between his arms.

"Touch yourself for me," he commands.

I slide my hand between us and massage my clit while Kelley continues his relentless pace.

"Atta girl," he breathes out. He lowers his face to my neck and sucks and bites at my skin, making me whimper and quiver, so close to release.

"You're going to come soon for me," he rasps into my ear and bites my lobe. "You're gonna come all over my cock."

"I am," I gasp. "Yes, yes, I'm gonna come."

When I feel myself start to shake, the beginning of an orgasm tingling deep inside, I rub my clit faster and buck my hips into Kelley's, once again matching his thrusts, spurring him on with my heels pressed into his lower back.

"God, Ivy," Kelley croaks, strangled and breathless. Almost pained. He chants in time with my thrusts, and he presses his forehead into my shoulder, growling through gritted teeth. "I need you to come, baby."

"Yes," I whimper, and my orgasm explodes through my body, curling my toes and arching my back. Kelley covers my mouth with his and swallows the sounds I make, his thrusts becoming erratic and rhythmless. I feel him swell inside my clenched walls, and he opens his mouth on a silent cry. His beautiful face is the picture of ecstasy as he spills his release into the condom.

We're both breathless and sweating. My body is still a mess of raw nerves and tingles, both burning up and shivering. Kelley drops down next to me, and I turn my head to look at him.

To marvel at this man.

My best friend.

My best friend who knows me better than anyone.

My best friend who would do anything for me, who cares for me and loves me unconditionally.

And who just owned my body and made me come harder than I ever have before.

I am literally in freaking awe. I'm gaping again. I can't help it.

When he meets my eyes, my breath catches at just how perfect he is.

"Who *are* you?" I pant out, and a lopsided, boyish smile takes over his face.

"I'm Kelley Allen Pierce." He waggles his brows playfully. "Your first friend." He kisses my cheek. "Your table buddy." He kisses my nose. "Your *best* friend." He kisses my lips chastely and presses his forehead to mine, whispering "And you're my everything."

I gasp and he swallows it with another kiss, deeper this time, and just as I'm about to lose myself in him again, he wraps his arms around me, quickly flips me over the top of him and drops me on his opposite side.

I squeak out in surprise. "What was that for?" I giggle.

"Can't have my everything laying in the wet spot, can I?" His eyes are mischievous and playful, and I snort a laugh.

"And they say chivalry is dead," I laugh again, and snuggle into him.

kelley

AFTER DISPOSING of the condom and taking care of Ivy, I move the comforter back onto the bed and we burrow under it. Ivy snuggles back up onto my chest, and I run my fingers through her hair.

This is how my first time should have been. It's how it was meant to happen. With her. Everything down to her childhood home and that fucking squeaky ass bed. It was fun and sexy and perfect.

In my head, from now on, this will be my first, because it's the only one that's ever mattered.

"Ask me a question or tell me a secret," she says sleepily.

"Secret," I say immediately. "You sure you want this one, though? It's kind of shocking."

"Give it to me, big boy." Ivy giggles and I give her side a little squeeze.

"Okay, well. Here goes nothing." I pause for dramatic effect. "I was almost a two-pump chump."

Ivy barks out a laugh before quickly covering her mouth with her hand. "What!" she whisper-shouts. "You mean just now?"

I nod solemnly. It's true.

"Yep. I had to recite Revolutionary War battle sites so I didn't come too soon. Wouldn't that have been some shit? I convince you to take a chance on me only to blow my load seconds after my first thrust." I chuckle morbidly. That would have seriously sucked. Travesty.

"Wait," Ivy giggles again. "You mean you were thinking about the Revolutionary War the whole time we were having sex?"

"Not the whole time," I defend. "Just right at first, and then again right at the end. The whole middle part was all you, baby."

Ivy's body is shaking with silent laughter, so I give her side another tickle. "You know, if I wasn't so confident in the fact that I just owned your pussy, I'd probably be hurt by your laughter."

"Oh, you think you owned me, do you?"

"I know I did. Your pussy is now mine. She answers to me from here on out. My dick will take very good care of her. My tongue will help."

Ivy gives me a shove. "You're ridiculous."

"I'm just telling you what I know, baby," I tease, then kiss her head. "Your turn. Question or secret."

Ivy is quiet for a moment. I hear her take a few measured breaths before she finally speaks.

"Does it bother you? How many guys I've slept with?"

I'm taken aback by her question, but my answer comes quickly and without doubt. "Not at all."

"Are you sure? I know that some people take issue with, you know, women who, um, embrace their sexuality, I guess." Her voice is quiet and thoughtful as she continues, "I've never worried about it before. But I don't know, you're different. I guess you're the first person whose opinion has ever mattered as much as my own."

"Ivy, listen to me now, because I don't want you to ever question this again. It doesn't bother me in the slightest that you've slept with other people. Was I jealous? Hell yes. The idea of you with anyone other than me burns me up with jealousy. But do I think less of you? Definitely not. Whether it was one or one hundred, you're still the same Ivy I've always loved. I actually really admire your confidence. The way you care fuck all what anyone thinks. It's sexy as hell. You spend so much time taking care of everyone around you. I will never, ever think less of you for doing something for yourself. As long as that thing isn't harmful, then do what you want to do."

Ivy snorts. "Are you saying that my hookups were a form of self-care?"

I laugh quietly and shrug. "Kind of, I guess. Yeah. You knew what you wanted, and you went for it. I don't think there's anything wrong with that."

Ivy sits up and turns to look at me. Her eyes trace over my face, studying. I wait, letting her look until she finds what she's searching for. She opens and closes her mouth twice, then shuts her eyes lightly, before she finally speaks.

"You don't know how good it feels to hear you say that," she whispers. "You couldn't know what it means." She leans back down and kisses me.

"There is one thing though," I add when she breaks the kiss and lays her head back on my chest.

"What's that?"

"You're mine now, and I'm yours. If you ever need anything and you're not getting it from me, if I'm not providing it, I need you to promise that you'll tell me so we can fix it together."

Ivy presses a kiss to my chest, just above my thundering heart.

"I promise," she whispers.

* * *

I dropped Ivy off at the testing center at 8:30 a.m. after taking her to the café for some much-needed caffeine and sustenance. The kiss she left me with was sensual and passionate and fucking phenomenal.

I am so gone for this woman.

Last night, I teased about owning her, but that was a lie. She's the one who owns me. She always has.

Ivy says she'll probably be done with the test around noon, so I text Jesse and ask if he's free to hit the gym.

Me: Just dropped Ivy for the LSAT. Gym in 20?
Jesse: *arm flexing emoji* *water emoji* *sweating face emoji*

I shake my head with a laugh.

Me: *running man emoji*
Jesse: *thumbs up emoji*

I walk into the campus gym exactly twenty minutes later. I keep a bag of clean workout clothes in my car, so I didn't have to stop at the condo. I change and set up on a free squat rack. I'm stretching when Jesse joins me five minutes later.

"What's that goofy smile?" He asks in way of greeting.

"What goofy smile?" I pop a brow.

He points his finger and waves it in a circle around my face. "This one. The dopey one. The one that's got you looking all love drunk and pussy high."

I stare at him and attempt to maintain a poker face, but Jesse sees right through it.

"Oh shit." His grin is Cheshire cat-like, and despite myself, I feel defensive.

"I'm not talking about it," I state. Ivy's not a hookup, and I won't be discussing my sex life with anyone but her. Not even with Jesse, my other best friend.

Jesse puts his palms up, but the smile remains. "I'm not gonna press," he reassures. "Even though I can tell y'all had sex."

I bristle at his chuckle.

"But you know I respect you, man. Ivy, too. You guys are my people. I couldn't be happier that my people are now officially each other's people, and we can be shiny, happy people together."

I squint my eyes at him and smirk. "This isn't gonna be a menage, J."

He barks out a laugh and tosses his towel at me. "Seriously, though. For real. I'm stoked for you guys. It's been a long time coming."

"Thanks, J."

"Also, I totally just won twenty bucks. Bailey bet you wouldn't hook up until after Ivy took the LSAT."

"You guys bet on when Ives and I would have sex?" I scrunch my nose up. *What the hell?*

"Yeah." He deadpans like I'm the unreasonable one.

"That's wrong, man."

"Whatever." He shrugs without remorse. "Wanna grab smoothies after this? I'm suddenly twenty bucks richer." I toss his towel back at him and he bats it away with a taunting laugh.

Our friends are asshats.

. . .

Ivy texts at 12:15 and lets me know she's finished, so I drive to the testing center to scoop her up. Then, I drive her back to her place trying to hide my excitement.

Nothing is out of the norm. Just another Saturday.

"Oh, I forgot to tell you what my mom told me," Ivy sits up straighter in my passenger seat and turns to face me. "You know that kid you teach? The one who was at the firm with his mom?"

"Yeah, Matthew Harrison. What about him?"

"Well, get this. His mom, Allison, actually works for my mom at the diner. Your mom and I had a talk with Allison last week at the firm, talked about some of her *options*..." She widens her eyes at me.

"Okay...?"

"I think she and her son might be moving in with my mom and Jacob for a while. My mom asked if it was okay that she turn my room into a guest room for Allison, and Matthew will bunk in Jacob's room. My mom is going to promote Allison at the diner and I'm pretty sure she is now working with your mom to utilize some of those *options*, and my mom is going to help her out."

"Wow." I blink. "That's amazing. Talk about a small world."

"I know. It's crazy." We hop out of the Jeep and walk toward her apartment. "I'm really thinking it's going to work out well, though. That man, Matthew's dad? He's, well, not really the best guy."

When Ivy moves to open her door, it's locked.

"Oh, weird," she says with a small frown. "I thought B was supposed to be home." She fishes her keys out of her bag and I step back, hiding my smile.

As soon as she walks through the door, she's hit with

flying confetti and a chorus of "SURPRISE!" from Jesse, Bailey, and me.

"Congrats on finishing the LSAT, my babe!" Bailey shouts and launches herself at Ivy.

"Group hug!" Jesse shouts just before wrapping them both up in his arms, so I join in, too.

"I baked you a cake," Bailey exclaims when we break apart, and she pulls Ivy by the hand into the small galley kitchen.

I take a moment to look around the room. When Bailey texted me this morning with the idea of throwing Ivy a little surprise party to celebrate all of her hard work, I was all for it. Jesse and I ran to the Party Town store and bought black and gold streamers, balloons, and Congrats banners. Then we came back and "decorated" the apartment while Bailey worked on the cake.

Honestly, it looks like a high school graduation and a fiftieth birthday fucked, had a baby, and that baby threw up all over the apartment.

J and I most certainly do not have futures in party planning.

The absolute joy on Ivy's face makes it all worth it. She's laughing with Bailey, and when she looks around at the celebratory embellishments we scotch-taped all over the apartment, her dimple is popped real deep, her face is flushed in happiness, and her brilliant blue eyes are dancing.

She's so beautiful it actually hurts. If I get to spend the rest of my life keeping that look on her face, I will die a happy man.

"So how do you think you did?" Jesse asks Ivy after we've eaten three quarters of the German chocolate cake.

"I think I did really well," she replies, licking icing from her fork. My dick twitches in my jeans at the sight, and the way she winks at me tells me that she knows exactly what she's doing. "Scores should be back in three to four weeks, and as long as I beat my last score, I'll be happy."

"Wait, what," I sputter. "Your *last score?*"

"Yeah, what's that mean?" Bailey cocks her head to the side and eyes Ivy.

"You took it over the summer, didn't you?" Jesse's sporting a knowing grin and nods his head slowly. "I had a feeling you already did."

"I took it in June," Ivy reveals sheepishly. "I didn't tell anyone because I was nervous and didn't want to have to share my scores if they were bad. I knew I'd probably be taking it again, anyway."

"How did you hide it?" Bailey asks, and I'm just as shocked and curious as she is. "You're literally always with at least one of us."

Ivy shrugs. "Not *always*. I studied a lot at the library. Used my phone app and stuff. I think I studied harder this time around just because I was determined to beat my other score." She takes another bite of cake.

"Well...." Jesse widens his eyes at her.

"Well, what?"

"Don't play. What was your first score?" Jesse demands. "You know we'll still love you, even if you tanked miserably."

"Oh, why thank you, that's so nice to hear," Ivy says dryly, but she can't maintain the unamused expression, and soon a toothy, proud smile is stretching over her face, and I know, I just know, that this brilliant woman aced that damn test.

"I scored a 172," she beams, and we erupt in cheers.

The highest score you can get on the LSAT is 180, and my girl scored a 172. She's so damn sexy, her and that big, beautiful brain.

I'm going to make her come so hard tonight.

When the cake has been eaten and the revelry has died down, Ivy comes up behind me and tugs me toward her bedroom. I'm ready to jump on her as soon as the door shuts, but she sits on the bed and pats the spot next to her for me to sit, too.

"Ask me for a question or a secret," she says quietly, and my heart starts thundering.

"You don't have to," I assure her. "I'm here whenever you're ready."

She smiles, but it's small and kind of sad. "I'm ready. Last night and today...they were so perfect, Kelley. I need to do this."

I nod, take her hand in mine, and whisper, "Ask me a question or tell me a secret, Ives."

"Secret," she says, her voice quiet but strong, her eyes closed. "I went to a party after high school graduation. At that party, I was drugged and raped." I squeeze her hand and do my best to calm the anguish and rage roiling in my gut.

"I, uh, I didn't handle it well." She chuckles sardonically. "I still to this day don't know how it happened. I had one drink. Just one, and I never put it down. I poured it myself. I did everything right. I was careful. But it happened anyway, and I hated how powerless that made me feel."

Her voice has grown frustrated, and she pauses to take a breath. When she continues, her words are measured and calm once more.

"After the ER cleared me and I filled out the police report, I had every intention of forgetting it all happened. There were so many emotions—regret, confusion, anger, sadness, *fear*. I wanted it out of my head for good, you know? The cops all but said there was no hope of catching the guy and I just needed to move on. But I was having these nightmares. They were terrible—I could go all day ignoring and pretending, but the moment I fell asleep, all those emotions...they took control. Then one night, I was having a nightmare and Jacob came in my room to try and wake me."

She stops to wipe a tear from her cheek, and I press a kiss to her head.

"I attacked him in my sleep. Terrified him. Scared Mom, too. That's when she called my aunt and sent me to Bowen. I started seeing a therapist." Ivy looks at me then with a small smile, her eyes glistening with tears. "Dr. Joyner—she's really great. She knows all about you."

"Good things?" I ask with a smile.

"There are only good things, Kell." She smiles again and then looks back at her lap. "Anyway, it was only supposed to be for the summer, but I struggled at first. Dealing with all the emotions. Processing everything. I just...it was such an invasion, you know? To have my control so forcefully stolen in a way that I wasn't even aware of until after. I just couldn't...I didn't want to accept it, I think. I wanted to ignore it and pretend it didn't happen, but the nightmares were so bad... So, I stayed longer. Went to the community college. Started self-defense training, too."

When she pauses, I take the chance and ask, "Why didn't you tell me?"

"At first it was because I was angry and then because I was scared. Part of me blamed you, even though I knew it wasn't logical, but I was such a mess, Kelley. It was like my rational mind had short-circuited. I kept telling myself that if you hadn't done what you did at prom, or if you'd have at least apologized, you would have been at that party with me and none of this would have happened."

Hearing those words knocks the wind out of me, guilt gnaws at my rib cage, and I have to physically rub at my chest because of the pain.

"I knew it was completely irrational to blame you, but I did it anyway. And then I would get angry with myself for relying on you like that—for not being able to take care of myself without you. You were the person I loved and trusted the most, but you were also the person my mind was choosing to blame. It was a vicious cycle. Still is, sometimes, if I'm being honest."

"You blame me still?" I whisper. She turns and rests her head on my shoulder, so I slide my arm around her waist and hold her tight. I can feel my shirt dampen from her silent tears.

"No," she pushes out. "Not even a little. But it's hard to feel myself needing you. I've spent so much time convincing myself that I need to be in complete control, that I can't rely on anyone but myself. Sometimes when I feel myself wanting to lean on you, that panicky part of my brain gets louder and tries to tell me that it's a weakness."

"It's not, Ivy. I'll never make you weaker."

How does she not see? She is the strongest person I've ever known.

"I know. I do. And it's ridiculous anyway, because I've always needed you, Kelley. Even when I didn't want to, or when I tried not to, I still needed you. You're my person."

My heart pounds. "You're my person too, Ives. Always have been."

She tilts her head up and places a soft kiss on my lips, and I can taste the salt from her tears.

"I need you to know that the panic attacks will likely still happen. Nightmares, too."

I cup her face with my hands. "I'm not going anywhere, Ivy. Remember? This doesn't make you weak. Fuck, baby, you're so strong. I'm in awe of you." I kiss her again. "I'm not going anywhere."

We rest our foreheads together, our soft breaths mingling, tickling my wet cheeks and lips.

"I'm sorry it took me so long to get here," she whispers after a moment.

"You don't have to apologize for the journey you had to take," I say honestly. "All that matters is that I'm where you ended up."

* * *

"Good morning, Sleeping Sexy," I whisper in Ivy's ear. It's 6 a.m. on race day, and she's snuggled naked in my bed, lying on her stomach with my grey comforter draped over her lower half. To say I don't want to leave is an understatement.

In the last month or so since I'd bared my heart and practically begged Ivy to give us a chance, and thank the fucking gods of whatever she agreed, things have been amazing. It's been weeks of laughter and kissing and sex and snuggling, and damn it, if I don't love the snuggling as much as the sex.

At the core of it, my relationship with Ivy hasn't changed. It's just *more*, now. More fun, more heart, more meaningful, more passionate, more at risk. The stakes are higher and so are the feelings, but I don't regret crossing the friendship line. How can I when I get to wake up every morning to the girl of my dreams?

Ivy has taken to sleeping at my condo on the weekends while I stay with her at her apartment most nights during the week. It took a while to convince her to stay over at my place at all, though. I ended up purchasing a very specific set of 800 thread count bedsheets to sway her.

"Mmmm," she murmurs, shuffling her feet under the covers. The movement pulls the sheets down more, revealing the twin dimples just above her plump ass, and I stifle a groan.

I've got a marathon to run in three hours, three hours that need to be full of race day prep, so I cannot get distracted by my girlfriend's tempting body.

She reaches her hand up and slides it into my hair, giving me a perfect view of the side of her breast, and I'm bowled over by the memory of sucking on her nipples last night until she was writhing beneath me.

Shit.

Revolutionary War battles.

Not my girl's perfect fucking chest.

"Do you have to leave now?" Her eyes are still closed, and her voice is the sleepy kind of sexy, which does nothing and everything for my now hard dick.

Powder Alarm. September 1ˢᵗ, 1774.

"Soon. I'm going to grab breakfast and then head to the park. I've got to check in and warm up."

"Mmmm," she hums again, dropping her hand from my hair and trailing it down my chest. When she opens her eyes, they're hooded, swirling with heat, and the deepest, darkest of blues. Sex eyes.

Fort William and Mary. December 14ᵗʰ.

"Do you think you can stay for just five more minutes?" She wets her lower lip and then bites it lightly.

Lexington. Concord. April.

"I don't know, babe. I need to be at the park soon..." My half-assed protest is weak, and she knows it. I mean, I don't know why I have to get to the park that early...

The naughty smirk she flashes goes straight to my groin. "Just five minutes," Ivy pleads, and just as I'm about to recall the dates of the *Siege of Boston*, she rolls onto her back, baring her entire front side to me.

Full breasts. Smooth belly. Glistening, swollen, sweet pussy.

All of it on display. All of it mine.

So, I do what any hotblooded human would do with a naked and willing Ivy Jean Rivenbark in their bed. I forget all about Revolutionary War battle sites and launch myself at her, laying claim on my girl's body with my tongue while simultaneously jerking my dick.

Six minutes later, she's sated and passed back out, and I'm ready to run a marathon.

TWENTY-ONE

WHEN KELLEY CROSSES the finish line with a time of three hours and twelve minutes, we're all waiting for him.

Me, Bailey, and Jesse are wearing matching t-shirts and have been camped out for the last hour, and when we finally see him heading toward us, we start jumping and whooping and cheering him on.

It's a blast.

Almost makes me want to run a....ew, no, never mind.

Kelley jogs up to us and immediately pulls me into a hug.

"Sorry I'm all sweaty," he pants as he peppers me with kisses.

"I like you sweaty," I tease.

"Well, how about we go get sweaty together?"

"Nope!" Bailey yells, "No dry humping in public!" I can't help but bark out a laugh. "I know you guys wanna boink like bunnies but we're going out to celebrate first."

"Beers first, bone later," Jesse snarks with a nod then grabs Kelley's shoulder. "You just ran a fucking marathon, my man. Ivy has submitted all of her law school apps and scored a 177 on her LSAT retake. Bailey signed up to do that bake-off thing—"

"That's not for certain yet," Bailey interjects. "But yeah, the goofball is right. *Aaaand* he got another acceptance email yesterday."

"No shit?" Kelley crows. "That's great, J. Is it—"

"Nope," Jesse cuts him off with a light shrug. "Haven't heard from them yet. This one was from Perelman. So still hella good. Which means we need to celebrate!"

"I'm definitely down for a celebration," I chirp. We deserve it.

"My soccer buddy's frat is having a party. A couple of them ran today, too. We could grab some food and then hit that up? I just need to go back and shower first."

"Yes! Plans made." Jesse claps once, does a little shimmy, and starts pushing Kelley toward the park exit. "Now let's get this man his post-race craft beer."

* * *

The house seems to be thrumming with energy. The music is loud, the front porch is packed with bodies, and everyone is holding a red plastic cup full of god knows what.

As we walk up the sidewalk toward the frat house, a guy in a polo bumps into Bailey, sloshing the liquid from his cup onto her shirt.

"Sorry," he grumbles and stumbles off.

"Yeah, it's cool." Her sarcasm is evident as she shakes the liquid off her sleeve. She lifts her arm up and sniffs, then turns to Jesse with a Cheshire grin. "Fireball and fuckery," she laughs. "You'll fit right in."

Jesse scoffs. "Please. Dr. Vanessa Hernandez raised no peasant. I'm much more refined. I'm more of the *Don Julio and*

Debauchery type." Kelley and I laugh loudly, and Bailey rolls her eyes.

"You're such an asshat."

"Ahem," Jesse says brusquely, pointer finger in the air as if he's about to make a crucial statement. "A *refined* asshat."

While they're snarking amongst themselves, Kelley's phone pings in his pocket.

"Huh," he says as he reads the message. "Preston is on campus."

"Preston from high school?"

"Yeah. When I ran into him a few weeks ago, I told him to hit me up if he was ever in town." He takes a moment to shoot off another text. "He's coming here. That cool?"

"Yeah," I say with a shrug. "I don't think he really liked me much but I'm sure we can get along for a night."

Preston was an entitled, jerk-faced weasel of epic proportions in high school, but maybe he's matured in the four years since I've seen him last.

Ugh. Please, let him have matured.

Kelley threads his fingers through mine and leads me through the door. We weave in and out of bodies until we reach the back of the house, then step outside onto a large deck.

"Kelley!" A guy I recognize from Kelley's soccer scrimmages waves us over.

"Scotty," Kelley says as they slap hands and do that weird bro-y handshaking back-pat thing. I'm so glad Kelley and Jesse just hug and don't bother with the extra *whatever* that was. "Ivy, this is Scotty. He's whose truck you've been driving."

"Oh!" I perk up at that information. "Thank you so much for letting me learn to drive manual on your truck."

"No problem. Anything for the Rocket Man's girl," Scotty

slurs with a grin. "Thanks for not wrecking it, though," he adds seriously.

"Thanks for the invite, man," Kelley says to him, and then he introduces Scotty to Jesse and Bailey. Bailey excuses herself to the edge of the yard to take a phone call, and Jesse bounces off in search of beer. When Kelley and Scotty are done chatting, Kelley laces his fingers with mine once more and pulls me in the direction of the makeshift dance floor. I wave to Bailey, so she sees where we're going, and she gives me a thumbs up.

The music is much louder when we enter the house, and some sort of bassy club song is pumping through two large speakers. When we reach the area where people are dancing, Kelley lifts my hand and twirls me, making my stomach flip and my heart skip. I swear I smile so much when I'm with him, my face hurts.

"You look gorgeous," he says once he pulls me against him. "Have I said that yet?"

"Mmm, I think you might have mentioned it once or ten times." I smirk at him and he nips at my lower lip. The pulsing beat of the next song is something slower, and we move our hips in time with the music.

Kelley runs his hands up and down my back. "This skirt is killing me tonight. And those fucking heels. You should let me fuck you against the wall when we get home. Heels and skirt stay on."

Mmm. Yes please. The weather is uncharacteristically warm for November in Indiana, so I took a risk and wore a black, patent leather skirt paired with a tight, black, cold-shoulder sweater. The desire dripping from Kelley's words tells me the risk definitely paid off.

"You sure you're up for that? You just ran a marathon. I

could always ride you instead—heels and skirt on." I raise a suggestive brow and bite my lip.

"Yes," he nods rapidly. "Yes to both."

"Then why wait until we get home." I run my hands up his chest as I speak, and he blinks at me, eyes flashing hot with need.

"Are you messing with me?" he asks after a moment, and I give a coy shrug. "Baby, the thought of taking you anywhere in that skirt makes my dick hard." He presses his pelvis into me so I can feel the proof of his words. "But you're mine, and I'm not sharing. Not even a viewing. So, I don't want to wait. But I will."

I whimper. "Can we go home now, then?"

Kelley snickers. "Soon, baby." He pulls me in for a kiss and it leaves me dizzy. The way he can completely disarm me with just a kiss? It's sinful.

Both of our phones go off at the same time, so we break apart to check them.

"Mine's from Bailey," I tell Kelley as I text her back. "She's getting an Uber back to the apartment." Bailey says nothing is wrong, that she's just tired, but I don't believe it. So, either she's upset about something or she's meeting someone. I'll get it out of her tomorrow. I text her back an okay and ask her to share her location with me, and when she sends not only the location but also a picture of her Uber driver, I put my phone away and look up.

Kelley finishes his text and puts it back in his pocket. "That was Preston. He's here somewhere."

Frick. I forgot about Preston. Now we can't go home and do naughty things to each other. Kelley must be able to read my thoughts through my pout, because he leans forward and captures my lips in a passionate kiss.

"Soon, baby. Give me an hour, and then we're going

straight home and we're not leaving until you come at least three times."

"Promise?" My voice is breathy and needy.

"Promise," he growls.

Gah. Stupid high school friends sex-blocking my sexy time.

I take a deep breath and peck him on the lips. "I'm going to find the bathroom."

"Want me to come with you," he asks, just as Jesse strolls up and hands Kelley one of the three beers he's carrying.

"It's fine. If I'm not back in fifteen, come find me." I kiss him again, then gesture to the beer in Jesse's hand. "Hold that for me, please."

I weave through the throng of people, make my way up the stairs, and find the bathroom. There's a group of girls inside, so I lean on the wall and scroll through my phone while I wait my turn.

Now that I'm not studying for the LSAT every waking minute, I've started reading some of the indie romance novels Bailey is always raving about. I was skeptical at first, because I tend to gravitate toward true crime stories, but once I started, I couldn't stop. Holy moly, do I love smut now. I didn't know there were so many different ways to describe a penis, though. *Fascinating.*

I pull up the e-reader app on my phone and select Bailey's newest recommendation, but I can't quite focus. The back of my neck keeps prickling and I get the strangest feeling that I'm being watched, but when I look around, I see nothing out of the ordinary.

When the group of girls leaves, I hurry in and do my business. The bathroom is actually communal with three separate toilet and shower stalls. It's a lot nicer than some of the frat bathrooms I've seen. Two of the three toilet stalls actually have toilet paper, too.

Color me impressed.

Go you, Sigma Nu Chu! Or whatever frat this is. Scotty deserves a high five.

As I'm washing my hands, the door opens behind me. I peer into the mirror briefly and see a muscular body enter, so I grab some paper towels and make my way to the door.

"Excuse me," I say, my eyes on the door handle as I attempt to sidestep the stranger, but his hand grabs my wrist and I stiffen.

"Ivy?"

My steps falter when I see that the man holding my wrist is actually Preston, Kelley's friend from high school, and my body relaxes.

"Preston," I say with an awkward chuckle. "You scared me."

He smiles. "Wouldn't want to startle Ivy Rivenbark, would I?" He tilts his head to the side as he speaks.

It's strange, the way he's assessing me, and I recall an image of a bird I saw in a pet shop once. It had beady, skittish little eyes and cocked its head creepily just like Preston is now.

"Right," I nod. "Well, I'm gonna go find Kelley."

I try to pull open the door, but Preston sticks his booted foot in front of it, trapping me inside, and all of my internal warning signals start to blare.

"Let me out, Preston," I say sternly, trying to hide the spike of fear, but Preston laughs.

The music is so loud. Would anyone hear if I screamed?

"I don't think I will," he quips almost playfully, and when he steps closer, I get a whiff of a spicy and cloying blend of leather and ginger. With the scent come the flashes of memory, and the pressure in my head grows.

"Juego Voss," I say, my heart hammering in my chest.

287

"You like that?" His voice is taunting, disgusted. The sudden shift in his tone sends chills down my spine. "I should have known you'd like the expensive shit. Gold-digging gutter whore like you."

He steps closer, and I step back, effectively trapping myself between the shut door and Preston.

A low rumbling voice. Navy curtains. A mesh jersey.

"You were wearing a Colts jersey," I recall out loud, my eyes rapidly scanning over Preston's face. Searching for a lie. For a sign that I'm wrong. He just raises an eyebrow and grins. I flick my eyes up and study his dark brown hair. It's cut short now, but in high school, I remember it being shaggier on top. An undercut.

I scan his body, taking in his bulked-out, football player physique. He's bigger than he was in high school, but the general shape is still the same. Gym rat. Big biceps. Exactly the kind of guy I was taking home before, testing myself.

I shudder.

"See something you like?" His voice sends ice down my spine, and when he steps closer, I get another whiff of his cologne.

I might throw up.

"Was it you?" I ask, even though I already know the answer.

At 4:06 a.m. the morning after our high school graduation party, I woke up in the backseat of my car with a pounding headache, one sandal, and no underwear. The ER confirmed that there was evidence of sexual assault, but my attacker likely used a condom, and while my symptoms were consistent with a Rohypnol dosage, no traces of drugs were found in my system.

Until now, all I had were flashes of memory.

Preston's voice is pleased and taunting. "How do you

think Kelley would feel if he knew I dicked you first?" He pulls on a strand of my hair, and I flinch. "He was always so obsessed with you."

I clamp my eyes shut and take steadying breaths through my mouth.

Think. Think. Think.

"Don't tell me you're going to play shy now. I've heard all about you, Ivy Rivenbark. Campus slut. Wild party girl."

His voice is rough, violent sounding, and it turns my stomach. When I force my eyes open, he's inches from me. Our bodies aren't touching, and I need to keep it that way.

"Preston, you're drunk and not thinking clearly. Kelley is probably going to come looking for me. We should really go back out there."

He slams his hand on the door right next to my head, and when I jump, he laughs. My pulse is erratic, and anxiety is swirling through me. My fingertips tingle. My head is foggy. My chest aches. *Breathe.*

"I don't think we will, Ivy," he snarls at me. "How did Kelley finally get you to spread those legs for him, huh? You fucked your way through campus, and he was all that was left? Little Ivy Rivenbark with a fucking golden pussy."

The anger in his voice is barely leashed, moments from being completely unhinged, and terror ricochets through me.

"I don't remember it being that good," he muses. "Maybe I should test it out again, yeah?"

I need to get out of this bathroom.

I scan the floor for my clutch which contains my pepper spray and phone and find it next to the door. I must have dropped it when he startled me. If I can't get to my clutch, then all I have is my body, and he's easily twice my size. I look him over as he prattles on.

Eyes, nose, throat, groin.

289

Breathe. Breathe. Breathe.

"How about you and me have some fun, Ivy? We could relive grad night." He presses in closer and sticks his hand roughly into my hair.

"That was rape, Preston." I scowl back, trying my best not to sob. "You *raped* me."

He yanks my hair, and I cry out in pain, but when he pulls back in rage, I flex my wrist and jab the palm of my hand upward at his nose. The connection makes a sickening crunch, and I drop to the floor for my clutch and immediately start to yell for help.

"You bitch," he screams, and with blood pouring from his nose, he lunges for me right as I get my hand on my pepper spray. I point the tiny bottle at him and push the button, and he thrashes away with a scream.

I clamber up and out the bathroom door.

"Help! Someone please help!" I scream, and immediately I hear footsteps pounding up the stairs. I press myself against the far wall just as Preston barges into the hallway and Kelley and Jesse reach the top of the stairs.

A crowd has formed behind them, and a few people have emerged from rooms on the opposite end of the hall too. A guy in a backwards Cubs cap catches my eye because he has his phone out.

I watch Kelley and Jesse take in the scene before them. I'm panting, tears are streaming down my face, and I'm sure my hair is a mess. And across the hallway, Preston's face is covered in blood, his eyes are bloodshot, and he's absolutely enraged.

I throw myself into Kelley's arms.

"It was him," I sob into his chest, and he stiffens.

"Bet you can't stand that I fucked her first, right, Kap?" Preston spits a mouthful of blood onto the carpet. "Always following after her, pining for her, whining about her. Maybe you want to compare notes now?"

"You raped me," I yell, and Preston sneers.

"You wanted it."

"You *drugged* me," I say on a sob, and Preston chuckles. Kelley passes me into Jesse's arms, and then launches himself at his former childhood friend.

Kelley lands one solid punch to Preston's jaw before Preston tackles him. Their bodies clash and fall to the ground, and I scream. Kelley is fast and athletic, but Preston is big, and when Preston wrestles himself on top of Kelley, the crunch of his fist fills me with terror.

"Stop! Stop it, Preston!" I yell and turn in Jesse's arms. "Get him off, Jesse! Help him!"

Jesse holds my thrashing body tighter. "In a second," he says, eyes on the fight. "Let our boy have a chance to mess him up a little."

I look back just in time to see Kelley slam his fist into Preston's already broken nose, then flip Preston onto his back. Kelley starts to pound on Preston's body, a flurry of fists at his torso and face, and I can hear them grunting with each hit.

One of Preston's fists crashes into Kelley's cheek, and Kelley rocks backward, but doesn't fall. Instead, he doubles back harder, his face furious and dripping blood from a busted lip and eyebrow.

"Get him off, Jesse, please!" I beg again, tears pouring down my face. Jesse waits another moment, until Preston's brought his arms to cover his face in an attempt to block Kelley's blows. Then Jesse nudges me aside and steps forward to pull Kelley off Preston.

"He's done," Jesse says as he grabs Kelley's shoulders and hauls him backward. Preston rolls over and spits out another mouthful of blood.

"You fucking pussy!" Preston yells as he gets to his feet.

"Shut the hell up, Preston," Kelley growls, and Preston laughs.

"I had her first. Can't change that." Preston spits again. "Next time you fuck her, remember I was there first."

Kelley breaks Jesse's hold and throws another punch at Preston, making him stumble backward. Preston runs at Kelley, crashing his big body into him, and just as they're about to get into it again, the cops arrive. Someone must have called them when I was screaming for help, and when the officers reach the top of the stairs, they break up the fight and arrest both Kelley and Preston.

"Ivy, call my mom," Kelley says as the officer cuffs his hands and leads him outside. "Tell her to meet me at the police station near campus."

"Okay," I croak.

"It's going to be fine," he says as they put him into the back of the police car, and then they're driving away.

As much as I want to crumple to the ground and cry, I have to focus on what I can control. I need to get to Kelley. I need to get to Preston. I can't let Preston get away with this, and this time, I've got a plan.

The wait time for an Uber is too long, and Bailey isn't answering her phone. Jesse is drunk and can't drive, so I dart into the house to find Scotty. The music has stopped and people are leaving since the cops crashed the party, but I manage to spot him on the deck. When I explain what happened, he hands me the keys to his truck and wishes me luck.

Then I rush back inside to find the jerk in the Cubs cap.

TWENTY-TWO

kelley

I LISTEN to Bailey and Ivy joke in the kitchen, laughing about something in a book they're buddy reading, but I can't focus on anything except Ivy's huge smile and her deep dimple.

My girl is always gorgeous, but she's even more so when she's happy.

In the two weeks since I was arrested, things have been a chaotic whirlwind of action.

When Ivy told me about what happened to her at the graduation party, I was angry for her. I hurt for her. I wanted justice for her. I wanted to do everything I could to help her heal.

But when we discovered that Preston was the one who hurt her?

I wanted to fucking *kill* for her.

I wanted to make Preston pay for the pain he'd caused, the damage he'd done, and the time I'd lost with Ivy.

He's actually really lucky the cops showed up when they did, or I might have done far worse than three cracked ribs

293

and a fractured cheekbone. I can't claim the busted nose—that's Ivy's work.

I was contemplating ways to hold Preston accountable for what he did to Ivy when my parents showed up at the station. I was prepared to do any and everything necessary to make sure he was thrown in jail, but it turned out Ivy didn't need my help.

My girl came strolling into the police station with three different cell phone videos of the fight, and all three incriminate Preston harshly. Then a fourth video was leaked online, and victims of Preston's from Stanford started coming forward.

It doesn't look good for him, and I hope he gets everything coming to him.

Ivy's been coping surprisingly well, all things considered. She had nightmares almost every night the first week after the fight, but they've decreased in severity, and her therapist has scheduled her for weekly sessions for the next two months just to be safe. She's chatting in her online support group daily, and she's even got me joining in on morning mantras and breathing exercises. These symptoms may never go away, but I'm going to be there to help her in any way she needs. Ivy doesn't hide from her scars, and she doesn't let them define her. I'm just in awe of her.

From my seat on the girls' couch, after two exhausting weeks, I feel like I can finally relax. Their apartment is decorated with tiny paper hand turkeys, the table is set with placemats that Jesse knitted, and the savory smells of butter and gravy and something else delicious float through the air. We're celebrating our second ever Friendsgiving dinner, and there is nowhere else I'd rather be.

"What about Piercenbark?" Jesse blurts randomly from where he's stretched out on the floor, and I bark out a laugh.

"Gross," Bailey calls from the kitchen. "Cool it with the ship names, J. They're just...bad."

"Kivy wasn't that bad," Jesse pouts, and Bailey laughs as she and Ivy join us in the living room.

"Kivy is *terrible*. And so is Ivelley and Kellenbark and all the others you've come up with."

As Bailey and Jesse get into the same argument they've been having for the last month, Ivy tiptoes behind me and leans over the couch. She slides her hands down my chest before whispering in my ear. "Come with me."

I'm out of my seat and following her into her bedroom in milliseconds.

"I have something for you," she sing-songs and wiggles her eyebrows.

"Is it you, naked, underneath me?" She snorts out a laugh, but I'm *very* serious. "I'm serious," I stress, and she laughs again.

"It is not...*yet*. Later, that can be arranged. But right now," she opens the top drawer of her dresser and pulls out a small white box, "you'll have to settle for this."

She hands it over to me.

"Are you giving me your zombie apocalypse badge?" I gasp jokingly. After Ivy drove my friend Scotty's truck to the police station, she wouldn't stop talking about how it validated her reasoning for needing to learn to drive stick. She talked about it so much, in fact, that Jesse knitted her a grey diamond-shaped "badge" with a blue Z on it. He told her it's the "official getaway driver of the zombie apocalypse" badge, and she beamed with pride.

"Heck no. That's mine forever. But this might be better."

When I open the white box, I'm surprised to see a small blue enamel pin.

"Uh...thanks..." I raise my eyebrow in question. "You want me to wear this?"

Ivy rolls her eyes. "Look closer."

I pick up the pin and study it.

A blue cornflower.

On the pin is a picture of a blue cornflower, and my eyes shoot to hers.

"This way your Bachelor's Button will never wilt," she says quietly, and my heart races.

"And what does that mean?"

Her smile grows and her dimple pops. "It means the girl you've fallen for returns your feelings."

I swallow, and work to wet my bone-dry throat.

"Ivy Rivenbark, are you saying you have feelings for me?" I tease despite my thundering heart, and she nods seriously.

"Very strong feelings," she whispers, running her hands up my chest and stretching on her tiptoes to press a kiss to my lips. "I'm saying I'm in love with you, Kelley Allen Pierce."

We're both smiling, and I press my forehead to hers. "I'm in love with you back," I say, and then I kiss her again.

epilogue

KELLEY

THE FIRST DAY of spring semester is in two days. My last first day of undergrad. It's strange. Part of me wants to savor it so I can bask in nostalgia, and the other part just wants to get it the hell over with.

Knowing all of the changes on the horizon, how we're all leaving one phase of life and standing on the cusp of another, fills me with excitement and dread. I'm excited to get into my own classroom, but I'm gonna miss undergrad.

I spent most of my winter break back home with Ivy and our families. With Allison and Matthew now staying with Ivy's mom, though, she stayed over at my house frequently.

It wasn't a hardship.

I smirk when I think about all the ways she and I *got comfortable* in my childhood home. I finally got to spread her out on my bed, just like I'd always fantasized, and I will never look at the pool table in my media room the same way ever again. Just the thought has me shifting my stance to relieve the tightness in my jeans.

As I'm unpacking my laundry and reliving every single moan I pulled from Ivy over the break, I hear my bedroom door open and my entire body erupts in tingles. I don't even try to fight the grin. I don't have to hide it anymore.

"Kelley," she croons behind me.

"Ivy," I greet back, then I shut my dresser drawer and turn to face her. "Hi, baby."

"Hi," she smiles sweetly, and I look her over. I just saw her this morning, but I swear I'll never get enough. I want to commit every look, every outfit, every mood, every smile to memory so that I am never without her. Until she's tattooed on the back of my eyelids.

"I love it when you look at me like that," she says as she leans against my now closed bedroom door.

"How?"

"With reverence. With love. Like I'm the most important thing in the room." She walks toward me, and I grab her hips to pull her close as soon as she's within arm's reach.

"The room. The city. The entire galaxy, Ivy Jean." I kiss her lips with a passion that I hope conveys how much I mean those words.

"Mmmm," she hums against my lips and walks me backward until I'm bumping into my desk chair, then she grabs my shoulders and nudges me down into the seat.

"You know what other look I love?" she asks seductively, and I watch as she pulls her shirt over her head and drops it to the floor, showing off her full breasts in a sexy blue lace bra. Then she hooks her fingers into the band of her leggings and pulls them down over her thick thighs, exposing a matching thong.

I can't tear my eyes away. My gaze drags over every curve, every dip, every inch of skin. I've touched it all, tasted it all, and it's all mine.

"That one," she whispers, and I lift my eyes from her

gorgeous body and up to her smirking face. "That look right there. Like you want to worship my body with your body."

I match her smirk and reach out, hooking my index fingers into the sides of the scrap of lace she calls underwear. "You like when I look at you like I'm going to finger fuck your pussy and suck on your clit until you're trembling?" I pull her closer. "Or like I want to sink my cock deep into you, pound into that sexy body until you're screaming my name?"

She nods, blue eyes swimming with desire. I squeeze her ass cheeks with my hands as my mouth clamps down on her nipple through her bra. The moan she releases goes straight to my dick. She pulls my shirt over my head and I unclasp her bra, but just as I'm about to lavish her chest with kisses, she drops to her knees in front of me.

I'm panting, the sight alone—Ivy Rivenbark, topless and breathless and kneeling between my legs—shoots sparks of need straight down my spine until I'm diamond-level hard. When she bites her lip and reaches for my zipper, I could come on the spot.

"Up," she commands, and I lift my hips so she can drag my jeans and boxers down my thighs until I'm sitting stark naked in my desk chair with my hard dick saluting her like the good soldier he is.

She flashes me a smile, then wraps her delicate hands around my cock and pumps twice. I reach down and gather her hair into my hands and watch as she licks me from base to tip.

"Fuck, baby," I rasp. When she takes me into her mouth, sucking on my head then pulling me into her throat, my answering groan is primal, and I thrust once, making her gag. She continues her torture, alternating between licking and sucking, pumping and laving. And I'm a mess, lost in the sensations her talented mouth creates.

"Yes, Ivy. Baby, you're so good. So sexy."

She hums around my shaft, and I growl, thrusting once, twice, three more times until she gags again and has to come up for air, pumping my dick with her hands.

"You like that, baby?" she coos.

"Fuck yes." I watch as she, again, puts my head between her plush lips. I can feel her tongue massaging the sensitive underside of my tip, and it's so good.

Too good.

As if Ivy can sense how close I already am, she gives me one final lick, then stands up and reaches into the desk drawer next to me, pulling out a condom. She rolls the condom down my shaft, straddles me on the chair, then pulls her thong to the side with one hand while lining my dick up to her entrance with the other.

"Shit," I ground out. "How did I get so lucky? How are you so damn sexy?" I pant the words, eyes jumping between her swollen pussy ready to swallow my dick and her blue eyes flashing hot with fire and lust. Ivy just smirks, then sinks down onto me with one long, low moan.

I swear I could spend the rest of my life between this woman's thighs. Dick or tongue, I don't care, so long as part of me is always buried inside her, drawing out those moans.

The velvet, hot feeling of her wrapped around me is euphoric, and I watch as she rocks, slowly at first, swiveling her hips. I run my hands up and down her torso, kiss her lips, suck on her neck and nipples, bite at the tender flesh of her breasts—everything I've learned that she loves. And when her hips start to speed up, I bring my thumb to her clit and massage it in the way that I know will make her detonate until her back is bowing and she's clenching around me, murmuring her pleasure in my ears.

Fuuuuck. She's perfection.

When she's ridden out her orgasm, I stand and walk us to my bed, then pull out and drop her on it. Ivy giggles as she bounces a little, then lays back, her eyes eating me up.

I reach down and grip the condom, squeezing my dick once.

"On your knees," I growl at her, and the excitement that sparks in her blue eyes is every damn thing I want.

Ivy gets up on all fours, then squeals when I grab her hips and pull her to the edge of the bed where I'm standing. When she looks at me over her shoulder, long blonde hair cascading over her back and pupils dilated wide, she is the erotic picture ecstasy. I run my hand over her spine, drag her thong down her thighs, then give her ass a playful smack, loving the way it jiggles and the needy whimper she releases.

"I'm going to fuck you like this now, Ivy." I drag my fingers through her folds and push one into her. She hums and pushes against me, begging for more.

"Please, Kelley," she begs. "Fuck me just like this."

Those words on her lips? I can't handle it.

I line my dick up and push into her until her ass is smashed up against my hips. Then I wrap my hands around her waist, pushing my thumbs into the dimples at the base of her spine, and fuck her just like she asked me to.

I'm entranced, watching how each thrust has her ass bouncing off my abdomen, rippling in the sexiest way. The way she gasps and whimpers, chanting "yes, yes, yes" when I speed up, has my balls tightening, my stomach tingling, and my toes curling. I know I won't last much longer.

"Touch yourself, baby," I command, and she does. Ivy rubs her clit until she's clenching tightly around my dick and I'm exploding my release into the condom, and we both fall onto the bed, sweaty, sated and drunk in love.

"Oh my gosh," Ivy pushes out between panted breaths, "that was so hot."

"Yeah?" I ask with a smirk, standing to dispose of the condom.

"Heck, yes. When you said 'on your knees, baby' I almost orgasmed right then. It was like Niagara Falls in my panties." The pure joy in her voice twists up my heart and stomach in the best way, and her tinkling giggle is music to my ears.

"You liked that, huh?"

"Yes, yes, I definitely did. Obviously."

"What about you with the thong, though? Pulling it to the side and riding me like that? Jesus Christ, Ivy. You're trying to kill me." I flop back on the bed and pull her on top of me.

"It's Bailey's books." She giggles and hides her face in my chest. "They're giving me *ideas*."

"Praise Romance Novels!" I say dramatically, and she pinches my side. "I fucking *love* reading."

I trail my fingertips up and down her arm, pleased at the goose bumps that pop up from my touch. It sounds corny as hell, but I didn't know it was possible to be this happy.

I'm about to tell her this, to express for the millionth time just how damn lucky I feel that she's mine, when her phone pings with a notification, and she shoots straight up.

Ivy rushes over to the floor where her phone was discarded and swipes the screen, then flicks her eyes to me, wide with nervous excitement.

"What is it?" I sit up and she walks to me, handing me the phone.

"Email notification from Chicago." She swallows and closes her eyes.

Ivy's been waiting on tenterhooks to hear back from the Law School at the University of Chicago for two weeks. She's already received an acceptance from the IU law school, which is right here in the city, but Chicago is one of the top law schools in the country.

"Do you want me to open it?" I ask when she doesn't reach out to take her phone back. She blinks.

"If I don't get in, I'm okay with it. Indiana University's law school is good. Tuition is significantly less. It's here in the city. It's only forty-five minutes from Mom and Jacob, and closer to Dr. Joyner," she adds, getting lost in listing her pros and cons.

"Dr. Joyner can meet with you from anywhere," I remind her. She raises her eyes to me.

"And you'll be here."

My heart thuds. My plan is to stay and teach here. The principal at Morgan County High already told me I have a job if I want it. But if Ivy gets into Chicago...

"University of Chicago isn't that far from here, Ives. Less than a four-hour drive." I keep my voice strong and reassuring. I will support her no matter where she goes and what she does. Me and Ivy? We're forever. "No matter what happens, you got this. *We* got this."

She nods her head. "Okay, go ahead and open it."

I click the notification and it takes me to her email app. I open the email and begin to read, and my heart races and a smile stretches over my face.

"You got in, Ives."

"I got in?"

"You got in!"

"Oh my gosh! I got in!" Her entire body is alight with happiness and excited energy, and I'm just so damn *proud* of her. This girl is going to change the world.

"Oh my gosh, I have to call Jacob! And Mom! And your mom! I have to call Dr. Joyner! I have to tell Bailey and Jesse!" Ivy makes for the door, but I wrap my arm around her waist and stop her.

"Baby, you can't go out there yet. You're naked."

"Oh." She stifles a laugh. "Whoops."

The energy in the room is buzzing as we hurriedly throw on our clothes, and the smile hasn't left Ivy's face the whole time, but when she goes to open the door, her hand pauses on the knob.

"Kelley?"

"Ivy." I have a feeling I know what she's about to say, and my stomach erupts with butterflies.

"What would you say if I asked you to come with me? To move to Chicago?" Her voice is quiet, hopeful but nervous.

"I'd say we'd need to get used to disappointment," I state seriously and lean on the wall next to her. I wait just a breath —long enough for her to hear me, but too quick for her to jump to conclusions—before adding, "because I hear being a Bears fan is fucking *brutal*."

Her eyes whip to mine and she takes in my stupid grin. "What?" she asks, a smile taking over her face, dimple popping back out in all its glory. "Does that mean you'll come with me?"

I grab her hips and pull her to me, lowering my forehead so it rests on hers. "I'll go anywhere and everywhere with you, Ivy Jean Rivenbark. As long as you'll have me, I'll be there."

She kisses me with a fierceness I used to be too scared to even dream about. She kisses me with passion and reverence and promise. She kisses me like a woman *in love*, and fuck if I don't try to give it back just like she deserves.

"I love you so, so much, Kelley," she whispers against my lips, and I smile.

"I love you back, Ivy Bean."

"We're moving to Chicago together," she says excitedly.

"Together," I repeat, and I press another kiss to her lips.

Because I'm proud of her, and because she's mine, and because I can. The reality still sends chills of elation through me—Ivy Rivenbark is mine. She loves me. She chose me.

I meant it when I said I'm going to love her better than anyone else can. Every day, for the rest of my life, and I'm lucky to do it.

the end

extended epilogue

KELLEY

I drop the last box on the living room floor and walk to where Ivy is putting away dishes in our new kitchen. She's wearing cut off shorts and a plain black tank top, her long blonde hair piled on top of her head in a messy bun. She's gorgeous, humming quietly to herself as she organizes the mugs in the cabinet.

I slide my hands around her waist and press a kiss just below her ear. The place that never fails to hitch her breath and send goosebumps skittering over her body.

I swear, touching her like this, loving her, it will never get old.

"That's the last of it," I say against her skin. She leans her head to the side, encouraging me, and I drag my lips down her neck, sucking softly where it curves into her shoulder. She smells sweet, like her mango body wash, but tastes of salt, a result of spending the morning moving boxes in the July Chicago heat.

"Mmm," she hums. "That feels good."

Ivy presses her ass into me, letting out a small gasp when she finds me hard.

I absoloutely love those gasps, but I'm not sure why she's surprised. I'm always hard for her. I've practically been a walking erection for the last ten months.

I grab her hips and pull her into me, and she snakes her hands up into my hair. We've got boxes to unpack, shopping to do, and a whole damn city to explore, but that's all going to have to wait.

A repeat of the Great Chicago Fire couldn't tear me away from this woman's body.

"I want you," Ivy moans, tugging my hair and grinding her ass on my dick. "I want you now, Kelley."

I groan and suck hard on her neck before spinning her around and lifting her onto the counter. Her legs wrap around my waist instinctively and our mouths connect in a desperate, sensual kiss. Her hands in my hair, mine running all over her body, squeezing and tugging. I still can't get enough. I want all of it under my fingertips, gripped in my hands, all at once, and forever.

"How about I fuck you on our new kitchen counter, baby," I growl onto her lips.

I'm half a second from tearing her shorts off and slamming into her, but my girl pulls out of my kiss and shakes her head slowly. Her baby blues are sparkling, a cloudless summer sky, and her swollen, just-kissed lips are pulled into a coy smile.

"That's not what I want," she whispers and pushes lightly on my chest. I shuffle back, just enough to let her climb off the counter, and watch as she slips her tank top over her head. I don't bother stifling my groan when she unhooks her bra and slides it down her arms.

I bend down and suck a pert nipple into my mouth, and Ivy's answering whimper makes my dick ache with need. I bite down lightly at the same time as I pop the button on her shorts and push them to the ground. With a soft moan, Ivy tugs my shirt up and I pull it over my head. The feel of her hard nipples dragging over my chest is torture and bliss.

Her tongue in my mouth, her breath in my lungs, I'm burning for her.

I cup her pussy and find her soaking, so I push her panties to the side and slip a finger into her heat. She moans loudly and clenches around me. I swear to god, the sounds she makes are musical. I add a second finger and thrust while pressing my palm onto her swollen clit.

"Yes," she pants, widening her stance before attacking my lips once more. I know what my baby likes. I know just how to make her sing.

Ivy pushes my gym shorts and boxers down my thighs. When I step back to kick them the rest of the way off, my fingers slip from her warmth. Before I can pull her back, she steps just out of arm's reach with a giggle. She crooks her index finger, beckoning, and darts around the corner into our living room. I chase her, like I always do, always have, and find her pressed up against our floor-to-ceiling windows that overlook the city and Lake Michigan.

Our one-bedroom Hyde Park apartment is...*lavish*, to say the least. If Ma and Pop weren't close with the owner of the building—another attorney and a U of C Law School alum—there's no way we could afford it on my teaching salary. If I felt at all guilty about taking advantage of my parents' connections, it all disappeared the moment I saw Ivy's naked form highlighted in front of a backdrop of the Chicago skyline from fifteen stories up.

She's a goddess.

And I'm going to worship her like one.

"What are you waiting for," she croons, rubbing her thighs together. "Come over here and fuck me against these windows like you said you would when we toured the apartment last month."

Hearing the word *fuck* come from Ivy's sweet mouth is sexy as hell, and my dick leaks precum. I squeeze my cock and swipe at the wetness at the tip.

"Does my dirty girl want all of Chicago to see me make her come?" The windows are tinted. No one will see what's mine, but my baby likes the fantasy.

"Yes, please." She pulls her plump bottom lip between her teeth, her blue eyes flash with heat, and my restraint snaps. I rush her, suck her tongue into my mouth and squeeze her ass with both hands. I start to slide down her body, needing to taste her, but she pulls me back up.

"Later," she rasps, desperate, and grabs hold of my dick. "I need you inside me now."

Fuck me.

I waste no time. Hitching one of her legs over my hip, I slam into her with a primal groan that matches hers.

"Oh, god, yes," she moans. Fucking bare is still new for us. The first time we did it, even reciting economic trends of the 20th century wasn't enough to keep me from blowing my load early.

I more than made up for it in the second round, though. And the third.

I feel her walls clench around me as I thrust. She's velvet heat and erotic perfection wrapped around my cock, and I curse at how good she feels.

"Fuck, Ivy," I grind out. "Baby, I'm never going to stop fucking you."

"Never. Never stop, Kelley."

Three more hard thrusts, and I pull out quickly and flip her around, so her forearms are braced on the window. The reflection of breasts swaying when I thrust back into her from behind and the sight of her plush ass pressing against my lower abdomen makes my balls tighten. I reach around and pinch her nipple with one hand while the other grips her waist. With each thrust of my hips, she pushes back into me, meeting my movements with her own. In fucking perfect sync.

I can't hold back my orgasm, so I slide my hand down and press hard on her clit, rubbing up and down just how she likes.

"Oh god, oh god," she cries. "Just like that." Her backward thrusts into my hips start to lose their rhythm, and when I feel her clench around me, I pinch her clit. She starts to cry out, so I wrap my other palm around the base of her throat and pull backward so I can capture her lips and swallow the sounds she makes.

Our kiss is frenzied. Ivy's back is arched and her breasts are pressed up against the window, and I quicken my thrusts, hard and fast, until I spill deep inside her pussy with one last groan.

"Oh my gosh," she pants out resting her head on my shoulder. "That was..."

"Yeah." She doesn't have to explain it. It's like this between us. Mind-blowing, our movements and desires flawlessly complementary, yet somehow always brand new. Always exciting.

Maybe we're still in the honeymoon stage.

Maybe these feelings will fade with time.

But judging by the last eight years, I'm pretty sure this is just *us*. Together, we're perfect.

I press a kiss to her temple, pull out, and sweep her into my arms to carry her to our bathroom. I set her softly onto the soapstone countertop, pull a washcloth from the moving box on the floor, and gently clean her up. She sighs, content and happy, and my chest tightens—the same *zing* feeling I get, that I've always gotten, when I know I've done right by her. I lean forward and take her mouth with mine in a soft, sweet kiss. Our foreheads rest together.

"I love you," she whispers, and I smile, the movement making my lips brush over hers.

"I love you back."

"I'm also hungry." She nudges me backward and then hops down. "Let's explore."

* * *

We grab dinner at a Thai place a few blocks from the apartment building. It's delicious, and Ivy makes sure to snag a take-out and delivery menu to bring home.

Home.

Our home. Mine and Ivy's. Together. My smile takes over my face at the thought of my reality. Who'd have thought it would end up better than I'd ever dreamed?

"What are you smiling about?" Ivy asks as we stroll hand-in-hand through Harold Washington Park. We decided against taking the L into the city tonight and instead chose to explore our new neighborhood. It's full of eclectic bars, restaurants, and shops, and we've been told it's got a great arts and entertainment scene, too. I've already found several routes to train for the Chicago Marathon, and Ivy discovered her new favorite café to keep her supplied with lattes once classes start.

"Just thinking about our life," I answer honestly.

"Yeah," she says with a sigh. "That makes me smile, too."

I bring our joined hands to my mouth and kiss her fingers. We cross the pedestrian bridge over Lake Shore Drive and walk until we're standing at the lake front. The breeze coming off Lake Michigan blows the loose strands of Ivy's hair back, tendrils dancing behind her, and her mango-sweet scent surrounds me. I breathe it all in. Her. Us. This new chapter of our lives.

Chicago will be home for the next three years. Maybe more. In August, I'll start my first real job teaching history to 9th and 10th graders at a local high school. I've also been hired as the assistant boys' soccer coach. The school is only a short walk and a nine-minute train ride from our apartment, and Ivy has already said she plans to be at every soccer game. Her classes don't start until September, but she's already figuring out how to get the course reading lists so she can get a head start on class work. Her and her brilliant brain.

This is how it's supposed to be. It's how it was always supposed to be. Ivy and me, together, enjoying life and making memories side by side.

I reach into my pocket for the small box I've been saving for a special occasion, and everything about this moment screams *special*.

"Hey, babe," I say to her, and she turns to me with a smile.

"Yeah?" The happiness radiating off her puffs my chest up, and her dimple is so deep that my heart skips at the sight. "What's up?"

Her eyes bounce playfully between mine, but when her gaze falls to my hands, spotting the black velvet box between my fingers, all levity vanishes. Her eyes widen, her mouth drops, and she takes one cautious step backwards, then another. She's all fear and nerves, her fight or flight instincts activated, and I know if I don't act soon, she'll either throw a punch or hightail it out of the park.

I try to hold back.

I try like hell to keep a poker face.

313

But the laughter bubbles up from my chest and out of my mouth anyway. I know this woman too damn well.

"Relax, Ives," I say through my laughter, and her brows and nose scrunch up.

"Excuse you! What the heck do you mean *relax*?" She's irritated, and she throws an incredulous finger at the jewelry box in my hand. "How the *frick* am I supposed to relax when you're holding...that...that *thing*."

I step toward her, and she bristles at my smirk. "And what exactly do you think *this thing* is?"

She huffs through her nose, and then whisper-yells, "an *engagement ring*."

I shake my head slowly, still smirking. "Always so conceited."

Ivy jerks her head back and her blue eyes flash lightning. She's pissed and confused, but she's also curious as fuck. The curiosity will win. It always does with her.

"Explain." That's all she says. A single command.

I grin, raise an eyebrow at her, and open the box, showing her what's inside.

"Oh," she whispers, and her eyes well with tears.

"You think I'd propose without discussing it with you first?" I question quietly and step toward her. "I wouldn't spring something like that on you, not before you had time to prepare. You know that."

"I just...I..." She reaches out and grazes her fingers over the necklace. A hexagon resin pendant with pressed cornflower petals inside on a rose gold chain. I had it made using flowers from the garden at our old high school. It's striking and unique. Just like her. She brushes away a tear and flicks her eyes to mine.

"It's beautiful," she murmurs.

"Can I?"

She nods and turns around. I gently take the necklace from the box, place it around her neck, and kiss her shoulder once the chain is clasped and secure. She turns back to face me and wraps her arms around my waist.

"Thank you," she says. "Thank you so, so much."

"I love you," I say in reply, and take her lips in a slow kiss. "I am going to propose," I say against her lips. "You will be my wife, but not until you're ready." I feel her smile brush over my mouth.

"Soon," she whispers. "Very soon."

PROLOGUE

Betrayal. Hatred. Despair. Guilt.

I'm seeing red. I want to scream. On the inside, I'm a mess.

I keep my face neutral, fight to keep my breathing steady, but all I can see is the date on the calendar. All I can think of is the deadline I won't reach, and the promise I'm going to have to break.

I let my guard down. I let someone in. And in doing so, I let *him* down. The only person worthy of everything good, and I've let him down. *Again.*

Tears burn the backs of my eyelids, welling up and threatening to spill, but I won't let them fall. I've had years of practice turning my outside to stone.

The man beside me shifts, and I can feel his gaze on me. His pleading gaze with his dark, chocolate brown eyes. I see his hands moving in my peripheral, his big fingers fidget, and despite his size, the movement is delicate. I know how those hands feel on my skin. I know how soft his touch can be.

I try to fight it, the way my heart clenches and aches. I try to focus on my anger, on the betrayal. I try to keep my sadness for the boy I've failed.

But deep down, I know the truth.

Underneath the fury, buried under the new-found hatred, is loss.

Loss and longing.

Mourning for the man beside me, the man I thought I knew. The man who is not at all who he lead me to believe he was.

* * *

CHAPTER ONE

Four Weeks Earlier

I smell like stale beer and French fries.

It's disgusting. I'll never let myself get used to it.

My shoes stick to the floor as I walk back and forth, wiping things down and replenishing what needs replenished. Limes, lemons, oranges, green olives, and my favorite, maraschino cherries. I snag one before putting the garnish tray back in the ice chest.

"I'm about finished here," I call to my manager, wiping my hands on my bar towel.

"You're good, B. Thanks for coming in tonight. I know you've got a lot going on."

"It's cool," I shrug. "I can always use the money. Even if it is a slow Wednesday, cash is cash."

I grab a toothpick from the jar on the bar and steal another cherry from the tray. Popping it in my mouth, I wink at the guy two bar stools down. He left me a decent tip earlier.

The least I can do is pay him one last bit of attention since he's likely to be back.

"Alright, girl, well head out and I'll see you on Saturday night. You're closing."

Jada pulls a draft for another guy and slides him the pint. A group of them came in to watch some sporting something or other earlier and then stayed. I couldn't care less about it, but it's the only reason I made any money tonight.

I say goodbye to Jada and head to the back of the bar to get my stuff. Switching out my hideous non-slips for my boots, I drop the shoes in my locker and grab my helmet and crossbody purse.

I should change my shirt, I know I stink like a bar, but I'm just too damn exhausted. I've been working more since Jada promoted me to lead bartender at Bar 31, my classes have been kicking my ass, and I've been spending all my free time trying to concoct the perfect cookie for the Bakery on Main cookie contest next month. My body is pissed at me and letting me know it, but if I can win that contest? The two-grand in prize money would make it worth it, and having my name and cookie displayed on their menu would be pretty great too.

I duck out the back exit and walk to my bike. She's my Baby. A black 2012 Honda Rebel 250. I bought it used from the guy who owns the auto garage back home for 1,500 bucks. It was a fucking steal, but I think he felt sorry for me and cut me a deal.

Sometimes there are advantages to being the girl everyone pities.

Putting my purse in the saddle bag, I swing my leg over the bike, put my helmet on my head, and start her up. No matter how tired I am, the rumble of her engine always gives me a jolt of excitement. Something about the freedom and the danger, maybe. I rev her twice, just for fun, and then cruise out onto the street.

It's already 12:15 a.m. when I pull into the parking lot of the convince store. It's late, I'm beat, and I only need one thing, so I'm braving it.

I hate having to shop so close to campus. I don't like running into people I know.

Working at one of the popular campus bars means a lot of people recognize me. Occupational hazard, and definitely not ideal. Unfortunately, there's not a lot of jobs where I can make 500 bucks on a weekend fully clothed, so when I'm on the clock, I fake it. Makes me quite a damn peach when I clock out.

After locking my helmet onto the backrest and grabbing my purse, I pop in my earbuds—a whole other level of antisocial. I spent the last three hours being *on*. Any more human interaction and I might develop a twitch.

My 2000's pop punk playlist is blaring in my ears, and I head to aisle six where they keep the baking stuff. I scan the shelf, find what I need and go to grab for it, then stop.

Shit.

This store actually has pure vanilla extract. I drop my hand. I was gonna get the imitation stuff—it's what I've been using—but if I want to win this contest, I need quality ingredients.

Shit. Eight freaking bucks for two ounces? I can get eight ounces of the imitation for $1.99.

I groan. This hurts. Like actually flipping hurts. It's that poor kid mentality.

I sigh, resigned, and reach for the bottle, just as another hand snatches it from the shelf. I whip around keeping my eyes on the precious bottle—the only one this stupid convenience store has—and huff.

I'm about to pop off, put this snatchy thief in their place, but my attention is stolen by the hand that's holding the bottle.

A big hand.

A strong hand.

A sexy hand.

Hmm.

I scan my eyes upward. A few woven bracelets are tied loosely around the thick wrist, and a dusting of hair covers the muscular, rigid, golden forearm.

That's a *nice* forearm, right there.

I move my gaze farther up, over a defined bicep and broad chest covered in a blue and white baseball-style t-shirt. A silver necklace of some sort hides beneath the collar of the shirt, the defined jaw is sporting a bit of light brown scruff, and soft, chestnut hair feathers just above the shoulders.

I bring my focus out, enough to study the whole hairstyle, to find it loose, kinda messy, with a bit of a wave to it.

Prince haired Harry hair.

When the mouth moves, I flick my eyes down to it to find plump lips quirked in a bit of a smile, and they move again.

The hulking man is speaking.

"Huh?" All I can hear is Patrick Stump in my ears.

His mouth moves a third time, the tiny smile turning into a full-blown grin showing off straight, white teeth.

Then I watch in slow motion as the other hand, the one not holding my bottle of pure vanilla hostage, raises up and tugs one of my earbuds out of my ear.

"You said Prince Harry," he says with a laugh.

"No, I said prince *haired* Harry," I correct. "And I didn't realize I'd said it out loud." He pops a brow in question, and I roll my eyes. "Google it."

"Okay," he continues, voice low and playful. "Are you okay?"

I bristle. "I'm fine."

"I wasn't sure. You're kinda just standing there staring."

"I was sizing up my new enemy." I tug out my other earbud.

"Enemy?" He laughs again. It's a good laugh.

"You just stole that vanilla from me. I don't make it a habit to befriend thieves."

"I didn't steal it. I just got it before you." He's still smiling. It's an attractive smile, damn it.

"I was clearly here first. I was clearly reaching for that bottle when you jumped out of nowhere and snatched it." I put my hand on my hip and pop it out. My roommate Ivy calls it my power pose. She says it's how she knows when I'm in a take-no-prisoners mode.

"You were here first, yeah. But you were standing there surveying the shelf for a pretty long time," he says with a smirk. "Some of us have places to be. It's not thieving to just sneak past ya and grab what I need."

"It's line jumping, which everyone knows is poor social etiquette, and it is thieving, because that bottle is mine."

"Poor social etiquette?"

"Mmhm."

"Is it poor social etiquette to blatantly check out a stranger at the grocery store, too?" He raises his eyebrows, grin still affixed to his mouth.

I huff out a laugh. "*Please*. I was not checking you out. I was surveying you for weaknesses in case I have to resort to violence."

His answering bark of laughter makes me lose my grip on my poker face, and I smirk.

Okay, maybe this particular social interaction isn't the worst.

"Resort to violence?!" He laughs. "I'm like twice your size."

"The bigger they are, the harder they fall," I croon. "Don't underestimate me just because I'm small. It could be your undoing."

He watches me for a minute, eyes sliding over my face, my body. I can actually feel his gaze on me, and I try to imagine what he sees. Amber eyes, freckles, nose ring, chap-sticked lips, turquoise dipped black hair. The old Green Day shirt and plain black distressed skinny jeans I'm wearing are snug and show off what little curves I have, and I'm rocking my Doc's. (Thrift store find. Twenty bucks. Fucking treasure.)

For a brief moment, I wish I would have taken the time to change and at least peek in the mirror before I left work. I'm sure I have helmet head from the bike, there's a damp spot on my jeans from a beer spill, and I smell like a bar. I feel just a teensy bit self-conscious, but then it passes. If he doesn't like what he sees, screw him. The big, beautiful jerk.

When his eyes land on my lips again, I clear my throat loudly and force a frown.

"So, Butch, you gonna hand over my property or do I have to overpower you and take it myself?"

"Butch?" He jerks his head back, amused and confused.

"Butch Cassidy? Train and bank robberies? A famous *burglar*. Don't tell me you're a thief *and* uncultured."

He chuckles and gives me a shrug.

"Just a pretty face, then," I shake my head and sigh. "Such a shame."

"You think I'm pretty."

"I have eyes." I fold my arms over my chest and look away, feigning boredom. "Doesn't change the fact that you're a criminal."

"I'll tell you what." He mimics my stance and hits me with an all-business stare. "I'll trade you for the vanilla."

I purse my lips before asking, "What do I have to give?"

"I'll trade you this vanilla for your number."

Oh. Well, okay then. This is a no-brainer.

"I told you before that I don't associate with criminals."

"But if I give you the bottle, then I wouldn't be a criminal. I'm not stealing; it's all just one big misunderstanding."

"And what if this isn't your first offense? How do I know you're not trying to trick me? Get my number, then make off with the goods?" I squint my eyes at him. "You could be trying to set me up for a bunch of cold calling campaigns. Or planning to put my number on a billboard or a bathroom stall. How do I know you can be trusted?"

Pretty sure I've got this boy eating out of the palm of my hand. He's trying so hard not to let his smile take over his face, trying and failing, and his brown eyes are dancing with humor. He's amused. He's having fun, and I'm suddenly not tired anymore.

"You bring up good points." He pauses. "I don't suppose you'll take my word for it."

I laugh and roll my eyes.

"Of course not," he chuckles. "I'll let you buy it first? You can buy it and put it in your car, and then give me your number."

I pretend to think it over.

"If we do it that way, you'll stay on the sidewalk until I've secured the product, and then I'll shout my number to you."

He laughs, giving an amused shake of the head before nodding his agreement. "Deal. Shake on it?"

He sticks out his hand, and I narrow my eyes at it. Then I meet his gaze, pop a brow, and slowly reach out to take his hand.

It's warm and calloused. His grip is firm, but not crushing, and I have a feeling his hands could do some serious damage if he wanted them to. The thought sends a shiver through me. The way his eyes flash with heat tells me he noticed, so I drop his hand and head to the check out.

He follows me out the door, the bottle of vanilla and the store receipt clutched in my hand. When we're on the sidewalk, I turn around.

"You stay here," I remind him, pointing to the sidewalk where his feet are planted. "No moving."

"Cross my heart." He uses his index finger to draw an X on his chest, and I have to hold back my smile at how serious he looks.

I take my first few steps backwards, keeping my eyes on him, until I'm about twenty feet away. Then I pivot on the ball of my foot and sashay to my bike. I'm not ashamed to admit it. I might not have much in the curves department, but what I do have, I know how to work. When I reach Baby, I put the vanilla and my purse in the saddle bag, unlock my helmet, then turn back around to face the guy. I lean on my bike lightly and smirk at his shocked expression.

People never expect me to be riding a motorcycle. It's one of the reasons I love it.

We stare at each other for a moment, me with my smirk and him with his wide, surprised eyes. The connection creates sparks, even with a parking lot between us, and I have to breathe slowly to steady my heartbeat.

"Is the package secure?" he shouts from the curb, and I reach down and pat the saddlebag.

"Snug as a bug in a rug."

"Okay. I held up my end of the bargain. It's your turn to hold up yours."

"Hmmm, what was my end, again?" I cock my head to the side and watch as he grabs the back of his neck and smiles at the ground. It's so boyishly adorable, so magnetic, that I kind of hate him a little. This guy is *dangerous*.

"Your number," he reminds me.

"Oh yeah," I say with grin. "Thirty-one."

"Thirty-one?" His handsome face scrunches up in confusion.

"Yep. Thirty-one." I stifle a giggle.

"Thirty-one is not your phone number."

"It's not," I respond slowly. "But you didn't specify what number you wanted." I shrug. "Thirty-one is the number you get."

As I swing my leg over my bike, I hear his rumbling laugh again, exasperated and amused. I'm just about to push my helmet on my head when he calls out.

"Sundance! Hey, Sundance," he shouts, and I can't help the huge smile that stretches over my face. That scoundrel said he didn't know Butch Cassidy, and here he is calling me Sundance. "I didn't get your name."

I look at him, smile wide, and roll my eyes. "Bummer for you."

Then I shove my helmet on my head, rev Baby to life, and cruise out of the parking lot without a backward glance.

When I get back to my apartment, it's past one in the morning, and I have a 9:30 a.m. class tomorrow. Ivy is probably asleep, so I move silently toward the kitchen. I put the vanilla in the cupboard and take a minute to admire it on the shelf. It's such a luxury. Makes me feel rich for a hot minute.

I flip off the kitchen light and walk to the sliding doors to our small balcony. I gaze longingly at my wicker bowl chair. I had plans that included that chair, my new romance novel, and a glass of wine tonight. Three of my favorite things: sexy romance novels, wine, and solitude. Hate love, but love romance novels. At heart, I'm basically a forty-year-old divorcee (who caught her ex cheating with the twenty-one-year-old secretary, so she dumped his lying ass and is now living comfortably on alimony payments without guilt. Duh.) Add in a pool boy and pack of Virginia Slims that "I only smoke when drinking" and I could practically be an ex-Beverly Hills housewife.

If I hadn't been called in to work, and then gotten distracted by the sexy stranger with the Harry Styles hair, I'd probably be able to bust out maybe half the book. Definitely would have gotten some dick. *Fictional* dick, but usually that's better anyway.

I smile at the thought of my convenience store thief, Butch Cassidy, and my chest warms. That was an in real life meet-cute if I've ever seen one. I didn't think that shit actually happened outside of books and movies. I guess forfeiting a few chapters of contemporary erotica to flirt with the hot guy in the baking aisle isn't a big deal.

In my bedroom, I take out the cash I made tonight and divide it up. Fifty bucks is pretty decent for a slow Wednesday night. I put forty of it back in my wallet to be deposited in my bank account to help cover usual expenses, and I take the remaining ten and shove it into the Crisco can I keep in the back of my closet. I update the total on the pink sticky note inside the can and scowl at it. I've been saving for six months and it's like I've barely made a dent in my goal. I'm hoping the promotion at work will help, but it's still taking too long. The sense of urgency, of guilt, is overwhelming.

It's been almost three years, already. Not for the first time, I curse myself for not starting sooner. For not thinking of it sooner.

If I can win this cookie contest... That two grand would be a game changer. I could make my deadline. He deserves *at least* that.

I have to win this contest. I kiss my fingers, press them over the tattoo on my chest, and murmur a promise. *I will win this contest.*

I shove the Crisco can back into my closet, grab a sleepshirt, and head into the bathroom that I share with Ivy. I need to scrub the bar smell from my body before I crash into bed. Then it's another day of classes and experimental baking.

Hopefully I can squeeze some fic-dick in there, too.

At least I don't have to work again until Saturday.

By the time Saturday evening rolls around, I've almost forgotten about the baking aisle boy. I did think I saw someone similar on campus today, and once yesterday I thought I heard his laugh. But otherwise, he's just a fuzzy memory, fading from my short-term memory, never to be fantasized about again.

Saturday nights at Bar 31 are always hopping. I'm closing tonight, so I can make a cool $200 at least, and it will be easy money. Rum and Cokes, vodka cranberries, and way too many Jaeger bombs.

College kids and their distinguished pallets. Ha.

Around 1 a.m., Thirty minutes before I get to climb on a stool and shout LAST CALL into the bar microphone, a familiar hand slides into my line of sight.

A sexy hand.

With woven bracelets tied to a thick wrist.

I allow myself one small smirk before meeting his chocolate brown eyes.

"You found me."

* * *

Better With You, book two in the *Better Love* series is available on most major retailers. Add it to your TBR now!

acknowledgments

Sit back, ya'll. This is gonna be a long one. (Or skim for your name. That's cool, too.)

I'm not too proud to admit that this book would be a trash heap of jumbled scenes and half-finished chapters if not for a handful of people. I would be too, probably. Between my self-doubt, flare-ups of imposter syndrome, utter lack of knowledge regarding independent publishing, kid-packed schedule, and fleeting attention span, the obstacles were ABUNDANT. I am beyond hashtag blessed to have had such an amazing support system cheering me on and moving me forward. If it weren't for you guys, well, I wouldn't be up at 2 a.m. writing these acknowledgements while drinking wine and crying happy tears.

First, to the ARC readers, bloggers, and bookstagrammers who decided to take a chance on a new author and picked up *Love You Better*. Thank you from the bottom of my heart. Every page read, every review posted, every like, share, and comment are so very appreciated. You elevate my purpose for writing. Releasing a book is kind of terrifying, especially when it's your first, and you all helped to make this a positive and memorable experience.

To Murphy Rae for designing this gorgeous cover. You used your creativity and talent to fill in the holes of my vision and brought it to life in a way that I never could have imagined. You captured Ivy and Kelley to a T, and the cover is the perfect representation of their relationship and this story. Not to mention, you're one of the easiest people to work with I've encountered so far. How are you so chill and cool? Teach me your ways.

Thank you to the authors and industry professionals in this community who graciously helped me through the self-publishing process. Thank you for putting up with my questions, and for never once telling me to STFU (to my face, at least). Navigating this process would have been so much harder and less enjoyable if it weren't for your guidance.

Trilina Pucci, Jenna Hartley, and Ella James, for taking the time to not only read this when you didn't have to, but to also provide detailed feedback, thank you so much. This book is lightyears better than the one I sent you months ago, and so much of that improvement is thanks to your suggestions and honesty. You ladies are absolute gems in the book world.

Lauren Asher, you deserve an extra special shoutout for putting up with so much shit from me. Your patience and kindness has been a godsend. One day, you'll regret giving me those digits. Hopefully that day is not too soon lol.

To my editor, Rebecca at Fairest Reviews Editing Services, thank you so very much for helping me transform my chaotic mess of story-telling thoughts into an actual, readable, well-written novel. You whipped this baby into shape like the pro you are, and you handled my frequent changes and love for flowery run-ons with poise and patience. My lane is your lane, friend. Enter as you please.

To my proofreader, Sarah at All Encompassing Books, your impact—both on me and this book—is immeasurable, and I am so grateful for you. As a proofer, a beta, and a friend —thank you for all the hats you wear. [Insert ornamental scene break here]. I couldn't have done this without you. Thanks for letting me ramble via voice message and text you at 3 in the morning when I was worried my plot was spiraling. [Insert another ornamental scene break]. My fellow Cancer baby, you're a gem and I appreciate you so, so much. Your skill, knowledge, and kindness helped me in more ways than you will ever know.

To Jess, who not-so-subtly hinted that I should change Ivy's career path, and then allowed me to ask a billion questions regarding LSATs, law internships, law firms, and fields of law in general. Thank you, and *you were right*. She's a better lawyer. That statement is here in print and PUBLISHED, so feel free to frame it.

To my sister, who inspired most of the Bailey/Ivy exchanges, especially the one in chapter six. Big doesn't mean better *cheers*. I fucking love you. Let's keep the real and ridiculous conversation topics flowing.

To my beta readers, Melanie, Dawn, Caitlin, Brook, Haley, Sarah, Jenn, and Ruth: Your feedback was crucial to giving Ivy and Kelley the story they deserve. Thank you, thank you, thank you for every word of critique and praise. (Please never leave me because B's book is hefty and Imma need you again pretty soon...)

Brook, your notes were SO FRIGGEN HELPFUL, so never again apologize for being thorough. You're not nit-picky, you're brilliant. Thank you x infinity.

Haley, my booksta-neighbor bae, your love for Kelley fills me with so much happiness. Thank you for being his first big fan (other than me). Let's get drinks soon and I'll let you know what I'm dreaming up for J.

Sarah, you got your shout out above but I'm putting you here, too, because you're just that special. And also so I can do this: [Insert ornamental scene break] [Random numbers].

Ruth and Jenn, my bestie and my seester, thanks for putting up with my bullshit for so long (like, literally over a damn decade) and also for joining me on this journey. Your support and encouragement mean the world to me. Please stay with me for many more decades. Margs and nachos soon, yeah?

Caitlin, a thousand scented novelty candles wouldn't be enough to fully express how much I appreciate and adore you. As a beta reader, as a human, and as a friend, you are amazing and strong and inspiring, and I fucking love you. You helped keep me leveled during this whole process and that could not have been easy. I'm going to write you that HEA with Jake the Jogging Single Dad someday.

To Dawn. You are my kindred spirit. I am so grateful to the Goddess of IG for bringing you to me. Thank you for always boosting me up when I'm feeling low, and for always having a kind and encouraging word. You are my fave hypeman forever, and I'll fangirl you til I die. You are an absolute light in my life. I hope I give you as much joy as you give me. I cannot wait for our world tour. It's gonna be a fucking blast.

To Melanie, the love of my Bookstagram life. Thank you for talking me off a number of ledges, for always being there to distract me with celeb gossip or booksta-tea when I need it, and for always being willing to give me the absolute truth when I ask for it. We're a two-person girl gang without a lunch table, and you're never getting rid of me. Ever. I'll have Arya draw you your very own picture of Humpty to show my gratitude. (Also, Danielle can eat a bag of crusty dicks *dancing lady emoji*)

To Jonathan, the love of my IRL life, my husband, my baby daddy, my partner-fun-haver for eternity, and my forever road trip buddy. Thank you for every single thing you've done to help me make this dream a reality. From the late nights, to the early mornings, the days of solo parenting, and the long conversations where I ramble about to-do lists and plot lines and you nod encouragingly and grunt at appropriate times.

This book quite literally could not have been possible without your help and support. You are the Nick to my Jess, the Ralph to my Vanellope, the popcorn to my Reece's Pieces. I love you so damn much that it's actually gross. Thank you for being mine.

And last but not least, to VENOM Presents on YouTube for releasing remastered versions of "Oh, Anna" and "Medicine" by Harry Styles. Thank you for giving me the best entertainment to enjoy during writing breaks when my brain felt otherwise numb.

And also thank you to Harry Styles. Because duh.

Until next time,

about the author

Brit Benson writes romance novels that are sassy, sexy, and sweet. She likes outspoken, independent heroines, dirty talking, love-struck heroes, and plots that get you right in the feels.

Brit would almost always rather be reading or writing. When she's not dreaming up her next swoony book boyfriend and fierce book bestie, she's getting lost in someone else's fictional world. When she's not doing that, she's probably marathoning a Netflix series or wandering aimlessly up and down the aisles in Homegoods, sniffing candles and touching things she'll never buy.

Made in the USA
Monee, IL
04 July 2023

37812631R10193